Danger in the Wind

Books by Jane Finnis

The Aurelia Marcella Roman Mysteries
Shadows in the Night (formerly *Get Out or Die*)
A Bitter Chill
Buried Too Deep
Danger in the Wind

Danger in the Wind

An Aurelia Marcella Mystery

Jane Finnis

Poisoned Pen Press

*For Carol Weston
in celebration of our happy friendship,
and with special thanks for her wise advice
during the writing of this book.*

Part of the province of Britannia in 100 AD

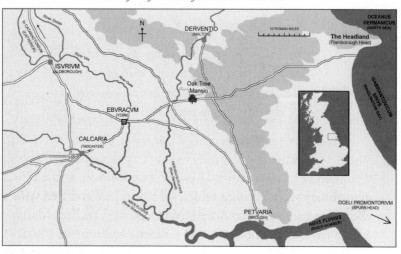

Chapter I

The letter arrived at breakfast. It jolted me out of my quiet morning mood and sounded an alarm in my head as shrill as a bugle.

I don't get many letters, and they still give me a childish thrill of excitement. Half the fun is trying to guess who they're from before I look inside. This one gave nothing away: it was an ordinary wooden note-tablet, folded in half and tied with a cord. It was addressed to Aurelia Marcella, the Oak Tree Mansio, coast road from Eburacum, and someone had written URGENT in large black letters above my name. But then everyone does that, even though we all know it makes precious little difference to how quickly the message arrives.

I gave up the guessing game and untied the cord. I was pleased to see the note was from my cousin, and the first few lines were cheerful enough.

Jovina Lepida to Aurelia Marcella, greetings.

I'm giving a patty at midsummer to celebrate my birthday, if indeed birthdays are truly a cause for celebration at our age. I'd love you to visit me and Marcus for a few days, to help me mark the occasion. Do say yes. It's too long since we were together.

So far so good. But then:

Please help, Aurelia. There's danger in the wind, and I fear the Greeks even when they bring gifts. Say nothing. Just come.

I read it through a second time. The alarm in my head grew as piercing as a whole cohort of buglers warning that barbarians were at the gates of Rome.

There was never any doubt that I'd accept the invitation. My cousin needed me, and that was enough. All the same, the sentence about danger was worrying. Yet how much danger could there really be at a birthday party? I poured myself a refill from the jug of watered wine and thought about it.

It was three years and more since I'd seen Cousin Jovina. I always call her "cousin," though strictly speaking she's not a first cousin, she's actually…never mind, cousin will do. We'd been friends as children, then for many years not seen one another, until we rediscovered our friendship when she moved to Britannia. She'd lived at Eburacum for some time, an easy day's travel from the Oak Tree. But her husband was in the army, so they never stayed anywhere for very long. It was at least three years since they'd been posted north to Isurium, and I hadn't seen them since their farewell party.

If you've never heard of Isurium, it's not surprising. It's a small, undistinguished fort with a small, undistinguished village attached to it. It's on the road to the northern frontier, but several days' march away from it, so for years there'd been no serious soldiering to do. Marcus and his fellow officers presumably passed the time hunting, drinking, and whoring, and now and then organising practise manoeuvres for their men. But it was dull for their wives, with nothing to do and hardly any female company to do it with.

That must be why Jovina was giving this party and inviting me to stay a few days with her. But it didn't account for the disturbing ending to her note.

Though the letter was worrying, at least it had created an interruption, and I was glad of that. I'd have welcomed any distraction at all, even a bill from our wine-shippers…well no, perhaps the situation wasn't quite that desperate, but it was a close thing.

Usually I'm happy in the mornings and enjoy the first meal of the day. This one was late and leisurely, and it should have been a special treat, because my brother Lucius had come to stay. He doesn't often visit us at the Oak Tree, so whenever he can manage a few days here, spending time together over unhurried meals is something we both relish.

But this time it was different. The food was good, the wine excellent, and I had no urgent chores to do. But Lucius had brought Vitellia, his latest lady-love. That was unusual to say the least. His romances lasted about as long as fashions in tunics, and as he's normally based down south, I hardly ever got to meet his young women. When he'd written to say he was bringing Vitellia to stay I'd been pleased, and immensely curious.

They'd arrived yesterday, tired after several days on the road from Londinium and happy to have reached journey's end. The first thing they did was drink a beaker of wine. The next was take a bath and change out of their dusty travelling clothes. By that time supper was ready, and at Lucius' insistence, we ate in the main bar-room, not the private dining-room.

"I want Vitellia to meet everyone," he said. Which meant, I realised, that he wanted everyone to meet Vitellia, so he could show her off. And she was lovely, with a beauty that made heads turn wherever she went. She carried herself like a goddess, and her delicate features, clear pale skin, and shining dark hair, would have made many of the more homely deities envious. She smiled a great deal, a captivating smile that made her look more beautiful than ever.

She didn't say much, and what she did utter was harmless but unimaginative, though made pleasant by her wide-eyed, innocent charm. "How nice" and "how interesting" were two of her favourite comments. Lucius did enough talking for both of them, chatting away to everyone, preening himself like a rooster on a dung-hill whenever she drew an admiring glance. He lost no time in telling us that her father was a leading man in Londinium, rich and influential, with a big town house and a country estate just the correct distance from the capital. In other words, Vitellia was a typical Londinium heiress, young and marriageable, and as beautiful as a butterfly. And probably about as intelligent.

When he announced that they were to marry, I was horrified, though of course I tried not to show it. She was the wrong girl for him, I was certain, although they seemed so happy. What would happen when the initial infatuation faded? But I fetched our best Gaulish red wine for everyone to drink their health, and I did my very best to be pleased for them, joining in the congratulations and the cheerful banter with every show of enthusiasm.

In truth I was dismayed. Lucius had never gone as far as marriage with any woman, and now here he was planning to buy a villa for himself and this child near to her father's property, and she was saying how nice and how interesting it would be to raise a family there.

I know, I know…I'm sounding like a sour old cat. I shouldn't take against someone just because her dull mind doesn't match her perfect body. And it wasn't that I disliked her; in fact if I'd met her casually I'd have said there was no harm in her. But she wasn't right for Lucius. He needed someone with more character, more spirit.

Lucius is my twin, and we've always been closer than most brothers and sisters. Partly, I know, the bond between us was strong because neither of us was married yet. I'd assumed he would eventually marry, of course I had, just as I assume I will some day. In my case I'm prepared to wait, because the only man I'd consider marrying is too completely absorbed in his work to think of settling down yet. And as for Lucius, I'd hoped he would choose a bride with a lively mind and a sense of humour, qualities that he possesses himself and Vitellia seemed to lack. Yes, her beauty was stunning, and her good family connections would doubtless help his career on the provincial governor's staff. Many men would say those advantages were sufficient. But they weren't, not for Lucius, not for the rest of his life.

I went to bed worrying about it. All I could do was hope that things would look better in the morning. They didn't. Our breakfast together was doing nothing to cheer me up.

We serve a good breakfast at the Oak Tree, though I say so myself, and this morning there was freshly-baked bread, still warm, and a choice of honey or some excellent soft cow's milk cheese, all washed down with a sweet Rhodian white wine. I'd even told the maids to lay out our best plates and beakers in the private dining-room and to put a vase of flowers on the table.

None of it helped. The girl was still dull, with no sudden lightning flashes of wit or humour to add spice to her insipid sweetness. She and Lucius were so absorbed in one another that I might as well not have been present. Conversation consisted of the kind of trivialities that strangers exchange, interspersed with long silences, which I found uncomfortable, and they didn't even notice. The relaxed, easy intimacy I'd shared with Lucius since we were children was gone.

I gave myself a silent talking-to. Maybe when you know her better, Aurelia, you'll learn to appreciate her better. If Lucius has chosen this girl, she must have more about her than meets the eye. Perhaps she's just shy, keeping quiet and making only conventionally polite remarks because she's not at ease. Well, you're an innkeeper, and putting people at ease is part of what you do for a living.

"Would you like some more bread and honey, Vitellia?" I pushed the loaf towards her on its wooden platter. "You've hardly eaten anything."

"Thank you," she answered. "It's very nice."

"Let me, Kitten." Lucius carved her a slice from the loaf and placed it on her plate, then he spooned some honey onto it and cut it into three neat pieces. It reminded me of my sister Albia feeding her small children.

"We're lucky to have so much honey left," I went on. "The bees did us proud last summer. Does your father keep bees on his estate?"

"Yes, he does. I find them a bit frightening, so I keep away from the hives. But the honey is very nice." She turned to my brother with a beaming smile that would have illuminated an entire forum. "Lucius isn't afraid of them, though, are you, dear?"

He smiled back, and they gazed into one another's eyes.

Why are you bothering with conversation, Aurelia? I asked myself. It was plain to see the pair of them didn't need anyone else just now. I felt left out, and the knowledge that this was childish and selfish of me made me irritable.

So it was a relief when one of the maids knocked and came in. "Sorry to disturb you, Mistress, but a messenger's just ridden in from Eburacum and delivered this note for you. He says he picked it up at garrison headquarters there first thing this morning."

I took the note from her. "He's made good time if he's ridden from Eburacum. You gave him a drink on the house, I hope?"

"I did. Like we always do for the lads that bring our mail."

The love-birds had barely noticed Baca's arrival, so I felt no compunction about opening my letter. After all, it did say URGENT on the outside. Having read it, I just sat staring at it, as if by sheer willpower I could make it talk to me and explain the meaning of those last few lines.

"Please help, Aurelia. There's danger in the wind, and I fear the Greeks even when they bring gifts. Say nothing. Just come."

The obvious explanation was too silly to take seriously. Jovina was writing from a military base, but I was certain she wasn't writing about military danger. Isurium was safe to the point of dullness. And even if something unexpected had happened to alter that, Jovina was an army wife, and knew that men didn't join the army expecting perfect peace all their lives.

No, this was something personal. And why was she talking about Greeks? "I fear the Greeks even when they bring gifts." A familiar enough sentence, a line from a poem. Which poem? I'd had to learn huge chunks of Our Great Literary Heritage by heart as a child, like any educated Roman. I cudgelled my memory.

Got it! This was from Virgil's *Aeneid*, never a particular favourite of mine. At least the quote came from one of the more interesting parts: the bit where Troy is about to be captured by the Greeks through that trick with the wooden horse, despite several Trojans uttering dire warnings of doom and disaster. In fact the doom-prophets were right, and the Trojans should have been deeply suspicious of Greek gifts, but as our grandmother often pointed out, when the gods have decided the outcome of a war, cautionary advice by mere mortals is a waste of breath.

So then, who was Jovina afraid of? She could mean literally a Greek, or just a person who appeared to be friendly but wasn't.

I realised something else about her letter. The two parts of it were in different styles of handwriting. The party invitation was neat and well-spaced, the work of a secretary probably. The call for help was in Jovina's writing, but small and squeezed in at the bottom, as if she'd added it to the letter herself afterwards. Why? Presumably because she didn't want anyone else to see her addendum to the innocent-seeming invitation she'd dictated. It was for my eyes only.

I felt a rush of excitement. There was only one way to find out what Jovina's troubles were, and that was to visit her. I'd give myself a little holiday. The gods knew I could do with one after the last few months. Jovina needed me, and I needed a change of scene.

A small practical corner of my mind told me I really shouldn't dream of going away just now. The date was impossibly close, for a start: midsummer was less than half a month away. And June is a busy time for innkeepers, the height of the travelling season when all the world and his wife takes to the roads throughout the Empire. I ought to be here to help.

"I'm going anyway." The words were out before I could stop them.

"Going where, Sis?" My brother tore himself away from Vitellia and gave me at least some of his attention. "Who's the note from?"

"Jovina. She's invited me to her birthday party, and to stay a few days with her and Marcus."

"Really? That's good. I thought we'd lost touch with those two. I certainly haven't seen them since they left Eburacum."

"Nor have I. That's why I'm keen to go. We've a great deal of catching up to do."

Lucius turned to Vitellia. "I don't suppose you know them, Vitellia. Jovina is a distant cousin of ours. We saw quite a lot of her when we were young, because she's like us, from Italia originally, but now settled here. So is her husband. He's Marcus Mallius Melandrus, he's in the army and quite senior now. They were in Lindum for some years, before they came up to Eburacum. They're a nice pair, we're fond of them both."

She shook her head, and the gesture didn't disturb her glossy dark curls. She was one of those women who remain perfectly groomed at all hours of the day and night. Makes you spit.

"No, I don't know them. I've never even been to Lindum." She gave Lucius her dazzling smile. "Until I met you, dearest, I'm afraid I'd always thought anywhere north of Londinium was rather…" She hesitated.

"Uncivilised?" I suggested, and was maliciously pleased when she looked flustered.

"Oh, of course not, Aurelia." Again she shook her head, and this time the curls jiggled, but not enough to spoil their fashionable arrangement. "It's just that I'm a town girl, I've lived mostly in Londinium, and it's—well, it's different here."

No, really? Well, as I often say, there's no law against stating the obvious.

My brother only laughed. "You're right there, Kitten."

I assumed they'd go back to making sheep's eyes at one another. But Lucius was still thinking about my letter. "Whereabouts are Marcus and Jovina based now, Aurelia?"

"Isurium."

"Gods, the poor things. That's a pretty dismal dump to be stuck in. No wonder she needs a party to cheer her up. "

"My thoughts exactly. It's not far away really, and the journey will do me good."

"Journey?" I had his full attention now. "I suppose it'll need two days, but you could take it in stages and rest in Eburacum for a day on the way. You're still not strong after your illness. Are you sure you're up to it?"

"Of course I am. Don't fuss, Lucius."

"I'm not fussing. I just want to make certain you're not taking on too much. You've been ill, and you've got to be sensible. Which I know you find hard," he added, with a touch of his old mischief.

I wasn't going to be put off. "A few days with Jovina is just the holiday I need. I know it's a busy time here, but the staff can manage. You're not going to begrudge me a holiday, surely?"

"Of course not, as long as you're well enough to enjoy it. What exactly does Jovina say about her party? May I see her letter?" He leaned forward and reached out to take it from my hand, but I pulled it away.

"No, you may not. It's private. Girl talk, not for your eyes."

He shrugged. "Girl talk? Gods, then I don't want to know."

Vitellia was looking blank. "Where exactly is Isurium? I've never heard of it."

"On the road that runs north from Eburacum to the frontier, Kitten."

She appeared none the wiser. "And your cousin lives in the fort with her husband? That must be grim for her. Is she allowed to, or does she have to keep out of the way? I mean I didn't think women were supposed to live inside a fort."

I laughed. "Jovina wouldn't be very good at keeping out of the way, and she doesn't have to. Marcus is the deputy commander, so he has his own accommodation inside the walls, and she's allowed to live there with him. But you're right, it is a bit grim, cooped up inside there. She and Marcus have built their own house in the village close by, and that's where she spends most of her time, she and her daughter. Her son's grown up and in the army, like his father."

"So you'll stay with her in the village? Among all the natives?"

"That's right."

"There aren't many of our own people settled there yet, are there? Romans, I mean…civilised people."

I smiled at her. She didn't know much, but at least she was taking an interest. "Some of the Brigantes consider themselves quite civilised, but I know what you mean, it isn't the same. Still, most of the natives have realised there's no point trying to fight Romans these days. We're here to stay. Far north on the frontier there's still hostility sometimes, but forts like Isurium are as safe as here. Aren't they, Lucius?"

"Oh, yes. The soldiers spend their time moaning that they're bored with endless drills and practice marches, and want to do some fighting."

"Then if it's really safe," Vitellia persisted, "why do they need a fort at all?"

A good question, in fact a very good question. I looked at her with renewed interest, but Lucius cut in before I could answer.

"Don't worry your head about it, Kitten." He patted her hand. "Just take it from me that Aurelia will be quite safe there."

She gave me her full, beaming smile. "I think you're awfully brave, travelling all that way on your own. You really don't think it's dangerous?"

"The only danger I can foresee is that I'll drink too much at Jovina's party, and a couple of strapping soldiers will have to carry me off to my bed."

She giggled. "That could be *really* dangerous."

Had she actually made a joke? We all laughed, I probably more loudly than the remark deserved.

"Well, then," Lucius smiled and raised his wine-mug, "Here's to a pleasant trip, and an excellent party."

The rest of the meal was easier. The love-birds started to make plans for the day, a drive around the countryside and a picnic. I wasn't included of course, but I didn't mind now, because I'd plans of my own to make. I'd have to get organised quickly. Jovina's party was at midsummer, and I wanted to arrive at least a couple of days in advance. I counted the days on my fingers, and realised how short the time was. It should have appalled me, but instead it simply added to the excitement to realise I must leave home the day after tomorrow.

I'm a great believer in making lists, and I took a wax note-tablet from my pouch and started to jot down a few of the more important things I had to arrange. Which of our carriages should

I take? Our vehicles were all serviceable but by no means new. Could I borrow something better for the trip from one of our friends? How many servants? Just a driver and a maid, and a couple of bodyguards. I'd need to have quite a lot of cash with me, because though I run a mansio, I'm not myself one of the favoured ones who can travel about and stay free at official accommodation.

It was only a two-day journey and the roads were good. I'd stop at Eburacum on the way, and I'd be able to stay at my sister Albia's town house there. She kept it staffed all year, even though she and Candidus rarely had time for visits to town in the summer. It was comfortable and well-placed for shopping. Yes, I'd stay an extra day and visit the shops. I scribbled "Write to A today" on my list.

So two nights in Eburacum and one more day's travel along the military road north would bring me to Isurium. Then Jovina's, the party, meeting her friends, helping her solve her problem, whatever it was…I was looking forward to all of it.

I hadn't felt so enthusiastic about anything, so alive with hope, for months. I knew for certain that I'd once and for all thrown off my illness and the black melancholy that had soured the spring. I was sure I would have a wonderful holiday. I was convinced nothing could go wrong, and if it did, I was confident I could easily deal with anything the Fates chose to put in my path.

I was mistaken on all counts.

Chapter II

I always like to stroll around outside in the mornings, to make sure everything is running smoothly and give the outdoor staff a chance to tell me if it isn't. The Oak Tree is an official mansio, (the best mansio north of the Humber, I always say, but then I could be biased) and also a posting-station, where travellers on imperial business change horses or mules, so the stables must always be smart and efficient. There was the farm as well, our horse-breeding enterprise in particular. And we were getting more and more business for our vehicle repair workshop. Mostly it was local carts or wagons, rough-and-ready jobs to be done as cheaply as possible and always, of course, desperately urgent. But sometimes there were unfortunate travellers whose official transport had let them down, and in that case there was genuine urgency, plus a captive clientele who'd pay extra for quick service.

At this hour of the day the paved area in front of the main door was deserted, but it would be busy later with animals and vehicles parked there by our thirsty customers. The morning was sunny and the breeze smelt good. I could hear a skylark high above my head, and nearby a blackbird sang from a branch of the giant oak tree that gives our mansio its name. It would be hot later—well, hot for northern Britannia, anyway. Not by the standards of our childhood home in Pompeii, but Pompeii was gone. Britannia is my home now, and I wouldn't change it, for all its imperfections. Father was right to bring us here as youngsters and set up the Oak Tree to give us all a future here.

He died before he could see what a flourishing success the mansio has become, but I think he'd have approved.

I shook off the past and concentrated on today. It was perfect haymaking weather, and Ursulus, the farm manager, would be putting every available man into the fields to mow. I must remind Margarita to have extra beer sent out to go with their midday bread. Haymaking is dry work, and I didn't want them sneaking back to quench their thirst in the bar.

Not that she'd need reminding, I thought as I turned to go to the stables. She was an excellent housekeeper, always well-organised. The Oak Tree would be in safe hands while I was away. She had been carrying much of my load anyway over the past few months. As soon as I'd done my rounds, I'd go and tell her my news. I felt sure she'd be pleased for me.

So would Secundus, who ran the stables. He'd been a cavalryman, and enjoyed reminiscing about army life, so he'd probably have some tales to tell me about the fort at Isurium. I headed for the stable-yard, but before I'd got halfway there I met him marching purposefully towards me. I opened my mouth to wish him a cheerful good-morning, but his worried expression stopped me, and instead I asked, "What's up, Secundus? Something wrong?"

"I'm not sure, Aurelia. That soldier who stayed here last night, the tall feller with the scar on his right arm. Terentius, was it? Has he left already?"

"No, not yet. Why?"

"One of his horses is missing, the dark grey gelding. And I can't find his servant. I'm afraid he's gone too."

"His servant? The thin boy with a runny nose?"

"That's the one. He slept over the stables with my horse-boys last night. He said his master didn't need him till morning, and he fancied playing dice with the lads. But he's not here now, and none of them have seen him today. He hasn't been over to the main house for breakfast neither, I've checked. Which makes me wonder…"

He didn't need to finish it. "Right, I'll go in and find Terentius himself, and ask him if he knows what's going on."

"Good. Because if the lad's run off that's one thing, but if he's still around somewhere it means the horse has been stolen by an outsider. Not that it's likely, I'd say. It was just a standard army nag, over-worked and under-fed. If thieves came snooping round here there are much better animals they could have gone for."

"There certainly are." I thought of our herd of black horses, the pride of our farm. "You're sure no other animals are missing?"

He nodded. "Certain, I've counted them up myself. Seems to me the lad and the horse must have taken the same road."

"Well, I know Terentius himself hasn't left. Last night he asked me to lock something away in the safe till this morning, something he obviously valued. And he hasn't collected it yet."

"I'm probably worrying over nothing then. He could have sent the boy off very early on some errand, before they start on their journey."

"Leave it with me. I'll let you know if there isn't a sensible explanation. Everything all right otherwise?"

"Aye, fine. Moon-cloud looks like she'll drop her foal today." He gestured towards a field where several black horses were contentedly grazing. "I'll move her into the small paddock, and make sure one of the lads keeps an eye on her every once in a while."

"I'll come and see her soon. It's a grand morning, isn't it?"

He smiled at me suddenly. "Aye, it is. And you're looking pleased with life. Have you had some good news? That early courier brought you a letter, did he?"

I smiled too. There aren't many secrets in a busy mansio. "Yes, he did, and you're right about good news. I've been invited to a party by some old friends at Isurium. I'll be away a few days."

"That's grand. Mind, I don't want to rain on your triumph, but it had better be a good party, because there's not much at Isurium otherwise."

"I think it will be. And I know it's a busy time, and I oughtn't to go away, but…"

"Of course you ought, if you want. We'll manage fine, you can depend on it." His smile widened. "It's nice to see you're feeling up to a bit of travelling. A holiday will do you a power of good. Go off and enjoy yourself, that's what I say."

"Thanks, I intend to. Oh, by the way, Lucius is going to take his young lady out driving, to show her round the district. Can you get one of the light gigs ready, with a decent pair of mules? Placid ones, preferably. He says he wants to drive himself, but he may not be keeping his eyes on the road."

"I reckon I'd have the same problem, driving that young lass around. He's a lucky feller. Is it true they're going to be wed?"

"Yes, it's true."

He offered congratulations, and I smiled and said I must get on with checking about the missing slave. I didn't want him asking me anything more, such as my opinion of my future sister-in-law.

Then I spotted my brother himself, standing under the oak-tree and beckoning me to join him there. He was on his own, thank the gods.

"Have you time for a chat, Sis? I was hoping to catch you before we set off for our drive."

"All right, but I mustn't be long."

"Nor must I. Let's go into the garden. We can be private there."

I wondered what he wanted as we walked round to the secluded garden which is overlooked by our private wing, but well away from the public area our customers use. We sat down on a stone bench in the sun, and I thought, I hope he's not going to ask me what I think of Vitellia.

"I'm worried about this trip of yours to Jovina's," he began.

"Now don't start all that again. I've already told you…"

"I know what you've already told me. It's what you *haven't* told me that bothers me. What's your real reason for wanting to visit her?"

"As I said, for her birthday party. And because I feel like a change of scene."

He grinned. "That's good, as far as it goes. But I said the *real* reason. I know there's more to it. Otherwise why wouldn't you let me read her letter? Girl talk, indeed! My guess is she has some other reason for asking you to stay, and the party, if it exists, is just an excuse."

"It exists all right. And the letter was just girls' chatter, as I said. Vitellia may let you read her private correspondence, but I don't have to, do I?"

"Stop being so prickly, Sis. I know you too well, and I'm right, aren't I? There is something else?"

I hesitated, which was answer enough.

"I thought so. Something she told you in confidence? But she knows you and I don't have secrets from one another. And I'm certainly not letting you go galloping north by yourself until I know what's going on. So tell me all of it. I'll keep it to myself."

When it came to it, I was glad to show him our cousin's note. He scanned it quickly, frowning. "Is this all she's told you?"

"It is. You're as wise as I am now."

"Which isn't saying much. But some of it's obvious enough. The main part of the message was written by her secretary or someone else with neat, official-looking writing, and she's added the last bit herself, in her own hand. Why?"

"Presumably she doesn't want anyone finding out that she's asking me to help her, as well as inviting me for a social occasion. And she might have thought a simple invitation would be too easy to refuse, whereas this…anyway, whatever her trouble is, it won't stop me going to see her, so don't…"

"…Waste my breath discouraging you? I shan't. I might even be able to help."

"Thanks, I may be glad of your help once I've seen for myself whether there really is some sort of danger. To be honest, I think Jovina's being a touch over-dramatic. You know what she's like, and *she* knows that I'm easily intrigued by anything mysterious. I bet her trouble will turn out to be something quite trivial that she's blown out of proportion. That wouldn't be so surprising, when she and Marcus live in a military base with only a few real friends."

He ran a hand through his mop of fair hair. "It's true, the atmosphere in a fort can get pretty poisonous, especially if everyone's bored and fed up because there's nobody to fight. If she'd just said there was trouble, I'd agree with you. But she says *danger*."

"It's to do with Marcus, that's my guess. He has a foul temper, especially when he's had a few drinks. Maybe he's quarrelled with somebody important. And of course he's got a roving eye, as I remember. Perhaps he's got entangled with the *wife* of somebody important, and now the man's found out, and is threatening him."

"Gods, Relia, you must be reading too much love poetry. I'm afraid it could be something much more important."

"More important than love?"

But he didn't react to my teasing. "Marcus is a senior officer in an important fort."

"Isurium? It used to be important twenty years ago. Now it's a fort where nothing ever happens."

"Where nothing has happened recently, you mean," he corrected. "But Vitellia had a point at breakfast when she asked why, if we were safe from native unrest, we need forts like Isurium."

"To make certain we stay safe. It'll be another generation at least before we can take it for granted that all natives in Britannia will behave peacefully all the time."

"Exactly. So anything that endangers a senior officer or his family might threaten the stability of the whole area."

Lucius seemed to be taking Jovina's danger even more seriously than I was, which gave me a nasty cold feeling inside.

He glanced at the note again. "What do you think she means by this quotation from the *Aeneid* about the Greeks bearing gifts? It makes no sense to me."

"Nor to me. I doubt if she's talking literally about Greeks, because I doubt if there are any at the fort, or within a day's march of her. The troops are all auxiliaries from across the German Ocean, and the officers are all Romans."

"There's Marcus himself of course," he said soberly.

"Marcus? Rubbish! He's as Roman as we are."

"By blood, yes. But have you forgotten how he's always enthused about Greece and Greek culture? It started when we were young, he wore Greek fashions, and even had his hair done by a Greek barber. We used to call him Graeculus, Little Greek, didn't we?"

"Ye-es, I do remember, now you mention it. But we were all just children. You can't assume he still feels the same."

"Not to the same extent, no. But he's given himself the nickname Melandrus because of his black hair. And what has he named his children?"

"Philippus and Chloe," I admitted.

"Quite. Greek names, not Roman."

"No, Lucius, if you're talking about some sort of treason, it can't be Marcus. He's a senior career soldier; the army's his life. If he's the man Jovina's scared of, it's for personal reasons."

"You could be right."

"I'm always right, it's a well-known fact."

He smiled. "Well then, let's assume Jovina doesn't mean literally a Greek. That doesn't make it much better. She's scared of someone who's offering a favour, an advantage, perhaps even an affair, and she thinks there's 'danger in the wind'. If she has reason to be scared, it makes me uneasy. I wish I could offer to come up to Isurium with you."

"Could you? That would be wonderful."

He shook his head. "There isn't time. I've promised Vitellia we'll have ten days here, so she can get to know you and all our friends, and we'll go over to see Albia and Candidus at the farm, too. Then I'll escort her home to Londinium. By that time the midsummer party will have been and gone."

I silently cursed Vitellia, even though I could see his point. A promise is a promise. "Can't be helped," I said, trying to sound as if I meant it. "A pity, though. It would have been good. And Jovina would have been pleased to see you."

"It would have fitted in very well. I've been wanting a pretext to visit the area north of Eburacum for a while now, without appearing to be investigating anything in particular." He sighed and stood up. "As you say, it can't be helped."

"What would you have been investigating? If I'm going to be there, I can keep my ears and eyes open for you."

"The usual vague rumours, nothing definite. I seem to spend my life following up half-baked reports of possible trouble among the natives."

"It gives you a good excuse for loitering in taverns."

"Do I need an excuse for that?" He grinned down at me. "The Brigantians around Isurium appear quiet enough, but one of our agents has picked up local talk about a young prince from the old tribal aristocracy who fancies himself as a leader against what he calls the Roman occupation."

"I'll see what I can find out. You never know, I might learn something useful."

"It wouldn't be the first time." He put his hand briefly on my shoulder. "And now I must go, and you must write to Jovina. Give her my greetings, won't you?"

"Aurelia! Aurelia, where are you?" It was Margarita's voice, and as she repeated my name, we could tell she was coming closer, and she sounded upset.

"In the garden, Margarita," I called. "What's the matter?"

She came running round the corner towards us, pale and out of breath, her hair flopping over her face. I was alarmed by her appearance. Margarita, usually so calm and collected, was in a serious panic.

"Aurelia, thank the gods, and Lucius too, that's even better," she panted. "Can you come with me quickly, please? Something awful has happened to one of the guests."

"Who?" Lucius and I asked together.

"Terentius. He's dead. One of the maids found him." She began to shiver uncontrollably. "It's horrible. He's been murdered."

Chapter III

"What a mess," Lucius growled.

I didn't know whether he meant the bedroom itself, or the dead body on the floor, or the unpleasant situation we were in, probably all three. We stood together in the doorway for a few heartbeats, reluctant to intrude into the ugly scene.

Terentius lay naked on his left side with his left arm bent under him. A gaping wound in his belly had bled freely. His dark-brown hair was tousled and his eyes were wide open. From the unnatural position of his limbs and head, he must have fallen, or been pushed, off his bed after he'd been stabbed.

Clothes and blankets and his few possessions were strewn about the room. I spotted a comb, a small leather pouch, and half-a-dozen coins, some of them silver. So the murderer hadn't come looking for money.

But without a doubt he'd been searching for something. The mattress and the pillows had been slashed wide open, and their wool stuffing emptied out in handfuls. It lay scattered everywhere, like a fall of snow, some of it even on top of the body.

Lucius was the first to move. As an investigator, he's used to dealing with sudden death, as far as anyone can be used to it. He bent and gently touched the dead man's cheek. "He's stone cold. And look, most of this blood's dry, especially here on the floor, and where it's stained the wool. He's been dead a good while."

"It must have happened in the night," I said, "when everyone was asleep You'd think somebody nearby would have heard a disturbance. One of the other guests…" I turned to Margarita. "I suppose nobody mentioned anything?"

She shook her head. "There were only two other men staying, and neither of their rooms were next door to this one. When they came in to breakfast I asked them if they'd slept well, as I usually do, and they said yes. I can't say I'm surprised about that. They all drank a fair bit yesterday evening."

"To celebrate Lucius' news, I suppose."

"They went on after you'd gone to bed. Terentius was buying, he kept telling everyone he was celebrating, too, because he'd just got promoted."

"Did they drink enough to quarrel or to fight?" Lucius asked.

"No, nothing like that. It was all very friendly. I wouldn't say they were even really drunk, but they had enough wine inside them to give them a good night's sleep…including this poor man. I suppose that's why someone was able to sneak in here and kill him."

"Have the other guests left yet?" Lucius asked.

"Yes, they went straight after breakfast."

"What about his slave?" I felt a twinge of guilt because I'd forgotten my promise to check up on the boy. "Secundus said he slept with the horse-boys over the stables."

"Yes, and spent the evening with them, too. That was after he'd had supper in the kitchen. He seemed a nice lad. He talked about his family, and how he wants to buy his freedom. Just an ordinary boy, nothing unusual about him that I can remember."

"But now Secundus says he's disappeared. He left here very early before anyone was up, and so did one of Terentius' horses."

Margarita's pale face turned ashen. "You're saying he could have killed his master in the night? But he was hardly more than a child. And he was in my kitchen? How dreadful!" She looked round for somewhere to sit, but the bed had no mattress and the stool was covered with the ruined pillows. She leaned against the wall, as white as marble, and I realised she was struggling to keep from fainting.

I pushed the pillows off the stool, which was luckily clean of blood, and helped her to sit down. "Try not to worry, Margarita. None of this is your fault."

"I know. But I feel there must be something we could have done to prevent it."

"I don't see what. I'm sure nobody from the Oak Tree was involved in it. Aren't you, Lucius?"

"Yes, I am. The man only arrived yesterday. I suppose it might possibly have been one of the other overnight guests."

She said thoughtfully "From the way they were talking, they hadn't met before, so if there was a quarrel, it was a very sudden one. I saw no sign of it. And there wasn't a trace of blood on either of them this morning, I'd swear to that."

"What about their rooms?" Lucius interrupted.

"Nothing. The maids who cleaned them would have told me."

"That pretty well settles it," I said. "His boy killed him, and then ran away, or rode away, rather. And for what comfort it's worth, it could have happened at any time and in any place."

Lucius, predictably, was more cautious. "We must do a thorough check. I'll have to report his death to the army, and they'll expect a proper investigation. Margarita, could you organise a search of the mansio—all rooms, including our private wing, and the baths. And would you ask Secundus and Ursulus to do the same with the outbuildings? If the lad isn't anywhere to be found, we'll be forced to conclude he's run away."

"I'll see to it straight away." Her relieved expression showed how much she wanted to get away from that ghastly room. "If we do find him, you want him caught, presumably? But if he's armed…"

"Good point. Tell everyone to search in pairs, at least one of each pair to be a man."

"Right."

"And we could ask Hawk whether he's seen anything unusual in the woods," I suggested. Hawk is the best of the native huntsmen in the Oak Bridges area. What's more, he's a friend, and would help if he could. "I'll send for him if we find the boy's run off. Now, just one more thing, Margarita. Which of the maids found Terentius here like this?"

"It was Baca."

"Is she all right?"

"More or less, though she was quite shaken. A couple of the other girls are with her. I told them not to leave her on her own for a while, and Cook is warming up some wine for them. Then I'll make sure they keep busy."

"Good," Lucius said. "Tell her we'll need to talk to her later. And," he added, "have some of that warm wine yourself, Margarita. You look as if you need it."

"You're right, I do." She hurried away.

Lucius said softly, "I can manage here, Sis, if you want to go and help Margarita."

I was tempted. Sitting in the kitchen with a comforting wine-mug, or even searching for the missing slave, would be preferable to being here. But I knew Lucius needed me to stay. The murder itself was grim enough, but the violent death of a guest under our own mansio roof turned the whole situation into a nightmare. Lucius is legal owner of the Oak Tree, though I'm the one who runs it from day to day. We were both well aware that a mansio whose customers weren't safe in their beds would soon have no customers at all.

So I said, "I'll stay. It'll be easier with two of us."

"Thanks. It will. Right then, the sooner we get on with this, the sooner we can get out of here. Could you start searching the room? Collect all his belongings together and see if there's a weapon or anything else useful buried under all this wool. I'll help you soon, but first I must take a proper look at the poor man. As Quintus always says, 'Start with the body.'"

"Gods, I wish he were here now." Quintus was an experienced investigator, and also my lover, when our paths crossed. If he were here, I thought, he'd know what to make of all this. But simply thinking of him cheered me a little.

First I put Terentius' few clothes and possessions onto the bedstead. Then I walked slowly round, using my feet to push the tufts of wool into one corner of the room. Finally I checked through the tufts by hand. I found a tiny bronze pin, and a couple of dry twigs that had been among the strands of wool since they'd come off the sheep. Nothing else.

"No weapon," I reported. "The killer still has it, presumably."

Lucius straightened up and turned away from the body. "The wound looks straight and deep, a professional blow, probably with a dagger. And there doesn't seem to have been a fight. There's only this one stab-wound, no other marks or bruises on him." He swept his gaze round the room. "Someone's done a pretty thorough search here, presumably whoever killed him. The servant seems the most likely, especially if he's really disappeared."

"I agree, he does. I didn't see much of them really, I only spoke to Terentius briefly when they arrived. I asked where he'd come from, and he said he'd just finished a three months' attachment down south, mostly in Londinium, and was on his way to Isurium."

"Isurium? Did he say he was based there?"

"He implied it. He said he was with a cohort of Batavian aux-iliaries, but he wasn't a Batavian himself, judging by his accent."

Lucius nodded. "Those auxiliary units usually have Romans as officers. Anything else you can think of?"

"No, not really…wait, of course there is. His package. I was almost forgetting."

"What package?"

"He asked me to lock away a small package in our own strong-box overnight. He said it was too valuable to leave in his room."

"Ah. Now we're getting somewhere. What's it like?"

"Small, about the size of my hand, but oblong. It's wrapped in a piece of soft cloth so I couldn't see what it was. It felt hard, like a box, and something rattled when I moved it. Coins, I'd say, but not many, because it's not very heavy."

Margarita appeared at the door, bearing a tray with a couple of wine-mugs and a jug that gave out a delicious spicy aroma. "I thought you could do with some, too," she smiled, and I was relieved to see she was her usual calm self again.

"Thanks, Margarita, we certainly could." We drank gratefully. Lucius asked how the search was going.

"We've looked everywhere in the house and stables. There's no sign of the lad. The farm and outbuildings will take longer, but nobody so far has seen hide nor hair of him since late yesterday evening."

"Excellent, thank you." My brother finished his mug of wine and poured himself another. "The boy had no business to be anywhere on the farm, so if he's found there, it means he's gone into hiding. But my guess is he's taken the horse and fled. He could be heading anywhere, to the coast, to Eburacum, or into the country on one of the native roads. He'll be miles away by now. There's no point trying to follow him."

"Maybe Hawk…?" I suggested.

He sighed. "We can ask him, but it's a long shot. Still, I suppose the authorities will expect me to have gone through the motions. Could you find him , Relia, and ask him to do what he can? I'll give him a day to see what he can find, and tomorrow I'll report Terentius' death to army headquarters at Eburacum. I'll send his body there, with a note explaining the circumstances. I don't think I need to go there myself. I doubt they'll want me to do anything more."

"We'll put his body in one of the outbuildings for now," I said. "We need to clean this room up. I suppose that means yet another donation to the temple priests in Oak Bridges to persuade them to come and purify the room."

Margarita nodded. "I've already sent one of the boys off with a message asking if a couple of them can come over straight away and perform the cleansing. They're usually very obliging."

"So they should be, given the fat purse of silver they always receive for their services." But there was no alternative. We had to get all the ritual purifying done today, before any more guests arrived and the room was needed.

"Vitellia has been asking for you, Lucius," Margarita said. "What shall I tell her? She's wondering when you're going to set off for your drive."

"*Merda!*" He put his mug hastily back on the tray. "I'd forgotten Vitellia. Well, not forgotten of course, but I mean…Does she know what's happened here? I don't want her to be scared."

"She knows, yes. She was with me in the barroom when Baca came and told me about finding Terentius. She was quite shocked, and wanted you to come to her. When I told her you and Aurelia were investigating how Terentius died, she asked why you had to be involved. Of course, she understood why when I explained that you had no choice but to look into everything. But I get the impression she's a bit disappointed that you can't take her out driving."

"But I can, and I will. I've promised to spend the day with her, and I can still do that. I think we've more or less finished here, haven't we, Aurelia?"

"Well, there's still…"

"Oh, I'm sure you can deal with anything else that needs doing. I must go to her and comfort her. She's quite shy, poor girl, and having someone killed here will worry her dreadfully. If we go out for our drive, it'll take her mind off the unpleasantness of it all."

"But what about…"

"So can I leave the rest to you, Sis? See to the cleansing, get in touch with Hawk. You can handle all that, can't you?"

"If I must. But you don't think that having someone killed here might worry *me* dreadfully too?"

His look of surprise gave me my answer. "I agree it's not very pleasant, but you're used to dealing with trouble. You can cope, I know you can."

I let it go. I suppose it was a compliment in its way. "You'll have to write the report for the army at Eburacum, but I can do everything else."

"The report can wait till tonight. After we—you—have spoken with Hawk."

"All right."

"Thanks, Sis. I'll just get us some food and wine from the kitchen, then we'll be off. I'll see you later." He strode out.

Margarita asked, "Are you all right, Aurelia? This is a shock for us all. And you've been ill."

"I wish everyone would stop reminding me that I've been ill. As if I'm likely to forget! I'm fine, absolutely fine. And if Lucius is too besotted with that precious girl to do his job, you and I will manage perfectly well without him."

"Of course we will."

"Oh, sorry, Margarita. It's just..."

"I know. Don't worry. Lucius is in love, that's all. Come back to the kitchen with me and relax for a while. The customers will start arriving soon."

"There's one more thing I have to do first. Terentius left a package with me for safekeeping. I ought to open it and see what's in it. It's in the safe."

"You think that's why somebody tore the room apart like this?"

"I suppose it must be." I picked up my wine-mug. "I'll take this with me, in case there are any more nasty shocks to come."

"You've made me curious. May I come too?"

"Yes, if you'd like to." It was good of her to offer. I knew I'd be glad of her company.

We went to my study, and I pulled the goatskin rug away from the floor-board that hid our safe. It was easy enough to raise the board and lift out the sturdy iron chest, but I felt absurdly nervous as I unlocked it, and was relieved to find Terentius' package still safely inside.

I took it out and handed it to Margarita while I relocked the chest and stowed it away. She gently turned the bundle over in her hands, and it rattled slightly.

I carefully unwrapped the cloth. Inside was, as I'd expected, a square box made of some light-coloured wood. It had a military seal over the lock, and some sort of design carved on its lid. When I looked closely I realised it was three initials, or rather one initial repeated three times. VVV.

"VVV must be the man who owns it," I said. "It's nicely made. Now, to open it. The question is how?"

"You didn't find the key in the bedroom?"

"No. Let's see now…" I broke the seal. "We'll have to get in by brute force, unless…I know. I'll take it across to the workshop, let Taurus have a go at it. He's not bad at picking locks."

Margarita smiled. "I'm not sure I like the idea of a slave who can pick locks. But as it's Taurus, we don't need to worry."

She was right. There never was a more loyal servant than Taurus, my handyman.

We found him outside on the forecourt, whistling through his teeth as he gazed at a dilapidated farm cart that was standing there, or to be more exact, almost falling over. It had a wheel missing. An old native farmer was striding off, shoulders hunched, face flushed.

"'Morning, Taurus," I said. "Cavarinus doesn't look very happy. Is this his cart?"

"'Morning, Mistress Aurelia. No, he isn't. But then if my cart was as much of a wreck as this, I probably wouldn't be either. I've said I'll try and see to it today, but we've one of our own wagons to mend this morning, and that can't wait, now the boys are haymaking."

"You're getting quite a few repair jobs for our neighbours now. You can manage to fit them in with your other work?"

"'Course I can. And I enjoy doing it. The new lad is a help." For the first time in his life, Taurus had an assistant, and he was proud of it.

"Good. He's settling in well, is he?"

"He's very willing, and an extra pair of hands is useful. Only with a lot of jobs, by the time I've explained how I want it done, and what to be careful of, I might as well have done it myself."

I laughed. I know that feeling, so does everyone who's ever trained an assistant. But I hadn't time for discussing the finer points of delegation. "I've got a small job for you. I need it done straight away, but it shouldn't take you long. Can you open this for me? I've no key, but if you can do it without damaging it,…"

His eyes lit up when he saw the box. "That's a beauty. Beech-wood, and well made. Even got some decoration on the lid. It's not local work, I'd say. What's in it?"

"That's what I need to find out. Can you open it up without smashing it to smithereens?"

"I expect so. I'll try and pick the lock, and if that doesn't work, I can get in through the hinges."

"Fine. Be as quick as you can, won't you? I'll be in my study."

"You don't need to go away. If you come over to the work-shop, I can probably do it while you wait." I followed him into his den, with its tidy workbench and its rows of tools hanging neatly around the walls.

The new lad was planing what looked like the leg of a stool. He wished us a polite good-morning as we entered.

"Fetch me the small wooden chest, Tappo," Taurus said, and when the boy brought it, he began to rummage about inside it. He finally produced a large bunch of keys and a couple of tools I hadn't seen before. He examined the box carefully. "Quite a simple lock; I should be able to manage. What I need to do…"

But before he could begin, Secundus came striding in. "Aure-lia, I've just heard the news about Terentius. A bad business. And his lad's not come back?"

"He hasn't. It looks as if you're right, he's made a run for it. And there's only one obvious reason why he'd do that."

"Aye. I came to give you this, in case it's important." He held out a shiny iron key on his palm. "We found it in the stall where the missing horse went from. Lucky to spot it in the straw. The boy must have dropped it while he was saddling up. I remember you said something about his boss leaving some valuables in the safe."

I pointed to the box. "Just in time. Well done, whoever found this. Tell him there's a jug of beer for him in the bar. Thanks, Secundus. By the way, I want to talk to Hawk today, in case he saw anything unusual in the night. Is his daughter still hanging around the stables? I think she's sweet on one of your horse-boys, isn't she?"

"Don't ask me, I can't keep up with all their romantic tangles. She's here now, that I do know. I'll send her to find him."

"Thanks." I took the box from Taurus and slid the key into the lock, and it fitted snugly and turned easily.

"That's good. I shan't have to spoil it now. Mistress, will you be needing the box once you've looked inside it?"

"I don't know. Why?"

"If you don't, could I have it please? I'd hate it to be thrown away, a nice little box like that."

"*If* I don't need it, you certainly can, but I can't say for sure yet."

"Thank you. Now I'll have Ursulus complaining if I don't get his wagon mended."

Back in my study, I opened the box. It contained three items only, all innocent-looking, yet a man had already died for them.

What took my eye first was a curious semicircular token made of silver. When I picked it up I realised it was one half of a coin. Someone had cut a silver denarius neatly into two, and this was one half of it. Where was the other? With the person who had originally given Terentius the box to deliver? No, more likely with the person who was destined to receive it, so he'd know this message was genuine even if he didn't recognise the bearer.

I put it aside and examined the next item, a small bronze brooch. It was a very ordinary-looking plain disk, the sort of thing a peasant might use to fasten a tunic at the shoulders, except of course such brooches normally come in pairs. Its only distinguishing mark was three letters incised on its surface. It gave me a shock to realise they were the same three as appeared on the lid of the box: VVV.

I showed it to Margarita. "I wish I knew what those letters could mean. Oh well, let's see if this tells us more." The last object was a standard wax note-tablet, tied and sealed. I was disappointed when I opened it to see there was only a single line scrawled on it, crude but quite legible.

"The opening performance of the Fall of Troy is confirmed for midsummer at Isurium. As agreed, the Greek is to play Achilles and Eurytus Hector."

Below were, yet again, the three letters VVV.

It was meant to look like the announcement of a play. There are plenty of dramas about the fall of Troy. But this couldn't be literally a theatrical performance. That wouldn't need secrecy, and knowledge of it wouldn't be worth killing for.

The reference to Troy must be the clue. Hector met his death at Troy. This message was threatening or perhaps warning that someone called Eurytus would die at midsummer, at Isurium... the same time and place as my cousin's birthday party. Terentius and whoever killed him believed this knowledge was urgent and valuable.

I didn't know what to make of it. I was out of my depth, like a swimmer in a fast current. All I knew was what I must do.

"Fetch Lucius, please, Margarita. He must see this."

"He and Vitellia are just setting off for their drive. He may not want to be disturbed."

"I don't care what he wants. This is urgent. Just get him here, and don't take no for an answer."

Chapter IV

Lucius came storming into the room. "What do you want, Aurelia? Whatever it is, it'd better be good, I've lost quite enough time…"

"Shut up and read this." I handed him the note. "It's what Terentius died for, and it looks as if someone else might be going to die too."

He read the tablet and his anger evaporated at once. He stood still for a few heartbeats, then flopped heavily down into my chair. "I'm sorry, Sis. You were right to call me. But of all the lousy luck! As if we didn't have enough trouble with a murdered soldier, he turns out to be a traitor too."

"A traitor? So you think it's some kind of death threat?"

He nodded. "It's not just the note itself. It's those letters at the bottom, VVV. And on the brooch too, and even the box."

"What do they mean? I can't think of anything except 'Veni, vidi, vici.'"

"This isn't a joking matter, I'm afraid. The letters stand for 'Vivat Venutius Victor.'"

"Long live Venutius the Victor? Who's Venutius?"

"Venutius was a Brigantian prince who made trouble quite soon after the original conquest of Britannia. There was a scandal among the native royalty because the queen left him and ran off with one of her bodyguard."

"But that was ages ago, long before our family settled in Oak Bridges. Surely he can't be still alive? If he is, he must be about a hundred and fifty."

"No, he's dead. But the slogan Vivat Venutius Victor has been taken up by his grandson, another Prince Venutius. He has quite a following among the young Brigantians, and it's rumoured he wants to put on his grandfather's armour, so to speak, attacking the Roman garrisons in his area, trying to drive the army out of Brigantia."

"His area? Does that include Isurium?"

"It does."

"So this message has something to do with a native conspiracy. What was Terentius doing carrying it all the way from Londinium?"

"That's the other worrying thing, the mention of Eurytus."

"I've never heard of him. Is he someone important?"

"Very. He's a senior tax official, one of Caesar's most influential freedmen. He's come out here from Rome to do Imperial audits all over Britannia. Apparently someone at court thinks that not all of Caesar's taxes are finding their way into the Imperial treasury. So this Eurytus is investigating. He's powerful and rich, and also a real bastard by all accounts."

"We've heard nothing about tax audits in this area."

"That's deliberate policy. He keeps his itinerary secret, to give as little advance warning as possible to anyone who's up to no good. Usually any town or fort he visits gets just one day's notice. He started in Londinium in the spring and is working his way north, and he's made himself very unpopular wherever he goes."

"So this note is a warning that he'll be visiting Isurium at midsummer, and someone will kill him while he's there. It says 'as agreed…' which must mean they already have some kind of plan ready, they're just waiting for confirmation."

Lucius nodded. "And the other things, the half-coin and the brooch, are to prove to whoever the message is for that it's genuine."

Margarita spoke, making me jump because I hadn't realised she had come back into the room. "What does it mean about Achilles and Hector? I'm a bit hazy when it comes to the Trojan War, but they were on opposite sides, weren't they, and Achilles killed Hector in single combat?"

I was about to mock her ignorance of one of the best-known parts of history, but remembered in time that she'd been born a slave and hadn't had much education.

"That's right. Hector was a Trojan prince, and Achilles picked a fight with him because Hector had killed his friend."

She said slowly, "This may be sheer coincidence, but I somehow don't think it is…"

"What?"

"Terentius' boy, the one who's run off. When he was eating his supper in the kitchen last night he mentioned Achilles and Hector, and even Isurium. I was busy with the meals for the guests, and it didn't make sense to me, so I didn't think anything of it at the time. But now…"

"Can you remember exactly what he said?" Lucius asked.

"I think I got the gist of it. He was boasting that he'd soon be rich enough to buy his freedom, because he and his master were on an important mission with a message for someone, and they'd earn a great deal of money. The other servants asked him what the message was, and at first he wouldn't tell, but they teased him and eventually he did. He said pretty well what's in that note: there's to be a performance of the Fall of Troy at midsummer at Isurium, and a Greek Achilles will kill an enemy called Hector."

"I wonder," I mused, "whether Terentius trusted the boy with the message in case something happened to him, or whether the boy sneaked a look inside the box one day?"

"And *I* wonder," Lucius added, "whether the lad has killed his master and run off to deliver the message himself, so he can collect the whole reward instead of only getting a small part of it?"

"And that would explain the state of the bedroom. Before he left he searched and searched for the box because he wanted the identification token as well," I suggested.

"So in plain Latin," Margarita said, "somebody Greek will kill Eurytus at Isurium at midsummer."

Lucius looked thoughtful. "As we were saying earlier, there aren't many Greeks in the army, especially here in Britannia."

"It could be an army doctor," Margarita suggested. "Most of them are Greeks. Most of the doctors in the whole Empire, come to that. Like my Timaeus."

It was so obvious, I knew she had to be right. "A medical officer? Of course! Well done, Margarita. Does Timaeus have any friends or contacts among army medics? He might be able to give us some names."

"He's never worked for the army, so I doubt it, but I'll ask him, certainly."

Lucius stood up. "Whoever the Greek is, this box means trouble, there's no doubt of it. And it means I've no choice but to go to Eburacum to report it. So much for my holiday plans!"

"You'll leave Vitellia behind?"

"I'll have to. I can't take her with me, and she'll be fine here, won't she? I'm sure you can take good care of her. With a bit of luck I'll only be gone a couple of days, though I suppose they may want me to go on up to Isurium to check on the situation there." He sighed. "Anyway, I must go and that's that. If our guesses are right, and there's to be some kind of incident at midsummer, there isn't much time." He added a few choice comments about Terentius and young Venutius. "But there's enough time for me to have today here, at least. After all, Hawk will need today to check around in the woods, won't he?"

"Of course he will."

"Then I'll leave at first light tomorrow. And now I'm going to make the most of what little time I have left with Vitellia."

"I'll go and tell her you're ready," Margarita said, and left us.

Lucius looked at me. "You realise what this means?"

"It means we could end up working together at Isurium after all." I felt a sudden surge of happiness. "You never know, I may be able to pick up something useful, through Jovina and Marcus and some of the others there. They'd confide in a civilian woman more than an investigator like you. But I couldn't be ready to leave tomorrow. I'll follow on as soon as I can."

He shook his head. "No chance. I'm sorry, but Terentius' message changes everything. You must refuse Jovina's invitation. If there is some sort of conspiracy going on at Isurium, a plan to assassinate Eurytus or even to attack the fort, it could be far too dangerous for you to be anywhere near."

"Now wait, you're not leaving me out of things just like that! If there *is* danger in the wind, as Jovina said in her note, she needs me all the more."

"And *I* need to be able to do my job up there without constantly looking over my shoulder to make sure you're all right. I know you're not bad at investigating…"

"Thanks, brother!"

"…but in a situation like this, you'd be more of a hindrance than a help."

"Nonsense, you know Marcus and Jovina will take care of me, as if I couldn't take care of myself. And if there's an advantage in secrecy, it'll be far easier for me to work undercover than you."

"Argue away as much as you like. I can't allow you to go up there now. It's too dangerous."

I sensed his growing excitement as he thought about the assignment. Sensed it, and shared it, and very much wanted to be part of the investigation. How could I persuade him that, far from being a hindrance, I could be an asset?

"Look, suppose you make sure Eurytus' visit to the fort goes off safely? He'll go away, you'll go away, but the hostility that's at the bottom of all this will still be festering underground, waiting to emerge again like a fungus lurking under a tree root. If you want to stop it for good, you've got to catch the leaders, not just chase them into hiding. You've got to work undercover. And I, a civilian woman going to a party there, will have a cover that nobody will suspect."

He rubbed his chin thoughtfully. "Yes, you're right, I shall need to be undercover, at least at first. But that makes me more determined than ever not to let you put yourself in danger by going there. I'd be worrying about you all the time."

"I don't see why."

"And I'd be worrying about Vitellia, left all alone here, if we were both away. Much better for you to stay together, safe and sound and keeping each other company."

"WHAT?"

"It's an ideal solution. A good chance for you to get to know one another properly."

Suddenly I saw where he was driving, and it made me very angry. He wasn't really worried about my being in danger at all. He was expecting me to refuse help to my cousin, not to mention the chance of a holiday, in order to stay at home and act as nursemaid to a silly little girl. Well, I wasn't having that. I wanted to explode, to shout at him and tell him what a selfish pig he was. But I knew I must keep calm, outwardly at least. If I let my anger show it would only make matters worse.

"I've got to go, Lucius. Jovina needs me, and it looks now as if the danger she's in is a good deal more serious than I thought. You'll either have to find someone else to take care of Vitellia, or give her a strong escort and send her home on her own. And it'll give her a taste of what her life will be like married to you, left by herself half the time while you go off on assignments."

"Look, Aurelia, you must see…"

"I see that Vitellia may be a child you can order about, but I'm not. I'm not abandoning Jovina, and you can't force me to."

Oh, me and my big mouth! Now I'd made him angry too.

He spoke softly, with the dangerous calm of someone keeping tight hold of his temper. "Indeed I can force you, if you persist in being so stupid. I'm the head of the family."

"But you're not all-powerful. I'm a free citizen, and legally you can't stop me travelling anywhere in the Empire if I choose to." I wasn't at all sure about this in fact, but from Lucius' answer, neither was he.

"I might not be able to physically prevent your travelling," he said slowly, "but I have power over this mansio and everything in it. I'm the legal owner, and all I have to do is order the staff not to help you, or let you take any of my property away from the Oak Tree. You can't remove even one horse or saddle, one slave, without my leave, let alone the proper escort you'd need for a journey north."

I stared at him in horror. Much as I hated to admit it, I realised he was right. In law, he is the owner of the Oak Tree, because of course as an official mansio, it can't be owned by a woman. We called ourselves joint proprietors, but the legal fact was that he owned it, while I ran it. This arrangement suited us both, and had never caused us a cross word. Until now.

But I couldn't bring myself to acknowledge that the law was on his side, so I said nothing.

"I hate this," he said, in a more normal voice. "I don't want to quarrel with you, Aurelia. I want to keep you safe. Is that so unreasonable?"

I was too annoyed to make peace. "It's completely unreasonable. If I have to stay here with Vitellia, I'll…well I *won't* stay here, and that's all there is to it."

"Enough!" he snapped, and I heard in his gruff tone an echo of our father's voice, when he'd made an unpopular decision and expected the family to obey him.

My mind was racing as I tried to think of a way out of this impasse. There must be something I could do, if I could only find it. There *must* be.

He said, "I shall talk to the senior staff, Margarita and Secundus."

"To tell them I'll be a prisoner in my own mansio?"

"Oh, don't worry, I shan't make it sound as if I'm having to forbid you like a naughty child, even if I am. I shall say you're in danger if you go north, and I'll hold them personally responsible if anything happens to you. I'll make it clear that you are not to leave the Oak Tree unescorted till I come back, and you're not to travel further afield than Oak Bridges."

"And Eburacum, surely," I protested. "I need to go there now and then for business reasons, you know that, if you're away for any length of time."

"All right, you can go to Eburacum if it's really necessary, but you must take Secundus as guard. That way you won't stay there an hour longer than you have to, because you'll know he'll be needed here."

And Albia's farm? My sister's name flashed into my mind and I almost spoke it aloud, but I swallowed it back just in time. My sister and her family live a day's travel to the east, and she'd help me, I knew she would. Lucius has no authority over her now that she's married to Candidus. If he hadn't thought of that, I wasn't going to remind him.

For now, I'd have to let him think he'd won, and wait till he'd gone and I could get help. But he knows me, and if I gave in too easily, he'd smell a rat. "You're being a bastard, brother," I grumbled, "and a stupid, pompous bastard at that."

"But I'm right, and you know it. Stop arguing, and give me your word that you'll do as I ask in this."

I gave him only a silence.

"I'm waiting, Aurelia."

"You'll have a long wait."

He shrugged. "Very well, you won't promise. That makes no difference. I'll give my orders and the staff will do as I tell them. Which means you will too. You live a pretty free life here, but you must accept my judgment about what's best. You'll stay away from Isurium until the danger there is over. Like it or lump it."

"I shan't do either, brother," I answered, but too softly for him to hear as he stalked out.

Chapter V

I daresay it will shock many people that I even considered disobeying Lucius. As head of the family he's duty-bound to take
decisions for all of us, if he thinks he's protecting us from harm.
But I was so sure I was right to go to Jovina and so angry with
him for wanting to prevent me that my decision was made in a
heartbeat, and once made, I never thought of changing it.

I believe the gods must have approved of my disobedience,
because everything was surprisingly easy. I've always been a good
organiser, so the practical details were straightforward enough:
I just had to make sure I could get away from the Oak Tree and
as far as Eburacum without assistance from anyone here. I knew
how I could arrange that. Then once I was in Eburacum, Albia
wouldn't refuse her help, and I could get to Isurium.

Lucius himself made it simpler for me than I could have dared
to hope. What he should have done was talk to the staff straight
away, because once he ordered them not to help me travel any
distance from the Oak Tree, everyone would have to obey him:
the slaves without question, the free staff from duty. But he was
so determined to spend the rest of the day with his beloved that
he and Vitellia set off for their country drive as soon as he'd
finished laying down the law to me, and I knew they wouldn't
be back till dinner time. I had all day to plan.

First I wrote to Jovina, accepting her invitation and assur-
ing her I was looking forward to her party, without of course

mentioning her request for help. I wanted it to reach Isurium as soon as possible, which meant one of our lads would have to take it as far as Eburacum, from where the army post would carry it north. But luckily a cavalry courier I recognised stopped by to change horses and have a meal on his way west, and in no time he'd agreed to add my note to the bag of official messages he was carrying, in exchange for a free skin of wine for his journey. Cheap at the price.

The second letter took longer. It was to my sister Albia, and I was asking two favours. I needed her to help me on my journey to Isurium, even perhaps lend me transport to drive there, and also to look after Vitellia at her farm while I was away. I was sure she'd agree. She knew Jovina as well as I did, and would want to help if she was in trouble. All the same she'd think my requests odd, and I didn't want to go into the problem of Lucius' attitude in my note, so I added a couple of sentences which would tell her there was more here than met the eye: "I know I'm asking a lot, Albia. There's a problem with a guest from Arpinum which is making all this a bit complicated." "Arpinum" was a kind of code word all the staff knew, going back to the old days when Albia was my housekeeper at the Oak Tree. It was a way of telling each other discreetly that we'd got trouble. She would remember.

I didn't expect the gods to find me a convenient army courier for this note too, but they did even better. As I headed for the stables to arrange for one of our own boys to ride to my sister's, I heard hoof-beats coming down from the main road. Onto the forecourt rode a young man I recognised, one of Albia's servants. He waved and called my name.

My heart missed several beats. A messenger from Albia? Was something wrong? Perhaps she was ill, or Candidus, or the children?

But he was grinning as he pulled up and jumped down beside me. "Don't look so worried, Mistress, there's nothing wrong. I've brought a message from Mistress Albia. She's gone to stay in our Eburacum house for a few days, and she invites you to visit her there."

"Albia's in Eburacum? That's wonderful. But surely…I mean why didn't she call in here as she was passing? I can't believe she wouldn't stop at the Oak Tree on her way."

"She didn't come by this road. She went by way of Petuaria to visit Mistress Tullia there. She wanted to see her new baby. Very taken with it, she was, and…"

"Yes, I see." Albia adores new babies. I can never understand it myself. "So she went direct to Eburacum from there?"

"That's right. She had some business to do for the farm. We got there last night. She sent me straight here to ask if you'll come and join her."

He pulled a note-tablet from his saddlebag and handed it to me. "This letter explains it all. I'm to wait for your answer and take it straight back today." He grinned again. "And I'm to say she won't accept any answer except yes."

"Then it's yes, I'd love to come. Get yourself something to eat, and a fresh horse. I'll have a note for you to take back by the time you've done that."

I hurried to my study, hardly able to believe my good fortune. An invitation to Eburacum! Exactly what I needed and wanted.

Albia to dear Aurelia, greetings.

I hope you're really on the mend at last. Your letter in May sounded more cheerful, and I've got just the prescription to get you completely well again. Come and stay with me in Eburacum. I'm here for a few days after visiting Tullia and her gorgeous baby. And I'm here alone, Candidus can't leave the farm with all the summer work, and I didn't take the twins with me to Tullia's, I thought she had enough to do without having them rampaging around her house. I've got a few business errands to do for the farm, but it's very lonely. Do say you'll come over and keep me company. Then I'll travel back with you to the Oak Tree, so I can see Lucius on my way home and meet this latest girl of his.

Remember, I'm not taking no for an answer.

The note I wrote to her now was as easy as the previous one had been difficult.

Aurelia to dear Albia, greetings.

What a wonderful surprise. Yes please, I'd love to come. I've been thinking about a little holiday, with Eburacum as the first stop, so thank you. I'll set off the day after tomorrow. I'm quite recovered, and looking forward to a change of scene, and especially to seeing you. And I've lots of news, including some from Arpinum.

Lucius has to go away on an assignment, unexpected but necessary. So Vitellia is staying here at the Oak Tree. I hope it's all right if I bring her with me.

I'm counting the hours.

I was watching the lad ride away with my note when one of the horse-boys came running to me from the direction of the stable-yard. "Could you come to the small paddock, please, Mistress?"

"What is it? Moon-cloud?"

"Not yet, but she won't be long. No, Hawk's got a message for you. He's waiting there."

I always enjoy chatting to Hawk, partly because he's a good friend and partly because he's the best native tracker I've ever seen. He knows our woods as nobody else does, down to the last tree and tuft of grass, and if anything unusual had happened last night or early this morning, he would very likely be able to tell me about it.

He was leaning on the fence talking softly to Moon-cloud and stroking her neck. Yes, she was very near her time. Mares usually give birth in the night, but this one looked as if she wouldn't wait till dark.

He turned and smiled as he heard me approach. He's a dark, slim man who can move like a cat through the trees. As usual, he had his large hound beside him.

"Good morning, Aurelia. How are you?"

"I'm well, thank you, Hawk. I haven't seen you for a few days. Have you been on your travels?"

"Yes, I've been hunting north of here. I took two of my sons. It's time they spread their wings a little."

"A successful trip?"

He nodded. "We caught a wild boar, and his sow and litter. A couple of deer, and the usual small birds, and several good big hares. I wondered if you'd like any meat."

"Very much, please. Deer or hares would be welcome. And what birds did you catch?" We discussed game and prices briefly, and shook hands on a deal. As usual, I spoke Latin, while he answered in native British. We always conversed like this, even though each of us understood the other's language perfectly well. After knowing him for almost twenty years I've forgotten why we started doing it, but it suits both of us.

And whatever language Hawk chose to speak, he was worth listening to. So when we'd finished our bargaining and he showed no sign of wanting to leave, it meant he had something else to tell me, but something he wanted to discuss in private.

"I need to get back inside," I said, "I've a mountain of paper-work waiting, but I'm glad of any excuse to put it off for a bit longer. Have you time to seal our bargain with a drink?"

"Thanks, yes, I'll take a beer."

He said nothing else till we were comfortably settled in my study, he with a mug of beer and I with some watered wine. I said, "We had a death here last night, and we think the killer is in the woods. Did you see anything unusual?"

"As it happens, I did. I was on my way to tell you when my daughter came to find me. I was up most of last night, our cow had a difficult calving and needed some help. Just after dawn Bran heard something that made him bark." He glanced down at the big brindled hound, more like a wolf than a dog, which lay quietly beside his stool. "I always take notice when he barks, so I went into the woods to investigate. I found a riderless horse wandering about looking lost. Dark grey with one white sock, rather skinny, but quite lively, and didn't mind being caught. I looked around for a while, and found the boy who presumably had been its rider. A thin spotty lad with lanky brown hair."

"*Had been* its rider? I don't like the sound of that."

"I'm afraid you're right. He's dead."

"How?"

"He was stabbed in the neck."

"Poor boy." I felt sorry for him of course, but mainly I was alarmed. We'd assumed he was the criminal in this affair, murdering his master and then escaping. Now it seemed there was another murderer…who was still free.

I told Hawk briefly about Terentius. I mentioned the locked box but not its contents. This situation was growing more complicated by the hour, and I felt instinctively that the fewer people who knew about that particular secret, the better. "We assumed the servant had killed his master, either after robbing him, or perhaps because of some grudge. I suppose it couldn't be that the boy felt remorse for what he'd done, and took his own life?"

"No, he was attacked from behind. And I saw his murderer's tracks."

"Did you now? Tell me."

"Here's what I think happened. The boy rode his horse through the trees, parallel with the road, coming from the mansio here and heading east up the Long Hill. He stopped and dismounted about a quarter of a mile from here, and paced about, as if he was waiting for something, or someone. A man's tracks came from further into the wood and met the boy's. They must have stood talking for a short while, and then the boy's tracks headed towards where he'd left his horse. The man followed him, came up behind him, and stabbed him. There wasn't even a struggle. The horse took fright and ran off, and the man didn't try to catch it, just went back into the trees on foot."

"Hawk, you're a wonder. You can tell all that from the footprints?"

"Oh yes. The attacker was wearing army boots with hobnails, some of the nails quite worn. I haven't seen those boots before, but I'll know them again."

"Again? You think he may still be about in the woods?"

"I don't know, but it's possible. That's why I didn't want to tell you all this outside in the open. The trees have ears." He drank some beer.

"What happened next?"

"I haven't had the chance to do any more. I assume he had a horse of his own waiting in the trees somewhere, or he'd have used the one belonging to the boy. He's probably miles away by now. Do you want me to look round and see what I can find out?"

"Yes, please, Hawk. Lucius will be sending a report to Eburacum, and he needs to add as much information as possible. Gods…Lucius is out somewhere driving with Vitellia. Suppose they run into the murderer?"

Hawk shook his head. "They won't. I saw him heading up the Long Hill. He didn't see me, he was too absorbed in his girl. Beautiful little thing, isn't she?"

"Yes. But suppose the killer…"

"They'll be safe enough sticking to the road. And anyway, I don't think this was a random attack on a passing stranger, do you? The two of them knew one another, else why would the boy have been hanging around in the woods? He had his horse, he could simply have ridden off. Why didn't he?"

"I see what you mean. The slave was actually waiting for the man who attacked him, and talked to him, and was taken off his guard by the attack. I wonder what he had to say? To report that he'd killed his master?"

Hawk gave his rare smile. "Now that's something I can't tell you, I'm afraid. Not yet, anyway." He finished his beer and stood up. "I'll see what more I can find out, and come and tell you before the end of today."

"Thanks, I'll really appreciate it. So will Lucius. He's taking the whole incident quite seriously."

"Not seriously enough to postpone his romantic outing, though?" Hawk asked, as we walked together through the barroom and out onto the forecourt.

"Gods, no, that would need a barbarian invasion, or Caesar dropping in here for a beaker of Gaulish red."

He nodded. "I don't remember ever seeing your brother in love before."

I couldn't think of a suitable reply, and Hawk, perhaps sensing my lack of enthusiasm, changed the subject. "I'll send my daughter over with your meat later. She'll bring the horse back too. What about the boy's body?"

"Lucius will want to see it. When your daughter comes, tell her to ask Secundus for a couple of men and a cart to go and collect it. And Hawk…"

He paused in midstride. "Yes?"

"Take care, won't you? Hunting wild boars is one thing. Hunting murderers…that's different."

He nodded. "I will."

I told Secundus about my conversation with Hawk, and then stayed by the paddocks a little while, making a fuss of the horses. Hawk's news had upset me, and I needed something to help me calm down. I always enjoy looking the horses over, and their contented grazing made me feel calm too, in spite of the possibility that a murderer might be about in the woods.

I tore myself away at last and went into the kitchen to find Margarita, because I realised that with all the drama earlier, I hadn't yet told her my good news. As I opened the door I heard raised voices, and paused to glance round. One of the girls had dropped a pot of hot sauce, which had smashed into a thousand pieces and created a pungent pool over half the floor. Cook was throwing a tantrum, yelling curses and insisting that the girl clear up the mess. She was crying, calling him a bully and a heartless brute. He could be both, but he was in the right here.

I couldn't see Margarita, so I had to deal with the squabble myself. As I opened my mouth to stop the row and back up Cook, I realised the girl in tears was Baca. She must still be shaken after her unpleasant experience earlier, and that made a difference, in my eyes if not in Cook's.

"Calm down, both of you." I said it loud enough to carry over their voices, and they both fell silent and gazed at me. "Cook, Baca's had a nasty shock today, she's not at her best. It's not surprising she's made a mistake. Don't be too hard on her."

"She's just a stupid…"

"No argument, please. Baca, you've been clumsy, but I'm sure you didn't mean to be. Apologise to Cook and clean all this up, and we'll say no more about it."

The door from the hall opened, and Margarita came in. "What's happened? Oh dear. A bit of an accident?"

"Nothing serious. Well, Baca? Cook's waiting for you to apologise."

"I'm sorry, Cook," she answered in a small voice. "I just…I don't know. It slipped."

Cook grunted. "Well, don't do it again. Clear it away, for the gods' sake." He gestured to one of the other girls. "Crispina, chop some more vegetables. I'll have to start all over again." He made it sound as if he'd have to prepare an entire replacement banquet, but I ignored that.

As he and everyone else went back to work, I had a useful idea. "Margarita, can I borrow Baca for a few hours this afternoon? I've some sewing that needs doing."

"Yes, of course. I'll send her to you when she's finished here."

Baca smiled. She was one of the best of the servants when it came to sewing, and I'd realised that at least one of my tunics and my travelling cloak were in need of repair before I set off for Jovina's. Also I must decide what I would be wearing for her party. I'd lost some weight over the past few months, and my best clothes would need taking in a little.

Margarita and I moved into the barroom, and I told her about my holiday. As I'd expected, she was delighted, and began asking me all about Cousin Jovina. But she was soon distracted, because the bar was filling up as customers started to arrive for their midday beaker of beer or bite of food.

I left her to it and went to my study to write yet another note. This was to my friend Clarilla, the sister of our local chief town councillor. They lived in Oak Bridges, only a mile or so away, and I wanted to tell her about my holiday, and also ask for her help in case I ran into problems getting round Lucius' prohibition of it. I sent one of the horse-boys over to her villa with a note asking if she'd be free later for me to drop in and tell her some good news.

By the time I'd had something to eat and set Baca to work reviving my clothes, the boy was back with Clarilla's answer: she was agog to hear my news and would be delighted to see me any time this afternoon.

I asked Secundus to get a small two-wheeled gig ready. I would drive myself, and take one of the horse-boys along as a mounted escort. It was a long time since I'd felt like driving anywhere, and my spirits lifted as I took the reins and set off for Oak Bridges.

Chapter VI

I found Clarilla outside in her garden, lounging on a cushioned reading-couch with a scroll on her lap. As it was still rolled up, I gathered she'd been doing more drowsing than reading, but she jumped up when she saw me.

"Welcome, Aurelia. It's lovely to see you." She turned to the maid who'd brought me to her. "Let the master know that Aurelia's here, and fetch the wine, please. Now, sit down and tell me how you are. Indeed I can see how you are—you look better than you've done for months, like your old self again."

We sat down side by side on the couch. "Yes, I'm feeling really well. It's like coming out of a dark cave into bright sunshine."

"That's wonderful. Though I'm a little disappointed you've come all alone. I was hoping you might bring your brother and this gorgeous new fiancée of his."

"You've heard about her, have you?"

"My dear, who hasn't? Everyone's talking about her…young and beautiful, and from a very good family too. In fact I thought that might be the good news you'd come to tell me. You must be delighted."

"Yes, I suppose I must. She's a mixture of the Goddess Aphrodite and Queen Cleopatra."

"Oh, dear. Don't you like her?"

"It's not that I don't like her exactly, but she's very immature, and just not the kind of girl I'd hoped he would marry."

"I'm sure as you get to know her better, you'll understand what he sees in her." She smiled. "Who knows, you might even come around to the idea of marriage yourself one of these days. You and Quintus Antonius, perhaps?"

I laughed. "I know you love matchmaking, Clarilla, but Quintus and I are very happy the way things are, so don't hold your breath. And no, it isn't Lucius and Vitellia I've come to tell you about. I've some happy news of my own. I'm going on a little holiday. First to stay with Albia at Eburacum, then to a cousin's birthday party at Isurium."

"How exciting. No wonder you're looking so full of life."

"My cousin's invitation only arrived this morning, and the party is at midsummer, so it's all a bit of a rush. I wondered if I might ask you a favour."

"Of course, anything." Clarilla paused as her stately major-domo arrived carrying a tray with a beautiful silver wine-jug and three matching goblets, and a silver dish of tiny round pastries. As he set them out on a small table, her brother Silvanius Clarus appeared from the house. He looked every inch a chief councillor, tall and elegant, immaculate as always in a gleaming white toga, even though this was an ordinary working afternoon. I knew the reason he liked to dress so formally: he was born British but had earned Roman citizenship, and he treasured the right to wear the toga whenever he could.

He greeted me with his usual mixture of warmth and pomposity. "Aurelia, my dear, it's a pleasure indeed to see you. I'm so sorry I was not here to greet you. Important meeting, I'm afraid. The price of responsibility…one is honoured to serve, but the work is onerous sometimes."

"You do a very valuable job, Clarus. I don't know what we'd do without you." And you love it, I added silently. Well, why not? We Romans depend on people like Clarus for the day-to-day governing of this province. He's devoted to Rome, and he has considerable power in our district, which he uses to bring Roman civilisation to his fellow Britons whenever he can. I don't begrudge him a little vainglory now and then.

Clarilla poured wine for us all, and Clarus smiled at me over the rim of his goblet. "It's good to see you out and about, Aurelia. You're looking better, if I may say so."

Clarilla said, "Isn't she? And she's going on holiday. Eburacum, and then Isurium. Is your cousin's husband with the army?"

"Yes, he's an officer at the fort there. I've never been to Isurium before, but you two know it well, don't you?"

"Quite well," Clarilla said. "We have a kinsman there, Brennus, and we still keep in touch, though it's a while since I visited. It's a quiet little place, no public entertainments of any kind, but it's very pleasant for a holiday, especially if there's a party. Clarus, we must give her a note of introduction to Brennus."

"Indeed yes. He's done rather well for himself, I'm glad to say. A citizen now of course, and an important local leader at Isurium. He has a most charming wife too. I'll write you an introduction. And perhaps you'd also take a personal letter from us to them both?"

"Of course I will. I'm sure I'll enjoy meeting them."

He frowned slightly. "And if there's any trouble while you're there…but then of course you'll be staying with your cousin and her husband, so you'll be well protected."

"Trouble? I thought Clarilla just said it was quiet."

"Certainly it always has been, but lately…I'm sure it's a storm in a wine-cup, my dear, but there are rumours of—ah—restlessness, discontent even."

"I see. So that explains it."

"I'm sorry?"

"Lucius is a bit worried about my making the trip. He seems to think there might be some unrest among the locals there."

"Your brother has heard the rumours too, has he? I'm not surprised. In his position he'll be well informed. The main problem, it seems to me, arises from this silly fashion for idolising Prince Venutius. Some say it is just the young people being overexuberant, but I consider it dangerous."

"I've heard a little about this young Venutius. Couldn't he be just another headstrong would-be warrior with too much ambition? Making a great deal of noise, but not a real threat to Rome."

"That's what I keep hoping. But Brennus is quite concerned about it. You see…I know I can trust your discretion, Aurelia, and this isn't public knowledge yet. The governor plans to make Isurium some kind of administrative centre for the Brigantes, with its own town council to run day-to-day affairs. As ours does in Oak Bridges."

"Our council here is a good example of how well that can work."

He beamed at the compliment. "Brennus and his friends would do an admirable job as town councillors at Isurium. The last thing they want is for a group of hot-headed young fools to cause the governor to change his mind." He sighed and sipped his wine. "I'm afraid there are still some benighted folk here who—ah—haven't fully accepted the finality of being a part of our great Empire."

"Actually, it isn't just Venutius that my brother is concerned about. It's this wretched tax auditor from Rome, Eurytus, who seems to be going round upsetting everybody. He's due in Isurium soon. Has your kinsman mentioned him at all?"

"Not by name, but his most recent letter said something about corrupt tax collectors in his district, and I've heard from elsewhere the gossip about Eurytus' very—ah—abrasive manner."

"He's downright unpleasant, everybody says so," Clarilla put in. "Rude and arrogant, and yet he's only a freedman."

"An Imperial freedman, don't forget," Clarus amended quickly, "and I realise he has a job to do. We must all pay our taxes, but he does seem to have the knack of causing friction, rather than smoothing it away."

"I suppose it's inevitable," I said. "Nobody likes taxmen."

"It's more than that, I gather." Clarus refilled our glasses. "As you say, he'll visit Isurium sooner or later, and there have been problems there caused by some—ah—overzealousness on the part of the local tax officials."

"Corruption, in plain Latin. Well, we all know there are some parts of the province where the tax collecting system is as bent as a catapult-spring. Isn't that what people like Eurytus are supposed to put right when they do their auditing?"

"Perhaps. But Caesar is interested mainly in gathering the right amount of taxes into his treasury. He's less concerned about exactly how that is done."

"Let's not depress poor Aurelia just as she's about to visit the place," Clarilla said. "You'll be fine if the army are looking after you. Now, you mentioned a favour. To do with your holiday?"

"Well…I'm only asking on the strict understanding that you'll say no if it isn't convenient. The problem is, our carriages are all on the elderly side, and a bit scruffy. I wondered if I might borrow a raeda from you for the journey."

"Of course, my dear, we'd be delighted. In fact you must take two. A big one for yourself, and a smaller one for baggage and servants."

"That would be excellent, if you're sure you can spare them."

She smiled indulgently. "Clarus buys far too many carriages. We could never use them all, if we travelled the Empire all summer long."

"And perhaps we can help set your brother's mind at rest about your journey too," Clarus said. "Would you like Brutus to escort you?"

"Clarus, that would be wonderful." Brutus, an ex-soldier, was one of Silvanius Clarus' best retainers, a kind of chief bodyguard, reliable and brave. "I can't think of anyone I'd rather have accompanying us. But can you manage without him? You or Clarilla might need him yourselves, if you're thinking of travelling anywhere."

Clarilla assured me that they had no journeys planned themselves till the middle of July. "And you'll be back in Oak Bridges long before that, won't you, Aurelia?"

"Yes, I will. And in any case I wouldn't dream of keeping him or the carriages there for my whole visit, only for the journey itself. They could return here straight away. Jovina's husband will provide vehicles and an escort when I travel home again."

"Then it's settled," Clarus said. "When do you leave?"

"The day after tomorrow."

Clarilla exclaimed in surprise. "However will you be ready at such short notice? I need at least half a month to prepare for a holiday."

"At least," Clarus smiled. "Now if you'll forgive me, I must get back to work, so I'll leave you to your women's talk. Have a wonderful time, my dear."

I left soon after too, pleading that I'd a mountain of work to get through before I went away. That was true, but the mountain was considerably less daunting now.

It was midafternoon by the time I reached home, and the barroom was almost empty. Usually there's a sleepy lull between the midday crowd and the evening drinkers, but this time I was aware of tension in the air. A stranger was talking to Margarita at the bar, and the remaining four or five customers were silently watching.

"Well, for the gods' sake, how long will she be?" The man had a gravelly, growling voice, as if he was recovering from a sore throat, but that didn't conceal his anger or impatience. "This is an urgent matter. I'm late already, and it's really very simple. All I want is to find him. Why can't you give me a straight answer? Is he here or not?"

"Ah, you're in luck." Margarita was relieved to see me. "Here's the innkeeper now, she'll be able to help you. Aurelia, this is Portius Niger, he's been waiting for you. He says he needs to find Terentius urgently. I think it may have something to do with that guest from Arpinum."

I looked the man up and down as I walked slowly across the room. He was tall and muscular, with very dark hair, either black or brown. It was hard to see much of his face, because his head was swathed in bandages which obscured most of it completely, or left it in shadow. I got an impression of a jutting jaw with a two days' growth of beard, a straight nose, and a confident, imperious manner.

"I'm pleased to meet you, Portius," I said. "Aurelia Marcella, at your service. How can I help?"

"I need to find one of your guests, a soldier called Terentius." The man stifled a cough with a hand in front of his mouth. "He's staying here just now, and I need to see him. But your barmaid won't go and get him for me, or tell me where he is."

"It's a little complicated," I said. "Let's get you a drink, and I'll explain. Come and sit down over here." I led him to a corner table out of earshot of the other customers. He followed with a bad grace, but despite his bandaged head he moved easily and didn't seem to be in any discomfort.

I gave him my brightest smile. "Now, what will you have? If you don't mind my saying so, from the look of those bandages, you could do with something to revive you."

"What? Oh yes, my wretched horse threw me. And I've a sore chest too." He gave another loud cough. "I'll take a beaker of red, thank you." He sat down, and I signalled Margarita to bring it. "Meantime, can you send someone to fetch Terentius for me, please? It really is important. He has property of mine, a small box which he's due to hand over to me. We were supposed to meet yesterday, and he'll be as anxious to see me as I am to see him."

Something wasn't right here. I caught Margarita's eye as she brought the wine over, and knew that she sensed it too. Then Secundus came in, unusually for the middle of the afternoon, and he strode straight over to me.

"Sorry to interrupt, Aurelia, but I'd like a word when you can. It's about Moon-cloud. I think we're going to have trouble."

"Really? I'll be with you as soon as I can, Secundus. Get yourself a drink, I won't be long."

He nodded, and I was glad to see him lounge against the bar with a beaker of beer. I'm not afraid of any customer as a rule, but this stranger was making me nervous, and Secundus' presence was reassuring.

Portius took a drink of his wine. "Well? Are you going to send for Terentius?"

"No. I'm afraid he's not here now."

The stranger frowned. "Not here? Where's he gone then?"

I hesitated, wondering how much to tell him. There was something threatening about him, a kind of tension, like a ballista about to hurl a stone. I decided to be cautious.

"I'm afraid," I began, "that there's been a—well, an accident here. Terentius is dead. It happened sometime in the night. His servant has run away. I'm sorry to have to give you such bad news. If you're a friend of his…."

"Dead? Oh, I see." His reaction surprised me. I could have expected him to be sad, or angry, and certainly to have asked how Terentius met his end. But his next question was, "What has happened to his possessions?"

"We have them here. We'll be sending them to Eburacum with his body tomorrow."

He looked relieved. "Ah, that's all right then. If you'll just give me his box? He was supposed to hand it over to me when we met."

I decided to move from playing cautious to playing ignorant. "Box? I don't know anything about a box."

"But you must! I know he was travelling with it, and I presume he gave it to you for safekeeping. It contains something of mine, something I need urgently. That's why we'd arranged to meet here, so I could take charge of it." He was leaning forward eagerly and staring into my eyes. "Just a small box, but very valuable, vitally important. Are you sure he didn't give it to you to lock away overnight?"

"I'm quite sure, yes."

"May I take you into my confidence?" Portius looked down, as if embarrassed, then glanced up again. "The fact is, he owes—I mean owed—me quite a bit of money, and I badly need some cash at present. And it's all in the box."

Oh really? And I'm the Queen of Brigantia. I'd been right to refuse him any information. Either he truly didn't know what was in Terentius' box, or maybe he knew only too well but was assuming I did not. "I wish I could help," I said. "I wasn't there when Terentius first arrived, so I didn't even notice him carrying anything. And his room's been thoroughly cleared out since he died."

"This is a disaster. Gods, what am I going to do? I must have that box, I *must!*" He put his head in his hands and repeated, "What am I going to do?" in a kind of moan.

Again there was no curiosity about Terentius' death. I could only think of one reason for that: he knew about it already. If he was the murderer, or if he'd told the servant to kill Terentius for the box and failed to get it, he didn't need to ask me for the details.

Suddenly I felt scared. Terentius had died for that box, and this Portius was responsible. Would he kill for it again? I must get him out of the mansio as quickly as I could. I stood up. "I'm afraid I can't tell you any more. I'm really sorry about your friend's death. As I said, his body is being sent to the garrison at Eburacum, because he said he was on his way there. Was he serving with the Ninth Legion?"

"No, with one of the Batavian units at Isurium. He'd been away though, seconded to Londinium, a special job for the Governor. He was on his way back to base." He sighed heavily. "Well, thank you for your time. If you haven't got the box, I won't hold you up any longer." He moved towards the door. Secundus opened it for him, and he marched away without a backward look.

I relaxed when the door closed. "I'm glad he's gone. And I'm glad you were here, Secundus. What made you think something was amiss?"

"Hawk sent me. He's just outside under the oak tree, and he wants to see you." He fell into step beside me as I walked out onto the forecourt. "Moon-cloud was just an excuse, the first thing that came into me head."

Hawk was standing in the shadow of the giant oak. He smiled when he saw us. "I'm relieved you're in one piece, Aurelia."

"I'm all right, though that man who just left gave me a fright."

He nodded. "I've been following his tracks, and there's no doubt he killed the slave-boy in the woods. Whether he also killed the soldier, or ordered the boy to do it, I can't say. I was worried for you when I realised he was paying you a visit. His trail was hard to follow, winding round and about, but he's been waiting in the woods all day."

"Perhaps he saw me go out and thought he'd have a look round."

"He certainly did that. Tied his horse up to the rails like any customer, and then went wandering among the outbuildings, as if he was looking for someone…or something. Nobody paid him much attention, most people were out at work, so I walked up to him and asked, very politely, if I could help him. He said no, and headed for the barroom. I slipped down to the stables and warned Secundus. You drove back onto the forecourt just then, and there wasn't time to stop you before you went inside."

"Thanks, Hawk, I really appreciate all this."

"What did he want?"

"He claimed to be a friend of the man who was murdered here this morning. But he wasn't exactly grief-stricken when I told him he was dead in an accident. All he was really interested in was the small box Terentius had with him, which he said actually belonged to him. He said it contained cash, which it doesn't, and he demanded that I hand it over."

"And did you?" Hawk asked.

"No, I denied knowing anything about it."

"Was he convinced?"

"I think so. I hope so."

"So do I, but take extra care for a while. He rode off heading westwards. My son's following him now. Between us we should be able to keep an eye on him, and see whether he might be thinking of doubling back and coming here less publicly."

"Thanks, Hawk. We'll certainly be on the alert from now on."

"I'm glad to help, you know that. By the way, my daughter brought your meat round earlier, and a couple of your men fetched away the servant's body."

Secundus nodded. "We've put him with his master. Lucius'll want to see them when he gets back."

"Gods, yes, the love-birds will be home soon, and I haven't even had time for a bath. I'd better hurry."

In fact I had ample time to bathe and change, check Baca's sewing, look into the kitchen, and pour myself a beaker of wine in the barroom, before they arrived home.

Vitellia came in first, flushed and happy. Lucius appeared a little later. I supposed he'd taken his chance to talk to the staff about my being forbidden to travel, but I could hardly ask him, so I chatted to Vitellia, pleased to find her more animated than she had been earlier. She was enthusiastic about the picnic they'd had at the summit of the Long Hill. I had to agree with her that once you've managed the stiff climb to the east of us, you can see for miles, and on a beautiful June day you feel on top of the world. I remembered going there with Quintus, and suddenly I no longer felt annoyed with my brother, but envied him. I wished Quintus were here with us now.

Lucius, too, was relaxed and cheerful, and made no mention of this morning's quarrel. Before he went for his bath, I took him outside into the garden to recount the day's happenings, at least those I felt he needed to hear about. I told how Hawk had found the slave's body and identified the murderer. When I went on to relate Portius' visit, he was shocked.

"Relia, you were in serious danger. You handled it well, as always. But I'm sorry. If I'd known anything like that would happen, I wouldn't have gone out today."

"The stuff from Terentius' box is obviously even more important than we thought, if this Portius is searching for it so intently."

"The quicker I get it to Eburacum the better. Terentius' body too. I've spoken to Secundus about it, it's all arranged for tomorrow."

"You won't take the servant's body, presumably?"

"No point. The authorities will only be concerned about a soldier's death, not a slave's. I'd better have a quick look at him, I suppose."

"I'll wait for you here."

He was soon back. "That's the boy, and it's murder for sure. And you know something? Nobody's searched him, including the murderer. Look!" He opened his hand and showed me three gold pieces. "They were in his belt-pouch."

"Stolen from Terentius, do you think?"

He shook his head. "His wages from this man Portius, more likely. Portius promised him money to find the box, and maybe to kill Terentius, or maybe Terentius woke up during the search and the lad acted in self-defence. And this morning the boy was all set to escape, but first he went to the woods to report back and collect his payment. That way Portius was certain of seeing the lad again."

"So Portius put him at his ease, handed over the money… and then killed him. I told you the man scared me, even here in the bar."

My brother heaved a sigh. "In lots of ways it would be simpler if the poor lad *had* killed himself after murdering his master. This Portius complicates matters."

"How do you mean?"

"One soldier, Terentius, conspiring with natives could be explained as a single unfortunate incident, caused by a grudge perhaps, or greed. Two soldiers conspiring together with natives could be the start of a mutiny. You're sure Portius was a soldier, not just wearing military gear as a disguise?"

"Quite sure. He had that military look about him, it's unmistakeable."

"Pity you didn't find out more about him."

"Sorry, I'm sure. Next time I have a murderer in the bar, I'll get him to tell me his life story."

He laughed. "Yes, and you would too! Most women run from danger like mice from a cat. You turn into a lion and take whatever comes." He paused, then briefly touched my hand. "I know you're disappointed about not going to Jovina's. I'm sorry. I haven't changed my mind. But I don't want us to part in anger. Wish me good fortune on my journey."

"I do, Lucius. May the gods be with you."

I meant it. I no longer even felt angry with him. But I hadn't changed my mind either.

Chapter VII

We were all outside to wave Lucius off when he left at dawn. I gave him a hug and wished him a speedy end to his assignment. Margarita, practical as ever, gave him a skin of good wine and a hearty snack for the journey. Vitellia gave him a passionate embrace and a long goodbye kiss, and to her credit, managed not to burst into tears until he was out of sight.

As I walked back towards the front door, I remembered I needed to find Taurus to pass on a message about a wagon repair from one of last evening's customers. The door to his workshop was closed, unusually at this time of day. I turned the handle and almost tripped over something—someone—lying just inside.

It was Taurus, flat on the floor and as still as death.

"Taurus! Oh, *Taurus!*" He didn't move, he simply lay there on the hard earth, with blood all over his face. "Taurus, it's me. What's happened? Can you hear me?"

Still no reaction. I felt near panic. Taurus was one of our most loyal slaves, the only one now left in our household who'd come with us from Italia twenty years ago. He was almost one of the family. If he was dead…

I yelled "Help! Help here!" and then knelt down beside him and felt his chest to see if his heart was beating. Yes, thank the gods, it was, and his flesh was warm. He was unconscious, but not dead.

I ran out onto the forecourt and almost collided with Margarita running towards me.

"Aurelia, are you all right? I heard you cry out…Oh gods, poor Taurus. What's happened?"

"I don't know, he's unconscious. We need Timaeus here quickly, please."

"I'll get him now." She set off at a run towards her own house, not far away from the main buildings. Her husband was a good doctor, he'd know what to do.

While we waited everyone rallied round to help. Taurus was a favourite with all of us, one of the kindest and gentlest of the slaves, despite his huge size and strength. One of the maids brought water and cloths, while another fetched two strong farm-boys with a plank to serve as a stretcher. But I decided to leave him where he was till Timaeus came, because I've heard him say often enough that too much damage is done to his patients by well-intentioned people moving them too soon.

I mopped the blood off Taurus' face and saw that it came from a nose-bleed, which must have started when he fell. What had knocked him out was a blow to the side of the head, which now had a huge lump on it, but the skin was barely broken.

I noticed his assistant had appeared and was standing in a corner, pale-faced and almost in tears. He was a nice lad, a junior version of Taurus—large, gentle, not over-bright. I couldn't believe he had anything to do with an attack on his master, but I had to be sure.

"Come here, Tappo, and tell us what you know about this. Have you any idea who attacked Taurus? When did you last see him?"

"I don't know nothing, Mistress. I ain't seen him since bed-time last night."

"What about this morning? Didn't you have breakfast with him and the other slaves?"

"No. I thought he'd got up earlier than us, he said he would, in case Master Lucius needed owt done before he left." He rubbed his hand across his eyes. "By the gods, if I catch the man what's done this, I'll tear him in pieces."

"Not if I catch him first," I said.

"Don't worry yourselves. I'm all right." The words startled me because they came from Taurus himself. With a great surge of relief I saw that his eyes were open now, and he was stretching his right hand up towards the lump on his head.

"Taurus, thank the gods! You had us all worried. How are you feeling?"

"A bit sore. Somebody hit me, someone prowling around in here last night."

"Can you remember what happened?" I asked him.

"I came back here just after moonrise, because I remembered I'd left my box behind. That little beech-wood box you gave me yesterday. I wanted to take it with me to my quarters. I didn't bother with a torch, there was enough moonlight to see. I got to the door and heard a noise inside, like somebody moving in the shadows. I came in but it was too dark to see. I heard someone behind me, and before I could turn, everything went black."

Timaeus bustled in and was relieved when he realised the situation. "Ah, he's awake, that's very good. No, don't try to move yet, let me examine you first."

He crouched down and gently felt Taurus' head, and peered at his nose. "This doesn't look too bad. Can you manage to sit up? Here, I'll help you."

Taurus sat upright. "I feel giddy. And my head hurts."

"You had a nasty knock, there's a bad bruise there. But there's hardly any blood." He smiled and patted the big man gently on the shoulder. "You'll live, my friend."

Taurus touched his face. "There's blood here."

"Just a nose-bleed. It's not broken. Now then, you'll be sore for a bit, but I can give you something to make it less painful. Just one more thing to check…what's your name?"

We all stared, including Taurus, but he answered promptly. "You know my name. Taurus."

"And what's my name?"

"You're Doctor Timaeus. Married to Margarita."

The doctor smiled and stood up. "Good. That's all right then. Sometimes a hard bang on the head makes men lose their wits. But not in your case, Taurus, I'm glad to say."

Taurus smiled back. "Everybody always says I haven't got many wits to start with, but they're all still here, I think." He started to get up, and Tappo came forward to help him. "Thanks, boy." He straightened to his full height. "I'm all right now, apart from a headache."

Timaeus nodded. "Then I prescribe some warm wine, and I'll add a little of my special powder for the pain. Rest this morning, and don't do any heavy work this afternoon. Some light jobs if you feel like it."

"You can rest for the whole day," I put in. "Tappo can look after things for you, can't you?"

"Yes, Mistress. I'll take care of everything."

"Then let's go over to the kitchen now, and we'll find you some wine. Timaeus will bring your medicine. Then you can go to bed and rest if you want."

"Some wine would be good. And some breakfast, I haven't had any."

"Neither have I, come to think of it."

"But first I must check if anything's missing from here. Whoever hit me must have come to steal something."

"I've had a look round," Tappo said, "and everything's in its place, like it should be. But your new box is gone."

"My box? Oh, Saturn's balls! Who would want to steal that? Nobody from here, that's for sure. We don't steal from each other here."

"I think I know," I said. "Wine first, and explanations later."

When we'd got Taurus comfortably ensconced in the kitchen, and both he and I were making up for having missed breakfast earlier, I told him about Portius' visit yesterday. He hadn't seen the man during the afternoon, but the barmaids had told him and all the other servants about him, and how he'd been desperate to find the box and its contents.

I said, "He wasn't at all pleased when I said I didn't know anything about it. He must have come back later to have another look for it, and spotted the box in your workshop. But it's odd he should steal it when it was empty."

"But it wasn't empty. I put some beads in it. Some special green glass beads I was going to make into a necklace for my girl's birthday. I hadn't locked it though."

"So when Portius found the box shut, and with something in it that rattled, he must have thought it was what he was looking for." I laughed. "He'll be disappointed when he opens it up."

Taurus yawned. "Whatever the doctor has put in my beaker is making me sleepy. I think maybe I'll have a nap, just till noon."

I sat for a while in the kitchen, oblivious to the morning bustle around me. We'd underestimated the resourcefulness of Portius, as well as the importance of the box. But what *was* the importance? And when he found the box contained only beads, would he come back to the Oak Tree yet again? I felt suddenly alone and alarmed. I wished Lucius were here now, or Quintus. I needed someone I could talk the situation over with. But there was no one.

So the best thing was to keep busy, and there was plenty to do. I consulted my list of jobs, but I knew that the most important task of all wasn't on it. I must speak to Margarita and find out what Lucius had said to her about my travel plans. I believed I could count on her not to hinder, even if she couldn't actually help. But all the same I couldn't take it for granted.

When I asked her to look into my study for a quick chat, she came straight away. We sat down and I took a deep breath.

"Margarita, can I trust you to keep something confidential… from the staff, and from your husband too?"

"You can trust me with your life, Aurelia. I owe you mine." For a little while we were both quiet, remembering a river-boat in Eburacum, where a terrified mother and child depended on me to protect them from being kidnapped, probably killed.

I shook the memories off. "This holiday of mine, visiting my cousin at Isurium. Lucius isn't keen on my going."

She nodded unhappily. "He said so to me. He thinks it isn't safe for you, and he doesn't want any of us giving you any help to get there. It's only because he cares about you."

"That's as may be. But I can't let him stop me."

Her worried frown vanished. "You're going anyway?"

"I've no choice. My cousin is in trouble, but not because the place isn't safe. She's got some personal problem, and she's asked me to help. I'm making arrangements to go without involving anyone here. Clarilla is lending me transport, and I'll stay with Albia on the way. I'm hoping you'll help too. But if you feel uncomfortable about disobeying Lucius, I'll understand."

"Of course I'll help you. After what you did for me and Spurius, *I* haven't got a choice either."

"Thank you. That's a tremendous relief."

"Did you really doubt it?" She smiled at me. "Just tell me what you need me to do."

"Clarilla is providing drivers and guards, so I'll only need to take one maid, I haven't decided who yet. That won't leave you too short-handed, will it?"

"No. Anything else?"

"Just not to mention what Lucius said to the rest of the staff."

She nodded. "Secundus knows, and he's prepared to turn a blind eye. It'll stay between the three of us."

"Thank you. That's excellent."

"If you think of anything else, you only have to say. Will Vitellia be going with you?"

"I haven't mentioned it to her yet, but I'm intending to take her as far as Albia's in Eburacum. After that, we'll see. She doesn't know Lucius has forbidden the trip, and it's better to keep it that way."

"There's just one thing that worries me then. What happens if you get to Isurium and Lucius is there already? He said he might be sent to the fort. When he sees you…"

"I'll make it very clear that you didn't give me any help at all."

"That's not what I mean. He'll be pretty angry when he realises what you've done. Won't he just send you straight home again with your tail between your legs?"

She'd touched on the one weak link in my chain, but I didn't want to admit its weakness even to myself. "I'll just have to brazen it out. He won't want a big family row in public, admitting to the world that he can't control his own sister. He'll have to make the best of things, and let me stay there at least one night to see Jovina. But I can talk him round, I'm sure of it."

"You're taking quite a chance all the same." She smiled at me as she got to her feet. "But you've obviously thought it all out. I'm sure you're doing the right thing, and *you* can be sure I'll take good care of everything here."

She went back to the kitchen, and I looked again at my list of jobs. They all seemed quite simple, now that I'd tackled the hardest.

I sorted out the clothes and sandals I'd need with me, and organised some presents for Albia—wine, and some of Cook's famous honey cakes. I discussed the farm work with Ursulus, who had everything well in hand. Brutus came round with Silvanius' two letters, and said he was bringing our vehicles, drivers and guards over to the mansio that night, so we could make an early start in the morning.

The only sad tasks in the otherwise cheerful rush were sending Terentius' body off to Eburacum, and arranging a pyre for his servant's remains.

About midmorning I realised I hadn't set eyes on Vitellia since her tearful outburst early on. I ought to see how she was bearing up, and tell her about the trip to Albia's. None of the kitchen-girls had seen her either, and she'd eaten no breakfast, which probably meant she'd gone back to her room.

Whatever I thought of her, I didn't like the idea of her moping alone all day, so I went to our private wing to see. As I walked along the passage, I heard voices, and stopped to listen. Probably a gossip session among the maids. Yes, I recognised Baca's voice, but to my surprise, I realised the other voice was Vitellia's.

"I can't bear it," she was sobbing. "How will I manage without him?"

"Don't be too sad, Miss," Baca said. "I know what it's like when your boyfriend is away. It feels like you've got a big hole inside you. But he won't be gone for long, I'm sure he won't."

"I don't know what to do with myself. I can't think of anything but him. I feel so alone here. Everyone's trying to be kind, but you're all so busy, nobody has time for me really. I miss Sosia, my maid. Lucius said there was no need for me to bring her up here because he'd be with me all the time, she'd just be sitting about with nothing to do. And now he's gone away."

"Perhaps I could be your maid," Baca suggested, "just while you're here. I could look after you, do your hair and that. You've got lovely hair. And I could do your sewing. I noticed the blue tunic you had on yesterday has a little bit of a tear in the hem. I can fix that for you if you like."

"Oh, thank you, Baca. But you've got your own work to do."

"I'm in the kitchen mostly. I'd much rather be looking after you." I heard her give a little giggle. "Believe me, sewing ladies' clothes is a lot nicer than chopping onions and pounding herbs. And maybe I could even come with you when you all go on your little holiday."

"Holiday? I don't know anything about a holiday."

Curse the girl, I thought, I was hoping to break that bit of news to Vitellia myself. Well, I suppose she had to find out sooner or later.

"Perhaps I've got it wrong then," Baca was saying. "Maybe it's just the mistress who's going. So how about if I look after you while you're at the Oak Tree? Of course if it doesn't suit you…"

"Oh, but it does, Baca. Only…would Aurelia let you, do you think?"

"I'm sure she would. Ask her."

"I don't like to. To tell the truth she frightens me. I don't think she likes me, and with Lucius not here to stand up for me…"

"Of course she does. And she likes that brother of hers too, she'd do anything for him. Don't you fret. She can be a bit sharp sometimes, but she's all right, is the Mistress. Her bark's much worse than her bite."

Thanks, Baca, I suppose that's a compliment of sorts. I crept back to the door that led in from the hall, opened it noisily, and strode down the corridor calling out "Vitellia! Vitellia, are you here?"

She answered from her room. I went in and managed to sound surprised and pleased when she shyly asked me whether Baca could serve as her maid.

"That's an excellent idea. I'm going to have to be busy for the next day or two, and you're bound to feel lonely without Lucius. The only thing is, Baca's not really very experienced as a lady's maid. Can you teach her what her duties will be?"

"Oh, yes. I know what Sosia does for me at home."

"Fine. And if you've any sewing to do, Baca's a good neat hand with a needle."

"Thank you." Vitellia smiled at me. "I know you're busy. I'll try not to be too much of a nuisance."

"You're not a nuisance at all. And I've got a treat lined up for you—for both of us. You know my sister Albia has a town house in Eburacum?"

"Yes, Lucius and I stayed in it on our way up from Londinium. Albia wasn't there herself though."

"She's there now, and she's invited us to go and join her for a couple of days. I think it would be fun. What do you say?"

Her face lit up. "That would be really nice."

"Good. We'll leave tomorrow first thing."

"And we may see Lucius there too. Wouldn't that be wonderful?"

Oh, wonderful! But I could hardly tell her my brother was about the last person I'd wish to meet in Eburacum. "I shouldn't count on it. My guess is he'll be sent up north to check on the soldier that was killed here yesterday."

"Won't he call in to see Albia on his way?"

"It's unlikely. He makes it a rule not to visit her if he's on an assignment, in case it might be dangerous for her if he's seen at her house. Anyhow, you and I and Albia can have a good time without him. We can all go shopping together. Baca, we'll need to take a maid with us. You can come if you like."

"Ooh, yes please, Mistress. I've never been to Eburacum."

As I left them, I caught the words, "Told you it'd be all right!" and some girlish giggling. I felt relieved. I'd expected to have trouble finding something for Vitellia to do, but now she had a companion she liked. When we got to Eburacum there'd be time enough to tell her I wasn't travelling straight back to the mansio, and give her the choice of coming with me to Jovina's or staying at my sister's. With a bit of luck she'd stay with Albia.

Next I decided I must go and have a look at Moon-cloud, who had finally produced a lovely ink-black foal in the night. As I leaned over the fence, Hawk stepped up beside me.

He nodded towards the horses. "That's a pleasant sight, isn't it? The foal looks a fine little fellow."

"Good morning, Hawk. Yes, he does. Did you have a quiet night?"

"Reasonably. I even managed to get some sleep after our friend with the bandages settled down in the woods. And I've brought you good news. He's gone this morning."

"Thank the gods for that."

"But I found tracks leading back here, fresh ones made in the night or early this morning, not left from yesterday afternoon. I think he was prowling around here before he left."

"He was, fairly early in the night." I told him about Taurus, and he was horrified.

"Gods, I'm sorry. I only went home for a couple of hours to catch up on some sleep, after he'd made himself a fire in the woods and apparently gone to sleep too. I was sure he'd stay put till morning." He frowned. "He's cleverer than I gave him credit for."

"He couldn't know you were following him, surely?"

"No, but he wasn't taking any chances. Military training, I suppose. Tell Taurus I'm sorry, won't you?"

"I will, but it can't be helped, Hawk, you can't stay up all night every night looking after us all; I know that. And the fellow has gone now, you say?"

"Yes, and before he went he had a wash in the river, and I noticed something unusual about him, something that might help you recognise him if you ever see him again."

"I don't think I want to see him again. But go on, tell me."

"He took off the bandages from round his head, had a good wash, then put them on again. There was no sign at all of a head wound. But he'd a sizeable chunk missing from his right ear, an old cut that's healed up but still visible."

"So the bandages weren't just to hide his face, but to make sure nobody saw his distinguishing mark. Interesting. And when he'd washed, he rode off straight away?"

"More or less. He hung about in the trees just off the road till Lucius left, and then he went back to fetch his horse, presumably to follow. Only it had mysteriously vanished." He smiled briefly. "My son took it and hid it out of the way. We thought it might be safer for Lucius. Bandage-man wasn't at all pleased when he realised he had no transport."

"Oh, brilliant! What happened then?"

"He tried looking around for tracks, but that got him nowhere, so he set off to walk westward, the same direction as Lucius. My son followed him at a safe distance until well past the Oak Bridges turning, and then saw him stop a farm cart going further west and get a lift. We'll be keeping an eye open in case he comes back, but I think he's gone for good."

"I agree, but I'll make sure everyone stays on the alert. And thanks, Hawk, you and your son have done just the right thing. Let's hope we've really seen the last of Portius now."

"You're on your way tomorrow, all being well?"

"That's right, first thing."

"Good. Take care then. And enjoy your trip." With a brief wave, he turned on his heel and melted into the trees.

Chapter VIII

Eburacum was looking its best in the afternoon sunshine. The trees were in full leaf, the wider roads were busy and cheerful, and the little unpaved alleyways were mostly free of mud. The rivers flowed peacefully and hadn't yet started to smell.

It isn't large like Londinium, though it always seems big to me compared with Oak Bridges. Nor is it one of those beautifully planned places with regular streets and decorative temples. It's a soldiers' town, dominated by the solid bulk of the legionary fortress. The higgledy-piggledy streets around it are home to the men's families and the civilians who provide for them. There's a regular market, so the forum is a reasonable size, and more and more shops are springing up. From bootmakers to brothel-keepers, from coppersmiths to cloth-sellers, they're all there trying to turn a more or less honest denarius.

Albia's house was among a group of pleasant civilian townhouses, quite central, not far from the larger of the two rivers. It was well built and roomy, with a lovely little courtyard-garden at its centre. As Brutus led our two carriages through the streets, Vitellia was gazing out like an excited child, and I was in no position to mock, because so was I.

Albia was at the door to greet us as we pulled up. We jumped down, not waiting for the carriage steps to be unfolded for a more dignified descent, and she gathered me and Vitellia into her arms and hugged us.

"Welcome to you both! Relia, how lovely to see you looking so well. And Vitellia, I've been longing to meet the girl who's finally going to persuade our brother to settle down."

My sister is one of those people who makes everyone feel at home straight away, and settling in didn't take us long. She gave Brutus directions about stabling for the horses and accommodation for the drivers and guards. He himself was staying overnight with an old army comrade at the fort. Then she led Vitellia and me out to the courtyard. Her steward Crotus brought us a jug of cool white wine, while his wife showed Baca where to unpack our things and we sat and relaxed. Really, I thought as I sank onto a cushioned couch, I don't understand why travelling makes one so tired, when all that's involved in sitting in a carriage and letting horses and men do the work. But it felt wonderful to be at rest now.

Vitellia, having stayed at the house already, was immediately at ease, calling the servants by name and needing no help to find her way around. As we chatted she grew livelier than she'd been since she came to the Oak Tree. That was my sister's doing. Albia always brings out the best in people.

Of course she asked whether Albia had heard from our brother, but she hadn't. "Lucius doesn't stay here when he's on an investigation, and often if he's very busy he doesn't even send me a note." Seeing the child's disappointment, she hastened to change the subject. "I hope you've got your shopping lists ready. Tomorrow's a market day."

Vitellia brightened at once. "Oh, that's lucky. Is it a big market?"

"Quite big, yes, though I don't suppose it's as grand as in Londinium. The country people bring in their produce from round about, but there's plenty to see from further afield as well. Traders come up from the south, and boats bring goods all the way up the river from the German Ocean."

"I love markets," Vitellia said. "And my papa gave me some money for my holiday. I haven't been able to spend any of it yet."

"I'm sure we can put that right," Albia smiled. "You'll find lots of things to buy. And you could get a present for your papa, perhaps?"

"Oh, yes, and Mama too. And something for Lucius. And then there's my little brother…" She chattered on for a while, and I was pleased to see her so animated. But I wanted to talk to Albia privately, and my sister must have realised it.

"You don't have to wait till the morning to see a little of the town," she said to Vitellia. "Aurelia and I have some family business to discuss that you'll find extremely boring. Would you like to take a short walk by the river before dinner?"

"How lovely! Can I really? And can I take Baca? She's never been here before."

"Good idea. And you'll also take a man along, of course. Respectable women don't go out unescorted in a garrison town. Crotus' son will go with you."

We gave the three of them stern instructions about not venturing into the poorer areas and on no account going into wine shops. They all agreed solemnly, and set off in high spirits.

Albia and I sat down again in the courtyard. "Now, Relia, I could tell you've got all sorts of news, and I'm dying to know what's been happening to you."

"It's amazing. I've been busier these last three days than in the whole of the last three months. I don't know where to start."

"With Arpinum, of course. You mentioned it in your letter, and I remember well enough that it meant trouble. So what's been going wrong?"

I told her about Terentius' death and his alarming locked box, the runaway slave's murder, Portius and his lies. Finally I showed her Jovina's letter and told her about Lucius' refusal to let me accept the party invitation. As I'd hoped, she agreed with me that I must ignore Lucius' wishes if I was convinced Jovina really needed help.

"But you must promise to take care, Relia. Whatever mess Jovina's landed herself in, don't you get too involved. And come straight back here if things get nasty, or if it turns out to be a wild goose chase."

"Thanks, Albia. I knew I could count on you."

"Of course you can. If there's anything you need, just tell me. There's only one problem that I can see. Lucius is presumably in Isurium already. He's going to be extremely angry when you arrive there. What if he sends you straight back to Oak Bridges?"

"I know. That's the one major weakness in my plan. I'm relying on the fact that he won't want a big public row, so whatever he does say to me will be in private. I'll try to change his mind so he'll let me stay, but even if I can't, I'll make sure he can't send me home there and then, because there won't be time for me to travel back here."

She nodded. "You'll aim to arrive late in the afternoon, too late to set off on the return journey? He won't want you travelling the roads at night."

"Exactly. So I'll be able to stay at least one night at Jovina's, which will give me time to find out what's bothering her. I'll go round telling everyone I've come specially for her party, and Lucius won't want to send me home early because it'll make him look bad in front of Jovina and Marcus and all the other officers."

"You hope." She smiled. "And I hope too."

"I'll manage somehow. I'm determined to go, and if I can't make him see sense and I have to leave before the party, at least I'll have done my best for Jovina."

"Is Vitellia going with you, or does she want to come back to the farm with me? She's welcome, if she'd rather do that. She seems a nice girl, a bit young, but no harm in her, and if she's going to be one of the family I'd like to get to know her better."

"Thanks, she'd probably much prefer to be with you, but I haven't actually broached the subject yet."

"Nor told her you've quarrelled with Lucius, presumably?"

"I didn't want to upset her. You won't say anything, will you?"

"What do you think? And maybe the thought of seeing Lucius very soon will make her want to tag along with you to Isurium."

"I hadn't thought of that. I'll ask her tonight."

Dinner was an excellent meal, roast kid in a damson sauce with cabbage, and some baked custard to follow. Vitellia was full of what she'd seen on her walk, and we all chatted happily about tomorrow's shopping. Afterwards when we were finishing the last of the good Gaulish red wine I'd brought from the Oak Tree, I raised the subject of Jovina's party and my trip to Isurium.

Vitellia took it in her stride. "Baca said you were planning to go to a party, and I saw the size of your travelling chest." She smiled. "Would your cousin mind if I came with you? I've brought a tunic that I can wear to a party."

"I'm sure she wouldn't. But are you certain? I mean it's a long way, and you won't know anyone there."

"I'll know Lucius, and he must be there by now, mustn't he? He was hoping he'd only be kept for a day or two and then he'd go straight back to the Oak Tree. But he hasn't got back so far, which means they must have sent him up north to Isurium to investigate there. So I'd like to come with you, please, Aurelia. That way I'll see him again sooner."

I cursed inwardly, but I couldn't fault her logic. "All right. One condition though, and it's important. You know what Lucius' work is, don't you?"

"Not really. He's told me he's an investigator, but he doesn't talk about his assignments, because they're secret."

"Good. And we must keep them secret. If we meet him at Isurium, or some other officer who's interested in his case, we mustn't admit we know anything about it at all."

"We don't, do we?"

I controlled my exasperation. "Not much. But remember that dead soldier at the mansio? He was travelling to Isurium. If anyone asks us about him we'll just say he was killed by his slave, who ran away, and that's all we know."

"It *is* all we know. You don't need to worry, Aurelia. I can say I know nothing about what Lucius is doing, because it's true."

"Good. So if my brother hasn't appeared by tomorrow night, you'll leave with me for Isurium the day after."

"Yes, please. But we've got a whole day at the market first, haven't we?"

Crotus knocked and came in. "There's a package arrived for Mistress Aurelia."

"For me? It can't be. Nobody knows I'm here."

"I found it by the door just now, someone had left it there. But it has your name on it, Mistress." He held out something small and square, wrapped in coarse cloth. My name stood out on a tiny piece of papyrus attached to it.

I groaned. "Gods, I suppose it's from the mansio. I haven't been away for a day yet. You'd think they could manage without me for a few hours!" A sudden alarming thought struck me, and I stopped grumbling and started unwrapping. "I hope there's nothing wrong." I hurried to pull the cloth away. What I found inside shocked me so much I almost dropped it.

It was a small square box made of light wood, with the letters VVV across its lid. The very same box, I'd swear, that Terentius had been carrying and his murderer had stolen from Taurus.

"Oh, *merda!* What's this doing here?" It wasn't locked, and inside was a small wooden note-tablet. Scrawled on it in black ink was one crudely-written line. "Go back to the Oak Tree now, or you won't live to go back later. VVV"

I felt cold in spite of the evening warmth. This package must have been brought here by Terentius' murderer. The box proved it. Why was he so anxious I shouldn't go to Isurium?

Albia's hand gently touched my shoulder. "What is it, Relia? Not bad news?" I realised I'd been clutching both box and note tight, and put them down on the table. She read the message. "That looks bad."

Vitellia glanced at me enquiringly. "What's happened? Is something wrong at the Oak Tree?"

"No. But you'd better see this." I handed her the note. There was no point concealing it from her, in fact it wouldn't be fair. She was coming up to Isurium with me.

She looked briefly at the box, then read the message and opened her eyes wide. "Who would write something so horrid?"

"I think it's a man called Portius."

"Why does he want you to go back to the Oak Tree? Is it something else to do with the dead soldier?"

"I think so, though I don't know what. There must be something at Isurium that Portius doesn't want me to find out."

"Will you still go?"

"Of course I shall." I made myself smile. "It takes more than a threatening message to keep me away from a good party."

"I think you're very brave," Vitellia said. "Lucius always says you're brave."

"I think she's quite mad." Albia sighed. "I suppose I can't stop her, if she's made up her mind. But you don't need to go, Vitellia, if you're unhappy about it. You're very welcome to come back to the farm with me."

"I'll go if Aurelia goes. It takes more than a threatening message to keep me away from my Lucius."

"Good girl!" I said, and I meant it, even while I hoped we wouldn't find Lucius there. Vitellia might not be the brightest child in the world, but she wasn't a coward.

Albia smiled. "Oh, well, in that case you're both mad." She yawned and stretched. "You know, I think I'm ready for my bed, especially as we've an early start in the morning."

I felt tired too, but sleep wouldn't come at first. Questions raced each other round in my brain like chariots in the circus. How had Portius found out I was travelling to Isurium? Why did it matter so much to him? Was there a connection between Terentius, his box, and my cousin's birthday party?

I couldn't answer any of them, and eventually I fell into a troubled sleep. I was glad to see the dawn.

Chapter IX

We set off early for the market, taking Brutus as our escort. Baca begged to come too, "to carry all the things you buy." We were in high spirits as we made our way through the crowded streets.

Albia wanted cloth to make tunics for herself and the twins. I hadn't thought about new clothes in a long while, but suddenly the idea seemed appealing. Vitellia announced she could do with a new cloak.

So we made our leisurely way in the direction of the cloth-merchants, who were mostly clustered together in a small road just off the main market. We took our time, pausing and looking at the displays on the shop counters or on makeshift trestles outside in the streets. There were stalls everywhere, and street-performers entertaining the shoppers, some quite good. I remember a little acrobat girl who bent her body backwards in a hoop till her hands touched the ground behind her. We threw her some coins, and so did everyone else.

The shopping took a long time, and we all enjoyed it, except perhaps Brutus, who ended up so laden with heavy bolts of cloth that we sent him home with them, but not before he'd had a drink at a pleasant wine-shop with benches and tables outside in the sun. Brutus ordered refreshments for us all, drank his own beer quickly and set off for Albia's, giving us strict instructions not to stray far away till he got back.

As we relaxed, I suddenly remembered one more errand. "I must buy a present for Jovina's birthday, Albia. I'll take it along from you and me and Vitellia. I wonder what she'd like? Something for her house, I expect. We passed a shop selling unusual blue pottery beakers…if I can only remember where it was, I'll get some. You can never have too many mugs, can you?"

Albia bit into her pastry. "We'll have a look in the market. There's a stall there that sells the most beautiful rugs. Rugs are something else you can't have too many of, and it'd be easier to carry on the journey than a box of pots."

"Who's that waving at you, Aurelia?" Vitellia asked suddenly.

A young man was trying to catch my attention. I recognised him at once: his compact, wiry figure, his red hair, and his wide smile. I waved back enthusiastically, and he hurried towards us as fast as he could through the crowds.

"Mistress Aurelia! Mistress Albia! I never expected to see you here."

"Titch, by the gods! This is a surprise. It's good to see you."

Indeed it was. Albia and I insisted he sit down with us and have a drink. We had known him for years, ever since he came to work at the Oak Tree as a young horse-boy. Now that he was grown up and working as an Imperial investigator, we rarely saw him, but it was always a pleasure when we did. A special pleasure for me, as it usually meant we'd also see his boss, Quintus Antonius Delfinus, also an investigator…and to me, much more than that.

I noticed Vitellia looking puzzled. "Sorry, Vitellia, I'm forgetting my manners. This is Gaius Varius Victor, a very old friend of all our family. Lucius may have mentioned him."

"If he did, he probably called him Titch," Albia put in.

"And this is Vitellia," I went on. "Ah, now there's our table-boy." I beckoned the lad over, and in no time we had another jug of wine, and beer for Titch.

He took a long draught and sighed contentedly. "Thank you, that's very welcome. I'm as dry as a camel's…a camel in a desert. Mustn't be too long though. The boss is expecting me to meet him at midday." He smiled at Vitellia. "And this is the lady who's to marry Master Lucius?"

She blushed, and I laughed. "Good news travels fast, I see."

He nodded. "It does. We heard all about you from Lucius himself. I'm pleased to meet you, Miss Vitellia."

"Thank you." She gave him her beaming smile. "Where did you meet Lucius? Is he in Eburacum now? It's ages since I saw him, and I do miss him so."

"Ages," Albia teased. "Three days."

Titch shook his head. "He's not here now. We saw him the day he arrived, just long enough to buy him a beaker or two and arrange for a proper get-together next day. Then he got orders to leave in a hurry."

"For Isurium?" I made it sound casual, but I felt tense. Despite my brave words to Albia yesterday, I'd been hoping against hope that he might not be there when we arrived.

"Not Isurium, no. He's gone further north, to Morbium. There's been trouble at the fort there, some poxy natives getting uppity, and the garrison commander here said it was an emergency and sent Lucius off to deal with it. He'll just call in at Isurium on the way, but he won't be stopping."

I felt enormously relieved, but tried not to look it. Vitellia was crestfallen, then brightened up. "If I write him a note, could you get it delivered to him at Morbium?"

"Aye, probably, but…"

"Best not, when he's working," I cut in quickly. "You know he doesn't like personal matters distracting him when he's on a case."

Albia saw where I was driving. "Aurelia's right. But talking of letters, Vitellia, have you written to your parents since you arrived at Oak Bridges?"

"No, I haven't, and I should send them a note, shouldn't I?"

"I'm sure they're longing to hear from you."

"I will. I'll write this afternoon."

"What are you doing up north?" I asked Titch. "I thought you and Quintus were working in Londinium this summer."

"We were. But we've come north on a special assignment. We're guarding a Very Important Person." His mocking tone was at odds with his words, yet I knew it must be someone quite unusual, to need an investigator as senior as Quintus in his retinue.

"Do tell us," Albia said. "The provincial governor? He doesn't come north often, and when he does he brings half Londinium along for the ride."

"More likely a top gladiator," I said. "You're protecting him from his desperate lady admirers."

Titch laughed. "That's a job we'd really enjoy. Whereas this one…" He shook his head. "I dunno if we're meant to be protecting Lord Eurytus from the world, or the world from Lord Eurytus."

Vitellia asked, "Who's Lord Eurytus?"

I said, "A tax collector from Rome. And he's in Eburacum now?"

"He has been, but he left for Isurium today. We're going up there too, but not till tomorrow. We have to see the garrison commander here for a briefing before we leave."

"You and Quintus will be in Isurium? That's very good news. Vitellia and I are heading for Isurium ourselves tomorrow. We've an invitation to stay with my cousin there for a few days."

"Why, that's grand. Wait till I tell the boss—he'll be really pleased." He finished his beer and stood up. "And I reckon I'd best be on my way to him now. Sorry I can't stop longer, but we'll meet again at Isurium tomorrow." And with a smile and a wave, he hurried off and was soon swallowed up in the market day crowds.

Albia and I lingered over our wine, while Vitellia and Baca wandered a short distance away from us. They stopped to look at a stall selling an unusual mixture of goods: square table mats of some solid-looking white material, large table-cloths of a fabric I didn't recognise, and next to them a big pile of travelling cloaks in different shades of cream and fawn. Again I couldn't identify what they were made of, certainly not the usual sheepskin or wool. Beside the trestle table, surprising on such a warm day, was a charcoal brazier with a steaming iron pot suspended over it.

A sandy-haired salesman was showing off his wares, helped by a pretty girl assistant, and his lively patter had drawn a small crowd. We strolled over to join it.

"Come and look, my lords and ladies, come and look what I've got here! Congrio's my name, Honest Congrio from Crete, and I travel the world to bring you something really special. See these wonderful table-mats and cloths? Just the thing to grace any dinner, even a banquet for Caesar himself. Look at the elegant shapes and the nice clean white colour."

He picked a square mat up and held it aloft. "All right, you say, what's so unusual? I've got dozens of table-cloths and mats. Well, I'll tell you, my lords and ladies, you haven't got any like these. These are made from a marvellous fibre that's grown far away in the east. I call it Vulcan's Shield. Why Vulcan's Shield? Because the blacksmith of the gods would give his immortal eye teeth for this stuff. It's proof against any amount of heat, it'll even stand fire and flame, yet it won't be burnt up. Watch this now. Here we have a brazier, good and hot. You can probably feel the heat from where you stand, my lords and ladies, and you can see the steam coming out of that iron pot there. Well then…"

With a dramatic flourish he threw the mat into the brazier. The girl took a short stick and stirred the embers, heaping hot coals onto the mat. The tip of the stick began to char, and she held it aloft so the salesman could point it out to us. The mat simply sat there, undamaged.

The crowd murmured in wonder, and the salesman signalled to the girl. She removed the mat with a pair of metal tongs and held it out to him He took it with his bare hands, not even wincing as he held it high once more. Apart from a few smears of ash from the fire, it looked as good as new.

Next he picked up a fawn hooded cloak and spread it out in both hands so we could all see that it was complete and unmarked. It looked much like any other thick cloth. Vitellia was intrigued by it, and the salesman noticed and smiled directly at her.

"Don't take my word for it, my lady, feel the quality for yourself. This wonderful cloth brings you good luck, and it protects whoever wears it from all harm, especially that most terrifying disaster, fire."

Before I could stop her, Vitellia stepped forward and felt the fabric. "It's not as soft as wool," she said doubtfully.

"Quite right, young lady. But would ordinary wool protect you from all the evils of the world? Could you do *this* to an ordinary woollen cloak?" He laid it out over his display of mats and nodded to his assistant, who collected a shovel full of hot coals from the brazier and dumped them onto the centre of the cloak. They had no effect at all, though they were clearly hot and smoky.

Again the crowd was impressed. Congrio picked up the cloak by its edges and carefully tipped the coals back into the brazier. He held the material up to show it was unharmed, and then calmly draped it round his shoulders. "And now, my lords, my ladies, who's going to buy a cloak like this? Or a set of mats, or a cloth to grace your table…"

Several people looked interested but Vitellia was the first to speak. She announced, shyly but with determination, "That looks a good cloak."

"Don't waste your money," I murmured in her ear. "It must be a trick."

The salesman was all smiles. "No, my lady, I promise you there's no trick. Your young friend is making a very wise choice." He smiled at Vitellia. "Tell you what I'll do, for such a beautiful customer. If you'd like to buy a cloak, I'll throw in a set of four mats free. How does that sound?"

"And if I buy two cloaks," Vitellia asked, "one for myself and one for my fiancé, can I have eight mats free?"

Everyone laughed, including the trader. "Well, well. I see you're as clever as you're beautiful, young lady. Of course you can."

I couldn't remember Vitellia making any sort of independent decision since I'd known her, so I was pleased she'd stood up for herself, even while I was irritated that she'd fallen for the salesman's pitch. And at least the table mats would make an excellent birthday gift for Jovina.

While the purchases were being chosen and packed. I looked round for Baca and saw her further down the street, gazing at a table of bead necklaces. I walked a few paces towards her. "Baca, come over here, will you? You'll have to carry some of this lot till Brutus comes back."

"Coming, Mistress." She turned slowly, and I saw then that there were two men with her, soldiers by their appearance and drunk by their behaviour. As she started to walk away, the taller of the two put a restraining hand on her shoulder and said loudly, "Don't go yet, lass. Come along with us. We know how to show a girl a good time."

Baca shook her head. "Leave off, will you? I've got my work to do. That's my mistress calling me. You'll be getting me into trouble." She was smiling as she tried to push his hand away. She'd done plenty of bar work at the Oak Tree and knew how to deal with drunks.

But these two were persistent. "There won't be no trouble, beautiful," the shorter man said, leaning down and giving her a kiss. "We're bodyguards to the Lord Eurytus, and all the girls love Eurytus' lads." He put his arm around her waist, so she was now pinned firmly between them. She flashed a glance at me, and though she still smiled, I saw she was scared.

Brutus must surely be back soon, but maybe not soon enough. I didn't want the two men marching Baca off into some tavern up an alleyway. They were drunk enough to do it, and strong enough. I'd have to deal with this myself, not something I wanted to do in public in the middle of the street. I glanced quickly around. The faces of the market people and their customers, even at the stall we'd just been buying from, were blank and unresponsive. They weren't going to intervene to help.

I smiled and walked purposefully towards the soldiers.

"I said come over here, Baca. Gentlemen, let the girl go, please. She's with me, and she's not free for fun and games just now."

The taller drunk took a small step back but kept his hand on her shoulder. "Is she yours then, darling?"

"She is. And she's got work to do. So why don't you go and find yourselves some lasses with time on their hands?"

"Oh, we shan't keep her long. What we've got in mind won't take long at all." He reached his free hand out towards me. "You can join us if you want, you know. Then me and my friend will have a girl each. Rich or poor, mistress or maid, we love you all. And after a few drinks, who can tell the difference?" Both men laughed.

I held my ground and kept my smile in place. I couldn't allow them to take Baca out of our sight, because if they did it would be dangerous to follow. I'd have to play for time. "Ah, well, if it's a drink you want, why not have one here?" I pointed at the wine-shop we'd just left. "Why don't I buy you a jug of beer, to make up for the disappointment of having to let my girl get on with her work. All right?"

"We can buy our own beer. We're Lord Eurytus' boys." The taller man lunged towards me very fast, taking me by surprise. He let go of Baca and put his arm round my waist. Bending so close I could smell the beer on his breath he began whispering in my ear. I expected it would be some bawdy suggestion or other, but was much more shocked by what I actually heard.

"Got a message for you, Aurelia darling. Stay away from Isurium. Keep your nose out of other folks' business. Got it, Aurelia?" He added in a raucous drunken voice, "Come on now, darling, give us a kiss."

"Are these idiots bothering you, Aurelia?" A cool voice behind me called out, and my heart gave a leap. I knew that voice.

"Quintus! Yes, they are."

I turned my head in time to see Quintus and Titch leap forward together and spring at the two men, who went sprawling, releasing Baca and me as they fell. We ran back to where Albia and Vitellia stood watching in horror.

Quintus addressed the men on the ground. "I don't know who you are, you scum, but you're not in Eurytus' service. If you were, I could have you crucified for this. So get back to whatever hole you crawled out of, and be thankful I and my friend haven't time to give you a good thrashing. Stand up."

They stood up, dusting themselves down. One of them whined, "It was only a bit of fun, sir…"

"Shut up. Apologise to these ladies."

They were cowed now, and rapidly sobering up. "Sorry, ladies. We didn't mean no harm," the taller one said, and his comrade echoed "Sorry, ladies."

"Now get out of my sight." As they slunk away, he turned to us.

"Well, now, Aurelia, and….Baca, isn't it? Are you all right?"

"Yes," I answered, trying to keep my voice steady. "Thank you, Quintus. I was never more pleased to see anyone in my life."

"Nor me," Baca said. "Thank you."

"It's wonderful to see you both," Albia said. "What a lucky coincidence you were here."

He smiled. "No coincidence. Titch told me he'd seen you in the market area and you hadn't a male escort. I thought I'd come and make sure you were all right. The streets are crawling with these drunks. I'm glad we got here in time. But why haven't you got a man with you?"

Brutus arrived just then, panting and dishevelled, and apologising profusely for having left us for so long. He and Quintus were old friends, but all the same Quintus gave him a stern look as he said, "Where did you get to? These ladies shouldn't be left on their own. The streets aren't safe."

"Don't I know it! I got held up by a street fight on the way back from Albia's. Couple of Eurytus' bodyguards were trying to rob an old couple, a shopkeeper and his wife. I stayed to help some of the army lads calm them down."

Quintus told him briefly what had just happened.

Brutus nodded. "Thank the gods you were here. I'm very grateful for your help, both of you. Now, the quicker I get these ladies back to Albia's, the better."

"We'll come with you," Quintus said, and we began to walk home. "The point is," he went on, "the two drunks here claimed to be Eurytus' men, but they weren't. And the ones who started your riot weren't either. They couldn't have been."

"How's that? They were wearing the badges his people all have, the head of a bull."

"But Eurytus left for Isurium this morning, with his whole guard. I'm not saying that they wouldn't be capable of getting drunk and molesting honest citizens. But today, it was someone impersonating them."

Brutus scratched his head. "But why? Eurytus is unpopular, most people hate him even when they haven't actually met him. So why would anyone pretend they're connected with him when they're not?"

"To make him still more unpopular; that's my guess."

We walked the rest of the way in a thoughtful silence. The others were presumably mulling over what Quintus had said. I was trying to work out who could have sent the men, whoever they were, to find me—me personally—and deliver yet another threatening message. They'd intended to frighten me, and though I managed to walk with a confident stride and my head held high, they'd succeeded.

Chapter X

Quintus accepted Albia's invitation to stay for a bite to eat, but Titch excused himself, saying he had a previous engagement.

"I hope she's pretty," Albia smiled. "Vitellia, would you show Quintus into the courtyard while I just check how things are in the kitchen? I'll send Crotus through with the wine."

She touched my arm to stop me as I made to follow them outside. "Are you all right, Relia? You've gone quite pale."

"I'm fine. They scared me a bit, that's all."

"Gods, I'm sorry. I wish I could have done something to help. By the time I saw what was happening…"

"There's nothing you could have done. It's all over now, and I'm not going to let a couple of drunks spoil a happy day. A beaker of wine and I'll have forgotten all about them."

"Good for you."

I drank three beakers of cool white wine, which went well with the pleasant meal of fresh bread, smoked sausage, hard-boiled eggs and lettuce. It did indeed make me feel better, and I managed to join in the chatter about the morning and respond to Quintus' teasing on the subject of women and shopping.

When we'd finished our meal, Albia stood up and said briskly, "Aurelia, you'll probably want to tell Quintus what's been happening at the Oak Tree. I know some of it's confidential, so Vitellia and I will take ourselves off, and you can be private."

He smiled. "Thank you, Albia, you're right as always. But I hate the idea of driving you out of your own courtyard."

"Don't worry. I've a hundred things to do indoors, and Vitellia has letters to write."

After they'd gone, he sat down on the couch beside me and took my hand.

"Before I saw you today," he said softly, "I was all set to give you a stern lecture on Roman family values. Now…well, I don't know. But I must admit I was taken aback to find you on your way to Isurium."

"Were you?"

"Lucius told me he's forbidden you to go there, because it's dangerous."

His serious tone surprised me, given how easy we'd been together so far. It also irritated me. "Quite true. But whatever Lucius says, I'm a free citizen, I can go where I please."

"You shouldn't be going anywhere against the clear wishes of the head of your family. That isn't the Roman way of doing things. Is it?"

This was not only annoying, but alarming too. He knew my secret now and disapproved of my action. So presumably he would tell Lucius what I was doing.

"I've been invited by my cousin to her birthday party, and she's asked for my help. I don't know what her trouble is, but she thinks she's in danger. Lucius says that Isurium itself could be dangerous. I don't know whether he's right, but if he is, Jovina needs me there more than ever."

"He'll be pretty angry when he finds out you've disobeyed him."

"Perhaps, *when* he finds out. But that won't be for a day or two. According to Titch, he's been sent off on an emergency assignment to Morbium. That's right, isn't it?"

Quintus nodded. "I met him here a couple of days ago. He was all set to go to Isurium, he'd cooked up a wonderful cover story about missing army records, and then he was ordered to head further north still. He was told to call in at Isurium and warn them about Terentius' message, but then to push on to Morbium, where apparently they've got some trouble already. It was quite a sudden change of plan, and he wasn't best pleased with it."

That thought gave me a perverse pleasure, and I smiled. "Serves him right. Being ordered to do something he doesn't want to do will give him a taste of his own medicine. I hope it chokes him."

Suddenly he leaned back on the couch and burst out laughing. He continued to laugh till the tears ran down his face. "It's no good, I can't pretend I'm angry with you when I'm not." He turned to me and kissed me full on the mouth. "Aurelia, what in Jupiter's name are we going to do with you?"

"If you don't know by now, you probably never will."

"You're quite impossible. And I love you." He kissed me again and slipped his arm round me. Relief swept over me like a wave. I relaxed, and ridiculous though it sounds, as the tension of the last couple of hours drained out of me, it was replaced by the fear I'd been suppressing. I found I was shaking.

"What is it?" he whispered, and I felt his arm tighten around me. "What's wrong? Those two drunks in town scared you, didn't they?"

"They weren't just ordinary drunks, Quintus. They'd come looking for me. Me specifically." I told him about the warning message.

He swore. "I'd no idea. I saw one of them whispering in your ear, I thought it was just the usual obscene rubbish…gods, why didn't you say? I'd have killed the bastards."

"Because they said they were Eurytus' men, and I believed they were pretty much above the law. I just wanted them to go away. It was horrible, realising they knew who I was and were trying to scare me."

"You're safe now. I'm here."

He held me tightly, and gradually I stopped shaking and was able to look at him. "Who were they, Quintus? You say they aren't Eurytus' men at all. But they were working for whoever it is that doesn't want me to go to Isurium….this man Portius, I assume. So who were they, do you know?"

"Native malcontents, I'd say. They want Eurytus to be hated. From what I've seen of him, he can manage to achieve that all by himself, or at least with the help of his real guards. But there's trouble brewing in Isurium, and they want it to come to a head."

"Is that why you're going there?"

"It is. And you're going because your cousin wrote to you about danger. Do you still plan to visit her? Even in spite of this morning?"

"Yes. I shan't change my mind."

He smiled into my eyes. "As a matter of fact, I was delighted to hear you're going to be there. As well as helping your cousin, you could be an enormous help to me. If you will."

"I'll consider it. As long as there are no lectures about Roman family values."

He laughed. "None, I promise."

"Then you know I'll help all I can. What exactly are you investigating?"

"I think it may be linked to your visit. So first, I want to know what is so desperately important that it's making you defy your brother and go haring off into danger."

I told him all of it, starting with Jovina's letter and following with everything that had happened at the Oak Tree. Finally I showed him the threatening message I'd received at Albia's.

He barely read the note, but pounced on the box like a cat on a bird. "Aurelia, this is just the evidence I need. Brilliant!"

"Evidence? So it's got something to do with why you're going up to Isurium?"

"It has a great deal to do with it. When Lucius told me about Terentius, I felt in my bones there was a connection between what happened at the Oak Tree and the trouble at Isurium. This box proves it."

"So Lucius was right that the situation there needs investigating?"

He nodded. "Without a doubt. He's also right about possible danger. You're sure you still want to go?"

"Haven't I just said so?"

"Yes, but…"

"Watch my lips. I still want to go."

"Right then. This is the situation. I'm supposed to be keeping an eye on Eurytus and his goings-on—I've been doing it ever since we left Londinium. It's not been too bad, considering what an arrogant man he is. Anyhow, as you know Isurium is the next place to have the pleasure of his company."

"He won't get much pleasure out of it, if Terentius' message is right. Someone wants to kill him there."

He looked thoughtful. "Yes, this mention of a Greek. What do you make of it?"

"Two mentions," I pointed out. "Jovina's note to me mentions 'Greeks bearing gifts.'"

"Lucius told me he has a theory about the identity of the Greek who's frightening your cousin."

"Mallius, you mean? I think that's nonsense, and I told him so. Margarita had a much better idea, the doctor at the fort. All the medics are Greeks, aren't they?"

"Most of them. And there may be others. You can help me find them."

"Are you officially there to act as nursemaid to Eurytus? It won't make you very popular. You may find people reluctant to talk to you."

"Gods, no! I'm officially going there to inspect a bridge. Titch and I still wear our bridge-surveyors' helmets occasionally, and they come in useful for something like this. We should be there already, but I stayed an extra day to talk to some of the senior men here first. And thank the gods I did, because Titch found out you'd be there, too. It couldn't be better."

I poured us out more wine. "What will you want me to do up there, apart from searching for Greeks?"

"What you do best. Keep your eyes and ears open while you're staying with your cousin, and report to me anything suspicious." He took a long drink. "There's unrest among the natives around Isurium, and the governor's getting reports that there's something wrong at the fort itself."

"You mean someone inside plotting with the Brigantes?"

"It wouldn't be the first time."

"But why? A man in the Roman army encouraging barbarians to attack the Roman army? It doesn't make sense."

"For money, perhaps, rather than conviction. And it's probably more than just one man. This message Terentius was carrying was intended for someone with army connections, someone with good Latin who'd have understood the reference to Troy. That could be a native, but a Roman seems more likely. Mind you, of course the message has been intercepted and never got to Isurium. I wonder if that means they won't go ahead with whatever they're planning for midsummer?"

"The gist of the message has almost certainly got through."

"What makes you say that?"

I told him how Margarita had heard Terentius' servant talking about Troy, Achilles and Hector. "He knew the outline of what it was, and very likely passed it on to Portius."

"I see. Yes, we have to assume he did. Then why has Portius gone on trying to find the other items in the box?"

I thought about it. "Maybe, if he's doing this for money, he needs the half-coin to identify himself to the rebels in order to get paid."

"That makes sense." Quintus picked the box up. "I'll take charge of this for now. Lucius has already given me the note and the other things that were in it. They all belong together."

"Be careful. That box seems to bring trouble wherever it goes."

"Anything marked VVV means trouble just now."

"That's what Lucius thinks. Silvanius too." I relayed what Clarus had said.

He nodded. "With Eurytus there, any sort of native discontent could turn into outright violence. That would suit Venutius and his friends very well. They need an excuse, a rallying-point to make the Brigantians turn against the settlers. And Isurium is regarded as sensitive at present. The governor especially wants to avoid trouble there."

"I know. Silvanius told me. He also said there's been a bit of unrest at Isurium already."

"There's been nothing near the fort itself yet but a bit of low-level violence in the area round about. Small bands of Brigantians attacking Roman soldiers away from base, picking on small patrols or lads on hunting trips."

"That's not so unusual, surely. Especially if discipline has got a bit slack."

"But the natives round Isurium have been a little too well-informed about troop movements, when and where new patrols are being sent out, that sort of thing. They can only be getting information from a contact in the army."

I took a sip of my wine. "And whoever that contact is, he could be the Greek mentioned in Terentius' message, the one playing Achilles to Eurytus' Hector? A potential killer, in plain Latin."

"That's our best guess for the time being."

"And Terentius, based in Londinium, got wind of Eurytus' visit to his own area before it was public knowledge locally and wanted to warn someone about it?"

"So it seems. We'll know more when we're established at the fort. You, me, and Titch…we make a good team."

"The only thing is, I shan't have much to do with the soldiers. My cousin lives outside, in the civilian village."

"But you're bound to have some contact. Your cousin's husband is deputy commander of the whole fort. Because of his Greek connections, he's one of the people we want to keep a closer eye on. His son is another would-be Greek, I'm told, so he'll bear watching too. So all you have to do is be alert for anything out of the ordinary, big or small, and report it to me."

"I don't much like the idea of spying on Jovina's family. Marcus is an old friend."

"But suppose Lucius is right when he says Mallius is the cause of Jovina's trouble, the reason she asked for your help? You'll have to look into that, even though you don't accept it yourself. So you'll be watching your cousin's family anyway, won't you? Now you'll be doing it for two reasons, not just one; that's the only difference."

I laughed. "I hadn't quite thought of it like that. When will you and Titch get there?"

"Tomorrow evening. You're leaving tomorrow too?"

"Yes. You'll be staying at the mansio, I suppose?"

"To start with, but I expect I can persuade someone at the fort to give me a billet. As I said, we're inspecting the Isurium bridge. It's in a dreadful state, I've heard." He grinned suddenly. "I'll need to be in the area several days, I'm certain. And it should be easy for us to meet casually. Two old acquaintances, one on duty, the other visiting relatives on holiday. What more natural than that they'll bump into one another occasionally?"

"I can try to visit the fort, too, if Marcus doesn't come to see Jovina in her own house. I've known them as a couple for ages, it would be odd if I didn't want to meet him. And then there'll be this birthday party. I might pick up a few bits of gossip there."

"I'm sure you will. All kinds of personal things that Titch and I can't get near. And I'll be there to look after you, if there's any serious trouble. But now at least we're ready for it."

"I may need looking after all the same, if Lucius gets to find out I'm there, instead of meekly minding the mansio."

"He won't find out from me." He got up reluctantly and stood looking down at me for a few heartbeats. "This is an important case, and I want you there to help." He kissed me again. "I'm not going to be the one to get you sent back to Oak Bridges. So I'll keep your secret, if you'll keep mine."

"Yours? Do I know any secrets of yours worth keeping?"

"Only this one. Who do you think it was who advised the Eburacum commander that Lucius was the best man to send to Morbium to deal with the emergency there, and that *I'm* the most suitable man to send to Isurium?"

Chapter XI

The journey from Eburacum to Isurium was hot and dusty, but
uneventful and not too slow. We set off early, because now that
I knew Lucius wasn't at Isurium there was no need to delay our
arrival till late afternoon. Eburacum was busy, and the main
highway northwest had plenty of traffic on it. Most of it was
military, soldiers marching along in formation, cavalry trot-
ting by and forcing civilians to give way to them in their usual
arrogant fashion. Almost all of it was heading north towards
the distant frontier, though we met one long convoy of army
supply wagons coming southward, complete with a mounted
escort. From the smell of them, they were carrying freshly tanned
hides. The gods know how the drivers stood the stench. I was
glad they weren't going in our direction. If you're unlucky you
can get stuck behind a wagon train like that for miles.

We reached Isurium in midafternoon, and drove straight to
the fort to ask directions to Jovina's house in the village. As we
approached the big main gate I had a pleasant feeling of anticipa-
tion, almost of homecoming. All the forts in the Empire are built
along the same lines, whether large or small, on a frontier or in
peaceful countryside. So when you've seen one, you've seen them
all. I've seen plenty in my time, having a centurion for a father.

Brutus and I approached the fort on foot, leaving the carriages
parked on the road outside. As we came to the gateway I knew
at once that this wasn't, as I'd expected, a quiet friendly little

base where nothing much happened. There was a tension in the air that said, as loud as any drill-master on the parade-ground, "Stand ready now. We're expecting trouble."

The four gate-guards on duty were certainly standing ready. They were on edge, and barely civil. The senior one barked: "State your names and business."

Brutus was equally brusque. "This is Mistress Aurelia Marcella, come to see your deputy commander, Mallius Melandrus. We're on our way to stay at his wife's house in the village. Would you tell the deputy commander we're here, please?"

The men looked at each other and relaxed slightly, but not much. The chief guard shook his head. "I'm afraid it's not possible to see him at all today."

Brutus drew himself up and stared at the soldier as if he was back in the army. "I'm sure he'll want to see us, lad, and he won't want us kept hanging about. He's expecting us." His tone clearly indicated that he wouldn't take no for an answer, and after a couple more exchanges, the chief guard sent one of his men off to headquarters to enquire.

"But we're busy just now," he added. "I'm afraid you may have a long wait."

"We'll wait," Brutus said firmly, and added, "I can see you've got some sort of a panic on. What's happening?"

The guard shrugged. "Nothing too serious. Some of the natives playing up, that's all."

"Just what you don't need, when you've got an important visitor at the fort," Brutus said.

The guard unbent a little. "You've heard about him, have you?"

"Aye, we've just come up from Eburacum. Look, can one of your boys get a stool for the lady?"

They fetched one, and while the two of them chatted I sat and looked around. Though this was quite a small fort, the familiar layout was reassuring. There were regular rows of barracks, workshops, stables, stores, all the usual buildings that keep an army going, with wide roads between, and the widest of all was the main street leading from the gate directly to the headquarters block. Everything was tidy, though some of the buildings looked a little dilapidated. The few men in evidence hurried on their various errands, and the sentries on the ramparts above marched purposefully and kept looking out, as if expecting some kind of attack.

"Here he is now," one of the guards said, pointing. A couple of soldiers were marching towards us, supporting a man who was so drunk he couldn't stand on his own. They steered him on a more or less straight course between the buildings, and as they approached us I realised with a shock that the drunk was Marcus. Greyer, fatter, and redder in the face than when I'd last seen him, but it was my cousin's husband all right. No wonder, I thought, Jovina is asking for help.

He began to sing a bawdy song, till one of the men with him said, "Hush now, sir, you'll wake the commander from his afternoon nap."

The gate sentries showed no surprise or disapproval, but stood to attention and saluted. "You wanted Deputy Commander Mallius, ma'am?" the senior one asked. "Well, there he is. Doesn't look as if he's expecting you, though."

The trio halted in front of us, and Mallius cast bleary eyes over Brutus and me. "By the gods, Aurelia Marcella! Surprise to see you. What are you doing here?"

"Hello, Marcus. We're on our way to stay with Jovina. You remember? She invited us to her midsummer party." I suddenly had the alarming thought that she might not even have told him I was coming.

He smiled fatuously. "Jovina? Of course, her party. I've been busy, you know. Under a lot of strain. But I remember now. Aurelia Marcella…Lucius' sister."

"That's right, yes. But Lucius couldn't come to the party, I'm afraid. He's busy too."

"Ah, Lucius, the dear boy." He embarked on another song. "Lucius loved the ladies, the ladies of the town…"

I cut his performance short. "We won't keep you when you're so busy, Marcus. But we need directions to Jovina's house please. Maybe one of your men could come along and show us the way?"

"Certainly. It's easy enough to find, not far at all. Only not now. She's not well, she's in bed. She can't see anyone today. Tomorrow maybe, I don't know."

"In bed? I'm sorry to hear that. What's the matter with her?"

"Don't ask me." He shrugged. "Women's trouble, that's all I know. I'm only the husband, I don't get told any of the details. Probably wouldn't like them anyway. Too much blood usually where women's troubles are involved. But she's in a bad way, or she wouldn't have said she couldn't put you up tonight." He hiccupped. "I could put some of you up here at the fort, but there isn't much room really. I know—you can share my room, Aurelia, how about that?" He laughed uproariously and tried to take a step towards me, but his two companions prevented him.

"Father! So here you are." A young soldier came to stand beside us, and he put a hand on Marcus' shoulder. "Get yourself to bed now, sleep it off. I'll deal with things here."

"Philippus!" Marcus exclaimed. "Good lad, you've arrived just in time. Aurelia, this is my son Philippus. Philippus, this is Jovina's cousin Aurelia Marcella. She's coming to the party."

"I know, that's why I'm here." He turned to me with a charming smile. "Welcome to Isurium, Aurelia. Mother sent me to meet you and help you settle in. I'm sorry I wasn't here when you arrived."

"I'm pleased to meet you, Philippus. Or should I say, meet you again? You were only a boy last time I saw you, so I wouldn't have known you."

"But I remember you. And you haven't changed one bit," he answered.

I laughed. "Thank you. I'm sure you say that to all the ladies." In truth I hardly remembered him, and I certainly wouldn't have expected he'd grow up so handsome. I suppose any young, healthy man in army clothes makes a striking figure, and this one was well groomed, his black hair fashionably long, indeed too long for a standard military cut. More to the point, he had a brisk air of purpose about him, in contrast to his father.

We shook hands, and I introduced Brutus. "Your father was just explaining that your mother isn't well. How is she now?"

"She's been very poorly, but I think she's on the mend at last. Only she really isn't up to entertaining anyone today. She sends her apologies, and hopes you'll delay visiting her till she's recovered a little. Tomorrow, I hope."

"Poor Jovina. I'm so sorry." Indeed I was, and not just for Jovina's sake. If we couldn't stay at her house, we'd need to look for accommodation at the mansio, and if the village was already full of Eurytus and his entourage, that might not be so easy. "Will there be room for us at the mansio, I wonder? Brutus, could you go over there straight away and…"

"Don't worry, it's all arranged," Philippus said. "Mother asked me to book rooms for you there tonight, and make sure you settle in as comfortably as you can. I've just been to check, and it's all in order. They'll find room for all of you. How many are you?"

"I've got a young lady with me, Vitellia, my brother's fiancée. She and I can share a room. We've just one maid, two drivers, and two guards. Brutus here is planning to look up an old friend at the fort, I think?"

"Aye, that's right. I don't need to add to the crush in the mansio."

Philippus nodded. "The servants may find it a bit crowded, but they'll have beds."

"Thank you." I was relieved, but then another worry occurred to me. "I do hope Jovina will have recovered in time for her party."

"She will, she will," Marcus answered. "It's going to be a grand and glorious celebration. Everyone who's anyone will be there." He waved his arms to encompass the whole fort, if not the whole Empire. "She won't want to miss it."

Philippus looked less certain. "I'm sure she'll be fine. She insists that all she needs is a good rest, and she hopes to be able to receive you tomorrow morning." He turned to his father.

"Now off you go, Father, you need some rest too." He added to the soldiers who were still holding Marcus upright, "Get him home to bed, you two."

The three of them began to walk slowly away.

"I'm sorry about that," Philippus said. "He's been under a lot of strain lately, and now with Mama taken ill…he'll be right as rain again soon."

"There'll be plenty of chance to see him later," I said. "I think we'd better head straight for the mansio, don't you?"

We clambered back into the carriages and set off behind Philippus, but we didn't get very far. We had to halt by the main road, which divided the fort from the civilian village, because a large flock of sheep was spreading all across it. A shepherd boy was driving them, his two dogs moving them along unhurriedly while he strolled behind them, holding a little girl by the hand.

Philippus cursed mildly and called out, "Get a move on, boy, we haven't got all day."

"Sorry, sir," the lad answered, but didn't seem to progress any faster. I jumped down from the carriage to stand beside Philippus. It was pleasant in the warm sunshine, listening to the sheep-bells and watching the dogs keeping the flock together.

Then we heard the sound of marching men and moving vehicles. Philippus exclaimed, "Oh gods, here comes trouble. Look out behind, boy!" As he shouted, the peaceful atmosphere was shattered by a bugle-blast, and we saw a small convoy approaching from the south. A dozen soldiers, German auxiliaries by the look of them, marched smartly in step, followed by a large open carriage, then a smaller closed one, and six more Germans forming the rearguard.

The shepherd lad gave them one frightened glance and began shouting at his dogs, while the entourage came steadily on, making no attempt to slow down.

"Is this Lord Eurytus?" I asked.

Philippus was now standing rigidly to attention. "It is. You've heard of him, have you?"

"Yes. But not seen him, until now."

So this was the man who was travelling Britannia upsetting everyone. He made a commanding figure as he sat in an open carriage pulled by two good-looking white horses. He was tall and dark, with an elaborate hairstyle, expensive clothes, and jewellery that caught the sunlight. But I only had a fleeting impression because the cavalcade still didn't reduce speed, and I turned to watch as the front rank of soldiers reached the sheep and ploughed straight in among them, kicking out at any slow-moving animals in their path. The boy, the girl, and the dogs were doing what they could to clear their charges off the road, but they hadn't a hope. As the carriages inexorably followed the infantry, the whole flock broke like a fleeing army, and scattered to the four winds. The two children had to jump for their lives as Eurytus' raeda headed straight for them, almost running them down. One of the horses stumbled, perhaps alarmed by the milling sheep, and the carriage slowed slightly. The driver slashed at the boy with his long whip, but missed. Eurytus called out something I couldn't hear, and one of the escort at the rear leapt sideways and pounced on the boy. He gave him a vicious blow on the head which knocked him to the ground, and added a couple of kicks before he rejoined the march. The girl ran off, crying.

I stood and stared in shocked disbelief as the small convoy turned off the main road and disappeared into the village. I heard Philippus swearing under his breath, and Brutus summed up my own feelings by saying, "By Mars, I'm no believer in mollycoddling natives, but that was unnecessary. Why couldn't he just have waited a while? The road's for everyone to use, not just jumped-up freedmen…"

"Careful!" Philippus hissed, making Brutus look round in alarm, but there was nobody about except our party. "Mind what you say, my friend. All of you. Eurytus comes direct from Caesar, with Imperial power to do whatever he likes. Those kids can think themselves lucky they got away without any permanent injuries, especially the little girl. Eurytus likes little girls, they say."

I felt a stirring of anger, but suppressed it. He was a man to be feared, it seemed, and in any case this wasn't my business. All the same I didn't like it. "Gods, Philippus, is he always like that?"

He answered softly. "He's been here since yesterday, and already everyone hates him. Romans and Brigantes, he's upset everyone. There'll be murder done if he doesn't show some restraint."

We looked over to where the boy was sitting up now, rubbing his head, while his sister crouched sobbing beside him.

Vitellia jumped down and came to stand beside me. "Aurelia, those poor children! Isn't there something we can do to help? Maybe if their family are in the village, we can find someone to collect up the sheep for them. Look, they've scattered all over the fields."

Philippus smiled at her, but shook his head. "If I were you I'd leave well alone. Their people will hear about this soon enough and come to help. And with things as they are, I don't think any strangers, especially Romans, should go walking around the village unescorted. After an incident like this there'll be bad feeling."

The boy pointed along the road northwards. A large man, a farmer by his looks, was striding towards him, and the lad jumped up and shouted "Grandpa Brennus! Grandpa Brennus!"

The big man broke into a run and came to stand beside the children.

"Look," Philippus said. "There's his grandfather. He'll be all right now."

I remembered my conversation with Clarus about a Brigantian called Brennus. Could this be the man, a Roman citizen, likely to be made head of the tribal council here? Clarus had said he was powerful and already feared that Eurytus' presence might cause trouble. How would he react when he saw what the freedman had done to his own family?

Philippus said, "We must be going now. I told the innkeeper I'd bring you to the mansio as soon as I could. With them being so busy, I don't want them thinking you're not coming and re-letting your rooms to someone else." So we climbed back aboard the carriages and set off again.

It was a decent enough mansio, slightly larger than ours, clean, and with a reasonably sized stable-yard to the rear. Philippus ushered Vitellia and me into the barroom, leaving the rest to unload our luggage and see to the transport. A stout, greying man came forward to greet us.

"This is the innkeeper, Nonius," Philippus said. "Nonius, these are the guests I told you about, come to stay with us for a few days once my mother is recovered from her illness. Make sure you look after them well."

Nonius smiled at us. "Good afternoon, ladies, and welcome to Isurium. Your room's all ready. We only have one room available for you both, but I'm sure you'll be quite comfortable. If you like to come with me…"

He led us through the main hall and along a corridor, and opened a door at the far end which led into a small green-painted room with an unglazed window. Thank the gods it was warm today, we shouldn't need the shutters. The walls could have done with a lick of paint, but the two narrow beds looked clean, and there was just room for a pair of stools and a small table.

"This will be fine," I told him. "Thank you for fitting us in here when you're so busy."

"We're always glad to help Philippus and his family. But you're right, we are pretty full just now. Lord Eurytus' visit, you see."

"Is Eurytus staying here?"

"Oh, no, not himself in person. Some of his men are with us, but our Chief Brennus has the honour of entertaining his lordship."

"Ah. I run a mansio too, down near Eburacum. So I think I know just how you feel about that." As a fellow innkeeper, I could imagine his relief at not having to have the "honour" of accommodating a demanding, overbearing Imperial official. I was right. He gave me a broad wink.

Back in the barroom we found Philippus ensconced at a table with a jug of wine and a tray of beakers. He was chatting to a good-looking man in his mid-thirties, with brown wavy hair and a pleasant smile. Philippus introduced him as Nikias, the fort's medical officer.

A Greek name, if ever I heard one. "I'm pleased to meet you, Nikias. Forgive my asking, but you aren't related to a doctor friend of mine, Timaeus from Crete? He has a cousin Nikias in the army somewhere. I just wondered...?"

"No, I'm from Cos myself, and we've nobody in the family called Timaeus."

"That's a pity. Timaeus is always complaining that he misses the company of other Greeks. I'd like to have told him I'd found one of his long-lost relations. People like me do our best to cheer him up," I added in Greek, "but he says we're no real substitute. I suppose it must be the same here at the fort. I bet there isn't another Greek for miles around."

"My assistant Pythis is Greek," Nikias answered, also in Greek. "He's my nephew. I think we two are the only true Greeks here. Of course there are some would-be Greeks like Philippus here and his father, and they're better than nothing. The way they carry on, they're more Greek than we are sometimes, aren't you, Philo?"

Philippus laughed, and replied in Greek. "Some day I'll get a posting to Greece. The cradle of all that's finest in our civilisation, that's how I feel about it. Oh well, never mind. For now I'll make do with Cataractonium."

Everyone laughed, but then Nikias became serious again. "Look, Philo, I'm worried about this illness of your mother's. Do you think I should call in and see her tonight? I hear she's had nobody professional attending her, only some wise-woman from the village."

Philippus nodded. "She insisted it was a woman's problem, so she wanted another woman to look after her. I'd like her to have a proper professional doctor, of course, but you know how stubborn she can be."

"Yes, that I do know. But you can persuade her to let me examine her. I know you can. Will you try? Please?"

There was the tiniest hesitation before Philippus answered. "All right, I'll try. Come over later and I'll do what I can. But I'm afraid she may simply refuse to see you."

The doctor got to his feet. "I'll drop by before dark. Now I must go. By the way, did you patch up your slave all right? Do you need any more bandages for him?"

"No, thanks. You gave me enough to poultice an elephant the other day. They worked, anyhow. The boy's fine now."

"Then I'm off. Sorry I can't stay longer to chat, ladies. We don't get enough pretty women visiting Isurium. I hope I'll see you again. You're here for a few days, are you?"

"I hope so. We've been invited to Jovina's party. She's my cousin, and I'm looking forward to a chance of catching up on family news."

"Good, very good. So we must make sure Jovina has all her health and strength back by then."

"Niki's an excellent doctor," Philippus said as he poured our wine. "Between you and me, he and Mother used to be something more than good friends, if you know what I mean. It's all over now, but that's probably why she's reluctant to see him."

A Greek bearing gifts… But I hadn't time for pondering because he changed the subject. "Is your room comfortable?"

We assured him it was, and we chatted about inconsequential things for a while: about Isurium, which he didn't think much of, and Eburacum, which he quite liked. Then he mentioned a plan to visit Londinium, and he and Vitellia began to compare notes about the place. It was so long since I'd visited the capital that I didn't have much to contribute, and I told myself that was why Philippus was devoting most of his attention to Vitellia. But I knew better, really. When you travel with an exceptionally pretty young girl, she's going to have the lion's share of the attention. You may as well just get used to it.

Vitellia was attracting admiring glances from several of the customers, and I noticed that Philippus himself was popular, judging by the number of people who smiled or waved or stopped to have a word. Almost all soldiers, of course. One in particular I remember, a short, wiry young man with cavalry insignia who grinned as he crossed the room to us and allowed himself to be presented to Vitellia, and even to me. But it was Philippus he'd come to talk to.

"You've been away, Philo, haven't you?" he asked.

"Just for a day or two, yes."

"Cataractonium, wasn't it?"

"That's right."

"How was it?"

"Oh, boring as always. The quicker I can get myself transferred back here, the better."

The young cavalryman raised an eyebrow. "You didn't get caught up in the fire then?"

Philippus shrugged. "Fire? No. It was something and nothing."

"Really? One of the lads today said it made quite a mess of the tannery."

Philippus' look of alarm was almost comic. "I…I…You mean it was actually in the tannery itself? Gods, how bad was it?"

The cavalryman laughed. "Got you! Don't panic, there was no fire. I was just testing out a theory of mine, that you told us a load of rubbish about being ordered to go up there. You were nowhere near the place, were you? You were away from base without permission these last few days. Let me guess…Eburacum?"

"You bastard, Fabianus. All right, if you must know, yes, I've been in Eburacum."

"And was it worth the trip?"

Philippus grinned. "Oh yes. She was worth the trip."

"Well, don't try sneaking off for the next few days. There's going to be trouble, the commander says. Even the tannery contingent will be on alert." With another guffaw, the cavalryman swaggered off.

"Well, well," I said softly. "You're a dark horse, Philippus, aren't you? Absent without leave?"

"That's not the half of it." He lowered his voice to a conspiratorial whisper. "I had a good reason to be there. A secret mission, something the commander wanted done but didn't want talked about. Couldn't say anything in front of old Fabianus. You'll be discreet, won't you?"

"Of course." I nodded solemnly, though this sounded like nonsense to me, a bit of boasting to cover an embarrassing revelation. It could be partly true; there were informers all over the place who helped investigators like Lucius and Quintus sometimes. But no, Quintus would have known if Philippus was even an occasional informer. This was a fiction designed to impress me and especially Vitellia.

And indeed it did impress her. She gazed at him with shining eyes and an expression of wonder, and asked, also in a whisper, "Are you an investigator then? Like my fiancé? Lucius Aurelius Marcellus," she added proudly.

"Now and then." He put a finger to his lip, "Best not to talk about these things."

"Quite right." I gave another solemn nod. Whoever or whatever he was, I didn't want him quizzing her about Lucius. "Lucius never discusses his assignments with us. Does he, Vitellia?"

Unfortunately she didn't take the hint. "No, he doesn't. Even his latest one, about the mysterious man at the mansio."

Curse the girl, if I didn't change the subject fast, she'd be giving Philippus far too much detail about this "mysterious man." I glanced over at the bar seeking a diversion, and yes, thank the gods, there was a familiar face among the customers. Congrio, the trader in magic mats and cloaks, was buying drinks and attracting quite an audience, doubtless hoping to do some business later. But like any good salesman he had eyes everywhere, and when I waved at him he smiled back.

"The man at the mansio?" Philippus was looking interested. "Sounds fascinating. Do tell."

"I don't know anything really. But while I was staying there…"

"Look, Vitellia, there's that trader with the fancy cloaks and mats." I beckoned him. "Congrio, come and have a drink with us."

He was probably surprised by my invitation, but came over willingly enough. "It's a pleasure to see you here, ladies. Will you introduce me to your military friend?"

I did so, and as I'd hoped, Congrio launched straight into his sales patter. My diversion had succeeded, the topic of conversation was safe. But I'd have to remind Vitellia not to get drawn into telling people about Lucius and his work.

I sat listening with only half an ear as Congrio enthused about his wares. Most of my mind was on Quintus and Titch, wishing they'd arrive soon. I watched the main door, which was standing open on this warm evening. A steady stream of people came through it: soldiers, a few farmers, a couple of traders, a flute-player who settled in a dark corner and began to play haunting tunes, some of which I knew.

An interesting mixture of customers. But none of them was Quintus.

Chapter XII

Like the professional he was, Congrio remembered that Vitellia was already a customer, recalled what she'd bought, and congratulated her on her choice. But he gave most of his attention to Philippus.

"Now, sir, I'd welcome some advice from an officer. I'm hoping to interest the military authorities here in my wares, and their families too, of course. Are you based here at Isurium, sir?"

"No, at Cataractonium. It's only a few miles up the road, thank the gods. I'm just visiting Isurium for a few days."

"Then it's my good fortune to have met you here. If you'd like me to give you a private demonstration of the wonderful remarkable properties…" Once again I stopped concentrating as he went smoothly into his well-rehearsed routine. I looked at the sea of faces all around me and wondered if the crowd included someone who had warned me against coming here. Perhaps the soldier Portius was among the drinkers. I doubted if I'd recognise him without his layers of bandages. I tried not to speculate on what he'd do if he saw me now and realised that I'd disregarded the warnings intended to stop me coming to Isurium.

A bar-girl came over to take our order for the evening meal. I asked whether the men would care to join us. Congrio excused himself and returned to his audience at the bar, and Philippus explained that he must go back to his mother's house before long, because a meal would be waiting for him.

"I'm staying at Mother's till after the party. Luckily I don't have to go back to work for a day or two."

"I hadn't realised you're based at Cataractonium. I'd assumed you were on the strength here."

He shook his head. "Unfortunately not at present. Special duties at the tannery."

I know enough about army life to realise that special duties at any tannery mean specially bad rather than specially good. I wondered what he'd done, but put the thought aside, because there was an important question I wanted to ask him before he left for the evening.

"At least stay and keep us company till the food comes. And have another beaker of wine." I poured him a refill, and went on before he could return his attention to Vitellia. "We had a visitor from this area staying at our mansio recently, a soldier called Terentius. I'm not sure exactly where he was based though. You know him, presumably?"

He nodded. "And he's on his way home? I'm glad to hear that. He's a good friend of mine. There'll be quite a party when he gets back. He's been in Londinium, seconded to the governor's guard for three months."

So he hadn't heard about Terentius' death. That meant Portius hadn't come back to base, which wasn't surprising if we were right about his part in Terentius' murder. And maybe, as I'd half suspected, he was lying and wasn't based here. I could check with Philippus, but first I must tell him the bad news.

I did it as gently as I could, making it sound as if Terentius had been killed by his slave in the course of a robbery. It was clearly a shock to him.

"Gods, that's terrible. Murdered by his boy? I can't believe it!" He sat silent a while, staring into his beaker. "I suppose there'll be an investigation? Wait—isn't your brother an investigator? I remember Mother saying something about it."

"He is, and he's reported the matter to Eburacum, but I doubt if they'll need to take things any further. It seemed clear that Terentius had been stabbed by his own servant. The boy ran away, which looks pretty conclusive. Very sad, of course, but…well, it happens."

"I see." He sipped his wine with a thoughtful air. "As you say, it happens. I'll miss him."

"Actually, I'm surprised the news hasn't reached here already. Another soldier, Portius, was at the mansio enquiring after Terentius, the day after he was killed. I assumed he was coming straight here to report what had happened."

"Portius? We've nobody called Portius in the unit. Wait, I think I vaguely remember Terentius mentioning a friend called Portius, but he was based down south somewhere. That's right. When Terentius was seconded to Londinium, he said something about meeting up with an old friend there."

"That explains it then."

"May I ask, what's happening to his body? Will there be a funeral? And his things…he had a long-term girlfriend here, I expect he'd want her to have them. "

"We sent them to Eburacum with his body. I assume the headquarters people there will have arranged for them to be returned to his own base."

He nodded. "Of course. What with being away for a few days, I'm obviously not up to date with the latest news."

"They're auxiliaries at Cataractonium, I assume?"

He nodded. "Batavians. Like they are here. Good lads, and most of the officers are all right too. The trouble is, being in charge of a tannery is hardly a plum posting. It's a sort of punishment really. If I'm a good boy there for a few months, I'll be allowed back here, which is where I belong. It can't come soon enough for me."

Now, I thought, maybe I'll find out what he's done to deserve what is in effect a demotion. But just then Brutus came in with Baca and the drivers and guards.

I waved to him and he strolled over to our table. "Horses and carriages all settled in, Aurelia, and we've all got somewhere to sleep. I'm off over to the fort for a beer or two with a couple of old friends there. They're putting me up for the night. The others can eat their meal here. Now, are you sure you're happy about me going back home tomorrow? I can easily stay an extra day or two."

"Thanks, Brutus. I'd appreciate it if you could wait till we see how my cousin is in the morning. If she's still poorly and she isn't up to receiving visitors, it looks as if the party will be cancelled. I might just call in on her very briefly, and then head for home again. Disappointing, but there it is." I turned to Philippus. "Could you send someone here with a message first thing, to let us know how Jovina is? After a night's sleep, especially if she's seen the doctor, she might be much better, but if not…"

"Of course. I'll come myself and tell you how things are."

"Fine," Brutus said. "I'll find you after breakfast, Aurelia, but we'll not get ready to leave till we've had the latest news. See you tomorrow."

"Enjoy yourself."

"I wish I could be more positive," Philippus said. "I know Mother's longing to see you, Aurelia, but we really must be careful not to over-tax her strength. I think I should be on my way back to her now."

"Well then, give her my love, tell her I'm longing to see her, too. And let's hope for better news in the morning."

"I'll drink to that. Ah, now here's Gambax. I wonder what he wants, as if I didn't know?"

A good-looking soldier was making his way over to our table. Lean, sunburned, fair-haired, almost as handsome as Philippus, but younger and with a certain hesitancy about his manner. And presumably junior, because he saluted as he approached.

Philippus acknowledged the salute. "Well, Gambax, what can I do for you?"

The boy frowned. "I was hoping you'd have a message for me."

"Really? Who from, I wonder? Not my mother, she's too ill. Not Father, he's resting. Not one of these lovely ladies, surely?"

"You know who. Hasn't she written? She promised."

"Girls' promises, Gambax, are as reliable as wax javelins."

"Oh, well, I expect she's been busy. Never mind. Could you take a message to her from me then, please?" He produced a note-tablet from his pouch and passed it over to Philippus. "It's to tell her I've got myself assigned to the work detail that's preparing everything for your mother's birthday party, and I'm on guard duty during the party itself. So I ought to be able to see her then. Isn't that good?"

"My, my, love's a wonderful thing. Yes, leave it to me, I'll see she gets it." Suddenly he smiled. "And now I think about it, there is a message for you. Not a note, but she says she'll be at the usual spot at the usual time tomorrow. All right?"

"Wonderful! Thank you. Tell her I'll be there too."

"And the usual messenger's fee?"

"Of course. Your jug of Felernian's waiting at the bar."

He hurried off, and Philippus went to the bar and brought back a wine-jug. "Try this, ladies, it's good stuff. Brought to us courtesy of my sister's latest lover-boy. There's a lot to be said for acting as a go-between. So here's a health to all young lovers. On one condition though: not a word of any of this to the parents, all right?"

"Our lips are sealed. Except for drinking of course." I sipped the Falernian, and found it considerably better than what we'd had already.

Philippus drank with relish. "I really must get home, so you ladies enjoy the rest of the jug. It's the most drinkable wine in this place, and I've developed quite a taste for it. Long may their romance continue." He set down his beaker. "I'll say good-night then. I look forward to seeing you tomorrow."

I pretended not to notice this last remark was addressed to Vitellia. But the young lady herself noticed all right, and gazed after Philippus with interest.

"Isn't he nice? You didn't tell me your cousin had such a good-looking son."

"Didn't I? It's ages since I saw him, I was still thinking of him as a boy. I suppose he is quite handsome now. A bit of a lad, though, I'd say, wouldn't you? "

"Perhaps. But definitely fanciable." That made me smile. "Fanciable" used to be a favourite word of Albia's, in the days before she was married, when she seemed to be forever in and out of love. She'd been susceptible to a charming smile or flattering male attention, until she met Candidus and decided he was the one she really wanted. Perhaps Lucius wasn't, after all, going to be Vitellia's one-and-only love? Being surrounded by admiring soldiers might make her realise that.

Our meal was adequate, a thick stew supposed to have pork in it but in fact consisting mainly of onions and turnips, and insipid gravy that could have done with more pepper. It was followed with some raisin cakes. The Falernian helped to wash it down. All in all, it could have been a lot worse, but I kept thinking that if we'd been at the Oak Tree it would have been a lot better.

"Aurelia!" I looked up at the sound of my name, and saw Quintus striding to our table. He bowed formally to us, but I caught the look in his eyes, and it made me glad.

"What a pleasant surprise to find you here, Aurelia. I thought you'd be at your cousin's house."

"We should be, but she's unwell, so her son managed to get us accommodation here."

"It looks busy. I hope they've room for me and Titch."

"If you haven't got a room booked, you may be sleeping in the stables. Most of Eurytus' retinue are here."

He shrugged. "I'm sure the innkeeper can find us somewhere for tonight. After that we'll be staying in the fort I expect. I'll have a word with him, and then bring some more wine. What are you drinking?"

"The Felernian's not bad."

"Praise from an innkeeper! It must be the nectar of the gods." He walked over to the bar, and I watched him talking to Nonius. I couldn't hear what they said above the customers' chatter, but the course of the conversation was clear enough. Nonius shook his head several times, but Quintus persisted, until Nonius began to show signs of impatience.

Then Quintus produced a small piece of papyrus from his belt-pouch, and I whispered to Vitellia, "He's showing his travel pass from the Emperor. It's a very high-powered one, it'll get him in all right. Yes, look, Nonius has just remembered he has a spare room after all."

Sure enough, the innkeeper was nodding now. I almost felt sorry for the poor fellow: he already had an inundation of Eurytus' entourage, and now here was another Imperial officer whom he dared not refuse.

Quintus laid a couple of silver pieces on the bar, glancing towards our table, and Nonius nodded again and led him out of the room. He came back almost immediately and brought a jug of wine over to us himself.

"You found our friend a room, then?" I asked.

"He's having my youngest sons' room for tonight, the boys can bed down on the floor somewhere." He spread his hands. "I don't see many travel passes like that one. He's got friends in high places, hasn't he?"

"He has," I agreed. "But don't worry, he's cast in a different mould from…from other Imperial visitors in this part of the province."

"I'm glad to hear it. Ah, here he is. Everything satisfactory, sir?"

"Very, thanks, Nonius." He pulled up a stool. "Now, I hear good things of this Falernian."

We drank and chatted for a while. Quintus took trouble to make himself agreeable to Vitellia, and she answered politely, but I noticed she was tired, and in the end she gave way to a huge yawn.

"I'm sleepy," she announced. "Please forgive me, Quintus Antonius. I don't mean to be rude, but I'm tired after all the travelling and excitement."

"We've had a busy time these last few days," I said. "Don't stand on ceremony, we'll excuse you if you feel like an early night."

"Thank you, I think I do. Will you be coming soon?"

Quintus smiled at her. "I'm afraid I'm going to keep Aurelia talking a bit longer. As you gathered yesterday, we haven't seen one another for a long time."

I summoned Baca from the corner table where the servants had finished their meal, and wished Vitellia good-night.

"I shan't wait up," she answered, with her dazzling smile.

"That child is developing a sense of humour," I said as she disappeared.

"Perhaps she was being serious. Lucius must have told her about you and me. She seems a nice enough girl, and she's quite a looker. Lucius always goes for the very pretty empty-headed ones, doesn't he?"

"Does he? I never get to meet his girl-friends."

"She's a typical example, and he must be really hooked, to be offering to marry her. He presumably thinks an alliance with her father will help his career, and he's right. I know him slightly, he's quite influential in the governor's circle, and very rich—his estates cover about half the countryside between Londinium and the south coast."

I didn't get the chance to suggest what he could do with his estates, because a servant came hurrying between the tables and stopped at ours. "Mistress Aurelia Marcella?"

"Yes, I'm Aurelia Marcella."

"I've brought a message for you. From my mistress, Jovina Lepida."

"Ah, good. Is she feeling better now?"

"A little, I think. She asked me to say welcome to Isurium, and to give you this." She held out a note-tablet. "And she told me to wait for your answer, if you please."

This is odd, I thought as I untied the cord. Why has she written to me when she's already sent Philippus to look after us?

The note gave me the answer.

"Aurelia from Jovina, greetings. Please come to visit me tomorrow. They are trying to stop me seeing you."

I managed to keep my face impassive as I looked up at the girl. She returned my gaze, and I saw the anxiety in her face.

"What's your name?"

"I'm Selena, the mistress' confidential maid."

There was a very slight emphasis on the word "confidential". I decided that if Jovina trusted this servant, then I could too.

"You know what's in the message, Selena?"

She nodded.

"Who does she mean?"

"Someone close to her. Someone she should be able to trust. He's being far too protective, and it's making her worse, not better."

"I'm not going to make her ill if I visit her?"

"Gods, no, Mistress, quite the opposite. She wants to see you very much."

"Then tell her the answer is yes. Come what may, I'll be there."

"That's good." She smiled, looking relieved. "Thank you. I'll see you tomorrow then. Good-night now."

When she'd gone, Quintus stood up. "Why don't we take our drinks into the garden? Where it's cooler."

And a little more private. "Why not? It's a lovely night."

It was pleasant to be away from the noisy, stuffy barroom, in the fading light with the first stars showing. We found a secluded bench near a laurel hedge, with nobody in earshot. I showed him Jovina's note. "I'll go and see her tomorrow first thing. I've got to find out what's wrong there. I suppose if she's really ill, her party will be cancelled, and we'll have to go home again. But it sounds as if she's better than we've been told."

"I hope so. I'm relying on you to get firmly established in her house."

"I haven't done too badly so far. I've seen two members of her family already. Mallius at the fort, and Philippus here."

"Good. Your first impressions?"

"Mallius was very drunk and probably won't even remember the meeting. From the way the men reacted, it wasn't unusual to see him like that. Philippus is charming, entertaining, in fact a likeable young man, though a scamp. He's based at Cataractonium, but he's staying in Isurium till after the party."

"What made you say he's a scamp?"

"He's got landed with some sort of punishment duty up at Cataractonium, supervising the tannery. And when we were chatting earlier, it came out that he'd recently been absent without leave. He'd told everyone he was in Cataractonium, but he wasn't, and he admitted he'd been down to Eburacum. A friend was teasing him about it, and he said he was seeing a woman, but then afterwards he told Vitellia and me he was doing 'secret work' as an investigator. Is he?"

Quintus laughed. "What do you think? But you didn't challenge him about it?"

"No, I assumed he was just showing off for Vitellia's benefit. But if he was in Eburacum—and of course we only have his word for it—I'd like to know what he was doing there."

"Have you found any Greeks yet?"

"I have." I told him about Nikias and his assistant. "And Philippus said there'd been an affair between the doctor and his mother, but it's finished now."

"Good, you've done well. I'll make a point of getting to know him at the fort. And if I call on you at Jovina's tomorrow, you can introduce me to the family. Assuming you can manage to get her to put you up, that is. And do you think she'd invite me and Titch to her party, as we're such old friends of yours? That would be a perfect opportunity to meet your family, and presumably some of Mallius' fellow officers."

"Not to mention a good excuse for free wine and party food. But I'll see what I can do."

"Titch and I have several jobs lined up for tomorrow. We must pay a courtesy call on the fort commander sometime, and then be seen to go through the motions of looking at the bridge. That'll give us a chance to get the lie of the land. But I'm sure I can make time to visit you. Maybe about noon…I'll do my best."

"Another busy day," I said, trying to suppress a yawn. "Sorry, Quintus. Don't take it personally."

"I'll try not to. But the jug's not empty. I don't want to say goodnight quite yet."

Neither did I, so we sat together for a while longer, till it was full dark with stars blazing down from a cloudless sky. I remember how peaceful it all was, and how I wished we could stay there undisturbed forever. But we both knew it was simply the calm before a storm.

Chapter XIII

Breakfast was nothing special, yesterday's bread with hard over-salty cheese. But I barely tasted it. I was anxious to get it over and visit my cousin. Quintus and Titch were nowhere to be seen, and the innkeeper's wife told me they'd eaten earlier still and gone out.

When Brutus appeared I almost laughed aloud. He was making a valiant effort to look like a man who hasn't got a serious hangover, and failing miserably.

"Enjoyable evening at the fort, Brutus?" I asked.

"Aye, not bad at all, what I remember." He rubbed a hand across his eyes. "Have you had news of your cousin?"

"Yes, and I want to drive to her house straight away. I think we'll be moving over there today. She's feeling better."

He grinned ruefully. "I wish I was. I'll get ready now. And I'll bring the other driver and both guards along as escort. My pals at the fort tell me the village isn't too peaceful just now. There are extra patrols out, though, so we should be all right."

The soldiers were plainly in evidence as soon as we crossed the road and entered the civilian area. There were some natives too, haymakers, milkmaids, and the shepherd lad we'd seen yesterday, and they were all hurrying and looking uneasily around them as they went. We passed no less than four VVV signs on walls, and two gangs of slaves with pails and brushes, urged on by soldiers to clean the graffiti off. I was glad when we reached Jovina's.

It was a large single-storey house on the edge of the village, on an unpaved road. Its front door faced the street so it presumably had a garden at the back. The door-keeper answered Brutus' knock promptly and appeared to recognise my name. He politely ushered us into a small sitting-room overlooking the garden, and directed Brutus to the kitchen entrance at the rear.

"Your mistress is expecting us," I told him. "Her maid Selena brought me a note from her yesterday evening."

"Very good," he said. "I'll tell my lady you're here."

So far so good. We'd hardly had time to sit down when Philippus walked in, and stopped in surprise when he saw us.

"Why, good morning, Aurelia...Vitellia. You're up with the lark today. I was about to come over to the mansio to see you."

"Good morning, Philippus. That's kind of you, but I'm sure you must be busy, so I thought I'd save you the trouble. How's your mother today? I'm hoping she's feeling better, at least well enough to see me for a little while."

He shook his head. "I'm afraid she's no better this morning. She had a restless night, and she's still very unwell. I've sent for the wise-woman to come as soon as she can, and until she's been, I honestly don't think she's up to seeing anyone. These women's troubles, you know..."

I gave him my most reassuring smile. "Yes, I do know. I wouldn't tire her; I'd just look in quickly to say hello. It might do her good, a visit from another woman. It would certainly do me good. I mean I'm really quite worried about her."

"We all are. But I promise she's getting the best possible care."

"Did the Greek doctor see her last night? What did he say?"

He shrugged. "Briefly, but she wouldn't take any of the medicine he suggested, she said she preferred the herbs the wise-woman brings her. She saw the woman again just before she went to sleep, which is better than nothing I suppose. Well, I hope it is." He sighed. "I'm sorry you've had a wasted journey. Let me offer you some refreshment, and then I'll escort you back to the mansio for now. You'll be more comfortable waiting there, and

I'll send you a message later to let you know when she's feeling more sociable."

Escort us back to the mansio? Oh, no you don't, sunshine. I don't give up so easily. "Couldn't you just tell her I'm here, Philippus? I know she's been thinking about me. She sent me a note last night."

"A note?" For a heartbeat he looked worried, but then he smiled. "I hadn't realised she had written to you. She really should be resting. But I suppose it's a good sign."

"I'm sure it is. It was just a line welcoming me to Isurium and saying she hoped I'd look in today."

He sighed again. "Well, in that case I'll ask her, of course. I'll send for some refreshments for you while you wait."

Vitellia and I sat and sipped our drinks, and I found myself listening to the noises of the house. There were the usual busy morning sounds, maids' voices, somebody whistling, a clatter of dishes from the kitchen, the swish of a broom over a tiled floor. And then I heard a louder voice, a young woman's, angry and strident and coming nearer.

"I tell you I'm going, Philo, and you're not stopping me. Honestly, anyone would think I was a slave in this house." A male voice answered something, but too softly for us to hear, then the woman's tirade continued: "I've said I'll meet him, and I will. Stop trying to tell me what to do. It's my life, and I'll do what I please with it. You're in no position to give me lectures about how to behave. Demoted to running a tannery, with gambling debts big enough to pay for a cohort of cavalry. So just leave me alone." There was the sound of running feet, and a heavy door slammed.

"Somebody's not happy," I said to Vitellia. "I bet that's Chloe, Jovina's daughter. She always had a temper."

Just then Selena came in, and smiled to see us. "I'm pleased you're here, Mistress Aurelia. My lady will be, too. I was afraid from what Master Philippus said that you weren't staying."

"I said I'd come. But Philippus tells us Jovina is still too ill for visitors. Is he right?"

"Jupiter's balls, I wish he'd stop…" She paused and continued more calmly, "He gets so protective sometimes. She's not too ill for you, Mistress, I promise. Master Philo just came to tell her you'd looked in, but you had to hurry away and would come back later. My lady was beside herself so I came straight here to ask you to change your mind."

"Don't worry. I'm going nowhere till I've seen my cousin."

"Good, because she's desperate to see you. She's still unwell, and she needs her rest, but fretting over when you'll be here is stopping her getting it. If you'll come with me, I'll take you to her straight away. The only thing is, if she finds she's getting tired after a while…"

"We're old friends, she'll tell me quickly enough if I overstay my welcome. Vitellia, will you wait for me here?"

"May I keep you company?" Philippus was standing in the doorway smiling down at her. "I'll show you round the garden if you like. There are some quite interesting statues."

"Thank you, that would be very nice."

I don't know how I'd expected to find my cousin: lying flat out on her bed, or limply reclining, supported by a heap of pillows. It was a pleasant surprise to see her sitting on a reading-couch, fully dressed and with her hair properly arranged. She had lovely fine fair hair that I'd always envied. She was pale, presumably from being ill, but that only emphasised her large dark eyes and full lips. She hadn't lost her beauty.

She got up, smiling, as Selena showed me in. "Aurelia dear, thank the gods! It's so good to see you."

"And you, Jovina." I went to her and we embraced. "And I'm so glad to find you out of bed. From what your menfolk said about you, I wasn't expecting that."

She looked pleased, and then her expression became a little embarrassed. "No, well, I had to keep everyone at bay for a day or two, except Selena and the healing-woman from the village. But I'm better now. Come and sit here next to me, and I'll tell you it all. Could you fetch us some fresh wine, Selena, please?

Aurelia and I have a lot of catching-up to do. And I still don't want any visitors. Absolutely nobody."

"I understand, Mistress. Not even Nikias, if he tries again?"

"Well…no. Definitely not. I should never have allowed him to see me last night, only …never mind. I don't want to see him again."

"Very good." Something odd about Selena's tone caught my attention. Had the handsome medic helped or hindered Jovina's quick recovery? Had she even been ill at all? You couldn't read it in her face. You might have said she'd had a bad headache or an uncomfortable time of the month, but nothing serious enough to warrant her refusing to see anyone for days. Or had it been Philippus, not she herself, who'd been keeping visitors away? And if so, why?

"I don't know what I'd have done without Selena these last few months," Jovina said as the door closed. "She's loyal, she's efficient, and she's one of the few people here I can really trust. Now, first things first. I'm so sorry you had to spend last night at that dreadful mansio."

"It wasn't too bad. Not the Oak Tree, but then I've always said I run the best mansio north of the Humber, so what could I expect? And I was grateful to Philippus for sorting out accommodation for us when the mansio was so busy."

"He's one of their regulars. He plays dice there most nights and makes a useful contribution to their bar takings." She smiled. "Boys will be boys, you know. Anyhow, from today you must stay here…no, no arguments, I insist on it. Get your things brought over straight away. Selena will organise it all. How many servants have you?"

"Only one maid. My drivers and guards are wanted back at Oak Bridges so they're going home today. And don't forget there's Vitellia, Lucius' betrothed. You did get my note about her coming to the party?"

"She's welcome—the more the merrier. I'll need all the help I can get to keep things cheerful. And now that it's been brought forward…"

"Brought forward? I thought it was on your birthday in two days' time."

"It was, but that's Midsummer Day, and there's some sort of panic on at the fort about it. We've had warning that the natives are up to something, and Trebonius, that's the commander, wants everyone on high alert, not relaxing at a party."

"I only just got here in time, then. I'm really looking forward to it. And of course we'd much rather stay here, if you're sure."

"Quite certain. It's wonderful that you've managed to get here. It can't have been easy at such short notice."

"Of course I've come. Your message didn't leave me much choice, talking about danger, and Greeks bearing gifts. What's it all about?"

She spread out her hands. "Where to begin? I've got so much to tell you."

"Begin with why you wrote me last night that someone was trying to stop me coming to see you. Whoever it was, they were presumably only doing what they thought was right for you."

She smiled. "Oh, that? I think I was being a bit silly. Philo is so overprotective sometimes, but he means it for the best. He was worried when I was poorly, you know how men are about women's complaints. I'm having trouble convincing him that I'm recovered now."

"And are you really recovered? Selena says you're not quite there yet. What's been the trouble? Have you been ill for long?"

"I was only really sick for a day, but I didn't want the menfolk asking all sorts of awkward questions. Marcus especially. So we told them all I was too ill to see any of them. Now we can say the village healing-woman has found a cure, and I'm myself again."

"Good. But what was wrong with you?"

Again she evaded the question. "I'll be fit for the birthday party, at any rate. But as to enjoying it… The nearer this so-called celebration comes, the more I'm dreading it."

"Why, for the gods' sake? You'll be the centre of attention and you'll have all your friends around you."

"That's just it. *All* of them. I shall be like a juggler throwing knives in the air and trying not to catch them by the blades."

This over-dramatic image was so typical of Jovina, it made me smile. "Nonsense, it'll be fine. *I* intend to enjoy it anyway. It's ages since I was at a party. And it'll be good for Vitellia to meet new people. She's led a fairly sheltered life."

"Chloe will like having some female company of her own age." Jovina sighed. "That child is a worry just now, I don't mind telling you. Marcus plans to announce her betrothal at my party, you know. A good marriage, with an old family friend. Statius Severus, from Lindum. I don't suppose you remember him, do you?"

"I think so, vaguely." A picture came into my mind, not a particularly attractive one: an old man who walked with a stick, grey hair, grey face set in a permanent frown.

"He's a lot older than Chloe, isn't he?"

"He's well past fifty, more than twice Chloe's age. That's part of the problem. She says she doesn't fancy him. And before you say it, I know young girls can't just marry whoever they please. But I can understand how she feels. Living on military bases, she's got very used to mixing with men nearer her own age. All she wants to do is run wild, lapping up the attention she gets from the young soldiers. It's a perfectly good marriage though. Apart from Statius being a long-standing friend, he's rich. We never have been, so it's important Chloe marries money. She'll give up her wild ways eventually. But I've asked Marcus not to announce the engagement tomorrow. I don't want the party spoilt by a huge row."

"Just between you and me, I wish Vitellia could show a bit of wildness now and again. They should suit one another."

Selena came in with the wine, poured it out, and left. I raised my mug.

"To a happy birthday," I said, "and a happy party to celebrate it."

She lifted her beaker to me. "I can face it now you're here. I'm still dreading it, but I feel I can get through it."

"We'll get through it together. You still haven't really told me why you're dreading it."

She shrugged. "Oh, don't mind me. Tell me all your news. This Vitellia, now…"

I did as she asked, but reluctantly, because it seemed all wrong somehow. It was *her* news I wanted to talk about. But she persisted, and seemed bright and lively, and much interested in all the Aurelius family were doing. Yet to me, knowing her well, it was a forced brightness, like a coat of garish paint concealing blemishes on the face of a marble statue.

After a mug of wine, I decided I must make arrangements for us all to move to her house from the mansio.

Vitellia was where I'd left her, chatting to Philippus. The pair of them seemed to be getting on very well, and that must be a good thing, I thought. If I was supposed to be keeping an eye on Philippus, that job should be much easier if he spent plenty of time with Vitellia.

I sent for Brutus and gave all the necessary practical instructions. "So you can head for home today, in plenty of time."

He looked troubled. "The more I see of this place, the more worried I am about leaving you."

"I'll be perfectly safe with my cousin and her family."

"I don't know as any Roman outside the fort is *perfectly* safe just now. I've been keeping me ears open, and so have the drivers. There's definitely resentment among the natives, and they all seem to think it'll come to a head on Midsummer Day. The fort commander's quite worried, he's sending to Eburacum for reinforcements, they say. And I don't like the idea of you and Miss Vitellia being here alone."

"Ah, but we shan't be alone. Quintus Antonius has arrived here."

"Antonius? That's good news. Maybe the commander sent for him too?"

"Maybe. But the point is, I've got someone reliable I can call on if I need to. You go home, you're needed there."

He nodded. "All right then, if you're certain. I hope you have a really good party. And take care, won't you?"

"I will, Brutus. You can be sure of it."

Chapter XIV

As I was returning to Jovina's room. Selena came hurrying past
me in the hall, a note-tablet in her hand. She slowed down long
enough to say softly, "This letter'll please my lady. From a certain
person up at the fort. Would you mind waiting here just a little
while? You'll get no sense out of her till she's read it."

"Of course." I wandered to the nearest window and looked
out into the garden, and caught a fleeting glimpse of the handsome soldier Gambax whom I'd met at the mansio, hastening
along a paved path towards a stand of trees. He must be here to
see Chloe. Well, it was none of my business.

When Selena beckoned me to come in, Jovina was smiling
and holding her letter aloft. "A note from Trebonius. He wants
me to go and see him today. To make final arrangements for my
party. He's organising it, you see."

"The commander is? I'd assumed it would be Marcus."

Her smile broadened, and she even blushed. "Well, Marcus
hasn't been in much of a state to organise anything lately. Trebonius offered to help, and he suggested we should invite a few
people from the fort and the village, people outside the family, I
mean. He thinks with everyone being so unsettled and on edge
just now, a bit of socialising will be good for morale. That's the
only reason."

Oh yes? And I'm the Queen of Brigantia. She looked more
like a romantic young girl with a note from the boy next door

than a senior officer's wife planning a social event to improve morale.

"Where will it be? Here, or in the fort?"

"Neither. It's going to be outside, in the open air. A lovely spot where the water-meadows slope very gently down to the river."

"In the open? In northern Britannia? What if it rains all day?"

"It won't. We're in for a long fine spell, that's what the village wise-woman says."

"And if she's not so wise after all?"

She laughed. "There'll be tents there, enough so we can all sit and eat under cover if we really have to. But the plan is for all the tables and couches to be out in the sunshine."

"It's a lot to arrange, but a fort commander must be good at organising people and supplies."

"He is. You must come with me this afternoon, he wants to meet you. Bring Vitellia too. He says he knows Lucius."

"He probably does. My brother has all sorts of contacts in the army. Talking of which, you've heard me mention Quintus Antonius Delfinus, the bridge engineer?"

"Bridge engineer, spy, and your mysterious lover? When are you going to introduce me to him?"

"Quite soon, I think. He's here in Isurium, I saw him at the mansio last night. I told him I'd be visiting you and he said he might call round here later on, if it's convenient."

"My dear, of course it's convenient, I've been telling you for years I want to meet him." Then her bright smile faded. "But why is he here? Is he expecting trouble of some sort? Yes, of course he must be, otherwise what's he doing in Isurium just now?"

"There's some problem with the bridge, he told me."

"The bridge? Gods, as if things weren't difficult enough!"

"You mean with this dreadful man Eurytus? From what I've heard and seen, he causes trouble wherever he goes. Between you and me—and please keep this to yourself, Jovina—I think perhaps Quintus' visit may be connected with him and his antics."

"Good. In that case Trebonius will be very glad of his help." She sipped her wine and gazed thoughtfully through the open window at the garden. "I love this house, away from the fort. But I feel vulnerable here, surrounded by civilians, and most of them natives. If they start damaging property, setting fire to things, what can we do?"

"Is that likely?"

"Vivat Venutius Victor," she muttered. "The gods curse him, barbarian oaf. Trebonius thinks we have to take him seriously. So does Marcus…when he's in a state to think at all, that is."

I took the chance to put a question I'd been wanting to ask. "And how are things with Marcus these days? I saw him briefly yesterday at the fort. I'm not sure if he really saw me."

She nodded. "Philo told me. Drunk as a senator, I gather. I'm so sorry."

"It's hardly your fault. Is he often like that?"

"Most of the time, I gather. Of course he's under a great deal of strain now that he's deputy commander, and he needs to live over at the fort mostly. He has quite decent quarters there. But I prefer to stay here."

"So you don't see much of him. That seems a shame."

She smiled faintly. "He says living in a military base is more peaceful than putting up with Chloe's tantrums. I can tell you it's more peaceful for me without him. We keep up appearances in public when we have to. We're supposed to set an example to the younger officers."

"Presumably he'll be at the party?"

"Oh, yes. He doesn't like Trebonius, but he can't let it show." She sighed." He and Trebonius were rivals for the commander's post when the previous prefect retired. Marcus has never forgiven Trebonius for winning. He still thinks he should have got the job. But I don't see why I should take his side when Trebonius is so much the better man. You'll like him. Everybody does."

"You and Trebonius…are you seeing much of one another?"

"Now and then. It's not serious, we're good friends enjoying a bit of fun, nothing more. I know he'd like more, but after all he's a married man, and I can't…I ought not to…Oh, Aurelia, I wish

I knew what to do for the best." Suddenly her face crumpled, and she began to cry.

I took her in my arms and hugged her till the tears subsided. "Tell me. I'm here, and I can help, I'm sure I can."

Out it all came. How Marcus didn't love her now, or even want her in bed, preferring the company of village women. How Chloe was not just refusing the marriage her parents had arranged for her, but threatening to run away from home unless she was allowed to marry a totally unsuitable young soldier with no rank and no money.

And Philippus was her biggest worry. "Running wild, gambling, chasing women, spending money as if he has his own mint. I don't know where he gets it from, and I don't want to know, it's bound to be something unsavoury, if not actually illegal. And now he's got demoted and sent to command a tannery, of all things. And the company he keeps…thank the gods Terentius has been away lately, but when he comes back, I don't know what will happen to Philo."

"Terentius won't be coming back," I said gently. "He's been killed in an accident. I know, because it happened at the Oak Tree."

"Terentius dead? Well, that's something. Oh, dear, how awful of me. I've been so worried. Aurelia, can I trust you with a secret?"

"You can."

"After Philo stayed here at the beginning of the month, the maids were cleaning his room, and they found…I'll show you."

She went over to her bed, felt under the mattress, and produced a small pouch. When she unfastened it I saw a bronze brooch. She brought it to me, but I recognised it without having to look closely. It bore the letters VVV.

"I hid it," she explained breathlessly. "I know what VVV means, but I don't know why Philo would have a thing like this. Of course he wouldn't get himself mixed up in a rebellion, but…well, if he's short of money, he might have been involved in a small way. Supplying information, relaying messages, I don't know. What do you think?"

"I think," I answered, "that it's extremely serious. If Philippus is even slightly connected with Venutius, he could be in real trouble. Have you asked him about it?"

"Yes. He admitted it was his, but he swore he didn't know what it meant, but had taken it in part-payment for a gambling debt."

"Did you believe him?"

"No. And I didn't know what to do. That's what made me write to you. I thought you might, or your brother…you've always been good at sorting out problems. I panicked. And you came, and I'm so grateful. Now that you're here, perhaps I can find out more about what's going on, and put a stop to it." She looked up at me. "You don't mind, do you? I assume you don't, otherwise you wouldn't have come."

"I don't mind helping, but if I'm to do anything useful I need to know all of it. You really have no idea what Philippus is up to?"

"No more than I've told you."

"Why in the gods' name have you hung on to the wretched brooch? Throw it out, that's my advice."

"I will, but I can't get rid of it in the house, someone would be bound to see it. I'll take it with me to the party tomorrow and throw it into the river. Oh, it's all such a mess! But when you're a mother, you never stop caring about your children, whatever they've done." She wiped her eyes. "He's such a dear boy really."

"And all these family problems are what's been making you ill?"

"No, that wasn't it. I found I was with child. And not by Marcus."

So now we were getting to the truth at last. "I see. Wouldn't he have accepted it as his? Even been pleased to think he'd fathered a child?"

She shook her head. "He and I haven't shared a bed for months. I'm afraid that's common knowledge."

"He might still be prepared to let people think it's his."

"I couldn't take the risk, he's so unpredictable now. He already suspects I haven't been faithful to him, and he's jealous, even though he himself has had a string of native women. Men are so unfair, aren't they? They're allowed to have any girl that takes their fancy, but if a woman looks for a bit of comfort and affection, that's quite another matter."

More tears followed, and when she was calm again she said, "I'm sorry, Aurelia. It's just such a relief to have someone I can talk to, someone who understands."

"Your illness. Are you still with child now?"

She gave a little shiver. "I got rid of it three days ago. The local wise-woman helped me. It was just like a miscarriage, painful and upsetting. Not the first one I've had. But it's the first one I've ever welcomed. Oh well, it's over now."

"I'm so sorry. What a horrible thing to have to do. No wonder you were ill."

"It didn't last long, and I'm all right now, just a bit tired. And a little sad. Well, life goes on." She gave me an over-bright smile. "I'm fit for my party, anyway."

"Does Trebonius know what you've done?"

"Trebonius? Gods, I hope not."

"But if he was the father…"

"He wasn't. It was none of his doing."

I stared at her blankly. "Then who…?"

"Nikias, of course."

"The *doctor*?"

"Don't look at me like that, please don't. You're thinking I've behaved like a common tart."

"No," I lied. "But I'm thinking you've got yourself in a very messy situation."

"I can't argue with that."

"Your letter spoke of 'danger in the wind.' I didn't realise the danger was of your own making."

"Not all of it," she answered.

"And the doctor is 'the Greek bearing gifts'?"

She nodded. "We had an affair over several months. It started when I was his patient in the winter, I twisted my ankle, and he found me some herbs for the pain. He's been so sweet, so gentle, he really loves me. He knows what Marcus is like; he can see what I have to go through."

"But you say you finished with him?"

"He finished with me. He asked me to leave home and run away with him. He said we could make a new start somewhere far away, even if it meant leaving Britannia. I was tempted, but in the end I couldn't. Marcus doesn't need me, but Philo and Chloe both do, in their different ways. When I finally said no, he lost his temper, and we had a most awful row and stopped seeing one another. Then I discovered I was pregnant. I couldn't ask Niki to help me destroy his own baby, could I? Selena found the village wise-woman, and she gave me native medicine. That solved the problem."

Solved the problem? What an appalling way of describing it. "And now you think everything will go back to normal?"

"Why not? Men come and go. I haven't got Marcus and I can't have Niki, but Trebonius has been letting me know he's interested. I'm sure he can help mend my broken heart."

I winced at the scorn in her voice, because I realised it was herself she despised, more than the men in her life.

"Doesn't the risk you're taking with all this bother you? Having affairs with other people at the fort...it's a small community, and presumably everybody knows everyone else's business. Can you be sure of keeping secrets?"

"Oh, yes, I'm very careful."

There was a tap at the door, and Selena came in.

"I told you I don't want to be disturbed," Jovina snapped.

"I know, Mistress, but the master's on his way, insisting on visiting you."

"Marcus? Why?"

"I want to see you, and I won't take no for an answer," came Mallius' voice from the corridor outside, and he brushed roughly past Selena and strode in. He was sober as far as I could tell, and he was angry. "I've had enough of being kept out of my own wife's rooms. Why have you been refusing to see me, Jovina?"

Jovina had the presence of mind to stand up and smile at him. "Marcus, don't be so silly. I haven't wanted to see anyone lately, I've been so ill. But I'm feeling very much better today. I think I've turned the corner."

"Better? Really? I'm glad to hear it. Because if you let me down over this party, after all the trouble I've been to…"

"All the trouble *you've* been to? It's Trebonius who's done all the real organising, you've been too sodden with drink to make any sensible contribution. Oh, yes, don't think I don't know how you behave at the fort. Well, listen to this, Marcus, and don't forget it. I'm going to enjoy this party, and I won't have you spoiling it. I expect you to be there for appearance's sake. But don't you dare bring along any of your native girls. It's bad enough the whole fort knowing you don't live as my husband nowadays, but I won't have you making a display of it. Understand?"

"Perfectly. I wouldn't dream of it. I can't think any of them would want to come anyway. And as for keeping up appearances, that goes for you too, Jovina. If I see any inappropriate behaviour, if I see you encouraging advances by anyone, I won't be responsible for my actions." He turned on his heel and left, his boots echoing as he strode down the corridor.

Jovina flung herself onto the couch and wept stormily. I sat watching her and feeling helpless, not sure whether to stay or go. Eventually I got up and started to move towards the door, but Selena shook her head. She went to a table by the far wall and poured out a small beaker of what looked like red wine from a squat black flask.

"Here now, Mistress, have a drop of your special medicine. Mistress Aurelia will sit by you for a while till you feel better. We've got to get you ready for your trip to see the commander at the fort, haven't we?"

Jovina sat up and sipped the drink. "I'm sorry, Aurelia. He's *impossible!*"

"I know. Never mind. Just drink your medicine and I'll sit quietly here."

She finished the wine, and whatever it contained must have done her good. She handed Selena her empty beaker and turned to me. "Now you see why this party scares me, Aurelia. Marcus is jealous, but he's not sure who to be jealous of and thinks it may be Trebonius, and he hates his guts anyway. Nikias is sulking because I wouldn't run away with him, and he's still trying to persuade me. Last night he tried again. I don't know if it might not be the answer. Leave Isurium, leave Britannia even."

"You'd seriously think of throwing everything up to be with him?"

"Yes. No. *I* don't know. And what if they all drink too much, and start boasting, or throwing insults at each other? What if they come to blows?"

"At a party, with the whole base watching? I don't think so. They're all grown men. They'll know how to behave properly in public."

"I hope you're right. But gods, I'll be glad when it's over. I wish I'd never said I'd like a big party. I've never done anything like this for my birthday before. But when Trebonius suggested we make it a really lavish affair, for the fort as well as for me, it seemed a wonderful idea. I was flattered, I won't deny. But I should have said no, I'd prefer to invite a few family and friends to dinner here."

"It's not too late to change your plans. Nobody would blame you, with all the tension in the village. Nobody can force you to hold it, if you don't want to."

"No. I must go ahead with it now. For everyone's sake."

"It's *your* sake we need to be concerned with. If a smaller celebration is what you want, then that's what you shall have."

"It's too late to worry about what I want. Trebonius has staked his reputation on this party, inviting all sorts of important people, including some of the leading natives. 'Showing the eagle,' he calls it."

"I remember Father using that expression. Making a good Roman spectacle to impress the barbarians."

"Exactly. And having decided to show the eagle, there's no question of changing our minds." She stood erect, like a tragic figure in a play contemplating death or glory. "We must all do our duty when it's required. We'll get through it somehow. Rome expects it. Even at the cost of our lives."

This was just the sort of pose she used to strike when we were children. She loved dramatic scenes where she could make mountains out of molehills, huge crises out of tiny inconveniences. As youngsters we were all used to this, and we either ignored it or one of us would tease her out of it. Though there was nothing childish about her present situation, there was about her reaction to it, and I took a chance.

"As the Divine Julius nearly said, we'll come, we'll see, and we'll conquer."

Suddenly she smiled, her mask of tragedy forgotten, "Oh, Aurelia, you're such a comfort, you always did know how to cheer me up. And you're right, there's no point in being melodramatic."

"I'm always right. It's a well known fact."

"Of course you are. Now, I must change into something suitable for visiting Trebonius. Then we'll have a bite to eat. Perhaps your Quintus will be here by then, and he can join us. Afterwards we'll go up to the fort. I shan't take long."

"Good. I'll leave you to it. I'll go and join Vitellia for now. Where is she, Selena, do you know?"

"She's in the garden. I think Master Philo is with her." She walked with me towards the door, and we paused just outside it.

"She seems to be very up-and-down in her moods," I said softly.

"She is, but you're doing her good. I can't talk now, I must get back to her. May I come and see you later?"

"Of course, any time. And try not to worry too much. We'll get through this somehow."

One of my particular talents, for good or ill, is sounding confident even when I don't feel it.

Chapter XV

Vitellia was in the garden, but not with Philippus. She was sitting on a small terrace some distance from the house, deep in conversation with another young girl, who was slight and fair-haired and so like my cousin in looks that I knew she must be Chloe. I paused to watch her for a few heartbeats, my mind calling up memories of myself and Jovina as youngsters. I wasn't intending to eavesdrop, but as I hesitated, Chloe's words floated over to me.

"And so they had a fight. Of course it was quite illegal, they'd have been thrown out if anyone had caught them. They each took along a friend as witness. Philo took Fabianus, and Terentius took…oh, I can't remember now. Philo won, but they were never friends after that, and then Terentius got sent to Londinium to be in the governor's guard. Shame, really, he was always good fun."

"But fighting!" Vitellia sounded shocked. "How horrid. Suppose Philo had got hurt?"

Chloe laughed. "Not much danger of that, he's one of the best swordsmen in the unit. And boys like showing off, especially doing something that's not allowed. He's always been a bit of a rebel, has our Philo."

So Philippus' transgressions included fighting. And it was interesting that Chloe said he'd quarrelled with Terentius. They must have patched things up, because Philippus had told me he was saddened by Terentius' death. Unless he was lying, but I couldn't think why he would.

Still, he was one of the men Quintus wanted me to keep an eye on, and I must learn all I could. I stood hesitating there, waiting for more revelations, but the conversation turned to Philippus' long hair, and how he refused to adopt a standard short military haircut.

I couldn't decide what to do. The girls still hadn't seen me, so I could simply walk across to them and pretend I'd only just arrived, and then later find a way of getting Chloe to talk about her brother's fight in more detail.

Shrill childish laughter broke into my thoughts, and I looked round. To my surprise, out from behind a small summer-house ran Philippus, pursued by a gaggle of tiny children, no more than three or four years old. He lumbered along quite slowly while they chased him with delighted yells. "Lion! Catch the lion!" they squealed, brandishing invisible spears as they ran.

Suddenly he spun round and dropped to all fours, making a fearsome roaring noise. "Yes, I'm a lion," he growled, "a big bad hungry lion, and I'm going to eat you for my dinner."

The children scrambled all over him, squeaking louder than ever as he gently pushed them away, continuing his growling threats to make a meal of them. Chloe and Vitellia turned towards the game, and everyone dissolved into laughter. Philippus got up and began to lumber towards the summer-house, with the children in pursuit.

"Aurelia, there you are!" Chloe called. "Come and join us." She stood up, and both girls beckoned. There was nothing for it but to go across to them.

"How good to see you again, Chloe. And how like your mother you are! I'd have known you anywhere."

"Yes, everyone says we're more like sisters than mother and daughter. At least I haven't turned out like Father."

I sat down and declined a drink, looking round the pleasant secluded spot. "This is a nice garden for enjoying the sun.

I thought I heard children playing as I came outside. And was that Philippus with them?"

Chloe shrugged. "He was having a game with some of the slaves. And his own two, of course. If it wasn't for his size, you'd think he was four years old himself sometimes."

Vitellia was startled. "You mean two of them…Philippus is their father?"

"That's right. Their mother is a peasant girl from the village. She looks after them at her father's roundhouse mostly, but Philo likes to bring them here sometimes. Do you want to speak to him? I can call him back if you like."

"There'll be plenty of time later. I wanted to tell you both that I've just come from seeing your mother. She says she's feeling better and she'll come and join us all for a bite to eat. Then she's planning to go to the fort to see the commander…something about preparations for her birthday party."

"That's good. It's several days since she's been out of her room. I knew it would cheer her up, seeing you. How did she seem to you?"

"Frankly I'm rather worried about her. Her moods seem to change in the blink of an eye, don't they? I began to think my being there had cheered her a little, and she said she felt better… and then suddenly she was in tears, telling me she was dreading the party. To crown it all, your father came in, they had words, and she was quite upset."

"Don't talk to me about that bastard. He'd upset anybody."

"I'm sure that deep down he cares about your mother, you know."

Her pretty face twisted into a sour grimace. "I'm not. He doesn't care for any of us these days."

I could guess where this was leading. "Oh dear. That sounds familiar. You're growing up to be a woman, and he still thinks you're his little girl?"

"He's trying to make me marry a dreadful old man, ancient enough to be my grandfather. He wanted to announce the betrothal at Mother's party, but I told him if he did I'd run away to Londinium. He says now he'll postpone the announcement till *my* birthday, which is in September. By then," she added in a lower voice, "it'll be too late."

"Some older men are wonderful," Vitellia pointed out.

Could she mean Lucius? Speaking as Lucius' twin, that shook me, and Chloe's reply didn't help.

"Your Lucius isn't all that old. Not like Statius, who's all grey and wrinkled like a horrible monkey. Ugh! No, Gambax is the boy for me."

"Is Statius coming to the party?" Vitellia asked.

"He is. He'll arrive here later today, unless the gods give me a break and his carriage goes off the road and falls into a ditch." She looked at me defiantly, but if that was a challenge, I wasn't responding. "He needn't expect me to be all lovey-dovey over him. I've promised Mother I'll be civil, because I don't want to spoil her day. Beyond that, I'm promising nothing."

"I don't blame you," Vitellia agreed.

I could see this line of talk going on far too long, so I changed the subject.

"Do tell me something," I said. "I'm afraid I was born nosey, and as I came out just now I couldn't help hearing you telling Chloe that Philippus has had some sort of a fight. He wasn't hurt, I hope?"

"Oh no, he just had a tiny flesh wound, nothing serious. It was months ago anyway, it's all healed up now. He tells everyone it happened out on patrol, but actually he had a fight with Terentius over gambling debts. It was all hushed up at the time, but I think Trebonius suspected something. He didn't want to have a full-blown enquiry because both Philo and Terentius are good soldiers, so he sent Terentius off to Londinium and gave Philo his posting at Cataractonium. Oh, look, Aurelia," she gestured up towards the house. "That's your maid, isn't it? Trying to attract your attention?"

"I'm expecting a visitor," I said. "He must be here. If you'll excuse me, I'll go and see."

But I was disappointed. Baca hadn't come to tell me that Quintus had arrived. Instead she brought a note for me from him, a few words apologising that he wouldn't be able to visit us this morning, but adding that he'd try to look in later.

"I'll leave an answer for him at the fort," I said. "Have you got all our things unpacked? What are our rooms like? I may as well see mine now."

It was small but comfortable, a single room too, which was a pleasant surprise.

"Miss Vitellia's room is next yours, and I'm in the servants' quarters sharing with Miss Chloe's maid." Baca giggled. "She's a bit of a wild horse, that Miss Chloe, isn't she?"

"You're right. And her brother's a rascal too. Listen, Baca, can I tell you something in confidence? Something you won't pass on to anyone, not even Miss Vitellia?"

"Of course, Mistress."

"You've presumably seen the way Master Philippus is flirting with Vitellia?"

She nodded. "He's a real charmer, though, isn't he?"

"He's attractive, yes. But I don't think he realises that Miss Vitellia is betrothed, or maybe he does realise and doesn't care. Now a bit of harmless fun is fine, but…"

"You don't want him to go too far? I daresay he'll try, but don't worry, I'll see he doesn't get anywhere. She's a lovely young lady, Miss Vitellia, but not very wise in the ways of the world, as you might say. She thinks it's just a game, letting a handsome young officer pay her attention."

"Exactly. But Master Lucius is her man now, and she's got his reputation to consider as well as her own. If you think there's a danger of things getting out of hand, I want you to tell me straight away. Can I rely on you?"

She nodded. "You can, Mistress. You and the master have always been good to me. I'll not let you down."

We ate a pleasant meal in the dining room when Jovina joined us, and I was relieved that Philippus and Chloe appeared to have put aside their bickering. They could both be very entertaining company when they chose, and Jovina was in high spirits by the time we set off for the fort. Vitellia excused herself because she wanted to stay with Chloe, who had invited a couple of young friends over for the afternoon.

The open carriage gave us a welcome breath of air, but I didn't enjoy the journey much. I picked up the same unpleasant feeling of tension I'd experienced before, with soldiers everywhere, very few natives on the streets, and several VVV scrawls on walls. As we crossed the empty marketplace I smelt smoke on the breeze. Though I tried to tell myself it was someone's cooking fire or the public bath-house furnaces, I couldn't help thinking it was probably caused by something more sinister.

The gate guards waved us straight through, though we had to slow down as we drove up to the headquarters building. Two soldiers were carrying a stretcher with a third man on it, his body motionless and his head running with blood. I wondered whether there'd been a barrack brawl, or maybe he'd been injured patrolling the village. He looked in a bad way. I hoped the Greek doctor could help him.

An orderly showed us into Trebonius' office, and he welcomed us warmly. I noticed how Jovina went to him as if expecting a kiss, and how he contrived to shake her hand instead without actually backing away.

We weren't his only visitors that afternoon. Quintus was there before us. When Trebonius began to introduce him, I explained that we were old friends, though of course we were very surprised to find that our paths had crossed so far from home.

"In that case, you must come to our party tomorrow," Trebonius said to him. "Any friend of Aurelia's is very welcome."

"Thank you," Quintus said gravely. "I'd be honoured to accept. That is…" he hesitated. "I couldn't help wondering, with all this unrest in the village, whether you might be considering postponing the party for a day or two. I hear it's to be a distance away from the fort, by the river. You're not worried about trouble from the natives, in view of Lucius Aurelius' report, the message intercepted when one of your men was murdered?"

Trebonius shook his head and smiled. "This party's been arranged for a month, and we've invited all sorts of people. There's no chance I'd consider cancelling it now. But we have brought it forward by a day, just to be on the safe side. Then we can all be available and on maximum alert for midsummer day itself." He glanced at me. "Terentius was murdered at your mansio, I believe, Aurelia?"

"He was. A sad business, and frightening too, to have some-one killed under our own roof."

"I can believe it. But you mustn't worry about the party, my dear. Thanks to you and your brother we're prepared for any-thing, well prepared. Some of the hot-headed young native boys would like to scare me a little, and I'm afraid Eurytus…well, no matter. We're ready for whatever comes. I'll have plenty of men on guard tomorrow, including some out of sight covering the road leading to the field, and the river bank. We'll be quite safe."

Quintus asked, "How many guests will there be?"

"Thirty of us altogether," Trebonius said, and then added smiling, "that is, thirty-one now. And it's an interesting mixture of people, I'm sure you'll enjoy it. We thought we'd make it an extra special celebration, didn't we, Jovina?"

She smiled. "You're doing me proud. I'm so looking forward to it. Now the only thing we can't control is the weather. Have you got all the tents organised?"

"I have. There'll be five very large tents and four smaller ones. Ample room for the cooks, and for everyone to take shelter inside if it rains."

"You're leaving guards there overnight, presumably?" Quintus asked.

Trebonius nodded. "Better to be safe than sorry."

They went on to discuss some of the guests by name, and I recognised Brennus and Eurytus. One could only hope Eurytus' party manners were better than his behaviour yesterday.

I watched the two of them as they sat together, poring over the list of guests, then checking the menu. Jovina was eager and excited, Trebonius calm and slightly reserved. I wondered whether Jovina's desire for this relationship was stronger than Trebonius', but decided it was probably just that he was more discreet by nature.

Eventually they'd got everything settled satisfactorily, and we took our leave. As we walked towards the gate of the fort, Jovina turned to Quintus.

"I'm very pleased to have met you after hearing so much about you from Aurelia."

"I've heard plenty about you too," Quintus smiled. "You and Aurelia were friends as children, I believe?"

"Yes, though we didn't see that much of one another. But the twins and Albia came to stay with us for a while after Pompeii was destroyed…oh well, it was all a long time ago."

"Sometimes it feels like yesterday," he said. "I was in Pompeii myself the day Vesuvius erupted."

"Really?" They began reminiscing about Pompeii, but I didn't join in. I was too busy trying to think of a way to get a private word with Quintus.

As we came to the gate, I had an inspiration. "By the gods, Quintus, I've just remembered. When I saw you yesterday you said you had a letter for me from Regulus, but you hadn't got it with you. I suppose you haven't got it now either?"

"Regulus?" he looked at me sharply.

"Yes. I'd really like to have it. Would you be able to send it round to Jovina's tonight? Or perhaps I could drop in at the mansio on our way home and collect it."

At last he got the point. "Yes, that's the best idea. Why don't you let me buy you a quick beaker of wine to make up for my absent-mindedness? You, too, Jovina, of course."

Jovina smiled. "My dear, I'd love to, but I can't. I'm expecting another guest to arrive any time, and I should be there to welcome him. Statius Severus, the man who's to marry my daughter Chloe. But Aurelia's got no plans until dinner tonight, have you?"

"No, unless you need me at home."

"Then go off and have a quiet drink, the pair of you." She gave me a conspiratorial wink to show she was enjoying playing

Cupid. "But Antonius, you'll escort her safely to our house, won't you? The village is restless today."

"I'll keep her safe and sound, never fear. And she'll be there in plenty of time for dinner."

We walked the few yards to the mansio. It was quiet at this time of the afternoon, but we still chose to sit outside as we'd done last night. Judging by the innkeeper's warm welcome and the fact that he brought out our jug of Falernian himself, Quintus was now a favoured customer.

Quintus grinned as he poured it. "A letter from Regulus... Not bad for the spur of the moment, Aurelia. Or had you been planning that little tactic for hours?"

"I've a couple of important things to tell you before tomorrow. You might even have something important to tell me, unless you've been sitting round in the bar all day."

"Not quite all day. At least Jovina's well enough for you to stay with her. That's good news."

"She's putting on a brave face, but she's worried about tomorrow."

"She seemed happy just now."

"That's because of the company she was keeping. Trebonius makes her feel happy, and probably she doesn't want to seem ungrateful for the party. But she said earlier she's dreading it. There are several quarrels going on, and she's afraid some of them may come out into the open." I gave him a brief summary.

"Did you discover why she wrote to you for help?" Quintus asked.

"Her immediate reason was to do with her son. She found a certain very recognisable bronze brooch among his things quite recently. One decorated with three letters. Want to guess which three?"

"Aurelia, you're brilliant!" He jumped from his chair and came round the table to give me a big bear hug. "Well done. This is just the sort of evidence I've been hoping for. I must admit I wasn't sure whether Philippus should be on our list of possible candidates, but that confirms it. So that's three Greeks we've found so far: Mallius, Philippus, and Nikias the doctor."

"Four," I corrected. "Don't forget the doctor's assistant Pythis is Greek, a nephew or cousin or something."

"I wondered if I'd find you here." Titch was heading for our table, carrying a beaker of beer and a dish of olives.

"He's been checking over the area where the party will happen tomorrow," Quintus explained. "He'll be on patrol in the woods."

Titch made a comic-tragic face. "While you're all eating and drinking, I'll be hard at work." He ate several olives and took a good swallow of beer. "I checked the other side of the river, but I don't need to cover that as well as the bank where all the guests will be. The river's too deep there to cross without swimming, nobody's going to get into the party that way. So I'll stay on the near side. There's plenty of scrubby bushes close to the water, and a few decent trees. So I can keep out of sight, but then so can other folks too, if they've a mind to."

"Will there be any soldiers patrolling there too?"

"Yes, a dozen or so, according to one of the lads I've got to know. Name of Gambax." He glanced at me. "He said he'd met you already."

"Yes, he's the boy who's in love with Chloe, and sends her secret messages by way of Philippus."

"Aye, so I gather. Anyhow, he says he'll warn the lads from the fort that I'm on duty too, in case they catch sight of me and wonder what I'm at." He drank more beer. "He's hoping for a quiet little interlude with Miss Chloe, if he can get it. I told him I'd make sure he wasn't disturbed, if he'd help me in return by telling me about anything suspicious his lads come across." He finished his beaker. "By the gods, that hardly touched the sides. I'm going for another. Shall I get more Falernian while I'm at the bar?"

"Better not," I said. "Sorry, but Jovina will be expecting me soon. Before I go, just tell me, what's the plan for tomorrow? Titch will watch the woods. I'll watch Jovina, I can do that easily because I think she'll be happy to have me near. And I should be able to keep an eye on the rest of the family if they don't wander away too far."

Quintus nodded. "I'll concentrate on the military guests, Mallius and Philippus and Trebonius, and of course this Greek doctor, if he comes."

"He's not coming," Titch said. "Gambax told me. Seemingly he was invited but he said he'd be too busy. And there's a wounded lad at the hospital now, brought in this afternoon. He was badly hurt in the village on patrol, so our Nikias can use that as his excuse. 'Course, he could still come secretly. I'll be watching out for him."

"What about Eurytus?" I asked.

"He'll have his own bodyguard present," Quintus said. "I hope they behave themselves."

Quintus delivered me home safely and declined an invitation to dinner. I didn't blame him. There was a strained, nervous atmosphere you could have cut with a spoon. Once Statius had arrived safely, Jovina had taken herself off to bed, saying the trip to the fort had tired her, so Chloe was acting as hostess and not enjoying it much. Philippus had excused himself because he was dining with friends at the fort. Presumably he was at one of his gambling sessions, and I was sorry he wasn't there, because we could have done with his cheerful company.

Statius, the derided older man, did indeed look ancient, grey and stooped, and with several teeth missing, which gave him an old man's lisp when he talked. But he had sharp black eyes like a bird's, and a sharp tongue, too, when he chose. He barely spoke to me or Vitellia. He was too busy either trying to engage Chloe in conversation or bickering with Mallius, who was still quite sober but probably would rather have had a drink or two inside him to deal with his crabby guest.

I don't remember much detail about the next few hours, except that I did my best to lighten the uneasy atmosphere but without much success. Tension was even reflected in the weather, which was no longer clear and warm, but stifling and sticky. I had a headache, which for me is often the sign of a thunderstorm to come.

We ate dinner early, so that Mallius could leave while there was plenty of light. The unrest in the village was growing, he explained, and he was ordered back to the fort overnight. On his way out, I heard him giving strict instructions to the servants about keeping doors and windows locked, and telling them to post a night watchman to the rear of the house, as well as the man who usually guarded the front door.

I was glad when the sky began to darken and I could make my headache the excuse for going to bed.

Chapter XVI

I stood waiting in the centre of the arena. I was quite alone. The seats all around teemed with people, I could see them and I could hear their excited shouting. But none of them would lift a finger to help me. Their yelling rose to a howling cheer as the iron gates clanged open, and the lion rushed out.

I heard it growl even above the people's demented baying. It was coming towards me, slow but unstoppable, and I was completely terrified. I wanted to stand there bravely, but I couldn't. My body was numb, only my feet would move and they were out of my control. They started carrying me backwards, away from…away from…

The monster slowed down as it approached, and I heard it speak. "Yes, I'm a lion. A big bad hungry lion, and I'm going to eat you for my dinner."

"No!" I screamed. "Get back! Don't touch me!"

With my last shred of self-control I tried to look into its eyes, willing it to stop. But I couldn't see its eyes, I couldn't see its face at all. Its whole head was swathed in bandages.

"Get back! Don't touch me!" I screamed again as it loomed over me. My feet went from under me and I felt myself falling…

"Aurelia, wake up! Wake up, Aurelia. You're safe, it's all right. It's me, Vitellia. Oh, please, Aurelia, wake up. Everything's all right, really it is."

I was trembling and sweating as I flung the blanket from me and sat bolt upright in bed. I didn't know where I was at first, all

I knew was the fear that filled my body and mind. I looked round the room. There was no lion, just two worried-looking people.

"Where am I?" I asked. It came out more like the croak of a bird.

"You're all right, Mistress," Selena said. "You're at Mistress Jovina's house. You've had a bad dream, but it's gone now, and you're safe."

She spoke as if she were soothing a child. I felt like a child, weak and frightened and disoriented. But there was something important I had to remember, something from that dream.

"I met a lion," I said, forcing the words out although my lips felt stiff and cold. "It was going to kill me."

Vitellia came to my bedside and took my hand. "It was just a dream. There's no lion here, only Selena and me. We heard you calling out and came to see what was wrong. Don't think about it any more. You'll feel better soon."

But I had to think about it, and I had to make them understand. "Listen, this is important. I knew that lion, I recognised its voice. It was Portius."

They gazed at me with concern but without comprehension. How could they understand? How could they know it terrified me to realise that Philippus' growling lion-voice which had so amused the children yesterday was the same as the hoarse, gravelly tones used by the murderer Portius?

Portius and Philippus were one and the same.

I lay back on my pillows and shut my eyes. At first sight it seemed so unlikely as to be impossible. Philippus, that handsome, charming rascal, who loved his mother and enjoyed playing with his children...a murderer?

And yet it wasn't impossible. Quite the contrary; it explained a number of facts that so far hadn't been explicable. He'd spent the last few days away from Isurium in secret, so he could have reached the Oak Tree. He'd known Terentius, and far from being his friend as he claimed, had become his enemy. He wore his hair long not only to defy army custom, but to conceal a damaged right ear, injured in a fight with Terentius. And I suddenly remembered the doctor's question at the mansio last night. "Did you patch up your slave all right?" And Philippus joked that he'd enough bandages to put a poultice on an elephant. They must be the bandages he'd used to make his disguise.

It had taken me long enough to recognise him. Now that I had, what in the gods' name was the best thing to do?

Quintus would know. But Quintus wasn't here, and there was no way I could see him until we met at noon. I thought about driving over to the fort, but dismissed the idea as impractical, and even if I could manage it, it would cause far too much comment.

My body gradually relaxed as I lay there, but my brain whirled as I thought things out. At all costs I must behave normally, however frightened I felt inside. I must concentrate on Jovina, because helping her would help me to stay calm too. Above all I must avoid Philippus if I possibly could. If I had to see him, I mustn't betray by a look or a word that I knew his secret, because if he realised I'd discovered it, I'd be in real danger.

Selena meanwhile had fetched some wine, and I drank a little because she and Vitellia insisted it would do me good. "What hour is it?" I asked. "Is it time to get up and dress?"

"It will be soon," Selena said. "It's getting light, look. The bath-house will be ready when it's light. You ladies can have your baths before breakfast if you like, then you'll have lots of time to get ready for the party."

Oh gods, the party! The realisation of what lay ahead of us all today hit me like a pail of water in the face. I was going to a party, and there'd be a murderer among the guests.

I don't know quite how I got through that long morning. It helped when I found out that Philippus, who'd stayed overnight with friends in the fort, wasn't coming back to the house but would go direct to the party.

By the time we'd all had breakfast, everyone had got to know about my nightmare, and they were all sympathetic, but I made light of it as well as I could and tried to keep my thoughts on getting bathed and dressed, having my hair nicely arranged, and keeping Jovina company while she did the same.

She, too, I supposed, was struggling to put on a cheerful face, and she did it very well. We talked only about happy things, including several birthday presents which had come for tomorrow, but she decided to open them a day early. A large bunch of beautiful pink roses had arrived, bearing a note saying "with all my love", but containing no indication of who had sent them. We all assumed they were from Mallius. Our gift of table mats was appreciated and caused great interest, especially when Jovina insisted on going into the kitchen and throwing one into a cooking brazier to prove it didn't burn. It survived unharmed, and she was so delighted that when she learned Congrio was staying in Isurium, she sent one of the servants over to the mansio to invite him to her party.

Chloe and Philippus had bought their mother a beautiful silk scarf in a delicate mixture of cream and pale apricot shades which went perfectly with her party clothes. Statius presented her with a pair of gold brooches which she also planned to wear with her new outfit. There was no present from Mallius, apart from the roses, or Trebonius, or the Greek doctor. I could only assume they were bringing their offerings to the party itself.

We all, of course, put on our favourite finery. Jovina's new tunic and over-tunic were an elegant peach colour, perfect for her fair hair. She used make-up to mask her pallor, but it was well done, and after all everyone knew she'd been ill. Vitellia looked stunning in cream, (she'd have looked stunning in a grain-sack, of course,) and Chloe chose a rich rose-pink for her tunic and sandals, and ear-rings with pink stones. Even old Statius was resplendent. His toga positively gleamed, and the stick he leaned on was a silver-topped cane. And I don't mean to boast, but my best peacock-blue outfit didn't look out of place either.

Eventually, about an hour before noon, the carriages came to take us to the river, and I was glad to be on the way, even though it meant I'd soon be seeing Philippus again. I debated whether to warn Vitellia not to let him pay her too much attention, but decided against it. If Philippus got the slightest inkling that I, or anyone, was suspicious of him…no, I didn't even want to think about it.

I don't particularly enjoy picnicking in the middle of nowhere. Give me a nice comfortable dining-room with cushioned couches, polished furniture, and a decorative mosaic floor. And the open air is especially unpredictable in a province like Britannia where the gods send more rain than sunshine. Today the weather was still, warm and humid, and I expected to see clouds creeping over the horizon soon. Whether they'd hold off from soaking us all till the end of the celebration, only the gods themselves knew.

But I had to admit Trebonius had chosen the party location well, and spared no expense or effort to make it comfortable. Couches and tables were set out on the grass in the middle of a large open space which had trees around it, except where the land sloped very gradually down to the river. Off to one side a huge fire blazed, with a pig and a lamb roasting on it, giving out the most mouth-watering aromas. On the opposite edge of the clearing were open-fronted tents of different sizes, army issue of course, but decorated all over with garlands of leaves and flowers to give them a festive air. Three of them were laid out like rooms, with rugs and couches and tables, in case we needed shelter from the elements. The others were mostly kitchens or food stores, where a cohort of servants were getting the rest of the meal ready.

Vitellia and I wandered round the main area, then down to the river, which was only a hundred paces or so off across the grass. I looked along the bank wondering if I could spot Titch, but of course I couldn't—he was much too professional to let himself be seen. We strolled back up to the clearing where the other guests were arriving. Philippus was among them, and he came to wish us good-morning and to ask whether we'd had a comfortable night at Jovina's house. I answered "yes" firmly, and chose a safe subject.

"This is impressive, Philippus. Did you have a hand in designing it all?"

"Well, I made one or two suggestions, but it's mostly the commander's work. He's really done an excellent job. Mother will enjoy herself, I'm sure. And," he said, lowering his voice, "I have high hopes for myself today. Now that the Mallius family seem to be in favour again, I hope he'll take pity on me and call off my exile in Cataractonium. I don't know how much longer I can stand being stuck away there. It's a horrible dump; it really is. Still, I mustn't be gloomy on a day like this. Vitellia, you must cheer me up. Let me show you the river. There's a deep pool where the kingfishers come sometimes. We might be lucky and see one."

I felt a small stab of alarm as they went off together, but suppressed it. I'd already been through all that, I told myself sternly. Vitellia was safe, we were all safe, as long as Philippus didn't suspect we knew he had a secret to hide.

A horseman appeared in the lane at the top of the field: Quintus, looking immaculate in his military gear. He rarely wore it, but at Isurium he was ostensibly inspecting bridges, so it was appropriate. He dismounted and strolled down towards us.

I must seize a chance to talk to him alone. I went to stand near Jovina, who was smiling brightly, though I sensed she wasn't completely relaxed. Quintus came up to greet her, and they chatted briefly.

"I thought you'd be arriving with the contingent from the fort," I said. "Are Trebonius and Mallius on their way?"

"They're close behind me," he said, and as we all glanced towards the lane, a big raeda drew up. Jovina's tension became more apparent as Trebonius and his wife Fulvina stepped onto the grass, but there was no sign of Mallius.

"Gods, where's Marcus?" she said, more to herself than to me. "Don't say he's not coming. He promised he'd come."

As if at a signal, Mallius appeared on horseback and cantered right down to where Jovina was standing. He dismounted and threw his reins to a servant. Seeing him smartly dressed and apparently sober, Jovina relaxed.

"Sorry I'm late, my dear," he said. "Business is brisk at the fort today."

"I'm glad you've come," she answered, and they exchanged a kiss. "Thank you for the bouquet of roses."

For a heartbeat or two he looked blank, then he nodded. "I'm glad you liked them."

Trebonius stepped forward. "Aurelia, Quintus Antonius, let me present Fulvina, my wife. These are the guests I told you about, my dear. Lucius Aurelius' sister Aurelia, and his fiancée."

She was a large woman, taller than her husband, strong-boned and while not exactly ugly, certainly nobody's idea of a classical beauty. But her mouse-coloured hair was well styled, and her hazel eyes were sharp. She was smartly dressed in a pale sea-green tunic, with brooches that looked like small emeralds. In contrast to Trebonius, who was urbane and easy-going, she exuded an air of toughness and determination. She could probably quell a mutiny at a hundred paces with just one look.

I enjoy the company of strong women, I find them refreshing rather than frightening, and that's how Fulvina struck me. As we stood together she pointed out some of the guests I didn't know, officers from the fort and one or two of the Brigantians, describing them all with a dry wit that made me smile. A likeable woman, but not a person to cross.

Old Statius limped over with Mallius, which made it easy for Quintus and me to slip away. As we turned towards the river I heard the old man say, "I wish you'd change your mind, Marcus. You promised me you'd announce my betrothal to Chloe today, and now you've gone back on it."

I paused in mid-stride, not wanting to miss Mallius' reply. "Look, Quintus...isn't that a kingfisher?"

He stopped too, long enough to hear Mallius say, "I'm sorry, old friend. It's just not possible for a few days. Chloe needs longer to accept that it's time for her to settle down."

"Longer to accept? She's only a child. You must make her do as she's told. Make her accept!"

"Easier said than done. She's threatening to run away if the marriage is announced. She'll come to see how foolish that is, but…"

"You're not having second thoughts about the marriage, I hope?"

"Of course I'm not. I just need a breathing space, that's all."

We'd heard enough, and I realised that now, with everyone mixing and mingling, might be our only chance for a private word. I continued scanning the river for nonexistent kingfishers and said very softly, "I've got something important for you. Before it all starts."

He gave no sign of having heard, and then exclaimed, "Yes, I saw something, but I'm not sure…"

"Definitely a kingfisher," I said loudly. "Come on, let's go closer." We walked slowly towards the river. Nobody seemed to notice.

When we were out of earshot of the rest, I said, "You remember the man Portius who came to the Oak Tree?"

"Of course. Terentius' murderer."

"He was in disguise, as we thought, and now I know who he really was. Philippus."

Again, he didn't give any indication that he'd taken in what I'd said, except to look at me sharply, and I saw the excitement in his eyes. "You're sure?"

"Yes."

"Does he know you've realised?"

"No. I only found out this morning, and I've hardly seen him since."

"Good. I'll tell Titch to watch for him. You and I must try to keep him under observation here."

"Can't you just arrest him? I'll feel much happier when he's under guard."

He shook his head and almost whispered his answer. "If he's involved in whatever's supposed to happen tomorrow, he'll be making final plans today. He could lead us to some of the other conspirators."

"I don't like it."

"I know. But at least now we're on our guard. You've done well."

"It begs one important question, though...*why* is he encouraging a rebel plot?"

"Better leave it for now. Listen, I think the show's about to start."

Faint notes of a bugle came to us on the breeze, the call for "Salute the Commander." But the commander was already present, standing with Jovina, Fulvina, and Mallius. Everyone else was scattered about in small groups, and they all had an air of expectancy, like actors on stage just before something dramatic happens.

Then Eurytus' bodyguard came in sight, followed by his open carriage. The driver jumped down and unfolded a set of steps, then opened the door. The bugle-call sounded again, and Eurytus stepped down, with the air of a general come to survey a conquered province.

"Eurytus," a voice hissed beside me. It was Statius, and if looks could kill, the taxman would have dropped dead before his feet touched the ground. "Nobody told me he was invited. If I'd known, wild horses wouldn't have dragged me here. Gods, it's too much. Too much!"

"You're right," Fulvina answered angrily. "As if this whole ridiculous party wasn't grim enough, we have to have a freedman as guest of honour."

"I don't think he was Jovina's first choice," I said.

Statius stalked away, turning his back. Fulvina laughed shortly. "I wish I'd pleaded a bad headache and stayed at home. Brennus' wife has managed to escape, it seems."

Trebonius and Mallius led Jovina to meet him, and she smiled graciously and welcomed him with elaborate politeness. He was certainly the most ostentatiously dressed person present; nobody, men or women, came close. The soldiers were impressive in their polished parade armour, and we women were as colourful as a bouquet of flowers, but Eurytus' tunic was shot through with silver and gold thread, and with his gold sandals and a huge gold chain round his neck, he sparkled in the sunlight whenever he made the slightest movement. You never saw anything so vulgar.

He stood glittering there in solitary state while we were all presented, lining up for our turn as if we were awaiting an audience with Caesar. The men were received first, and I noticed Eurytus acknowledged them mostly with a nod or a short greeting, except for Statius. I couldn't hear what passed between them, but it was plain to see that Eurytus said something which made the old man angry. After a couple of exchanges Eurytus waved him away, and Statius limped off. while the freedman smiled, as if he had just put down an enemy.

We ladies were vouchsafed a few words each, and the younger the lady, the more words she got. Chloe in particular seemed to be having quite a conversation with him. Fulvina and I got only a short sentence apiece. To me he said, "Ah yes, the innkeeper."

I nodded and answered, "That's right. I run the Oak Tree Mansio, east of Eburacum."

"I don't stay in any kind of mansio these days."

And far be it from me to change your mind, I thought as I moved off.

Quintus came to join me, and we walked a few paces away from the crowd. "By the gods," I said, "the man must be a superb tax auditor. Caesar certainly hasn't employed him for his charm or diplomacy."

Quintus laughed. "Never mind. The food looks good. I asked the major-domo if he could arrange for us to share a couch, and do you know what he said?"

I smiled. "That I'd bribed him already to keep you at a safe distance?"

"Something much more surprising. He said Jovina told him there is no prearranged seating plan for the guests, we all just do as we please."

"That's unusual. I assumed we'd all be shown to our places. But that means you and I can definitely sit together. I know you'd rather share with Chloe or Vitellia, of course."

"Definitely. About as much as you'd prefer to share with Eurytus." We made our way to a couch on the opposite side of the clearing from the more elaborate seating that was presumably intended for the guests of honour. We couldn't sit down before they did, but everyone was moving towards the couches now, and there were plenty of them, so with luck we'd have one to ourselves. When the first of the roast meat was brought to a central table and carved up. I realised I was hungry.

"I hope your cousin knows what she's doing," Quintus said, as a slave brought us wine.

"She's always been eccentric. I remember a dinner party she gave when they were in Eburacum, when we didn't recline on couches at all, but everyone sat on chairs round a long polished table. It felt just like the dining-room at the Oak Tree on a busy night."

"Being eccentric is one thing. But not organising who sits where, with the present selection of guests, could cause unpleasantness. Look at the Great Man."

Eurytus was seating himself next to Jovina, and it would have been usual for Mallius to join them, or perhaps Trebonius as the giver of the party. But the freedman beckoned Chloe to the third place on his couch. We could see how this annoyed both Mallius and Trebonius, and Statius turned as red as an erupting volcano. If any of them could have altered matters, they would have done. But they couldn't, and he knew it.

Trebonius took the adjacent couch, and signalled Mallius to join him and his wife. I saw Mallius say a quick word to Philippus, who was deep in conversation with Vitellia. He took her across to where Statius waited, and the three of them sat down. The other guests sorted themselves out without trouble, and then everyone simultaneously realised that Brennus, the most important of the Brigantian guests, was standing alone near Jovina's couch, and he had no dining companion.

"That looks bad," Quintus said softly in my ear. "Insulting the local chief is the last thing we want. Sorry, Aurelia, but I think we'd better do the honours."

He strode quickly across to Brennus, smiling and holding out his hand. "Ah, Brennus, that's fortunate. I was hoping I'd have the chance of a talk with you. You're a kinsman of a good friend of ours, Silvanius Clarus."

Brennus came to sit with us, his polite smile showing more than a touch of relief. When Quintus introduced me by name, it became a smile of pleasure.

"Aurelia Marcella, it's good to meet you. I got the note of introduction from Clarus, and thank you for sending round the letter for my wife from Clarilla too."

"You're very welcome, Brennus."

"Why don't you both come to visit us while you're staying in Isurium? My wife and I would be honoured to welcome you."

"That's very kind," I said. "The problem is, we'll be quite busy, my cousin has planned various things for us to do while we're here. And you must have your hands full just now, entertaining your distinguished guest." In truth I was trying desperately to think of an excuse not to accept. If Eurytus was occupying Brennus' house, that was one place I definitely didn't want to visit.

Brennus understood my hesitation correctly. "Do come if you can. Lord Eurytus has the use of our house while he's in Isurium, so we're in my son's. It's next door to ours, on the road north out of the village. You'll be welcome any time. My wife will be delighted to meet you. She—she wasn't able to come today, as she's unwell."

A diplomatic illness, no doubt, and I couldn't blame her. There were few enough women at the party, and we were all Romans. I could imagine how a Brigantian, only newly a citizen, might feel shy about attending.

"Thank you," Quintus said. "We'd be delighted, as soon as your wife is well again."

Brennus himself seemed relaxed now, and Quintus and I made sure he felt at ease. I told him all the news from Oak Bridges, such as it was, and we began asking him about life at Isurium, and congratulating him on the governor's plans to make the town a tribal administration centre.

"It's a great honour," he said. "A responsibility too, of course. That's why…" he lowered his voice and glanced at Eurytus, who was in close conversation with Chloe. "That's why I'm so anxious that the next few days go well. If Lord Flavius Eurytus takes an unfavourable report back to Caesar…"

"I'm sure he won't do that," Quintus said. "It's the tax revenues that interest him, not the status of individual towns."

"I know, but we've had some problems with the collectors here. That's one reason why he's doing an inspection. I've tried to persuade the people they must stay calm, no protests, above all no violence. This business with young Venutius…But we shouldn't talk about such heavy matters at a party."

"I really don't think you have anything to worry about, from what I know of Caesar."

"You know Caesar? You've actually met him?"

"I have. I was in Rome last winter. And let me assure you, Eurytus isn't the only one capable of guaranteeing that Caesar will read his reports, if there's a need."

Brennus looked deeply impressed. "Thank you, sir. That's very reassuring."

"If I were Caesar," I put in, but very quietly, "I'd award you a laurel wreath in recognition of what you're having to put up with just now."

Brennus allowed himself a broad grin. "Commander Trebonius probably deserves one too. But I'll do what I have to. And after all, tax auditing must be a very demanding job, don't you think?"

"Undoubtedly," Quintus said, and we all laughed.

Conversation moved on to lighter matters as the servants brought around the food and wine, which were excellent. Besides the roast pork and lamb, there were roast chickens and ducks, a selection of summer vegetables, and fresh bread still warm from the oven. Apricots stewed in wine followed, and a very sticky light pastry stuffed with nuts and coated with honey. Three different kinds of cheese made up the final course, with more warm bread. There was no break between the courses, as there would be with a long formal banquet, but we had music to accompany the meal, a girl who played the kithara and sang Greek songs in a sweet, high voice.

As the servants started clearing away dishes and plates, I leaned back, feeling content and pleasantly surprised. This had been an excellent celebration, with no hint of trouble either from the native rebels outside, or the quarrelsome family actually present. Even Jovina seemed to have thrown off her initial nervousness and to be really enjoying herself. "It's gone well, hasn't it?"

Quintus answered, "It has. But it's not over yet."

Brennus was startled. "Are you expecting some sort of trouble?"

"Not trouble exactly," Quintus smiled. "But there's something we still have to face, and there's no escape." He signalled to a slave to refill our beakers. "Don't look so alarmed, we can survive if we put our minds to it."

Brennus did indeed look worried. "Survive what?"

"The speeches, of course."

Chapter XVII

Trebonius stood up, and his major-domo called for silence.

"Welcome, everyone, to this very special party. It's to mark a very important milestone for my friend and deputy commander Marcus Mallius Melandrus and his family. We are here to celebrate the birthday of his dear wife Jovina." He turned to her with a bow, and she blushed. "She's warned me she'll murder me if I reveal exactly *which* birthday it is." We all laughed dutifully. "So I'll simply say she must have discovered the Fountain of Youth here in Isurium, because I swear she looks younger every year. Let us all raise our beakers and drink a toast. To Jovina!"

We all cheered and drank the toast, and Jovina rose to her feet and said, "Thank you. Thank you all for coming, and thank you, Trebonius, for giving me this wonderful party. Please feel free to mingle and wander about as you will. I'm going to come around and thank you all individually."

"I wish all speeches were as perfect as those two," I said. "If I'd had to listen to any long rambling oration there's a danger I'd have gone to sleep. I'm going to congratulate the birthday girl."

Everyone was getting up and walking about. Jovina moved to the open space beyond the tables and began chatting to some of the officers from the fort. I looked round for Quintus, but he was already strolling off with Brennus. Eurytus, still seated on his couch, continued his conversation with Chloe as if they were the only two people in the world.

Statius soon put a stop to that. He came up and took Chloe by the hand with a proprietorial air that even the freedman couldn't ignore. "Come, my dear, you mustn't tire our guest with your girlish chatter." When he raised her to her feet she had no choice but to go with him, back to his own couch.

Eurytus didn't look best pleased. He took a long drink of wine, then walked over to where Mallius and Trebonius were chatting to Congrio. I could see even from a distance that Mallius was now quite drunk, but he seemed calm enough, and the four men stayed talking together. Philippus was still paying Vitellia close attention.

I realised I was one of only two people on their own, the other being the commander's wife Fulvina. I joined her, and she smiled and said, "We owe you thanks, you and Antonius. For looking after Brennus. He has a lot to put up with just now, and the last thing we wanted was for him to be treated so rudely. But with a certain person here…anyway, your Antonius saved the situation nicely."

"You're very welcome. We found him good company, and very eager to please. You know, it takes me back to my childhood days, coming to Isurium. My father was a centurion and my brother and sister and I used to visit him at various military bases. So all forts remind me of my childhood. Happy memories."

"Lucky you," she said. "I mean if you only visited, not lived in a fort. Being cooped up in a place like this is no fun. Even the men get bored, and it's far worse for us women. We ourselves have a house in the village, as your cousin does. But I still feel as if I'm in prison a lot of the time."

"Can't you get away sometimes?"

"It's not so easy, now my husband is commander. And I never quite know what may go on when my back's turned. I think it's best if I stay here and keep an eye on things." She glanced at her husband, who was talking to Jovina. It was clear enough what she meant.

"The other officers' wives, you mean? I suppose you must feel responsible for them, being the senior ranking lady here. I'm sure they look up to you for an example."

She laughed scornfully. "The forts your father served in must have been exceptionally well run, my dear. Or else you were too young to see what was really going on."

Jovina came up, wearing a fixed smile that looked as if it was painful, but she spoke graciously. "Fulvina, thank you again so much for letting your chef provide such a wonderful meal today. It was a triumph."

"It was," I agreed. "Really excellent. And the wine too."

"Well, we couldn't let the occasion pass on a diet of army rations, could we? By the way, Jovina, I've been meaning to ask you. I don't see Nikias here. Isn't he coming?"

"He sent his apologies. Unfortunately he'll be too busy. This outbreak of sickness among some of the men, and then Tribune Fabianus getting an arrow in the face on patrol yesterday. I understand his wound is quite inflamed, poor boy."

"I'm sure Nikias will manage to cure him," Fulvina said. "He has a very gentle touch, they tell me."

"Really? I wouldn't know."

"But haven't you just been ill yourself?"

"A little indisposed, but nothing worth bothering Nikias about. Women's trouble, you know. There's a healing-woman in the village. She found the herbs to put me right."

"How useful. I'd hate to think you and Niki had fallen out." There was an awkward silence, until she said brightly, "Well, well, I must mingle a little," and moved off towards the river.

"Sour-faced cow," Jovina said venomously. "It's no wonder poor Trebonius…never mind, she's gone now." She beckoned one of the servants. "More wine here. I know—we'll try out one of my birthday presents." She gestured towards her table. "Fetch the two glass goblets from there, boy. We'll drink a toast from those."

"They're beautiful." I don't possess any glass goblets myself, and when I'm lucky enough to drink from one, I love to swirl the wine round and admire the way the colour shows through. "A birthday present, you say? Who from?"

"You."

"Me?"

"That's what I told Marcus. They arrived last night, and I was determined to bring them today, only I had to think up a story that wouldn't make him wildly jealous. Yours was the first name that came into my head. Actually they're from someone else… someone who shouldn't be giving me extravagant presents."

"Now listen, Jovina, what you get up to is your own business, but I'd really rather you didn't involve me."

"Nonsense, you're just helping an old friend tell a harmless white lie." She raised her goblet. "To friendship, and to love."

"Now there's a toast I'm happy to drink."

She took a long swallow. "You know, I wasn't looking forward to today. But it's not going too badly, all things considered."

"It's going fine," I agreed. "They all seem to be enjoying themselves, *and* behaving themselves. I told you they would."

"You were right. Will you do me another favour?"

"Of course. Unless you're asking me to go and make small-talk to a certain Imperial freedman. Family loyalty only goes so far, you know."

She smiled, a proper smile this time. "I think I may soon feel like a stroll in the woods, just to catch my breath, clear my head, get away from the crowd. If you notice I'm gone, don't say anything, will you? And try to stop anyone else from looking for me. I shan't be away long."

"On your own?"

"What do you think?"

"Be careful, then. It's going well. Don't mess it up."

"I shan't. But some things are worth a little danger."

That's as maybe, I thought as she turned away to talk to other guests, but I'm not letting you go wandering off all by yourself. I'll watch and I'll follow.

And I could do with some help. I looked round for Quintus, but couldn't see him anywhere. Jovina was still in plain view though, so I walked over to where Vitellia and Philippus stood with a couple of the young tribunes. As I came nearer, Vitellia called out, "Aurelia, come and join us. We're going to watch the duck race."

"A duck race? That's a new sport to me."

"It's quite popular here," Philippus said, as we headed for the river, "especially among those of us who like a flutter now and then. The results are always completely unpredictable."

"Ah, but surely you have specially trained racers, super-athletes bred from generations of champions?"

Everyone laughed, recognising the most famous chariot-team slogan in Rome.

"But of course. And they're destined for a glittering career. Today, the people's darlings. Tomorrow, the people's dinner."

We stopped by the water and went to view the racers, six ducks of assorted colours and sizes quacking and pecking in a pen. Everyone crowded round and there was plenty of good-natured betting. Philippus joined in eagerly, and though I couldn't tell exactly how much he wagered, I did notice that he was handing over silver coins, whereas everyone else was content with coppers.

I realised with a guilty start that in the brief time it had taken me to reach the water, Jovina had disappeared. She was off in the woods, presumably. Trebonius wasn't to be seen either. So it could be the commander she'd sneaked off to meet. I'd assumed it was the doctor.

I silently cursed my carelessness, and began to walk upstream away from the people and the ducks. With a bit of luck I might spot her in the woods…

"Aurelia! You're going the wrong way!" Philippus called out. "They're racing downstream, not up. Have you put a bet on yet? They'll be starting soon."

"Do come and join in," Vitellia said, and I remembered I was supposed to be keeping her and Philippus under my eye too. Oh, well, Jovina was a grown woman. She'd be able to look after herself. This child was far more vulnerable, and she was my responsibility. So there was really nothing else to do but turn and go back to the duck-pen.

Most of the other guests were here by now, even old Statius who was sitting on a folding stool and looking slightly less grumpy than usual. Mallius was near him, leaning against a tree-trunk for support. Fulvina was in conversation with Congrio. Brennus stood watching the proceedings with an air of bewilderment; clearly this wasn't his idea of Roman sport. Eurytus wasn't in evidence, and neither was Chloe. I hoped they were not together, and even found myself wishing that the silly child had taken advantage of her mother's absence to steal off into the woods with her soldier-boy.

But then I spotted Gambax, and Chloe wasn't with him. He and another young soldier seemed to be in charge of the racers, and when someone blew a bugle and announced, "Ready for the off," they opened up the pen and urged the ducks into the river. Another bugle-call was followed by a strident voice yelling, "They're off!" But you'd never have known it from the attitude of the competitors. The birds simply swam about in circles, unable to fly off to somewhere more to their liking because their wings were clipped.

Two more young soldiers did their best to make them race downstream, with no noticeable effect at all. They even waded into the water, shouting and splashing about in the shallows, but the birds only looked more confused.

The audience on the bank called out various suggestions, some helpful, some physically impossible. One or two voices began urging the two men in the stream to forget about the ducks and enter the race themselves. All good party fun, I suppose. I'd have been far more interested if they'd been racing their horses, and far happier if I'd known where Jovina, Trebonius, and Quintus had got to.

A flash of lightning made me look up, and I realised how dark the sky was. Leaden clouds were piling up over us, blocking out the sun. The rain wouldn't be long now.

Gambax walked some yards downstream along the bank and scattered pieces of bread on the water, which caused the ducks to head in that direction. Everyone cheered, and he shouted, "I'll run further down with more bread. Finishing line is supposed to be the big grey rock, isn't it?"

The ducks eventually made their way to the rock, we onlookers following them along the bank. There was at least a winner, a large brown-and-white one, and everybody settled up their bets amid a good deal of cheering and joking.

I strolled over to Vitellia while Philippus was chatting to Gambax. "Enjoying yourself, Vitellia?"

"Oh, yes, it's a lovely party. It's a shame Lucius can't be here too, of course. But Philo is wonderful company. He asked if he can take me out driving tomorrow. I'd like to go, but…what do you think? It'll be all right, won't it?"

"I'm afraid not. Not by yourselves, anyway. It wouldn't be proper. If a group of you go out all together, that would make it all right, I suppose." Seeing her look of annoyance, I made my winning throw. "You wouldn't want to upset Lucius, would you?"

"No, of course not. Then that's what we'll do. I'll see if Chloe and Gambax can come."

Jagged lightning and a rumble of thunder made us all look at the sky. The storm was almost on us.

"Let's go and find shelter before the skies open." I headed up towards the tents in the clearing, and then stopped at the sound of my name.

"Aurelia!" I looked round hopefully, but it wasn't Quintus calling me. Trebonius was hurrying towards me. "Are you enjoying the party?" he asked me. "I'm afraid the weather may spoil the end of it, but there's plenty of shelter."

I assured him that I was having a splendid time, and complimented him on his arrangements.

"I can't find Jovina," he said. "I suppose you don't know where she is?"

That's clever, I thought, it must mean he's been with her. Otherwise he wouldn't need to tell me and anyone within earshot that he hadn't.

"No, I haven't seen her for a while. She'll be coming up here to shelter, I expect."

"I hope she hurries. Here comes the rain." Indeed a few big drops were splashing down and bouncing off the dry ground. "I'd better go and look for her, I think."

That wasn't so clever, announcing he wanted to see her. Or perhaps it was…Or was he being honest, indicating he hadn't seen her at all? In which case, who had she been going to meet when she left the clearing? I would only need one guess.

By the time I reached the biggest tent the rain was heavier and I was glad to get inside. As I entered, I heard Statius coming up behind me as fast as his limp would allow. supported by his servant and panting from unaccustomed exertion. "Shocking weather," he grumbled. "I told Marcus it was over-ambitious holding an outdoor party."

He stopped short just inside the entrance as he realised that Eurytus and Chloe were sitting side by side on a couch, too close together. I knew my cousin wouldn't like to see the way she preened herself, pleased to be the centre of his attention, nor the smile he wore, like a cat that's playing with a mouse. They both glanced up, and Chloe moved away from him, but only slightly.

Statius advanced towards Eurytus, and they glared at one another, plainly spoiling for a fight. For all his frailty of body, Statius exuded anger like a furnace radiating heat.

Luckily the arrival of two servants caused a distraction. One came in with lighted lamps, which dispelled the gloom inside the tent, and the other was carrying a tray of steaming beakers of mulsum.

"Who'd like a nice hot drink, ladies and gentlemen?" he asked cheerfully. "Guaranteed to keep the damp out. My lord…Miss Chloe?"

They each took a mug, and so did I. The hot, sweet liquid was welcome. But Statius shook his head. "Nothing for me. I'm going to order a carriage to take me back to the house. The damp's getting into my bones. I need a hot bath. I'll see you there later, Chloe." He left, almost colliding with Vitellia as she hurried in.

I was relieved to see she was without Philippus, until she said, "Has anyone seen Philo? He was with me down by the river, but now he's disappeared. I've looked in the trees, but he's nowhere to be found. He'll get soaked when the storm really starts."

"He'll have found shelter somewhere, I expect," I said.

A couple of the young officers came in, followed by Congrio wearing one of his own fawn cloaks over his smart party tunic. I wondered if he ever stopped being a salesman, even in bed. I half listened as they argued cheerfully about how to improve duck racing as a sport, and came to the conclusion that it was a hopeless task and they should stick to competing with chariots.

My mind wandered back to what was for me the matter in hand. Where had Jovina got to? For that matter, where was Quintus? I must find him, storm or no storm.

My thoughts were interrupted by a commotion outside. I couldn't tell the direction, but it was growing louder, and I heard a woman scream, and a couple of men shouting. Then Quintus' voice called my name, and Quintus himself appeared at the entrance and beckoned me urgently to join him outside. One look at his grim face was all I needed to make me hurry out after him.

"Quintus, I wondered where you'd gone. What's happened?"

"Where's Mallius? Have you seen him?"

"I've no idea. Sleeping under a bush somewhere, probably."

"And Trebonius? Is he in there with the others?"

"No, not in this tent. Why?"

"Something serious has happened, I'm afraid. Jovina…"

My heart sank inside me. "Jovina? Tell me!"

"I'm sorry, Aurelia. She's dead."

Chapter XVIII

My body turned to stone, my mind felt frozen. I saw again Jovina's pale face as I'd seen it yesterday when she said, "The nearer this so-called celebration comes, the more I'm dreading it."

And I'd told her it would be fine. I was supposed to be looking after her.

Eventually I said, "How?"

"Her body was floating in the river. Titch spotted it and pulled her out."

"You mean she fell in and drowned?"

He answered grimly, "She fell in...or she was pushed."

Again her words echoed in my head. "Some things are worth a little danger."

"I must go to her," I said. "Where is she?"

"I'll show you. But I'd better talk to Eurytus first." He opened his belt-pouch and took out his Imperial pass as he hurried into the tent.

Eurytus must have sensed trouble, for he had released Chloe and was sitting upright on the couch, his body relaxed but his eyes alert. "Is something wrong, Quintus Antonius?"

"I'm afraid so, yes. There's been an accident by the river—someone's drowned. I can't find either the fort commander or his deputy, which makes me the senior army officer here."

"Really?" The freedman's tone was only just short of insolence. "You're the bridge builder, aren't you?"

Quintus held out his Imperial pass so the freedman could read it. "I presume you have no objection to my taking charge of proceedings?"

"I see." Eurytus sat up straighter still, almost to attention, and looked at Quintus with a modicum of respect. "I didn't know you were so much in Caesar's confidence. I've no objection at all to your handling this. I've got enough to do with my tax work. The last thing I want is to be involved in the death of some drunk at a party. So carry on, Antonius, by all means."

He nodded to one of his guards. "Fetch my carriage, will you. It's time I went back to somewhere more civilised. If that's a term you can use to describe anything this far north." He laughed as he turned back to Chloe. "I'll see you again, my dear. I'll send for you tomorrow. You'll come, won't you?"

I wondered how Chloe would deal with this, and was prepared to intervene, but she kept her head. "Mother doesn't let me go out of the house alone with gentlemen, my lord. Even very important gentlemen." She smiled. "But please do call on me any time. Mama will be delighted to see you."

"I shall. Thank you, Antonius, that will be all."

"Bastard," I muttered as Quintus and I walked down to the river. "He never even asked who was dead, or what had happened. Just assumed it was 'some drunk'."

"Be thankful. Do you want him breathing down our necks while we investigate this?"

We strode on in silence to the river, then turned upstream and walked perhaps thirty paces till we came to Jovina's body. Titch was standing a short distance away.

"I'm so sorry, Aurelia," he said. "A rotten business, this."

"Yes, it is. You're sure she was dead when you got her out?"

"Aye, certain sure."

"Off you go then, Titch," Quintus said. "Two men and a stretcher, and somewhere private we can leave her. Quick as you can."

Jovina lay on the grassy bank, water running from her hair and her bright party clothes, her cheeks puffy and her eyes staring. Death is never beautiful, I know, but it seems especially savage when it turns a once-pretty face into an ugly mask.

"I'm sorry, Jovina," I whispered. I stood for a few heartbeats, looking down into her still face. I sent a prayer to the gods of the Underworld and to Diana, my guardian goddess, asking her to look after my cousin.

I felt a sudden wave of anger, not only with her murderer but with myself. Hadn't I come here to help her? And what had I achieved? Nothing. "By the gods, Jovina, whoever's done this, I swear I'll find them, and I'll see you are avenged."

Quintus touched my hand briefly. "And so will I. Let's start with the body. We've got to establish whether she died because she fell into the river and drowned, or whether she was killed on land and then thrown into the water."

"She was a strong swimmer." I remembered some of our childhood adventures. "And the river's deep, but not exactly a raging torrent. My guess is she was either pushed in and held under, or killed on the bank."

"There are no obvious signs of a struggle on her face or the front of her body. Help me turn her over, will you? Wait now... watch where you step, or kneel down. There's broken glass scattered in the grass."

"Glass? *Merda,* it's everywhere." I bent down to pick up a shining shard, and was shocked to recognise it. "Gods, Quintus, she had a pair of lovely goblets given for her birthday. She and I even drank wine out of them. It looks as if one or both of them is broken."

"So perhaps there was a struggle of some kind. Let's turn her over."

I hesitated, feeling slightly squeamish, and Quintus was all concern. "I'm sorry, Aurelia, I'm forgetting she's your cousin. If you want to go back to the tents, I can get one of the soldiers to give me a hand here."

"It's all right. I can manage."

We gently turned Jovina onto her front so we could see her from the back. There was a large gash in her head, splitting her skull open. Her hair all round the wound was matted with blood, though there wasn't as much as I'd have expected, given the size of it. The water had presumably rinsed most of it off.

"Brutal," I said. "As savage as an animal."

"At least it must have been quick. A sudden blow on her head, and she can't have been conscious by the time someone pushed her into the water. Better than drowning."

"Better than drowning? What difference does it make? She's dead just the same. And I was meant to be protecting her."

"You aren't to blame for this, Aurelia."

"I should have taken more care of her." My anger was still there, but mixed with guilt, and also with a feeling of nausea. I stood up and deliberately turned my back. I took several deep breaths, until I heard Quintus exclaim, "Ah, good, here's Titch."

With him were two soldiers carrying an army stretcher. They moved towards Jovina's body, but Quintus stopped them.

"Wait, we'll do this properly." He said a brief prayer for Jovina's shade, then signalled to the men, who gently lifted her onto the stretcher and covered her with a blanket.

"Have you found a place for her?" Quintus asked Titch.

He nodded. "We'll take her up to the clearing. There's several empty tents now the cooks have all gone. We'll put her in the smallest one. There's another small tent next door that we can use ourselves. We'll want somewhere we can talk to people without an audience."

"Good work. We'll follow you very soon."

Titch led his men away from the river. I started to follow them, but Quintus said, "Before we go inside, let's have a look round this area. See if anything else has been dropped or left here, apart from this broken glass."

"I suppose so, if we must. What are you expecting to find?"

"I don't know, really. I'd like to see the spot where she was pushed into the river." He began to pace about, eyes fixed on the ground, circling the spot where Jovina's body had been, then moving slowly towards the river's edge and turning upstream. I walked beside him till we paused by a clump of thorn bushes that grew close to the bank. One of them stood out because some of its small branches were bent or broken, as if a heavy animal had forced its way through…or a heavy weight had been dragged. I knelt down to peer underneath it, cursing as the prickly branches caught in my hair.

"We could do with Hawk for a hunt like this…Gods, Quintus, look."

In the grass under the bush lay a small bronze brooch, a plain disc bearing the initials VVV. It was identical with the one in Terentius' box, and the one Jovina had showed me yesterday. Perhaps it was even that same one…but no, she'd intended to throw it into the river, and she'd had plenty of time to dispose of it. This one must be yet another example.

"By the gods," Quintus said. "Well done. Now how did that get here?" H picked it up. "The pin's quite badly bent, see? It won't fasten properly. It's been torn roughly from a tunic or whatever it was attached to, without the pin being undone first."

"Look!" There was a tiny shred of cloth caught on the pin, the peach-coloured material of her tunic. Another larger scrap was impaled on a nearby branch. "That's the colour she was wearing." Somehow it upset me as much as seeing Jovina's body. I wanted to cry.

He put his arm round me. "I'm sorry, Aurelia. I was fairly sure one of her family was involved with this Venutius conspiracy. I didn't expect it to be Jovina. But it explains why she wrote and asked for your help. She couldn't tell anyone at the fort."

I pulled myself together. Tears wouldn't avenge Jovina. "I don't think she was involved. I can believe she'd got into a mess over her love affairs, she told me as much. But I can't accept she was conspiring with barbarian rebels. Does it seem likely to you?"

"It seems unlikely, but anything's possible. And if not, why was she wearing this brooch?"

"But she wasn't. She wore a pair of gold brooches at the party. She made a point of it; they were a present from Statius."

He stood upright, pushing a strand of wet hair out of his eyes. "You're right, and now I think of it, she's still wearing them." He helped me to get to my feet.

"I'm convinced she wasn't involved with the rebels, Quintus. From what I know of her and from the conversations I've had with her, I'd stake my life on it. There must be another explanation. Suppose whoever killed her deliberately pinned this disk onto her tunic, so if her body was found it would look as if she'd been murdered because of the conspiracy."

"It's possible."

"And then he dragged her down to the river and threw her in, but the brooch caught in the bush and came off. Why choose this spot, though? Further along the bank there aren't any thorns, it would have been much easier."

"He must have been interrupted, and had to get her into the water in a hurry. This was the nearest place. Then he ran for it along the bank."

"I wonder if whoever he saw spotted him, too? We'll have to question everyone, I suppose."

Quintus wiped the rain off his face with his sleeve. "There were thirty-some guests at that party, and at least the same number of servants, and then the guards. Interviewing that lot will take us half a month."

"Then we'd better make a start. At least let's get out of the rain."

"One thing though, let's keep this find a secret for now." He slipped the brooch into his belt-pouch. "We can't disguise the fact that she was murdered, but the less we reveal about what we know, or think we know, the better. Agreed?"

"Agreed."

We walked back along the bank in silence. As we turned to head up to the shelter of the tents we heard a shout and the sound of running feet coming towards us. A cloaked figure hurtled down the path, shouting as he ran.

"Hello! Is the commander there? I need Trebonius urgently."

"No," Quintus called back, "he's not here. What's happened?"

The man was swathed in a heavy cloak and hood against the rain. A small separate corner of my mind recognised the garment as one of Congrio's. It wasn't till he was almost on top of us that we recognised the man inside it as Philippus.

He skidded to a halt beside us. "Aurelia! Antonius! What in the gods' name are you doing out in the storm?" Without waiting for an answer he hurried on. "When I saw someone down here, I thought it was bound to be Trebonius. Something awful has happened. I need to find him."

"I'm afraid you're right, Philippus," Quintus said. "Something truly awful has happened. But how did you know about it?"

"How did I *know?* Because I've just heard him with my own ears, that's how. I must find the commander. We need a senior officer to deal with this. Father's gone quite mad."

"We'll find him. Meanwhile I have authority to look into what's happened," Quintus said. "So tell me what your father's done."

"I don't understand this. You said you knew something awful…"

"But not about your father. What's he done?"

"He's raging and crying and telling everyone he's murdered my mother."

I felt a shock, almost like a blow. I couldn't get any words out.

Quintus said levelly, "Do you believe what he says?"

"Of course not. It's some kind of madness, probably too much to drink, or…I don't know. Mother went home ages ago. She had a headache and left a message that we were to carry on with the party, but she needed to lie down for a while. Then the rain started and everyone began to leave anyway. I heard one of the young tribunes saying there'd been an accident down by the river, and I couldn't find Trebonius, so I went to tell Father. He burst into tears and said that Mother was dead and he'd killed her."

"You say your mother left a message? Who brought it?" Quintus interrupted.

"*Who brought it?* How should I know, and what does it matter anyway?" He must have read something in our expressions, because he grew pale. "That's right, isn't it? Mother's safe at home?"

"I'm afraid not." Quintus looked at me, then back at the young man. "I'm sorry, Philippus, but she isn't at home."

"Then where...gods, you're not telling me it's true?"

"No, not that exactly. But I'm sorry to say your mother's dead."

We told him what we'd found and showed him the place where she'd been pushed into the river. At first he was incredulous, then he became deadly calm. His face turned into a mask, empty of all emotion. It was sadder and more frightening than weeping or passionate anger.

He turned to face Quintus. "She was a good swimmer. She couldn't have just drowned. Somebody murdered her and threw her body into the river."

Quintus nodded.

"Do you think my father did that?"

"I don't know. It's too early to say what happened. But I can promise you this: we will find out."

We walked him gently to the tent where his mother lay. Titch was standing guard outside it, and after the two of them had stepped in, he said softly, "Mallius is telling everyone he killed her."

I put a finger to my lips. "I know. Later, I think. Where is Mallius now?"

Titch nodded towards one of the other small tents which had a soldier in front of it. "I put a man on watch outside. We can't leave him loose, can we? Do you think he did it? I don't." He lowered his voice to a whisper. "He wasn't by the river any time. But other folk might think he's guilty and take the law into their own hands."

Quintus and Philippus emerged just then. Philippus was shaking now, and sobbing.

"Oh, my poor Mother. How could this have happened? She hadn't an enemy in the world, not really. Even Father...I can't believe he'd hurt her. Where is Father now?"

Titch pointed out the tent.

"May I see him?"

"Not for a little while, I'm afraid," Quintus said gently. "There are some questions we need to ask him."

"You don't think he did it? He can't have done, he wouldn't…"

"In view of what he's saying himself, we'll have to talk to him first. And anyway, there's something else I'm hoping you can do."

"Of course. Anything."

"Somebody has to break the news to your sister."

"Oh, gods, you're right. I'll go and find her."

"Shall I come with you?" I dreaded the thought of it, but I wanted to help.

"That's kind of you. But I must do this alone." He began to walk away, then turned back to me. "Thank the gods you're here, Aurelia. She may need your help later. We all may."

"You know I'll do whatever I can."

"What I want is the truth about who killed Mother. Whoever it is, I want them brought to justice."

"That's what I want too," I said. "That's what we all want."

Chapter XIX

Quintus pulled his Imperial pass from his belt-pouch and handed it to Titch. "Find someone reliable to guard Jovina's tent. Then look for Trebonius, but don't waste much time on it, because we need to move fast. If you can't find him, use my authority. Eurytus has agreed I can handle this until Trebonius turns up."

"Right."

"Keep everyone here who hasn't left yet. Get them all together in one or two tents, and keep them there till we come. Try and make a list of everyone who's gone already."

Titch pulled a face. "They aren't going to like it."

"Then they can lump it. Aurelia and I will talk to Mallius. If he really killed Jovina, it simplifies matters, and we can let all the rest go."

Titch said quietly, "Like I just told Aurelia, I don't believe he did. I didn't see him down by the river alone this afternoon. He was with the crowd. And he was very drunk, unless he was pretending."

"He wasn't pretending." I said. "By midafternoon he could barely stand, let alone commit a murder."

"Then why in the gods' name would he confess to one?" Quintus grumbled.

"There's only one way to find out," I said. "Come on, let's get it over."

The tent where they'd put Mallius was small and uncomfortable. The wet grass underfoot made everything damp, and all he had to sit on was a folding stool. But in fact when we went in he was sitting on the ground, his back against the leg of a rough table. Not much light penetrated the leather, and a tiny oil lamp made little impression on the gloomy interior. In the shadowy half-dark his slumped figure looked sad and defeated.

He didn't attempt to rise as we entered, but lifted his head and looked first at Quintus, then at me.

"Antonius…and Aurelia. Philippus has told you what's happened?"

"Mallius Melandrus," Quintus said gently, "we're very sorry to hear about your wife's death. And you've told your son that you killed her. Is that true?"

"Yes, I killed her." His words were slightly slurred, but fluent enough. "It's all my fault. I killed my wife. I don't deny it, and I shan't try to escape the consequences."

"Tell us what happened," Quintus said.

"And why," I added.

"I did it this morning before the party."

"This morning?" Quintus and I exclaimed together.

"I mean that's when I started it. Of course I didn't know how long it would take to work."

Quintus stared blankly at him, then glanced at me, but all I could do was shake my head. I didn't understand either. Mallius didn't notice our silence.

"It was after I saw those glass goblets she had for her birthday. She was so pleased with them, she insisted on bringing them to the party. They were from a lover. I know they were, although she tried to tell me they were from you, Aurelia. But they weren't, were they?"

There was no point lying about it now. "No, they weren't."

"Who gave them to her, do you know?"

"She wouldn't say. She was very mysterious, and said they were from someone who shouldn't be giving her extravagant presents."

"That's what I thought. That means it must be Trebonius. And I was so angry that someone was giving her something so expensive, and that she was going to flaunt it in front of everyone.

She and Trebonius…there are rumours about them everywhere. I made up my mind I wasn't going to be treated like that, and I did it." He got up and stood unsteadily, one hand on the table for support. Yet his gaze was defiant. "Do you blame me?"

Neither of us answered, but again he didn't notice.

"I didn't know how long it would take to work," he repeated. "How could I? I've never done anything like that before. I just had to wait. And the party began, and I started to calm down and wish I hadn't done it. But it was too late."

His head dropped into his hands, and suddenly the defiant bluster went out of him, and he began to sob. "Too late. Too late! Now what will become of us all?"

"I still don't understand, Mallius," Quintus said. "You did something this morning but it only took effect this afternoon. What was it? Did you give Jovina poison?"

"I don't want to talk about it. I *can't* talk about it. All I know is I did it, and now I'm sorry. Oh, gods, I'm so sorry."

He collapsed slowly onto the ground and lay still. When I bent over him I realised he'd passed out.

"What do you make of this?" Quintus asked.

"I don't believe him."

"Nor do I. Yet he's confessed, we can't just ignore that and let him go. I'd better arrange for him to be arrested, at least overnight. I need to find Trebonius for that."

He looked out of the tent entrance. The soldier on guard was still there, and from his shocked expression he'd heard what had been said inside.

"Stay on duty here," Quintus ordered. "He won't try to escape, I'm pretty sure of it. Do you know where the commander is?"

"No, sir, I don't."

"We'll find him. Stay here until we do. Understood?"

"Understood, sir."

We set off in search of Trebonius, but in fact he found us. He strode down from the road towards us, and he looked very angry, indeed.

"Antonius! What in the gods' name is going on here? My men tell me there's been some sort of accident, somebody found dead in the river."

"I'm glad you're here, Trebonius. We couldn't find you, and the matter is urgent. It wasn't an accident, I'm afraid. It was a murder."

"A murder?" His expression changed from anger to disbelief. "A *murder?* Who's been murdered?"

"My cousin Jovina." I watched him closely as I said that. His reaction of horrified astonishment seemed completely genuine, just what I'd have expected.

It cost him a great effort of will to say quietly, "Tell me what's happened."

I admired his calmness under pressure, the mark of a good commander, even while I wondered how much of what we were telling him was really news to him. When we'd finished explaining how Jovina had been found, we took him to the tent where she lay.

He gazed at her for a long time, then he left the tent and said, "Thank you for what you've done. I'm grateful you were here."

"It was the least we could do. We did try to find you, but we couldn't. Were you called back to the fort?" Quintus asked casually. "Nobody seemed to know where you were."

"I escorted my wife home. She wasn't feeling well. Then at the fort there was a report of an incident in the village, some stone-throwing outside Brennus' house. Not aimed at Brennus, of course. My lads banged a few barbarian heads together and it was soon over, but I didn't want to come back here till I was sure everything had quieted down. I'll take charge now. So first things first. Have you any idea who could have done this?"

We told him about Mallius' confession, and how we didn't believe it.

"I'm afraid I believe it," he said gravely. "The poor fellow's not been himself for months now. It's common knowledge he sees—I mean saw—as little of Jovina as possible, and he was insanely jealous if any man so much as said good morning to her." He sighed. "He's drunk now, I suppose?"

"He was. Now he's unconscious," Quintus said, "in that tent over there."

"Very well. I'll arrange for him to be put under guard for tonight, and we'll talk to him again tomorrow when he's sobered up. It's a sad business, and frankly an inconvenient one at this time. I've got my hands more than full without being an officer short. Not that Mallius...well never mind."

"With respect, Commander," Quintus said, "could I make a suggestion? I'd like to look into this a little further. We must be completely certain that Mallius' confession stands up. I'd hate to see an officer convicted of murder when there's no evidence for it except his own maudlin ramblings."

"That's very commendable, Antonius, but as I've just indicated, I haven't the time or resources for any investigations for the next day or two. I'm a simple man, and I don't see the need to complicate things. There's been a murder, a dreadful murder, but we have a self-confessed killer in custody. What else do we need to do?"

"I realise you yourself will be far too busy," Quintus said. "But I have some experience of investigation work, and with your permission, I could continue to look into the circumstances of Jovina's death, just until we're sure Mallius was responsible. I'll report to you, of course, but not get in your way at all. You'll be on high alert tomorrow, as I understand it."

"You can say that again. Tomorrow is midsummer. The day when, if you believe that note Terentius was carrying, we can expect another murder, when Eurytus is killed by 'the Greek'."

"You don't sound as if you believe it yourself, Commander." Or is it just that you're not overly concerned about whether Achilles kills Hector tomorrow? I added, but only to myself.

"I don't know what to believe; I really don't. All I do know is that we must take every possible precaution. Eurytus may already have had enemies before he arrived here, and he's made a few more since."

"Such as?" Quintus asked.

"Brennus for one. He's made a play for his daughter, the younger one, and he and his party almost ran down a couple of his grandchildren on the road the other day. If you want my opinion, that's why Brennus' wife didn't come today. She couldn't stand being anywhere near him. Brennus himself had no choice. By the way, thank you for looking after him so well, Antonius."

"Eurytus put you in an awkward situation," Quintus said. "He seems to think he can do whatever he likes and nobody will dare stand up to him. I hope he's prepared to take some extra security precautions tomorrow."

"I've tried to persuade him to stay within the fort, we can guarantee his safety there. But he refuses to be, as he puts it, imprisoned by a bunch of barbarians. He says he has to talk to Brennus and one or two of the other native leaders, and he'll do it at Brennus' own house. I suppose that's his way of humiliating the provincials even more…gods, he's really an odious little man."

"But a powerful one. So then, you agree that I and my assistant Victor should do a little more checking into how Jovina died? And once you've got tomorrow out of the way, we'll hand over the whole case to you."

He hesitated, then nodded. "All right, yes. And if there's any practical help you need, let me know. "

"Actually there are two things," Quintus said. "First, could you confirm to your men that you don't mind our detaining a few people here for a short time while we ask some questions?"

"I'm afraid It's too late for that. I've told them all they're free to go. I can't keep guests penned up here like prisoners. If you need to talk to them, you'll have to find them for yourselves."

Quintus stiffened, but controlled his temper. "We'll do that."

"And the other thing?"

"Could you let us have a small office within the fort? We'll need somewhere we can talk privately or interview people. Just for a couple of days."

"Certainly. Talk to Junius about it." He beckoned one of his aides, who was waiting nearby. "Junius, arrange for an office for

Antonius and his assistant, will you? But first we need to see about Mallius." He began issuing a string of orders. We went back to the small tent Titch had commandeered for us.

It was hardly less depressing than the tiny one where we'd talked to Mallius: wet grass, nothing but folding stools to sit on, a crude apology for a table, and one inadequate lamp. But at least Titch was there, and he'd managed to find a jug of wine and even some leftover party food. He was the only one who was hungry, but we all took a drink. It didn't do much to dispel our sour mood.

Quintus said what we were all thinking. "How could we have let this happen? There were three of us, all meant to be making sure things went smoothly today and seeing that no harm came to Jovina. And what have we achieved? Nothing."

"I blame myself," I said. "I promised her she'd be safe, and I was supposed to be looking after her. I can't help feeling I'm responsible for her death."

"You did what you could." Quintus sighed. "We all did. It was an impossible situation really, out in the open with trees close by. We were up against somebody too clever for us."

"But Jovina told me just after the meal that she wanted to go off alone into the woods, and she asked me to cover for her."

"Cover for her? How do you mean?"

"Not draw attention to the fact she wasn't there and fob off anyone who asked about her. I said I would. I wasn't happy about it, so I tried to follow her when she left the rest of the guests. But I lost her."

"She didn't say why she wanted to get away from everyone?"

"Not in so many words. She seemed excited, and I assumed she was going to meet somebody privately. I did warn her to be careful, and she smiled and said, 'Some things are worth a little danger.'"

He shrugged. "Well, it's still not your fault. It's the fault of whoever she went to meet. One of her lovers, would you say?"

"I can't think of another reason why she'd want to meet someone secretly. It was either the doctor or the commander."

"The doctor or the commander," Titch repeated. "I saw both of those down by the river. At least I'm pretty sure I did."

"Pretty sure?" Quintus asked sharply. "Why not completely sure?"

"They were both wearing cloaks with hoods up, hiding their heads and most of their faces. Them fancy things Congrio has been selling to everyone."

"That Vulcan's Shield stuff," I said. "Yes, there seem to be quite a few of those in evidence today. I don't think they're very attractive myself, but they're popular."

"They're a cursed nuisance," Quintus growled, "if they make it harder to identify people."

"Well, like I said, I'm pretty sure I saw Trebonius—I got a glimpse of him face-on. And the doctor…he was the right size and build, and the walk was right. Yes, I'd say it was Nikias. Trouble is, I didn't see either of them with Jovina."

"Nikias would be my guess," Quintus said. "Aurelia, didn't Jovina tell you yesterday that her affair with him had finished, but he was trying to persuade her to revive it?"

"She did. And she said she was tempted, but undecided."

"He could easily have walked to the party across country from the fort," Titch put in. "I spotted him lurking in the woods just after everyone got up from the meal. About a quarter of a mile upstream from the duck-racing place, very close to the river. There's a big old willow tree there, the sort that would make a good landmark if you wanted to arrange a meeting. I almost missed him—he was quite well hid."

"What was he doing?" I asked, and simultaneously Quintus asked, "Was he alone?"

"Alone, yes, and seemingly waiting for someone, but nobody came near. Kept glancing up at the sun, when there was any sun to see. Then it clouded over, and he started pacing about, getting more and more impatient but still keeping in among the trees. He must have been around a good hour. When the thunder started he headed across country towards the fort. I followed him a short way, till I was sure that was where he was bound, then I came back. Trebonius was behaving much the same, but later on, and he only stayed a short while."

Quintus sighed. "I was trying to keep watch on Trebonius, which I thought would be easy because mostly he was walking about in full view doing his duty as the gracious host. I saw Jovina wander down to the river, just about the time the sun went in. But like you, Aurelia, I couldn't keep her in sight. You were chatting to Philippus, I think."

"That's right, trying to keep an eye on him as we agreed. I went to join the crowd at the duck racing and he was there throwing his money about. But you'd gone, and so had Jovina, and Trebonius too."

"He disappeared in the blink of an eye while I was checking up on Mallius down by the river. Statius started bending my ear about how awful Eurytus is. They've crossed swords in the past apparently. I paused for just a couple of sentences of his ranting, looked round the clearing…and Trebonius was gone. It was neatly done, as if he knew he was likely to be followed. I couldn't find him in the trees."

"There was one odd thing," I said, "or perhaps one very clever thing. Trebonius asked me at one point whether I knew where Jovina was, and I said I didn't. If he had actually been with her already, he was covering his tracks. Or maybe he genuinely wanted to find her and couldn't."

"So on the evidence we have, which admittedly isn't much, we've got two possible murderers," Quintus said. "The commander or the doctor."

"Not the commander, if you ask me," I said. "Why would Trebonius kill her? They were lovers. He'd shown how he cared for her by giving her a wonderful party. Whereas Nikias was a former lover, someone from her past, perhaps still bearing a grudge, resenting the way she'd refused to go away with him. For my money he's the more likely."

"I don't see that," Titch objected. "They were lovers some while back. If he was bitter enough to kill her because she threw him over, he'd had plenty of time to do it. Why wait till now?"

I considered Jovina's various revelations about her love affairs. "Perhaps he only got really angry when he discovered she was having an affair with Trebonius. Jealousy is a strong emotion. Or—I know—supposing he'd just found out that Jovina had got rid of his unborn child? Now that might make a man angry, don't you think?"

Quintus nodded. "So…Jovina was prepared to take Nikias back, or at least consider it. She let him know she wanted to talk. He couldn't be a party guest, so one or other of them suggested they should meet secretly in the woods. But his reasons for the meeting were quite different. He wanted to get her alone in order to kill her."

"Or maybe he didn't plan to go that far. They quarrelled when they met, either about the baby or about her not wanting to leave Isurium, and he lost his temper and became violent."

"That makes sense so far," Quintus agreed.

"But," Titch put in, "suppose it was Trebonius who suggested a private meeting by the river? She'd jump at it because she was in love with him, but he wasn't thinking of romance in the woods. He wanted to tell her to be a bit more discreet, or mebbe even to finish with her. You said she was making all the running, Aurelia, and perhaps he was finding it embarrassing, or his wife was cutting up rough. She could have threatened him that if he didn't go on seeing her, she'd tell everyone they were having an affair."

"Or maybe," Quintus suggested, "he'd heard a rumour that she was thinking of taking up with Nikias again, and that made him jealous. Either way, when they met they quarrelled, and he killed her." He scratched his chin. "Yes, that makes sense too."

I shivered at the thought of such cold-blooded murder. Someone had lured my cousin into the woods as if for a secret assignation, and then killed her…a man she loved, or had loved. She had looked for romance and tenderness because they were absent from her own marriage, and I realised I could forgive her being unfaithful to a drunken husband who made no secret of the fact that he no longer cared for her. Whichever of her two lovers had murdered her, she had deserved better than this callous act of betrayal.

Quintus stood up. "I don't think asking each other questions is going to get us any further forward. Let's start asking people who might know the answers."

Chapter XX

The fort had its own hospital block—only a small one, but then this was only a small base. There was an outer room where would-be patients waited, a surgeon's room where Nikias and his assistant carried out operations and major treatments, a large ward with beds for the seriously wounded or sick soldiers, and three smaller rooms for men who needed to be kept isolated.

Nikias wasn't in any of these, but in the storeroom, one corner of which he used as an office. He and a younger man, his assistant presumably, were poring over a pile of note-tablets on his desk by the light of a couple of lamps that gave illumination but didn't dispel the clinging damp in the air.

They looked up to greet us as we entered, and I didn't need to ask whether they'd heard the news about Jovina. They were both pale and tense.

I introduced Quintus to Nikias, who in turn introduced his assistant Pythis and then dismissed the lad and invited us to sit down.

"We're sorry to intrude at a sad time," Quintus said. "Jovina Lepida was a good friend of yours, I understand."

"A friend? Oh, yes, a friend. And I wanted…I hoped she would be so much more."

A good start, though a slightly surprising one. If he wasn't going to make a secret of his feelings for Jovina, then we needn't beat about the bush. I said, "My cousin mentioned that you and she had been very close."

"We were, in the winter and early spring. But it finished. I wanted her to leave Mallius and come away with me, go somewhere far from here and make a new start. I'm an experienced doctor. I could always find work. But she wouldn't."

"Because of her husband?"

"Partly, and partly because of the children. Sad, isn't it? She had a drunken husband, a crooked son, and a spoilt little daughter…and in the end she preferred them to me."

I was longing to ask why he called Philippus crooked, but resisted the distraction. "As you know, I only arrived here two days ago. But my cousin did hint to me in conversation that she regretted the quarrel you'd had."

"She said so to me, too, the night I went round there. Only we couldn't talk. There was too much danger of one of the servants or the family interrupting us. I wanted to see her privately, to persuade her that we could be together again, but the only way it would work would be somewhere away from Isurium. I couldn't stand the secret, furtive way we would have to live if we stayed here. I wanted to make her see it must be all or nothing. A new life with me…or finish altogether. No going back."

I asked, "You gave her that magnificent pair of goblets, didn't you, for her birthday?"

"Yes. Did she like them?"

"She did. She insisted we drank a toast from them, she and I. You sent the roses too?"

"I did. She loved flowers."

Quintus took up the questioning. "About this afternoon. You were hoping to talk with Jovina. So you arranged to meet her during the party?"

"How could I? I wasn't there."

"You weren't a guest, but you were seen by the river. I repeat, were you hoping to have a quiet talk with Jovina?"

"And I repeat, I wasn't there. I wish I could have been. I wanted to be, and I admit I did hope I could walk down along the river for a short while and meet her. But I couldn't because I have sick boys here to look after."

"You told Jovina you would meet her there?"

"I said I'd try. She knew what my work can be like. If I've got patients who need me, I can't go off and leave them, however much I want to."

"So you claim you weren't at the party at all?"

"For the third time, no, I was not. If you don't believe my word, ask my assistant."

"We will. Because whatever you say, you were seen."

"Impossible. Somebody made a mistake. If it was after the rain started, maybe there was someone the same size as me, in a cloak like mine. It wasn't me."

"What's your cloak like?"

"It's new, made of some fancy fabric called Vulcan's Shield. There's a trader staying in Isurium who's selling them, I bought one yesterday as a curiosity. They're supposed to bring a person good luck, and you can set fire to them and they won't burn."

"He seems to have sold quite a few of them," Quintus said.

"He has. I don't think Jovina had one…Oh, if only I had seen her, just once more. I never dreamed something like this would happen. She always said she was a good swimmer. How could she have drowned?"

"She didn't…" I began, but Quintus cut in quickly.

"She didn't have much of a chance, I'm afraid."

"I wish I could have seen her," he repeated sadly. "If only we hadn't been so busy here."

"How many patients are in the hospital just now?" Quintus asked.

"One seriously wounded, Fabianus, who was ambushed yesterday while he was on patrol. He's the reason I had to stay here. He's in a bad way and frankly I'm surprised he's still alive. Then I've several with this fever that's going around just now, they get diarrhoea and throw up for a couple of days and then they recover. Mostly anyhow."

Quintus nodded. "I think that's all for the present, we'll leave you to your work. We'll probably need to talk to you again in the morning."

"Could *I* ask a question please?" Nikias said.

"Of course."

"They're saying Mallius killed her. Is that true?"

"He's admitted it," Quintus answered.

"Then why are you asking all these questions? Don't you believe him?"

"So far we only have his word. He's very upset and very drunk, and the commander has asked us to check the facts for ourselves, to make absolutely sure."

"I see. Yes, you must be sure. She was a wonderful person, truly wonderful." He wiped a hand across his face. "Everyone who knew her will want to see her avenged. So if there's anything I can do, anything at all, you can count on me."

"Thank you. First, may we have a quick word with Pythis?"

He summoned his assistant, a pleasant-looking young man with an easy manner.

Quintus asked, "Pythis, you've heard about the tragic death of Jovina Lepida?"

"Yes, sir."

"We're checking up on everyone's movements this afternoon, mostly so we can eliminate them from our investigation. Where were you between the midday meal and when the thunder started?"

"I was here at the hospital. We've got several sick men at the moment, especially Fabianus."

"And was Nikias here, too, for some of the time?"

"All the time, sir. He was here all the time."

"All the time?" Quintus smiled. "He must have left briefly during all those hours. To relieve himself? To get something to eat?"

"We have lavatories here in the building, sir. And we can get food sent in, or we have a small kitchen area for preparing warm drinks and medicines. Neither of us had to leave at any time."

"Was that a bit too smooth?" I murmured to Quintus as we left to go in search of Titch. "Or am I getting over-suspicious?"

"I don't think an investigator can ever be *over*-suspicious," he said. "We'll talk to him again tomorrow when Nikias isn't there."

Titch was chatting to Gambax near the main gate. "I was just asking Gambax about who he saw wandering around by the river today, so we could compare notes."

"Let's discuss it in our new office," Quintus said. "An aide called Junius has found us one. I haven't even been there yet."

Titch went to inquire and soon came back with the good news that we'd been allocated a room in the quartermaster's block near the headquarters building. "Quite a good size, and dead handy," he said, and he was right.

When we were all inside, Quintus said, "Now let's hear your report, Gambax. We'll be glad of any help you can give us."

"Victor asked me whether I noticed anything unusual down by the river this afternoon. I saw three people on their own, Philippus and the commander and someone else in a cloak that I couldn't be sure of, but I think was Nikias."

"What were they all doing?"

"Philippus only came down briefly, as if he was looking for someone, and went away again. The other two seemed to be waiting around, but I don't know what for, or who for. I didn't see either of them with anyone else."

"Anything else unusual?"

"Yes. I heard something that struck me as odd at the time, and now…I thought I'd better tell someone."

"Go on," Quintus encouraged.

"A woman's voice, shouting. I wasn't sure whose, because I couldn't see, but Chloe…" he stopped.

I smiled at him. "It's all right. We know Chloe was hoping to have a quiet word with you this afternoon."

"I wasn't with her long, but we heard this woman really raising her voice. Chloe said it was her mother. And she sounded really upset."

"Could you hear what she said?"

"Pretty much. 'I won't. I can't. You know I can't give you up, I love you. Then why are you tearing me in two? If you really loved me, you wouldn't put me through this. No, talk all you like but I shan't change my mind.'"

"Who was she talking to?"

"That's just it, we couldn't tell. We heard a man's voice a couple of times, but very quiet."

"It doesn't sound as if she gave him much chance to put a word in," I said. "How did it end? Did one of them walk off in a temper?"

"We didn't stay till the end. Chloe said to me, 'We haven't got long together, and I for one don't want to waste it listening to Mother yelling at Trebonius, if that's who it is. Let's go further away.' So we did. Now, of course I wish…but it's too late."

"Chloe thought it was Trebonius with her?" Quintus asked.

"Well, as I said, neither of us could be sure. But everyone knows…that is, there are rumours about…I mean…"

Quintus nodded. "I know. It could have been the commander. Thank you, Gambax, that's useful. We may have more questions for you later."

"Please sir, I wonder…would it be possible?…" He stopped, looking embarrassed.

"Would what be possible? Come on lad, spit it out."

"I liked Mistress Jovina. She was always kind to me, and she wasn't above turning a blind eye when I wanted to see Chloe. Is there any way I can help you find out who's done this dreadful thing? You two are experienced investigators, but you'll need someone to do the running around, fetching and carrying and delivering messages. I can do all that if I can get permission from the commander."

"We'd be very glad of your help," Quintus said. "Not just for the running-around jobs, but because you know the fort and the area here far better than we do. I'll fix it with Trebonius. Meet us first thing tomorrow morning, and we'll make a start."

"Are you staying here at the fort?" Gambax asked.

"No, Titch and I are planning to stay at the Mallius house, to guard it tonight. Philippus has to be here at the fort, which only leaves Statius and a few male slaves there. We'll be back here early tomorrow."

Quintus and I went to tell Trebonius what we planned, and asked whether he could spare Gambax to help us. He agreed willingly enough to assign him to us tomorrow, but said he needed every available man on guard overnight.

"I'd like to see all of Mallius' household moved from the village into the fort here," Trebonius said, "but it's too late to start tonight, too dangerous in the dark. Can you organise it for the morning?"

"Yes, we can," I said. "But what about Jovina's funeral? Won't the family want to be in their own house?"

"We're holding that here tomorrow," he answered. "There's a field where we put up pyres for our own people, and the priests know how things should be done. Philippus has agreed, and I've already had her brought here for tonight, I think it's safer."

"How is Mallius now?" Quintus asked.

"Still unconscious. I assume it's the effect of the drink, but given the state he was in earlier, I've put him in the hospital block for the night. With a guard, of course. I can't take any chances."

"May I ask a quick question, Commander?" Quintus said. "We're trying to get a picture of what happened down by the river this afternoon about the time Jovina must have been killed. Aurelia says she met you looking for Jovina at one point. Did you find her?"

"No, I didn't."

"Any particular reason you were searching for her?"

"Only that I hadn't seen her for a while, and one or two people had started to leave the party. I thought she'd want to say good-bye. Then the rain began in earnest, and I came back to the tents, and after that I escorted Fulvina home, and went on to the village…I've told you all this."

"Yes, you have. Thank you. We won't hold you up any more."

As we left him and went to find our raeda, Quintus murmured, "Another one who's a bit too smooth? Or is it my turn to be over-suspicious?"

"Ah, but you said it's impossible to be *over*-suspicious, didn't you?"

We set off before dark, Quintus and I in a *raeda*, Titch riding alongside leading Quintus' horse, and two soldiers escorting us. As we clattered through the deserted streets the village seemed dead, like a place stricken by plague. We found ourselves talking in hushed tones, but in fact we didn't say much at all, glad to be able to relax quietly for a spell.

Jovina's house—that's how I still thought of it—was quiet too, because nearly everyone had gone to bed. Selena was in charge, and though she was red-eyed from crying, she was as efficient as ever and very pleased to see us.

"We'll be thankful to have some strong men here, sir," she said to Quintus. "Master Statius offered to stand guard, but his soldiering days are long over, so I said we could manage with just the servants. It's good we don't have to."

"We'll take watches in turn," Quintus said. "I'll go and arrange it."

"All the boys are together in the kitchen, sir. I'll take you to them."

She was soon back, and I asked, "How's Chloe?"

"Dreadfully upset, and so is little Miss Vitellia. They've both been crying their eyes out most of the evening. Losing her mother's bad enough for poor Chloe, but when she heard her father has confessed to killing my lady, she went to pieces altogether."

"She doesn't believe it, surely? We don't."

"She doesn't want to believe it, no. But there's been bad blood between her and the master for so long, she doesn't know what to believe. It breaks my heart to see her in such a state."

"When we've proved his innocence, and I'm sure we can, perhaps they'll be drawn closer together."

"I doubt it. You'll have gathered what they quarrelled about, this marriage with Statius the master is arranging. Chloe kept on hoping my lady would help her to argue him out of it, or at least get it postponed awhile. Now she feels she's on her own, and the master might force the wedding through any time. She's threatening to run away, but that's just wild talk." She sighed.

"I've given them some wine with poppy-seed to help them sleep. At least if they get some rest tonight, Chloe may be calmer in the morning. And they're sharing one of the big guest bedrooms. Better if they're not alone, I reckon."

"You've done all you can. Shall I look in and see them before I go to bed?"

"My advice is leave it for now, Mistress. I think the medicine has started to do its work, and you can be sure Baca and I will be keeping watch over them through the night. She's a good girl, is Baca. For all she's young, she has a sensible head on her shoulders."

"She's not the only one. I'm grateful for everything you're doing, Selena. And if you need me in the night you'll come and wake me, won't you?"

"Thank you. We must all do our best for my poor lady." For a few heartbeats her brisk manner faltered, and I thought she was going to cry, but then she got control of herself again and said, "You've spoken to him, Mistress—the master, I mean. I'm so relieved you don't think he killed her."

"We can't rule it out completely until Mallius has sobered up, but I find his confession incredible. Although I realise they were on bad terms, I saw that for myself yesterday. You know them both far better than I, Selena. Do you believe he would murder her?"

She shook her head emphatically. "I don't. Mind you, the drink has made him very strange lately, unpredictable, easily angered. But no. He didn't do it."

"Then you have an idea who did?"

She hesitated. "I think so."

There was a longer pause, and eventually I said, "You know I've vowed to avenge Jovina and see that her killer is brought to justice. Any information you can give me, anything at all, will help me."

"I promised I'd never tell anyone ever, you see. But that was before…Gods, I hate this. Tittle-tattling about my lady now she's gone. It feels so disloyal."

"It's not disloyal, quite the opposite. Tell me everything you think might help—then we can find out who killed her. That's what you want, isn't it?"

"Of course it is."

"Then what's this secret? Is it about the party?"

"It is. My lady planned to meet someone secretly by the river."

"I found that out myself this afternoon. After the meal she told me she wanted a little time alone with someone, but she didn't say who. I was uneasy about it, and when she slipped away I tried to follow her. But she vanished into the trees. That was the last time I saw her alive."

We were both silent for a few heartbeats. Selena said, "She told me it was the commander. She said they arranged a meeting when she was up at the fort yesterday."

"Trebonius? No, that can't be right. At least they didn't make any arrangements at the fort. I was with them the whole time. They didn't discuss secret meetings, and I'm sure they didn't exchange any notes. I thought you were going to tell me she planned to see Nikias. He gave her those beautiful glass goblets, he's admitted as much."

"Has he? They arrived without anything to say who they were from, and my lady was very coy about them. The same with those lovely pink roses. From Nikias too?"

"So he said."

"Well, I don't think it was the commander she was intending to meet in the woods."

"Why not?"

"It seems a lot of trouble to go to, when he could see her at the fort quite easily. Though I suppose once the party was over, there'd be fewer chances for that…but no, I still think it was Nikias the Greek she went to meet. He couldn't be at the party, but he could have come across the fields and along by the river without anyone seeing."

"But why would she lie to you? I know she trusted you completely; she told me so. I'd have thought she would tell the truth to you, of all people."

"I expect she knew I'd argue with her, try to put her off going. She knew I don't like Nikias. I didn't approve of how he tried to persuade her to leave the master, and then flounced off in a rage when she wouldn't. Yet she still cared for him."

"But you accepted her affair with Trebonius?"

"Only because it wasn't a real affair. Nothing happened, if you know what I mean—it was all for show. She wanted it to look like he fancied her, to persuade Nikias she'd stopped thinking about him. Persuade herself, too, I reckon." She shook her head wearily. "No, the commander's much too canny to get tangled up with his deputy's wife. It couldn't stay hid long in a place like this, and it would cause no end of trouble."

"Yes, I can imagine. I thought when I saw them together she was making most of the running. And yet he organised the party for her."

"Oh, that was agreed long since, he couldn't get out of it. The master forgot her last birthday altogether, and she was quite upset, so the commander promised her that next time he'd make sure she had a proper party. I suppose he hoped she wouldn't remember, but she did, and he couldn't go back on it. So he decided to make it a special celebration, and invite half of Isurium along to it. 'Course she told everyone it was all because of her."

I thought back over how Jovina had poured out her heart to me the day before the party. "She told me she was tempted to run away with Nikias, but she couldn't make up her mind."

"No more she could. But if he suggested a secret meeting, she couldn't resist going to it, could she? And if they did meet, and nobody saw her after, he must be the man who killed her."

It was possible. Up to now I'd considered that Nikias' work in the hospital gave him an unshakeable alibi for the whole afternoon. Yet he could have been lying, and if his assistant was prepared to lie too, he could have been absent for a while.

"So you think that she went to meet Nikias and he asked her to go away with him, but she refused, so he lost his temper and murdered her?"

She looked doubtful. "Either that, or she accepted, but he was only playing a game with her. That's my guess…A game of revenge."

I realised where she was driving. "He found out she'd got rid of his baby, and that made him kill her?"

"That's what I think."

"There's one problem. Nikias says he never left the hospital all afternoon."

"He would say that, wouldn't he?"

"Spoken like a true investigator, Selena." I didn't realise that Quintus had slipped quietly into the room, and was listening to our discussion. "You're quite right. We can't take Nikias' word alone for where he was today, or Trebonius' word, or anyone else's for that matter. We need more evidence. And tomorrow, we'll find it. But first we must get through tonight."

He outlined the arrangements he'd made for guards around the house and garden. He'd done what he could with the small number of male servants available, and Selena and I assured him we could sleep easy knowing we were well protected.

Indeed I had a more restful night than I might have expected, I suppose because I was bone-tired after an eventful day. As I drifted into sleep, I reflected how it was unkind of the Fates to arrange that the first time in months Quintus and I had the chance to share a bed, he was occupied with guard duties all night long. But the hours of darkness were uneventful, thank the gods, and I got up with the dawn as usual.

Quintus, Titch and I ate breakfast early, very soon after dawn. Baca told us Selena had gone to snatch a couple of hours' rest, and Chloe and Vitellia were still in their beds.

"We took turns to watch through the night," she said. "They calmed down once they'd had some of Selena's special wine. Do you want me to go and wake them up?"

"No, let them sleep if they can," I said. "But we do want them, and all of you here, to move into the fort this morning and stay there for a day or two, till things around the village get back to normal."

She nodded. "Selena said there's trouble brewing. Some pesky prince, she said. Don't worry, she knows all about moving to the fort. She's got most of the arrangements made. We'll be there well before noon."

"Make sure you are, because if you stay here you may be in danger. So I rely on you, Baca, to help Selena get everyone out of here as soon as possible. And to make sure Miss Vitellia isn't too upset by it all."

"She's sad for Miss Chloe," Baca answered. "But she's taking it all in her stride, really. Master Lucius would be proud of her."

"That's good. I'm sure you're helping her through it all. We'll see you later."

"You will, Mistress. I've never lived in a fort before. It'll be quite exciting."

As we set off for the fort, I found myself hoping there wouldn't be too much excitement there.

Chapter XXI

I was glad to be in the shelter of the carriage, because although last night's rain had gone, it was windy, with clouds chasing across the sky, and very little sunshine.

The village was quiet. There were no Brigantians to be seen, only scores of soldiers in patrols, armed and alert for danger. Their display of force was impressive, and so far it seemed to be deterring whatever was planned for today.

"So where do we start, Quintus?" I asked. "By interviewing everyone we can find who was at the party and in a position to see what happened down by the river? That should keep us out of mischief for most of the day."

"Unless Mallius sticks to his confession once he's sober. That will make our lives a lot easier."

"I don't believe he will stick to it. Do you?"

He shook his head. "I think we've established that it was either Nikias or Trebonius. All we have to do," he added with a grin, "is prove which."

The guard on the gate had been doubled, and there was a centurion in charge today. He was one of the officers we'd met at the party, so I gave him a smile and called, "'Morning, Ennius." He waved us through and smiled back.

Gambax was waiting for us in our office, and he'd even arranged breakfast there for us. "There's a cookshop been set up near the food stores, for all the people that are coming into the fort for shelter today," he explained. "You can go there for grub whenever you like."

Quintus and I contented ourselves with some wine, but Titch helped himself enthusiastically to bread and cheese. "Great. I'm no good for anything on an empty stomach."

"I don't know where you put it all," Quintus smiled. "If I ate that much, I'd be so fat I couldn't find a horse strong enough to carry me."

"I reckon it's down to hard work and a virtuous life," Titch answered.

The joking stopped when we began to make our plans for the day. Everyone knew, and nobody admitted, that we had far too much to do, and far too few people to do it.

Quintus and Gambax began compiling a list of the people we needed to interview, some of those at yesterday's party and the soldiers who'd been guarding it. Titch went to check discreetly on Philippus' whereabouts. We didn't intend to talk to him immediately, but Quintus wanted to keep track of his movements.

My first job was to visit the hospital to see how Mallius was, and if he was still unconscious, make sure they let us know when he woke.

Before I could set off, Titch came back to report that Philippus had left the fort at first light, telling the gate-guard he had orders to ride to Cataractonium.

"He'll surely be back here in time for his mother's funeral," I said. "That's going to be late this afternoon, I believe. One of Trebonius' aides is organising it."

"I wonder if he's really gone to Cataractonium," Quintus mused. "It seems odd Trebonius should send him up there, if they're desperate for every available man here."

"Wherever he's gone, I must confess I'm relieved he isn't in the fort. I'm frightened of him, now I know what he's capable of."

"But he doesn't know that you know, don't forget," Quintus said. "And you're safe enough in the fort, anyway."

"Safer if he's not here, certainly. But I'd like to see the man arrested."

"Soon he will be, or at least that's what I'm hoping. If he's run off or gone to make contact with the rebels, it may take us longer. We must try to find him if he's still in Isurium. I want to know where he goes today, who he sees."

"Hadn't we better check with Trebonius whether he really has been sent out on some sort of mission?" I suggested. "While we're at it, we ought to find out about Eurytus' plans for the day."

Quintus nodded. "I'll go and see Trebonius now. Titch, could you have a word with the stable-master, make sure that if we need horses later we can get them without any hold-up or fuss."

He grinned. "Already done last night. The horse-master here has been in the cavalry since Romulus was a lad. I discovered he used to know me dad in his army days. His name's Septimus, and he says if we ask him personally, he'll make sure we have any mounts we need, whatever else is going on."

"Good. Then you can help Gambax with this list of people to interview. I'll go and see the commander, and Aurelia will visit the hospital. Meet back here as soon as possible."

The waiting-room in the medical block was deserted, but I heard sounds of activity coming from the office-cum-store. I knocked and entered, and found Nikias standing with his back to the door, pounding away with a pestle at a large mortar that gave off an unpleasant smell. I preferred not to speculate what it was, knowing the weird and horrible things that go into some medicines.

Nikias turned as I came in, and I realised it wasn't Nikias but Pythis. They were similar in appearance from behind, the same build and the same brown hair, but I hadn't realised that last night because their faces were different. This boy was pleasant-looking, whereas Nikias was decidedly handsome.

"Good morning, Mistress," he said politely. "The doctor has gone to get some rest, it was quite a disturbed night for us. Fabianus was delirious and had convulsions, and then of course the deputy commander gave us a fright."

"Mallius? What's happened to him?"

"I'm afraid he tried to take his life," the lad said. "Opened a vein in his wrist. But we found him in time and he hasn't gone to the Underworld yet. He's in a deep sleep, as still as a dead man, but the master says he'll pull through."

"Gods, as if that family hasn't suffered enough. Does Philippus know?"

"I couldn't say, Mistress, but I doubt it. He hasn't been here since he visited his father last night, and we haven't told anyone except Commander Trebonius."

"May I see Mallius now?"

Pythis shook his head. "I'm sorry. The master said he wasn't to have any visitors just yet. Of course, as it's you…but I don't like to go against his direct orders. Could you wait until he comes? I'm expecting him later this morning. And there really is nothing to see, just a poor wounded man who needs his rest. He'll be all right eventually. We found him in time," Pythis repeated the reassurance and I had to be satisfied with that.

I said a quick prayer for Mallius at the little shrine to Apollo outside the medical block's entrance, and went back to report the disturbing news to Quintus and Titch. "Chloe hasn't arrived, I suppose? She ought to know about this. Philippus too."

"No, Chloe's not here yet. I've asked the lads at the gate to send us a message when she turns up." Quintus was staring thoughtfully out of the small window. "You know, the fact that Mallius has tried to commit suicide ought to confirm that he murdered Jovina. But it doesn't, to me. It makes his behaviour even more incomprehensible, that's all."

"I agree. I don't see how he could possibly have followed Jovina through the woods during the party in the state he was in. But he could have intended to. Suppose he'd poisoned her food or wine at the party with something to make her drowsy, meaning to kill her later on, but then was drunk and couldn't do it? And someone else attacked her…no, that's too far-fetched."

"Did she seem sleepy when you spoke to her? She didn't look it."

"No, you're right. When I talked to her after the meal she seemed bright and alert, and excited about the idea of disappearing into the woods."

I stopped because there was a loud, familiar voice outside, calling out to somebody further away. "Is this Antonius' office? Good." There followed a peremptory knock at the door.

My heart sank inside me as Quintus called "Come in," and my brother stepped into the room.

"Lucius, welcome," Quintus said, rising and moving forward to shake his hand. "This is wonderful. I'm very pleased to see you. We've got too much work and not enough workers, as usual."

"Quintus, I'm glad you're here. I've just heard about yesterday, about Jovina....*Aurelia!*"

"Good morning, Lucius. This is a pleasant surprise."

"What in the name of all the gods are you doing here?"

"I told you I planned to come and visit my cousin. I was right, she did need me here."

"But I gave you strict orders to stay at home."

"Which I managed to get around, because it was important. I travelled here without any co-operation from the staff at the Oak Tree. Albia helped me. She agreed with me you were being ridiculous. And I do have other friends, you know, who will rally round when I need them."

"Other friends? You mean Quintus!" he almost shouted, whirling round to face him. "Did you have a hand in this?"

"No. The first I knew of it was when I met Aurelia in Eburacum and she told me about her cousin's letter and what had happened since. By then she'd made all her arrangements, and not least, she'd made up her mind. I'm sorry you're angry, Lucius, but as things have turned out, I'm very glad she came. She's been a great help in my investigations."

"Really? She doesn't seem to have helped Jovina much."

It was a cruel comment, but I couldn't deny it. "I don't think anyone could have done, Lucius. I intend to help now though, to avenge her and bring whoever's killed her to justice. You were right about one thing. There's something seriously wrong here at the fort. I don't know yet how deeply Jovina and her family are involved."

"We shall find out. That's Quintus and Titch and I. Not you. I'm taking you home today myself. I don't feel I can even trust you to go on your own under escort. We can stay at Albia's tonight, and get to the Oak Tree tomorrow. Presumably Vitellia is still there?"

"Of course not. Do you think I'd leave her all alone at Oak Bridges? She's here at Isurium. She wanted to come with me, in the hope of seeing you. The gods know why."

"*Here!* You brought Vitellia here, into danger, against my express wishes…by the gods, Aurelia, that's unforgivable."

There followed a long, fierce row, with Lucius ranting and me defending myself as best I could. I've had many arguments with Lucius—what brother and sister haven't quarrelled, even when they are as close as we are?—but never one as brutal as this. I didn't notice when Quintus and Titch slipped out of the office, but they obviously thought we were best left to sort out our differences in private.

It went on for ages. We are both stubborn, and we were both angry and convinced we were in the right.

We might be arguing there still, if Quintus hadn't come back and said without preamble, "All right, you two. I'm going to have to interrupt your family council. Something bad's happened, and I need your help. If you can't or won't give it, I need you to get out of my office so Titch and I can deal with it."

We both stared at him. Lucius said, "What is it? Not Vitellia…"

Quintus shook his head. "Eurytus has been murdered in the village. The commander is threatening to take punitive action. The natives know about it, and the whole place looks fit to explode like another Vesuvius."

The silence was so absolute that I clearly heard marching feet somewhere outside, punctuated by sharp words of command.

Eventually Lucius asked, "Where and how?"

"The body was found on the road just outside Brennus' house, which is on the edge of the village. He was stabbed with a silver-handled knife which was left beside him. The commander has sent men to arrest Brennus and he's ordering all Roman civilians inside the fort."

"So Achilles has killed his Hector," I said. "Will the next act in the drama be the Fall of Troy?"

"I don't know. Let's hope we can find out who played Achilles before it's too late."

"Vitellia and Chloe," Lucius said, "are they here yet?"

"No. They should be soon though. They were supposed to be following us here. No doubt they're just not aware of the urgency. I'll send Titch over for them with a couple of men."

"Vitellia should never have been brought to Isurium," Lucius snapped. "Aurelia, if anything happens to her, I'll never forgive you. If you'd done as I told you…"

"How many more times? I will *not* do as you tell me, when what you tell me to do is unreasonable. You can't order me about…"

"That's enough!" Quintus shouted. He rarely shouts, and the effect was frightening. "*I* can order both of you to do as you're told, if I choose. And if all you're going to do is squabble like children, then I order you to get out of my office and out of this fort. I've two major crimes to investigate, one of them so serious that if I don't come up with an answer the whole of this village will be torn to pieces and none of us may survive, anyway. Curse you, you idiots, can't you see I need your help? But I'll do without it sooner than put up with your nonsense. So work with me and each other sensibly, or go. *NOW.*"

There was another long silence, which I broke.

"I'm sorry, Quintus." I turned to Lucius. "Shall we call a truce, brother? We're all on the same side, here to do the same job. Isn't it better if we work together till the job's done?"

He hesitated for a few heartbeats, then answered gruffly. "Yes, it is. A truce…All right. I'm sorry too, Quintus. Tell us what you want us to do."

"Thank you. Lucius, I suggest you and Titch go to Mallius' house and fetch Vitellia, Chloe, old Statius, and the servants. Leave only a couple of the male slaves there to watch over the house. On your way, Titch will tell you the details of what's been happening. I'll go to Brennus' house and try to find out how Eurytus met his death. If I haven't returned to the fort by the time you've brought everyone safely in, come and join me there."

"I will. The house is fairly close, isn't it? I shouldn't be long. Anything else?"

"Not yet. We'll have to plan on the hoof as the day develops. And make sure you keep Aurelia informed about what's happening, your progress and your plans. I'll be doing the same. She'll be staying here as our contact point. We've no choice but to split up, and it's important there's someone here who has all the information we're collecting." He turned to me. "All right, Aurelia? You'll be holding the fort here, more or less literally by the looks of things."

"All right, if you think that's best."

"It's vital. Eurytus' assassination has to take priority for now, because of the way the natives are getting worked up. But we still need to investigate Jovina's death, find out whether Mallius is sticking to his confession, and if not who else we should be looking at. Can you handle it?"

"I'll do my best."

"Good. But stay inside the fort, won't you? Don't leave it without me or Titch or Lucius for any reason whatever."

"But…"

"No buts. Promise me."

"I promise."

Gambax knocked and came in. "I've got four mounted men for escort, sir. That's all the commander will spare us. The rest are out patrolling, or standing guard here." He grinned. "I know you wanted more, I made sure to pick good lads."

"Better than nothing. Two will go with Lucius and Titch to fetch everyone from Mallius' house, then follow on to Brennus' place as soon as they've done that. The other two will come with you and me, Gambax. We'll go straight away."

After they'd all left I sat alone in the office for a while, letting the tension of my quarrel with Lucius gradually drain out of me. I felt limp and exhausted, but this was no time for allowing tiredness to stop me working.

Fresh air and a change of scene would help. I'd walk over to the medical block again and see if Mallius was awake yet. And I'd try to catch another word or two with Nikias' assistant Pythis.

As I reached the hospital I heard raised voices from inside. A feverish patient in a delirium? No, as I entered the building I recognised one of the voices as Nikias', though speaking Latin, not Greek.

I hesitated outside the surgeon's room, unwilling to walk in on yet another argument. I'd had my fill of rows for one morning.

"I wasn't asleep, Master, honestly." It was a very young voice, too high-pitched to be Pythis, talking in Latin with a Brigantian accent. Another assistant? Perhaps a slave? He sounded scared, whoever he was. "I was sleepy, but I made myself stay awake. You said it was important somebody was on watch all night long."

"Don't lie to me, you little runt. You were asleep." That was Nikias' voice for sure, also speaking Latin. It was followed by the sound of a hard blow, and a yelp.

"Please, Master…"

Nikias' angry answer was accompanied by another blow and a louder yelp. "Gods, I wish I'd never bought you, you useless lump of lard. Get out of here!"

I just had time to step aside as the door flew open and a small chubby boy rushed out, one hand clutching his left cheek, his eyes streaming with tears. I don't believe in striking slaves, especially children, but this wasn't my affair, so I didn't move as he ran off.

The door was swinging shut again, and I heard Nikias say, in Greek this time, "Pythis, you're not much more use than he is. What did you put in that medicine for Fabianus? How many times have I told you to be careful about quantities?"

"I looked in your notes," Pythis answered, "but they didn't always give the exact amounts, so I did my best. The poor man was raving, trying to escape, mad from the pain. I had to do what I could to calm him."

"But you know as well as I do that quantities are all-important in medicines. Some of the herbs we use are beneficial in small doses, but lethal in larger ones."

I decided that, row or not, I couldn't wait all day for a discussion on the properties of herbs. I knocked and pushed open the door.

Nikias and Pythis were both looking angry, Nikias flushed and his assistant impassive.

"I'm sorry to trouble you again," I said, "but I'm wondering how Mallius is getting on. His daughter will be arriving here soon, I'll have to break the news of—of what happened last night. Is he by any chance awake?"

"Not yet, but I don't think it'll be long," Nikias said.

"May I see him?"

"I suppose so. Just let me go and check."

As he left the store-room I saw Pythis shoot an angry glare after him, and wondered if he, like the boy, had been a victim of Nikias' temper. His next words gave me the answer.

"Don't mind the master. He's a touch grumpy this morning."

"Lack of sleep, I expect," I answered. "It goes with your job sometimes, I imagine."

"Woman trouble." He stopped guiltily, as if he'd said too much. "Or not enough sleep, as you say."

"Don't worry, I can keep secrets. I was in my cousin Jovina's confidence, and she told me about…about somebody she hoped to meet yesterday afternoon at the party. Did he manage to get there all right?"

He nodded. "It's bad enough having to do his work as well as mine while he goes out for hours, but then he comes back in a foul temper and says after all that he couldn't find her. And Fabianus was delirious from his fever, and I'd made him up some medicine, but he said I hadn't done it right. And now of course he's devastated, because the lady was killed." He stopped, looking guilty again, and said in a lower voice, "Don't say I told you, please don't. He doesn't like it known that he leaves me in charge on my own."

"He's lucky to have such a conscientious assistant," I said, just as Nikias came back into the room.

"Come through with me. Mallius is sleeping very lightly now. It won't be long before he's conscious."

He led me to the small room where Mallius was in bed. The guard lounging outside straightened up and saluted as we entered.

He lay on his back, his left wrist bandaged. He was pale and calm, and I could see he was breathing regularly. But there was something odd about the way he was lying. I looked down at him and tried to work out why he looked strange, but I couldn't. It must be because he was unconscious and his limbs were awkwardly stretched out.

As we approached his bed, he turned his head towards us and opened his eyes.

"Could someone fetch me a drink of water please?" His voice was husky, but clear.

"Deputy Commander, you're awake again. That's very good. How are you feeling?"

"Thirsty. And sore. And confused. What are you doing here, Nikias?"

"Two of those problems I can remedy." Nikias went out and returned with a jug of water. He poured a beaker, which Mallius drank straight off. "You ask why I'm here? It's because you're in the fort hospital. You passed out at the party. Then later you had a bad time. Do you remember anything about yesterday evening?"

"Not much."

"Jovina's party," I prompted. "We were all by the river celebrating her birthday."

"Jovina…gods, yes, I remember. They found her dead in the river. And I killed her."

He was sticking to his story then, and there was no doubt he was sober now. "It was all my fault. I'm sorry…so sorry." There were tears in his eyes.

"You told us that," I said. "Then you collapsed. The commander had you brought here to the hospital."

"I remember the news about Jovina, but not much more." He moved restlessly. "Why is my wrist bandaged up? Was there a fight?"

"No," Nikias said. "But something happened after you'd been brought here and put under guard. You really can't recall anything about it?"

"Not a thing, no. Did somebody attack me?"

"I'm afraid you cut your wrist and opened your vein."

"Did I?" He looked down at his wrist, then back at the doctor. "I did this?"

"Yes. You were feeling so wretched about your wife's death, you lost your reason for a while."

"Well, if you say so. It's just so unlikely."

"I'm sorry. But at least we found you in time."

"I've no memory of it, none at all. But my thanks to whoever found me. Was it you?"

"All part of our job, Deputy Commander. So you don't remember anything after you collapsed at the party?"

"Nothing. I can only remember Jovina. Jovina…oh, I'm so sorry. What was I thinking of? How could I have done such a thing?"

I felt anger rising in me. He really had murdered my cousin. But I controlled it, because some instinct told me I could only get him to talk fully about it if I spoke softly.

"Doctor," I said, "I wonder if it might be possible for me to have a few words with Mallius in private? I won't tire him, but I do need to discuss one or two family matters with him. You feel strong enough to answer a few questions, Marcus, don't you? Just one or two things we—er—weren't able to clear up last night."

Just for a heartbeat I fancied there was a flash of understanding in his eyes, then it was gone. "Certainly, Aurelia. Yes, there are one or two things…is that all right, Nikias?"

"Of course. I'll be within call if you need me."

When he'd gone, I said, "Let's not beat about the bush, Marcus. You told us last night that you wanted Jovina dead because you were jealous of her lover. How did you kill her? Some sort of poison in her food, or in her wine?"

"Poison? No, of course not."

"But you said you started before the party, and then had to wait for the outcome, and it happened quicker than you expected. What was it you started?"

"The curse, of course. I put a curse on her."

"The *curse*?" I felt a shock of understanding and relief. I'm not sure whether I believe that curses work at all, but certainly if they do, then they are performed by the gods themselves, not by other mortals. The point was, Mallius believed it and was convinced it had worked.

"There's a small sacred spring about a mile from the fort," he went on, his words tumbling out now that he'd decided to tell me. "A shrine to Taranis, the natives use it, with a deep pool for petitions to the god. They write their curses on pieces of lead and throw them into the water. I hadn't any lead, I wrote on a note-tablet and weighted it down with a stone. I threw it into the pool yesterday on the way to the party. That's why I came on horseback, and alone." He began to sob. "I'm sorry. I'm so sorry…"

I asked, "What was the curse, Mallius? That she'd become ill again and die?"

"To drown her in the river."

"In that case, your curse didn't work."

"Of course it did. I heard them say she was floating in the water. That's when I realised the gods had granted my wish. Only by then I'd stopped wishing it. Oh, Jovina, Jovina…" He cried like a child.

"She wasn't drowned," I said.

"Not drowned? But she was in the water."

"Listen, Marcus, Jovina's dead, but not by drowning. Some-one killed her by hitting her on the head, and then they put her body in the river, hoping it would be carried away downstream. That was an evil deed done by an evil man. But it wasn't because of you."

It took me some time to make him understand what had happened, get him to accept that he wasn't to blame. Then his guilt turned to anger, and he began to rage against whoever had killed Jovina.

"By the gods, Aurelia, I want to know who's done this, and I want him punished. Will you help me?"

"Of course I will. But the important thing now is for you to rest and get your strength back. And, Marcus, if you really want to help us avenge Jovina, there's something you can promise me now."

"Anything. Just tell me."

"Don't get drunk like you were yesterday, or like you were when I first got here. It seems to me you're relying too much on Bacchus and not enough on Mars just now. Will you promise me to try to stay sober? We need you clear-headed and active, not incapable or unconscious. Will you promise…for Jovina's sake?"

"I promise. May the gods be my witness, I promise."

"May they help you, and all of us. Now I'll go and see Trebonius and get you released. Till then, you'll have to stay here. There's a guard outside. Take the chance to rest and recover. I'm sure the doctor will give you some medicine."

"What I'd really like is a bath," he said. "I feel as if I've just come off a battlefield."

"I'm sure that can be arranged." On the little table by the bed was a bronze hand-bell, and I rang it vigorously.

Nikias came in at once. I assumed he'd been waiting close by and had heard everything Mallius had said, so I didn't need to give lengthy explanations. "I'm satisfied that Mallius didn't kill his wife," I said. "There's been a misunderstanding, but it's clear now."

"Really? That's good news. So do I release him then?"

"I'm going to see the commander straight away; better wait till he authorises it. But if you can look after him here for the rest of the day, he'll get back his strength all the quicker."

"I shan't need that long," Mallius said. "I'll do better in my own home, Nikias."

The doctor agreed. He could hardly do anything else. But he wouldn't hear of his patient going to the bath-house, saying firmly that he wasn't strong enough for that, but a wash would be in order.

He went to the door and yelled "Onion!" and the small boy I'd seen before appeared, not crying now but with the beginnings of a bruise showing on his face.

"Get some hot water, boy, and help the deputy commander wash himself."

I left them to it, promising Mallius I'd return later to see how he was progressing. I wasn't particularly happy about leaving him in Nikias' care, because I knew there was no love lost between the two of them, but I'd no alternative, and it wouldn't be for long, just until Chloe and Selena arrived.

Chapter XXII

I made my way to Trebonius' office in the headquarters building, feeling an odd mixture of relief, sadness, and anxiety. I was extremely glad Mallius hadn't killed my cousin, yet sad that he had tried to, in his own fashion. Above all, I was worried because, from what Pythis had said, we were right back at the starting-gate. Nikias had been to the party. He might or might not have seen Jovina there. His bad temper could indeed have been caused by not finding her, but a quarrel with her followed by a murder was even more likely to put him in the worst of moods. And there was still Trebonius…

Fulvina came out of the main door, and I wished her good morning. She gave me a cold and distant reply, but she didn't look at me or slow her pace. She preferred to ignore me, did she? But I wanted the chance of a word with her, so I decided to ignore being ignored, and fell into step beside her. "I'm glad you're recovered, Fulvina. I was sorry when Trebonius said you'd had to leave the party early because you were feeling unwell."

She stopped then, and turned to face me. "I wasn't unwell in the medical sense. I was just sickened by the whole thing."

"The party, you mean?"

"What else? I'd had enough, if you want the truth. It was like some dreadful comedy, and I told my husband I was going home, I'd done my duty for the day. He said he wanted to see how things stood here and in the village, but he couldn't announce that he was leaving before all the guests had gone. He came with me to the gates of the fort, and then I believe he went into the village before returning to the party. By then Eurytus had left, presumably, so the atmosphere would be more civilised." She laughed scornfully. "Really, I don't care how important that man is. He's an oaf and should never have been invited to our party. The way he treated the women…not the servants I mean but the guests! A couple of the officers' young wives had trouble escaping him, until dear little Chloe caught his eye. She's still only a child, and he was all over her, literally."

"I saw. I'm afraid she found it rather flattering."

"She would. Like mother, like daughter. I suppose it's a family trait."

I recognised this as a challenge and decided not to take it up. However formidable this woman was, I needed her on my side.

"Fulvina, I know you and Jovina had your differences. But whatever she did, she's paid for it now. What I want to do is investigate what happened, find out who killed her, and get justice done for her. I've no quarrel with you, and I'd like to feel I can call on you for help if I need to."

She looked at me steadily, then nodded. "I'm sorry, that was uncalled-for. And whatever I thought of your cousin, I never wished her dead. You say you're investigating her death, but I heard her husband killed her?"

"He said last night that he had, but it was the wine talking. Today he's sobered up and come to his senses, and knows that he wasn't responsible. I'm on my way to tell your husband now. We're still looking for the murderer."

"I see. I hope you catch him soon. I don't like the idea of a killer at large. And yes, you may call on me for help, if you feel there's anything I can do."

She went on her way, leaving me wondering how long Trebonius had been away from the party altogether, and whether his absence coincided with the time, just before the rainstorm, when my cousin was killed. Fulvina had given him an alibi of sorts, but not a very useful one, unless we could tie up the times more precisely.

I had to wait a while before the commander was free, which was hardly surprising in view of the alert. But at least when I eventually saw him he made no trouble about releasing Mallius, once I'd explained that his confession was the result of a misunderstanding and too much wine.

"That's excellent. I'll authorise his release straight away." He called in a secretary and dictated a brief note to Nikias, ordering him to treat Mallius as an injured officer and no longer as a prisoner.

"I must say it's a relief," he said to me. "You were right to persevere with him. I'd hate to think he could have been convicted of a murder because we hadn't fully understood what he meant. And that's one more man back on the strength."

"I doubt he'll be fit for much today. The doctor's keeping him in bed."

"I don't mean Mallius. He'll need time to recover. I mean the guard I left watching him. We're holding down the natives by force of numbers, and I need every single man who's fit to fight. Even so, if any Brigantes come from outside Isurium I can't guarantee to hold the village for long. I've sent out for reinforcements, so let's hope there isn't some sort of general native rising that affects other forts as well."

"Ah, so that's why Philippus went off so early," I said. "I hope he'll be back soon. I'm sure it will comfort Mallius to see him."

"Philippus? He hasn't gone anywhere that I know of. He's in the fort somewhere."

"The gate-guard says he left at dawn for Cataractonium."

Trebonius swore and then apologised, but I smiled and assured him that, having a centurion for a father, I wasn't easily shocked. "I'm puzzled though," I added. "I wonder where Philippus has gone?"

The commander frowned. "Really, that boy! Sometimes I think it must be his fault that his father's taken to drink. When am I ever going to teach him army discipline?"

"A bit of a rascal, is he?"

"That's putting it mildly. A bit of a troublemaker, more likely, with his gambling and fighting…I ought to have thrown him out of this unit months ago. But he's one of our best fighters, and especially good at scouting, keeping under cover and observing from a distance. Perhaps that's what he's doing now, reconnoitring the situation in the village. If not, I don't know where he is or when he'll be back. Your guess is as good as mine." He stood up, indicating our meeting was over. "Well, thank you for bringing me one piece of good news. I haven't a homicidal deputy commander to deal with, on top of everything else."

On my way back to our little office I saw Congrio, walking slowly and dejectedly towards the stables. "You don't look very happy, Congrio."

"I've just heard the news about Eurytus being killed. And bad news it is for me, I must say."

"Really? I hadn't pictured you as an admirer of Lord Eurytus. Or did you see him as a potential customer?"

He laughed. "You're right on both counts. But nobody's allowed out of the fort today without express leave from the commander, and he's so busy he won't even see me. Just sent a message that I'm to stay within the walls or I'll be arrested."

"That must be annoying for you. I don't blame you for wanting to leave us, with everything that's going on."

"I've sold all my cloaks now, and most of the cloths and mats. It's been a good trip for me, and I need to get more stock. I've a warehouse at Eburacum, with more supplies coming up the river all the time. Only now I'm stuck here for at least a day, maybe longer. I'd be safe enough on the road. I've got good bodyguards and I've no quarrel with the native Britons—they respect traders. But the commander says it's too dangerous." He grumbled on for a while, but I'd a question I wanted to ask, so I waited patiently till there was a pause.

"You've sold all those cloaks! Well done. That means practically every soldier in the fort must have bought one."

"Just about." He smiled proudly. "I suppose I shouldn't feel too badly about the unrest among the natives. The arson in the village has made everyone a bit jumpy about fires."

"The doctor was very pleased with his."

"He bought one for his assistant Pythis…his nephew, I think he said. I got the impression they were pleased to meet a fellow Greek. Trebonius and his wife each bought one, and three of the tribunes, and Philippus of course, and even a couple of the locals. Their leader Brennus, the one who was at the party yesterday, got a couple more for his sons." He grinned. "Pity I'm not allowed to sell my knives here, but the commander's absolutely forbidden it. Still, you can't win every race, can you?"

"Knives? I didn't realise you sold anything that wasn't made out of Vulcan's Shield."

"I always carry a few small items, and I got a couple of dozen very fine knives while I was in Eburacum, from a friend of mine who trades in the market. I had to promise him not to sell them there. He didn't want the competition, but I reckoned they'd go well in the fort here. They would have done too, but Trebonius says he doesn't want any offensive weapons sold to the troops just now, there's enough brawling without making it any easier for them. Can you believe it?"

I had to laugh. "No, I can't, Congrio. He's got a fort full of soldiers, trained to kill and equipped with the best Roman weapons…and he's worried about a few knives?"

He laughed too. "So he says. Pity, because they're nicely made, decent sharp blades and good wood handles with silver inlay."

"Silver inlay? That's unusual." I remembered Quintus had said that Eurytus was killed by a knife with a silver handle. It couldn't be one of Congrio's…or could it?

He shrugged. "But I don't want bad feeling with the army, so I'm doing what I'm told, and I haven't sold a single one. I did give one away to young Philippus, as a thank-you for helping me sell the cloaks. It was when he bought one that all the others started to take an interest. He doesn't live here, so I can't see the harm."

I can, I thought, given Philippus' liking for brawling. Still, it was done now.

Congrio must have sensed my disapproval, and mistaken it for envy. "Perhaps you'd like one yourself, Aurelia? You did me a good turn the other night introducing me to Philippus. So I'll be delighted if you'll take one with my compliments."

"Thank you, that's really kind of you. I'd like one very much. Could you drop it into our little office? I'll be in and out of there all day."

"Of course, as soon as I can." He broke off and turned towards the main gate. "There, look, more people coming inside for shelter."

Several carriages were rumbling in, accompanied by a couple of dozen servants on foot, and four mounted men. I recognised the riders as Lucius, Titch, and the soldiers they'd taken as escort. The carriages must contain Mallius' household. I watched as they pulled up some distance inside the gate and disgorged old Statius and his two servants, and a dozen or so of Mallius and Jovina's slaves, mostly women and children. Selena was among them, but neither Chloe nor Vitellia were, and I couldn't see Baca either.

I ran across to Lucius. "Is everything all right? Why aren't the girls with you?"

"Nothing's all right." He pulled a note from his belt-pouch and thrust it at me. "It's addressed to you, but I've read it. Titch, could you report what's happened to the commander, please. Get more men to help search. Then we'll go straight back and look for them."

"Look for them? What do you mean?"

"Read it," Lucius snapped, and I opened the note-tablet. To my surprise I found it was from Baca, in childlike writing and badly spelt, but that couldn't disguise the appalling message.

Mistress Aurelia from Baca.
I'm sorry. Miss V and Miss C are going to the river. They won't say why, to meet boys, I think. I can't stop them so am going too. I don't like it.

I didn't like it either. Quite apart from the danger they were putting themselves in, it was completely the wrong way to behave, going off to secret meetings so soon after Jovina's death.

"The stupid, stupid children…Lucius, what can I say? I'm so sorry. I never thought of them doing anything like this."

"No." He jumped from his horse and came to stand close to me, speaking quietly. "Chloe's presumably at the bottom of this?"

"Yes. She's been sneaking off regularly to meet a soldier she thinks she's in love with, a lad called Gambax. But he won't be going to any secret rendezvous today. He's helping our investigations and he's with Quintus now at Brennus' house."

"The note mentions 'boys', more than one. Who else would they be going to meet, do you know?"

"Philippus, I expect. He's been…" I almost said "flirting" but stopped just in time. "He's been looking after Vitellia while I've been with Jovina. Which is good of him," I added with a sudden inspiration, "considering she never stops talking to him about you."

"Philippus? But Titch told me he's the killer who came to the mansio."

"He is, but that's a different matter, quite separate from this. Vitellia's in no danger from him because she doesn't know anything about our investigations. Her innocence will protect her. And anyway he won't get to the assignation either. He's ridden off to Cataractonium this morning."

"This gets worse and worse. It's bad enough the two silly girls having gone out on their own, but now when they get to the river they'll find nobody waiting for them, nobody to look after them. And the whole area seething with hostile natives!"

"They'll come back when they realise nobody is going to turn up." I was trying to reassure myself as well as my brother. "Back to the house, or probably straight here. They'll realise being out in the open isn't a good idea, what with Eurytus' death…"

"They won't know about Eurytus' death," Lucius retorted.

That took the wind from my sail. They were a pair of thoughtless little girls, off on what they believed was an amusing secret outing and probably feeling very daring, but with no real idea of the danger all around them.

"Gods," Lucius said softly, almost to himself, "I can't help thinking maybe I could have prevented Eurytus' death if I hadn't been sent away up to Morbium. Guarding him should have been my job."

I opened my mouth to throw back the remark he'd flung at me, about not being much help to the person I was supposed to be guarding. But I didn't say it. Instead I said, "There are some things that can't be helped, brother, however hard we try. Jovina and Eurytus are dead, and we each feel responsible. But it's the people who did the killing that are truly responsible. All we can do is make sure justice catches up with them."

He nodded, then looked me in the eyes, and I felt an understanding pass between us, the way it used to when we were children and each knew what the other was thinking.

"I'm sorry I shouted at you, Sis."

"And I'm sorry Vitellia is in trouble now. I hadn't foreseen anything like this."

"I know." He reached out and briefly touched my hand. "Friends again?"

"Of course. We need one another, and Quintus needs both of us."

I looked round as Titch came riding up. He didn't say anything, but from the way he dismounted I could tell he was very angry.

"I need to talk to you in the office, Lucius," he said.

"Can't it wait? You can tell me on the way."

"No, it can't, and Aurelia needs to hear it too. Now, please."

Titch wasn't usually so brusque, or so incandescent. Lucius and I followed him to our little office and closed the door.

"That Trebonius…" Titch let loose a torrent of curses. "He'll get this fort destroyed, and all of us along with it. D'you know what he's doing? He's assuming Eurytus was killed by Brigantians, which is fair enough. He thinks Brennus probably knows who's done it. Again, fair enough. So he's sending out men to take twenty Brigantians hostage. When the killer is handed over, they'll be set free."

Lucius said, "That's not such a bad idea."

"Wait, I've not done yet. If the killer isn't handed over, Trebonius will execute two hostages a day until, as he says, they come to their senses."

"*What?*" Lucius almost shouted.

"Once the hostages are rounded up, he'll send out messengers to announce the news to Brennus and the other leaders, and make a proclamation in the forum. If nobody's given any useful information by tomorrow, the first two will die at dawn."

"And then the whole village will erupt," Lucius growled. "What does the fool think he's doing?"

"What about the Fall of Troy?" I said. "If we've read Terentius' message right, there are plans for an attack on the fort today, as well as on Eurytus himself. So the conspirators will be prepared anyway, probably raring to go. We might just have stopped them by patrolling every street. But once Trebonius begins killing natives…"

"Didn't you tell him Quintus is still in the village? And Vitellia and Chloe could be anywhere?"

"Of course I did. But he wouldn't change his mind, and he's the commander, when all's said and done, I couldn't force him."

"So we've got till tonight to bring everyone in." Lucius glanced up at the sun. "It's not long to noon, so let's get started. How many men did he give us for escort?"

"None."

Now it was Lucius' turn to swear. "But we've still got the two who came with us to Jovina's house, I suppose?"

"No, they've already been ordered out on patrol."

"Then we must join forces with Quintus and search together. We'll go to Brennus' house first, warn him what's about to happen, and then all go out to look for the girls."

Titch nodded. "Aye, that's the only option we've got really. Gambax is there with Quintus and a couple of soldiers. We can take them with us to the river, find the girls, and bring them in. We should be strong enough."

"We'd better be."

"I'll come too," I suggested. "I can ride, and…"

"No!" they said in unison.

"But this is urgent. I want to help."

"And if you stay here, you will be helping," Lucius said. "No, don't look like that, I'm not fobbing you off with something unimportant, quite the reverse. You're our contact point. We'll probably have to split up, but if we can get messages back here, or send here for information, you'll know what's going on, and be able to keep the whole group informed."

There was sense in that. "And I can keep an eye on what the garrison is doing, and I hope, get advance warning of what they're planning."

"Good. We'll see you later then."

I wasn't happy to be left behind. Still, at least Lucius and I were friends once more, and as long as they reached Quintus in time he'd be safe. But what about Chloe and Vitellia, and Baca? The silly girls were exposing themselves to real danger, and maybe leading the men who searched for them into danger as well. I thanked the gods for Baca's quick thinking in leaving me a note and sent a prayer to Diana asking her to look after the runaways until help could get to them.

I went back to the office to wait, and to think over what I'd learnt from the conversations I'd had at the fort today, and last night. Now that we'd discounted Mallius' foolish confession, it seemed clear that Jovina's killer was either her former lover or her current one, either Nikias or Trebonius. But which?

Both men had reasons for wanting her dead. Both men could have persuaded Jovina to meet them in secret by sending her a message. Both men had been missing for a while yesterday, out of the public view while the party was happening. Both men had been seen alone by the river, as if waiting for someone. That someone must surely have been Jovina. And then there was the brief snatch of a quarrel that Gambax and Chloe had overheard. The words Jovina had used could have been addressed to either man. "No, I won't. I can't. You know I can't give you up, I love you. Then why are you tearing me in two? If you really loved me, you wouldn't put me through this. No, talk all you like but I shan't change my mind." She could have been pleading with Nikias to resume their previous relationship, but at Isurium, not in some faraway place. Or she could equally well have been appealing to Trebonius not to finish with her, but to continue the affair they'd only just started.

A knock at the door made me jump. I looked round nervously, then pulled myself together. "Come in."

Selena opened the door and stood hesitating on the threshold. "They said I'd find you here."

"What can I do for you?"

She stepped in cautiously, and I could see how uneasy she was. She perched uncomfortably on the very edge of a stool, nervously fidgeting with a fold of her tunic, not meeting my gaze. And she should be uneasy, I thought. Much as I liked her I couldn't help feeling angry with her. She shouldn't have let Chloe and Vitellia go out unsupervised from the house on a day like this. How could she have been so careless?

The silence lengthened. Eventually she said, "I'm sorry, Mistress. I'm so sorry. They were too crafty for me."

"Chloe and Vitellia, you mean?"

"Yes. They must have planned and schemed and worked out how to leave the house without me knowing."

"You'd no idea what Chloe intended? I assume Chloe's responsible really, and Vitellia…well, she's easily led."

"Yes, I'd say so." She sighed. "There was some wild talk last night, Miss Chloe saying she wanted to run away because now my lady isn't there, the master will make her marry Statius. I didn't take it seriously—you know how she likes to make a drama out of everything. But I didn't foresee anything like this."

Her words, the very same ones I'd spoken to Lucius, dispelled my anger. This poor woman was as shocked and upset by the girls' disappearance as I was. And like me, she felt guilty.

"None of us foresaw it, Selena. You mustn't blame yourself. All we can do is try to put it right. First tell me all you can about what happened after we left this morning. The girls were still in the house then, presumably…or at least Baca was, and she said they were in bed."

"When it began to get light, they were certainly in bed. I looked in on them and they were asleep. Or that's what I thought. Baca suggested I should get some rest—she could manage for a while. I was bone-tired—we'd been up all night—so I was glad to. I thought once it was day; we could relax a bit. I went to my room and slept for a couple of hours. The rest did me good."

"You woke up after we three had had breakfast and left for the fort?"

She nodded. "About an hour after you went, I'd say. Baca wasn't about, and I knew she wouldn't have gone to sleep, so I thought she must be in the girls' room and went to see. That's when I realised they'd gone. I found the note Baca left for you, but I didn't like to read it. I sent a couple of the lads to the fort to fetch Master Philippus, but they found he'd left already. I didn't know what was best to do. I wondered if I ought to go out and look for them myself, but then I thought, perhaps they'd just gone for a short while and would come back again soon, and I ought to be there if they did. I knew we were all supposed to be going to stay at the fort. Lord Statius went into the village to see what he could find out…"

"Statius? By himself?"

"With his two men, of course. I thought he was foolish but he insisted, and he wasn't gone long. He didn't find any trace of them, or anyone who'd seen them. I was really worried by then. I was so relieved when your brother arrived to take charge."

"I don't think Baca was involved in planning how to get away." I told her about the note. "I trust her. I believe she really thinks she's doing the best thing, going with them, though the gods know three girls are no safer than two as things are. Anyhow, we'll know for sure when we find them."

She looked up at me. "You truly believe we'll find them?"

"I do. My brother and Victor are already out searching."

"I pray you're right. This family's in more than enough trouble. The mistress dead, the master saying he killed her, Miss

Chloe swearing she'll run away. As for Master Philippus, I don't know what's to become of him now my lady isn't here."

"There's one bit of news that might comfort you." I told her about what Mallius had said this morning, and how he was now a free man, though a sick one.

"That's a relief, at least. We were right, you and I. We said he hadn't killed her." She smiled at me. "Now all we've got to do is find the bastard who did."

"From what you told me last night, I think we may have found him," I said. "But proving it, that's something else entirely."

"I'm sure if anyone can do it, you can." She rose to go.

"One more thing. What made you say that you don't know what will become of Philippus now his mother is dead?"

"Nothing really. Only that he'll be sad. He loved his mother."

"Selena, I thought we'd agreed you must tell me everything, and I know there's more to it than that. Jovina was worried about him, wasn't she? She told me about finding a bronze brooch with VVV on it among his things, and being anxious because he was spending more than he could possibly be earning."

She sat down again and nodded. "He gambles far too much. Sometimes he wins, but more often he loses. My lady had to pay off his debts more than once."

"Did he get money from anyone else? His father, for instance?"

"Never. He was too proud to ask, and anyhow his father would never have given him anything."

"Then how did he manage? My cousin told me she was afraid he was taking payment from the Brigantians. Was he involved with this silly VVV business?"

"No, at least not the way you mean. He's no traitor, Master Philippus. But he's always trying to make a few extra sestertii any way he can. When Terentius was here, it was even worse—they used to encourage each other to spend money like senators. I'm pretty sure they had some minor rackets on the go, disposing of surplus army stores from Cataractonium, selling them to traders

and no questions asked, that sort of thing. He's in charge of the
tannery there now."

"I know. Some sort of punishment, I understand. What had
he done to deserve a demotion like that?"

"Word got around that he and Terentius had a fight. They
quarrelled over money, so the story went, but I don't know the
details, and of course it was meant to be secret. But you can't
keep secrets for long in a fort. The commander didn't want to
dismiss either of them. They're good soldiers, and both Roman
citizens, which is more than most of the men are. So he sent
Terentius down to Londinium for three months, and Philippus was posted to Cataractonium. He made a great fuss about
not wanting to be there, but I don't suppose it's very hard for
the officer in charge of a place like that to sell a few raw hides
privately, even some tanned leather."

"It'd be fairly unusual if there was no stealing at all," I agreed.
"But making enough money out of it to pay for serious gambling…that's a different matter."

"You think he was up to something else as well? It could be
so. But you know, Mistress, really I can't believe he'd do anything
too terrible. He was a loving son to my lady, and he's good with
his children, even though their mother's only a village girl."

"That's as maybe." I couldn't think what else to say. Selena
was right. It was hard to keep secrets long in a fort, but there was
one big secret which Philippus had managed to keep from his
mother, and it was a great deal more serious than petty thieving
at a tannery.

Fortunately the sound of hoof-beats outside provided a
distraction.

"Maybe someone has news of the girls," I said, and we got
up and went outside to see.

Lucius and Titch were dismounting, looking tired and dishevelled. A few paces behind them came the two soldiers that had
escorted them, one riding and the other marching, leading his
horse, which had a body tied across its saddle, looking patheti-
cally vulnerable in spite of its rich tunic and golden sandals.

I hurried over to them, Selena beside me. "I'm glad you're safely back. But where are Quintus and Gambax?" I glanced at the body on the horse. "Eurytus, presumably?"

"Yes," Lucius answered. "We couldn't leave him at Brennus' house for the mob. We were only just in time getting there. Half the village were gathering outside it, yelling and chanting, working up the courage to go in, and I don't think Quintus and the others could have stopped them. They backed off when they saw us."

"But where's Quintus now? And Gambax? Why haven't they come back with you?"

"I showed them Baca's note about the girls. Gambax got very excited, said he thought he knew where they'd have gone. There's a special place by the river, quite near Jovina's house, a little hut where he and Chloe used to meet sometimes. He insisted on going to look, and Quintus couldn't let him go by himself, so he went as well. They sent us back with Eurytus, and then we're to follow them. Gambax gave us directions."

"But that's madness, Lucius! Why didn't you stop him and make him come back here with you, and then you could all have gone out to the river together? They shouldn't be taking risks like that. Why didn't you insist?"

"Insist?" Lucius growled. "When was the last time you managed to persuade Quintus not to do something he'd set his heart on, however mad it was?"

"All the same…"

"And he has a point," Titch put in. "Time's running out. The patrols that are in the village now can't hold things together much longer. The commander'll have to send out more men still, or else call everyone back in and bar the gates. We want the girls back in here by then. If it's possible, Quintus can do it."

"And if it isn't possible? If it's too late already?"

Nobody answered. Beside me Selena gave a low moan and began to cry. "The gods help them, the poor children," she muttered, and walked away.

I echoed her prayer, adding, "The gods help us all."

Chapter XXIII

Lucius broke the silence. "Time's short, so let's get moving. I'll go and report to the commander. Titch, can you find somewhere suitable to leave Eurytus' body for now? Then go and get some fresh horses, preferably solid old nags that won't be spooked by crowds or fire. Aurelia, could you organise some bread and a skin of wine? We'll take it with us, we may be out for some time."

"I will. But can't you eat here? Then you can tell me the details of what's happened."

He shook his head. "Titch is right. Time's short. We'll tell you everything when we get back. By the way, has anything happened here?"

"No arrests yet, but I've one or two useful bits of information."

"Good. Then the quicker we set off, the quicker we'll be back to hear them."

I found them some food and went to watch from the gate as they rode away. I was thankful they had with them the same two soldiers who'd been their escort earlier. But they were only four men, venturing out into a hostile village full of angry tribesmen. I was frightened for them, and for Quintus and Gambax, and especially the girls. Three girls on their own, even if they were outside the village itself…it didn't bear thinking about.

I went to our office, thinking I'd better eat some food, as breakfast seemed a very long time ago. It was simple army fare, flat-bread and sausage with slices of onion, and rough red wine to wash it down. I didn't mind that, but when it came to it, I found I wasn't hungry—I was too worried.

I gave myself a mental shake. Worrying would do no good, and I had work to get on with. I pushed the plate aside and decided I'd pay yet another visit to the hospital.

There came a timid tap at the door. I called "come in" automatically, and then wished I had some sort of weapon to hand. Too late. I stood up and moved to stand with my back against a wall.

I felt foolish when the door opened slowly, and a small boy came in, looking nervously round. He was the slave I'd seen at the hospital, the one Nikias had been chastising. Apart from recognising his chubby features, I couldn't miss the bruise on his cheek.

"Come in, boy. What can I do for you?"

He gazed at me silently. I realised he was frightened, and wondered whether he'd had another beating, or whether he expected one from me. Perhaps he was bringing me bad news, or maybe he regarded all adults as potential bullies.

I said gently, "You're from the hospital, aren't you? The lad they call Onion. I saw you there this morning."

He nodded but was still silent. I noticed he was shivering slightly. I wanted to put him at ease, partly because I felt sorry for him and partly for a less unselfish reason. It occurred to me that a youngster might be a good source of information about life at the hospital, especially one like this who was being bullied by his master.

"Have you brought me a message from Mallius?"

"Yes, Mistress. He says to let you know he's about to move into his own quarters this afternoon and he asks if you'll go and visit him there. He wants to talk about a family matter, he says."

"Good. Tell him I'll come and see him very soon."

"I will." He rubbed his bruised face, and as he raised his arm I noticed a red whip-mark across his wrist.

"Thanks, Onion. You know, I've never met anyone called Onion before, it's an unusual name. How did you come by it?"

"It's what I've always been called. My mother used to belong to a wine-shop, and I helped in the kitchen. Then she died and the owner sold me to the doctor here, and the name had sort of stuck by then. And I do like the taste of them." I saw his eyes flick briefly to the table, which held my uneaten snack of bread, sausage, and onion.

"Are you hungry? They've sent me a whole lot of bread and sausage, and I can't eat it all. Would you like some?"

His face lit up. "Yes please. Only my master might be cross."

"Then we shan't tell him. Help yourself to the onion, Onion."

He grinned, and demolished the food as if he hadn't eaten for days. "Thank you, Mistress. I got no breakfast today. My master said I didn't deserve any."

"Oh, dear. Why was that?"

"He said I went to sleep when I should have been watching last night. But I didn't. I was awake all the time. And it was me that found the deputy commander after he cut his wrist."

This was exactly the sort of inside knowledge I'd been hoping for. "It's a good thing you did, otherwise he might not have recovered. How's he doing now? I saw him this morning when he'd just woken up, and I was thinking of looking in again soon."

"He says he's feeling better, but I think he's going to be poorly for a while. I helped him to wash himself this morning, and he was very clumsy, we both got a splashing from his bowl. He kept complaining how difficult it was, saying he felt awkward doing things with the wrong hand."

The wrong hand... It was like a flash of lightning, making everything suddenly clear. Of course! Mallius was left-handed. I should have known. Indeed I must have known it years ago, and simply forgotten. No wonder I'd had an uneasy feeling that somehow he looked wrong as he lay in bed. A left-handed man who wanted to open a vein would have cut his right wrist, not his left one.

I wondered if the boy realised what he was saying? Apparently not, because he was still chattering on about having to change his wet tunic when he'd finished helping Mallius. But something in my face made him stop and his scared look returned.

"It'll soon dry," he said, meaning the tunic presumably. "And at least there was no blood on it. The master gets furious when I mess my tunic up with blood." He trailed off again.

I gave him a reassuring smile. "It'll be all right; I'm sure it will. Now then, Onion, can you keep a secret?"

He nodded. "Yes, if it's something I mustn't tell the master. I'm quite good at those sort of secrets, otherwise I'd be black and blue." He touched the bruise on his cheek.

"This is a secret you mustn't tell anyone. I want you to promise."

"All right, I promise."

"You've discovered something important. The deputy commander is left-handed, that's why he was so clumsy with the other hand."

"Of course, that must be it! He never said it in so many words. I didn't realise. So his right hand was his wrong hand, wasn't it?" He smiled, and I saw that there was a cheeky little scamp lurking somewhere beneath the outwardly timid slave. The lad wasn't cowed yet.

But I had to make him see the danger he was in. "That's a good way of putting it. You see what it means, don't you? It means he didn't try to kill himself. If he had, he'd have used his left hand to cut his right wrist."

"Then if he didn't cut his wrist, who did?"

"I don't know yet. But I mean to find out. Will you help me?"

"Yes, if I can. But I don't know anything important, really."

"You've already proved that you do. Have you told any of this to your master, or Pythis?"

He shook his head. "They get annoyed if I criticise the patients. Though some of them are…well, I'd better not say. But the master was in and out among the patients most of the morning. I suppose he could have seen for himself what a struggle Lord Mallius was having. He's getting better now anyhow, so I don't suppose it matters."

"It matters very much. I want to find out who tried to kill him. It was an evil thing to do, don't you think?"

"Well…they say he killed someone himself, so perhaps he deserved it."

"He didn't kill anyone. I can promise you that. So he didn't deserve to be killed."

"Then it was evil. Do you think I should tell my master?"

"No. As I said, it's got to be a secret. Remember, you've promised me you won't tell anyone else. When the time comes, I'll tell everyone, but not yet. Do you see why?"

He looked puzzled, then slowly realisation dawned. "You think the master will be angry with me if he thinks somebody has sneaked in from outside and tried to kill the deputy commander, and I didn't notice?"

"Quite right." That seemed a less alarming reason than the true one, and it should convince the boy to keep quiet. "You don't want to make him angry, do you?"

"No. I understand. I'll keep the secret."

"Just for now, till we've found out what really happened to Mallius. I'd like you to tell me as much as you can about last night. Were you the only one on watch?"

"I was the main one," he said proudly. "My master slept on a bed in the waiting-room, and I had to rouse him if anything happened. It should have been Pythis really, but the master said he'd take the watch, because the deputy commander was one of our patients."

"If you stayed awake all the time, you'll have seen most of what went on, I expect."

"I wasn't watching by Lord Mallius' bedside. I was in the store-room most of the time, cleaning the master's instruments, sharpening some of them, rolling bandages, that sort of thing."

I grinned. "You get all the glamorous jobs, don't you?"

His smile returned briefly. "Oh, yes. But store-room work is better than emptying slop-buckets. That's the absolute bottom of the glamorous list." Then he was serious again. "The small rooms where the patients sleep are all along one corridor. The store-room's at one end of the passage, so if you're working in there you can see all the way down it from inside."

"And each small room has a curtain in front of it instead of a door. That must make it quicker for the doctors to get from one patient to another."

"Quicker and quieter, with no doors slamming. Actually it's one big room split into three, with screens dividing one patient from the next."

That made me stop and think. "So a doctor, or anyone, could go from one room to another by moving one of the screens aside, not going out into the corridor and in again?"

"They could, but they don't. Quite often they're carrying things, trays of instruments or bowls of water. It's easier to go through the curtains."

"And there were just two patients last night, Fabianus and Mallius?"

He nodded. "And some in the big fever ward, but one of the other boys did that watch."

"Then we'll concentrate on the three small rooms in the corridor. From the store-room you could see if anyone went in or out?"

"Yes, and hear what was going on in them. That's what I was really there for, to answer if anyone called out, and fetch the master."

"And did anyone call out?"

"Fabianus did. He's the man who got wounded on patrol. He was restless with his fever, and started shouting and trying to get out of bed. I fetched the master to him, and he stayed by his bedside for ages."

"Did Mallius call out?"

"No. The only sound from his room was from the people who visited him. They spoke to him a bit, and the master tried to rouse him of course, but he didn't answer any of them."

"If he didn't call out, what made you go into his room?"

"It was when the daylight came. My master had told me I could go to bed at sunrise. So I wanted to get permission to leave, but I knew he'd ask me whether I'd checked that the patients were all right before I went to bed; he always does. So I went into Fabianus' room and he was sound asleep at last, and then into the deputy commander's. There was blood everywhere, and his wrist was all slit open. I fetched the master and he was furious. He said I should have realised Lord Mallius was trying to cut his wrist. But I didn't hear a thing."

"You said people came to see Mallius. Who were they? Did any outsiders come in?"

"I don't think so. There was the commander of course, he came just before the moon rose, but he's not an outsider. And the deputy commander's son, Philippus, I think they call him, but he's not an outsider either."

"Maybe 'outsider' is the wrong word. I mean anyone who wouldn't normally have been in the hospital at night-time. Trebonius, Philippus…anyone else?"

"Oh, I see. I don't think so. There was a guard in the waiting area. He might know for sure."

I said gently, "Then *you* don't know for sure? Is it possible, just possible, you fell asleep for a little while?"

"Well…I did get very sleepy. But it wouldn't have been for long, only a few heartbeats." He looked frightened. "You won't say anything to my master?"

"I won't breathe a word. You've been such a help to me, the last thing I want is to get you into trouble."

"Have I? I'm glad. Now I'd best be getting back, or he'll be grumbling."

"And not a word about this conversation to anyone, all right?" I tossed him a copper coin.

From his joyful reaction, it could have been a gold piece. "Thank you, Mistress. That's the first money I've ever owned."

"Take care of it then. Off you go."

I sat for a while pondering what he'd said. Two people had visited Mallius in the hospital during the night. Could either of them have tried to kill him? I thought I could rule out Philippus, not so much because of his filial loyalty, which was dubious where Mallius was concerned, but because he of all people would be bound to know his father was left-handed. If he'd planned to fake Mallius' suicide he'd have done it properly. Besides, I really didn't believe he had killed his mother, and I felt very strongly that Jovina's death and Mallius' near-death were linked.

But Trebonius…that was a different box of beetles altogether. He was definitely under suspicion of killing Jovina. He'd been seen in the woods alone at the party, he'd been missing from the party field for a substantial time when he claimed to be taking Fulvina home. And he had a motive, or rather a choice of two: either he wanted to be Jovina's lover and she refused him, or, more likely in my opinion, she desperately wanted an affair with him but he didn't.

And if I was wrong in concluding the murder and the attempted murder were committed by the same person, Trebonius had yet another reason for wanting Mallius dead: to avenge Jovina, after he'd heard Mallius confess to killing her. Making it appear as a suicide was a clever way to leave himself completely clear of suspicion. Add to all that the fact that Trebonius and Mallius had been rivals over many years. Perhaps Trebonius had been biding his time till he could dispose of a troublesome enemy, and had seized the chance with both hands.

It looked an overwhelming case. And yet it failed to convince me completely. Right from the start of this investigation there'd been two runners in the field, the doctor and the commander. The doctor was still in the running, it seemed to me. Pythis had told me he'd been to the party field, and Jovina herself had talked about the possibility of renewing their love affair. And then there were the pieces of broken glass in the grass where her body had been found. Had she taken his beautiful present so they could drink together at their secret tryst…and had he smashed it in a fit of temper?

We'd already found two powerful motives that could have induced him to kill Jovina: discovering about his unborn baby, or becoming enraged because she wouldn't run away with him. And the same logic applied with him as with Trebonius: if he hadn't killed Jovina and believed that Mallius had, there was an additional motive. And there was one more thing to bear in mind. Of all the people in the hospital last night, he was the one with most opportunity to arrange Mallius' "suicide," especially since he'd insisted on remaining on night duty even though it wasn't his turn.

If it hadn't been for little Onion's finding Mallius in time, one of those two would have got away with murder.

Chapter XXIV

I strolled over to the main gate with the excuse of checking whether Lucius or Quintus, or anyone at all, had sent me a message. They hadn't, but to be honest my main reason was the need to be outdoors. All this talk of the hospital at night, with somebody creeping about bent on murder, left me feeling anxious not to be cooped up in the office and in need of an outdoor breeze and some ordinary, friendly sunshine. I was unlucky there, because the sky had clouded over and a blustery wind blew, but it did at least provide fresh air.

Centurion Ennius was still in command at the gate. I asked him how things were going.

"All according to plan, Aurelia," he said with an over-hearty smile. "Don't worry, we have everything under control." That's the standard answer that officers always produce to reassure civilians, which it usually doesn't.

"Jolly good," I answered. His meaningless reassurance deserved an equally meaningless response.

But then came something more interesting. "The hostages are all safely under guard now. They tried to get that native leader Brennus, but he's vanished. Picked up one of his sons though. The commander reckons the natives will soon come to their senses."

It's Trebonius who needs to come to his senses, I thought, and set off to visit Mallius.

The deputy commander's house was considered large by the standards of the fort, but seemed small by comparison with civilian accommodation. Outside it stood a huge soldier with muscles on his muscles and an unwelcoming expression. He eyed me suspiciously and grunted, "The commander's resting. He ain't seeing nobody."

I debated correcting his bad grammar, but decided against. "He'll see me, because he sent a message asking me to come. I'm his wife's cousin, Aurelia Marcella."

He turned and hammered on the door, which was opened by another man, even larger and surlier.

"Here, Ajax," the outdoor guard said. "This woman says the deputy commander wants to see her. I doubt it myself, she ain't his type. But go and ask him, will you?"

"All right." He shut the door, leaving us outside, but was back very soon, and addressed me with what, for him, must pass for politeness. "He's expecting a Mistress Aurelia Marcella. You got any identification? Can't be too careful, the way things are."

"Identification? Don't be ridiculous. Show me in at once. If Mallius doesn't recognise me you can show me out again."

"Well, I suppose so. Come along o' me then."

He led me into the main room, where Mallius himself reclined on a reading-couch. I was pleasantly surprised by his appearance. His wrist was still bandaged, but he wore a clean tunic and was freshly shaved. And he wasn't drunk. The room was neat and clean too. I wasn't surprised, though, to see that the table beside him held a wine-jug and beakers.

"Aurelia, come in and sit down." He glanced at the guard. "Thanks, Ajax, I'll call you if I need you. While Mistress Aurelia's here I don't want to be disturbed by anyone. Understand?"

"Sir." He saluted and left.

"What's all the security for?" I asked him. "You're completely free again now, aren't you? That's what Trebonius told me."

"Oh yes, quite free. And I know I owe that to you. You stood by me and wouldn't take my silly rant of last night seriously. So thank you."

I felt embarrassed, and could only come up with the inadequate reply, "You're welcome."

"I'll explain everything properly. First let me pour you some wine." He filled a mug slightly awkwardly with his right hand, and I took it from him and sat down on a stool near his couch. He raised his beaker to me. "To your health, Aurelia."

"And to yours, Marcus. I must say you're looking better than you did this morning. How are you feeling now?"

"Not too bad. My wrist is sore, and I've a thumping headache, which I know I could cure with plenty of wine, but I want to keep my wits about me, so I'm not going to drink much."

"Good. I mean good that you're not drinking much. I'm surprised to see you here, actually. I thought you'd take the chance to rest in the hospital, at least for today."

He began to shake his head, and winced with the pain. "I wanted to be out of the place. It scared me, I'll tell you that for nothing. Gods, I'm glad you're here, Aurelia. Someone I can talk to. Someone I can trust." He stopped and looked at me keenly. "I can trust you, can't I? I want your help, and I'd like your friendship, too."

I honestly didn't know how to answer. After the way he'd treated Jovina during the past few months, could he really expect me to be his friend ever again? And if he did, was I prepared to be?

"I'll help get justice for Jovina," I said. "You didn't kill her, and I'll find out who did. You can trust me for that."

"Thank you. No, I didn't kill her, although I didn't treat her well these last few months. I'm as anxious as you are to avenge her." He took a small sip of wine. "I think I know who did murder her, and because of that somebody tried to kill me last night in the hospital. It was meant to look like suicide, but I assure you it wasn't."

"I know. A left-handed man would never have cut his left wrist."

He let out a huge sigh of relief. "You realised that? I was hoping and praying that you would. It's the strongest proof I have that I didn't try to kill myself."

"Were you awake at all last night? For instance, when some-body came into your room and opened your vein?"

"Yes, I was. Half-awake anyway. It's all nixed up in my head. At first I was too drunk to be aware of anything. I know I had some vivid dreams, very strange but mostly not unpleasant. Jovina was in one of them, she was down by the river, and I was with her…" He stopped.

I must steer him away from this sad subject. "Did you dream about anyone in the hospital?"

"Once or twice, and I thought I was truly awake, only I couldn't move or speak, and I got confused. Then in the last of the dreams, I felt a pain in my wrist. I thought it was part of the dream to begin with. It didn't hurt much."

"And you think that was when someone was opening your vein?"

"I'm certain of it. I came partly awake. I didn't know where I was, I only knew I felt sick and thirsty, and someone was holding my wrist and cutting it."

"Gods, I'm not surprised you're glad to be away from there. What did you do?"

"Nothing at all. Although I know now that I was half-awake, at the time I thought I was dreaming and I felt too weak to struggle. Someone had put a pillow over my mouth—not my nose, just my mouth, so I could still breathe but not call out. And I couldn't see much, it was very dark. There was only a faint glimmer of light from the window, and the man was in silhouette."

"You can't even remember whether he was tall or short, thin or fat?"

"No. And although I could hear what he said to me, it was in a soft whisper, so I wouldn't know his voice again."

"What did he say? Can you remember?"

"I'll never forget it. 'We both know who murdered your wife. You should have kept your eyes shut and your mouth shut. You will pay the price, and I will risk the wrath of the Erinyes.'"

I shivered in spite of the room's warmth and the bright daylight outside. The Erinyes, the Daughters of Night…their name alone seemed to bring dread into the house. My mind was filled with the ugly shapes of the three terrifying winged goddesses whose job is to punish wrongdoers by making them ill, even driving them mad. And their torments last for ever…

"Diana preserve us from them," I prayed, and the dreadful images faded. "What happened then?"

"The pain was sharp and short, soon over, and I felt blood starting to flow. But I was too tired and confused to think properly, and I didn't realise I was in danger from it. It still seemed to be a dream, and I thought, if I just lie here and keep still, soon I'll wake up and find this never happened. Of course I realise now what he was trying to do. He could just as well have cut my throat to kill me. It would have been quicker, but it would look like a murder, whereas this way people would think I'd committed suicide."

"Yes, I understand that much. Whoever murdered Jovina wanted to pin the blame on you, making it look as if you had killed yourself in a fit of remorse. But what did he mean about you keeping your eyes and mouth shut?"

"He must have thought I saw him killing Jovina down by the river."

"And did you?"

"No, of course not. If I'd seen that, I'd have stopped it."

"You weren't all that close to the river, Marcus. We had people watching, and nobody saw you by the bank. You were also pretty drunk."

"But not blind, and not so completely incapable that I couldn't have done something to save my wife."

"Did you see anyone at all?"

"Yes, several people, but too far away to recognise."

"How far?"

"Oh, it wasn't the distance so much, it was that everyone looked the same." He scratched his chin thoughtfully. "They all had similar cloaks, with the hoods up because of the weather.

Those new things that are supposed to be lucky. Waste of money, if you ask me, and I haven't bought one, but practically every officer in this fort has. Several people had brought them along to the party yesterday and put them on when the thunder started. That Greek trader will be laughing all the way to his banker."

"It all fits together," I agreed. "We think the killer was interrupted by something, from the traces left in the grass…"

"Don't tell me, I don't want the details. I don't want to think of her like that."

"Then finish telling me about last night. What happened after your wrist was cut? Did the attacker say anything else?"

"No. I remember he stood over me for a little while, I don't know how long he was there. I drifted back into sleep. I didn't wake again till dawn, when I found Nikias beside the bed, bandaging up my wrist and telling me everything was going to be all right."

I took a good sip of wine. "Thank the gods for the little lad who found you."

He nodded. "Nikias bound me up and cleaned away the worst of the blood, and gave me some medicine he said would make me sleep. He said I mustn't blame myself for anything, and I mustn't try to open the vein again. I knew I hadn't opened it to begin with, but I wasn't going to admit that of course. It would be like accusing someone in the hospital of trying to murder me. So I just lay there and said as little as possible, till he said he'd leave me to rest. I pretended to go back to sleep, and stayed like that till you came to see me. But I wasn't asleep. How could I sleep, knowing someone was trying to kill me?"

Throughout Mallius' horrifying story, I'd felt a mixture of emotions: fear inspired by his appalling experiences, but also, I confess, excitement. Everything he told me confirmed the suspicion that Nikias had tried to murder him. And if Mallius was correct in remembering his last words, he'd also killed Jovina. He had discovered how she had got rid of his unborn child, or had lost patience with her when she refused to go away with him.

Or both. Either of those possibilities could have driven him to kill her. But how were we going to prove it?

"And you really have no idea who it was who cut your wrist?"

"Oh, I know who it was. I mean I know who it must have been. I've no doubt who killed Jovina even though I didn't see it happen. That person thought I did see him, and wanted me dead. Wants me dead, if it comes to that."

"You're assuming he'll try again?"

"Of course. Hence the big lads I've drafted in as bodyguards. Four altogether, I'm not taking any chances. They'll keep the enemy away till we have enough evidence to arrest him."

"You still haven't told me who the enemy is."

"Trebonius, of course. My esteemed commanding officer."

That stopped me in my tracks. "*Trebonius?* Why?"

"Last night when he heard me confess to murdering Jovina, it must have seemed to him like a gift from the gods. He knew I hadn't done it—of course he did, because he'd killed her himself. But he was the only man who knew for certain I'm innocent. If he could make it appear that I'd taken my own life out of remorse for taking my wife's, then everyone would believe it, and he'd be free of any suspicion."

There was sense in that, as far as it went, but that wasn't very far. "That could explain why he wanted to kill you. But why would he kill Jovina? They were…I'm sorry to be blunt, Marcus, but they were lovers, weren't they?

"They were, and I admit I was jealous. Trebonius and I have never liked one another. We were rivals for the commander's post here, and that was bad enough. But being rivals for a woman… it's too much to bear. She knew I disliked him. It was one of the many things she and I quarrelled about."

"But if Trebonius loved her, why would he kill her?"

"Isn't it obvious? Because of the baby."

"The baby?"

"Don't pretend you didn't know. She was carrying Trebonius' baby, and she got rid of it."

I opened my mouth to protest that this was wrong, but he didn't give me time.

"You don't need to defend her now, Aurelia. I'm sure you were in her confidence. I wasn't, but there are ways of finding out these things. Selena wouldn't say a word, but some of the other servants were less discreet, especially when I gave them the impression I knew all about it anyway. I found out from the door-slave that the village wise-woman attended Jovina several times. One of the young house-girls said it was because of some 'woman's complaint.' The cook mentioned she'd lost her appetite, and started asking for unusual foods, things she didn't normally eat. We've had two children together, I can recognise when a woman's expecting a child. And I can count months and days," he added bitterly. "I know when she started throwing herself at Trebonius. And it really hurt me, Aurelia. That she could even think about having an affair with one of my enemies." He laughed without any humour. "I was pleased when I found out she'd got rid of the baby. I thought that would mean the affair would end…but it didn't, not until he himself ended it. Well, I'll tell you this. I've sworn vengeance on her killer, and I'll make sure he answers for what he's done."

I felt as though I were wading into a morass. I'd believed Jovina absolutely when she said her unborn child was Nikias'. But could she have been wrong, or simply lying to me to protect Trebonius? And if the child was the commander's and he found out, would he be angry enough to commit murder? Yes, probably he would. Or his wife might decide it was her duty? No, that was going too far, surely.

He interrupted my thoughts impatiently. "You sit there as if you've never heard any of this before. Surely Jovina told you?"

"Most of it, yes. But she thought you didn't know; in fact she was desperately anxious that you shouldn't find out. Or anyone else, for that matter. She especially didn't want the commander to know the cause of her illness."

"I can well believe it. But secrets don't stay secret for long in a place like this. He was bound to hear rumours."

"True enough. And if it really was Trebonius who attacked you last night, he may have trouble keeping that quiet too. The small slave-boy I mentioned noticed him, for one, but thought it was natural that he'd come to see how his deputy was faring. Maybe other staff there were aware of his visit."

"Which means it's all the more certain that he'll make another attempt to kill me as soon as possible," Marcus said. "I'm ready for him, when he comes."

"*If* he comes," I said.

"He'll come."

Someone knocked on the door. It made us both jump. Mallius called, "Go away. I've already told you I'm not to be disturbed."

A gruff voice outside answered. "You've got another visitor, sir. Commander Trebonius is here to see you. Shall I show him in?"

Chapter XXV

Mallius sprang up from the couch and shouted through the door, "Ask him to wait till I get dressed." To me he added softly, "I must find a weapon. Anything. Are you carrying a knife?"

"Don't be silly, Marcus. He can't do anything here and now. The guards are outside, and I'll stay with you. Let's see what he wants. He may have news."

"I suppose so." He turned to the door and shouted, "I'm ready now. Show him in."

Trebonius strode in briskly, followed closely by the big body-guard, but there was no feeling of aggression or threat. His smile appeared genuinely warm and friendly, though it couldn't hide the lines of weariness and anxiety on his face. "Thank you, Ajax. Wait outside within call," he ordered, and the soldier had no choice but to leave us.

"Mallius, it's good to see you out of the hospital and back in your own home. Sit down, man, you look tired still. And Aurelia, I'm glad you're here to keep him company." He pulled up a stool and sat near the couch.

"He's looking better, isn't he?" I said.

"He is. How are you feeling?"

Mallius sat down on his couch and relaxed a little, smiling back. "Not too bad, thank you, sir. May I offer you some wine?"

"Thanks, yes, that would be welcome. I've just been out in the village with one of our patrols. Thirsty work, what with all the dust and smoke."

Mallius poured him a beaker and handed it to him.

Trebonius took a long swallow. "That's good! I shan't stay long, but I wanted to see how you are. And to tell you not to worry about anything, take whatever time you need to recover from this dreadful business."

"That's good of you, sir, especially when you're so busy."

All this ever-so-courteous formality struck me as incongruous in light of what Mallius had just been saying to me, but as I'd observed at the party, they'd got accustomed to hiding their mutual dislike under masks of pleasantness.

"There's one thing I need to ask you," Trebonius said. "Jovina's funeral. I discussed it with Philippus last night and we'd intended it to be today, but that really isn't possible with everyone on alert. Our funeral field is outside the fort," he explained for my benefit. "And in any case, with neither your son nor your daughter here, it doesn't seem right. I'd like your agreement to postpone it until tomorrow, Mallius."

"I agree. Thank you for taking on the organisation. There's no news, then, about Chloe or Vitellia?"

"No. I'm afraid they haven't returned yet, neither have the investigators who are searching for them."

"Can you send out more search parties? The girls haven't had time to go very far from the village, and perhaps they went into hiding somewhere by the river when they realised the danger of being outside."

Trebonius sighed. "I can't spare anyone till my reinforcements get here. I'm sorry, but given the situation in the village…"

"What exactly is the situation? Are our patrols managing to contain the unrest?"

"For now, yes. There are groups of young Brigantians moving round the streets, but they aren't carrying arms, or not openly at any rate, and they aren't challenging our patrols directly. There are rumours that Prince Venutius will arrive to take charge before nightfall, but so far he hasn't shown up."

"I suppose there's some arson—it's inevitable. Any looting?" I was pleased to see that now they'd both abandoned their false civility, and were simply two soldiers discussing a military problem.

"Some fires, and some looting of Roman property. We're doing all we can to deter it, but we've barely enough men. I've sent to Eburacum for reinforcements. They should arrive tonight or first thing tomorrow." He drank more wine. "Meanwhile I've taken twenty hostages, and I've sent messengers out to let everyone know I expect the Brigantians to hand over Eurytus' killer by tomorrow at dawn; otherwise, I plan to execute two hostages a day till they do."

"*What?* Sir, is that wise?" I realised that this was the first Mallius had heard of Trebonius' scheme. "Won't that simply inflame the villagers all the more?"

Trebonius was unruffled. "Probably, but we can hold them down indefinitely once reinforcements arrive. And I have no choice. I must do everything I can to discover who killed Eurytus. We can't let the death of an important Imperial official go unpunished."

"It's to be hoped Quintus Antonius can find out who the murderer was," I said. "He was confident he could, given enough time."

"So he told me. He has till tonight. Time is the one thing we're short of. And talking of that, I'd best get back to work." He finished his wine. "I'm glad to find you recovering, Mallius. I realise you've not been well, but when does the doctor reckon you'll be fit for duty?"

"I'm to rest for today, and after that it's up to me. So I shall be back in harness tomorrow."

"Good man. I'll see you then."

I felt the tension slacken a little as the door shut behind him. "I've got to say, Marcus, he didn't look like a murderer to me. He was the picture of a concerned commander."

"He's a very good actor," Mallius answered. "You saw how gracious he was at the party, when all the time he was hating my guts, and waiting for the chance to make love to my wife…" He seized his beaker and gripped it so hard I thought it would break, but with an effort he regained control of himself and put it down. "He got away with it that time. Thank you for staying, Aurelia. Your presence made sure he behaved himself."

"I'm glad. It's certainly given me something to think about."

"You still don't believe he's a murderer?"

"To be honest, I believe he'd be capable of murdering you. You've implied that you're capable of murdering him, and I believe that too. After all, you're soldiers. You're also rivals. If he believed you when he heard you confess to killing Jovina, he might have decided to avenge her and make it appear you'd done away with yourself in a fit of remorse. All that I can accept."

"Well, then?"

"But I can't bring myself to imagine him murdering Jovina."

"Why not? They were lovers, and they had a lovers' quarrel."

"Selena has told me that though they liked one another's company, they never went to bed together. And she said she thought Jovina was keener on the relationship than Trebonius was."

"Stuff and nonsense. She was just trying to protect her mistress. No, Trebonius is the man, there's no doubt. Think about it, Aurelia. You'll admit it fits the facts?"

"It fits quite a few of them, yes," I admitted. "Trebonius was seen alone down by the river during the party. Jovina told Selena that she planned to meet him for a private talk, and there was a stretch of time when nobody knew where he'd got to. He'd have had long enough to meet her, to quarrel with her, and yes, to murder her…except I just don't think he did."

He was finding it hard to keep his patience. "Then if he didn't kill her, in the gods' name who did?"

"It could have been Nikias."

"Nikias? You're joking…But no, you're serious, aren't you?" He looked genuinely surprised. "I don't think that's likely. For a start, why? He and Jovina stopped seeing one another months ago. If he was angry with her for throwing him over, surely he'd have killed her then."

"Suppose he tried to start the affair again? He admitted to me that he wanted to see her, but he couldn't because he wasn't invited to the party. In fact, though, he could still get to the field by the river, by going across country where no one would see. What if he was really the one that Jovina planned to meet by the river, but she considered it so secret that she didn't even tell Selena? Then afterwards, when you confessed to the murder yourself, he had the same idea you're attributing to Trebonius: he'd dispose of you, making it look like suicide. Being in the hospital himself made it very easy to do, and nobody to be any the wiser."

"But he didn't go to the field by the river. However much he wanted to, he didn't."

"How do you know?"

"Because he told me. Believe me, I'd had the same idea as you, that he wanted to be Jovina's lover again, and killed her when she refused. I challenged him about it this morning. He was adamant that he never left the hospital at all yesterday afternoon, and his assistant confirmed it. So he's in the clear," he finished triumphantly.

I realised how much he wanted his enemy Trebonius to be proved a murderer for personal reasons as well as in the interests of justice. I must be wary of letting his own hatred of the commander cloud my judgment. Yet the mere fact that the two men loathed one another was surely an important reason why Trebonius could have killed his subordinate.

"I must go," I said, "but I promise I'll think over what you've told me, and so will Quintus and Lucius. And you must take care. Be on your guard all the time, and not only against Trebonius—against anyone who could possibly be your enemy in secret."

"I shall, never fear. He'll try again, and I'll be ready for him."

I left him and wandered aimlessly around the fort, trying to get my thoughts in order. Mallius' conviction that Trebonius had killed Jovina, that he was the father of Jovina's child, was so strong, it caused me to think again about my own conclusions.

On my way back to our office I saw Congrio coming from the direction of the main gate. "Here's the present I promised," he said, and handed me a small thin bundle wrapped in leather. "Only small, but it's a good little knife, sharp as a razor."

"Thank you, Congrio. That's much appreciated." I unwrapped it cautiously, and found a well-made knife with a sharp iron blade and a wooden handle inlaid with silver. "This is beautiful, thank you so much. And very timely, too. I'm going to keep it with me. On a day like today, even a peaceable innkeeper feels like carrying a weapon. And this one's small and neat enough to fit into a pouch." I tucked it into my belt-pouch straight away.

"I hope you never have to use it in anger, but if you do, may it bring you victory," he said. "Just don't show it to Trebonius, that's all."

"Any news at the gate? I saw you talking to the centurion there."

"The usual. 'Everything under control.' As if anyone believed that."

"I wish I knew what's happened to the two missing girls… well, three in fact, because they took a maid with them."

"I'm sure we'll hear something soon. Try not to worry."

The more people tell you not to worry, the harder it is not to. And I couldn't help feeling anxious and dispirited as I headed back to my office. I'd gone as far as I could with my investigations into Jovina's death, but I still hadn't found her murderer. I didn't know what to do next. I wished Quintus or Lucius were here. I needed someone to talk over the case with, a fresh pair of eyes to look at the information I'd assembled, and with luck see some pattern, some logic, that I'd missed.

But they weren't here, and the gods alone knew when they'd be back.

Chapter XXVI

"Any news of the girls, Mistress Aurelia?" Selena came up, looking as unhappy as I felt.

"Not a word, I'm afraid. We must just keep on hoping. How are you all settling in?"

"It's a bit crowded, but we'd rather be here where it's safe than at the house, waiting for Jupiter knows what to happen. I made sure they gave Lord Statius a room to himself."

"Isn't he staying with Mallius?"

"No, the master's keeping his spare room for Miss Chloe when she comes back. At least that's his excuse, but I was in the hospital this morning and I overheard them having a falling-out, a real argument. Statius went to visit him to tell him he doesn't want to marry Miss Chloe after all."

"Really? Why?"

"Because of the master saying he'd killed my lady. I know he's gone back on it now, but Lord Statius doesn't believe that. He keeps going on and on about how there's truth in wine, and no smoke without fire, and…"

"…and all the usual sayings people come up with when they can't think of anything original."

She laughed. "That's about it. The main thing is, he's decided he doesn't want an alliance with the Mallius family."

"How extraordinary! You'd imagine he would be only too glad that Mallius is innocent, and want to support him. Do you think he means it, or is it just a fit of temper? He does seem to have rather a—well, an irascible character, from what I saw yesterday."

She shrugged. "You're not wrong there. He walked out of the hospital in a real rage, that's all I know. I've always felt sorry for Miss Chloe, having the prospect of Statius for a husband. He's rich, certainly, and the family never seems to have enough money even though the master is a senior officer now. Sometimes I'm quite glad I'm a freedwoman and can marry anyone I like. Well, anyhow, Miss Chloe will be delighted if Lord Statius has permanently changed his mind. Though whether that means she'll get her soldier-boy…"

"I need to come over and have a word with Statius myself. Didn't you say this morning that he went out early into the village looking for news of Chloe and Vitellia? I'm wondering if he might have seen something to do with Eurytus' murder. He hasn't said anything about it, I suppose?"

"Not about that. But," she lowered her voice, "he says he's delighted Eurytus has been killed. He hated him. One of his lads let it slip that they've been enemies for years, over some of Statius' property in Italia."

"He was telling me about it yesterday. And of course the way Eurytus more or less took possession of Chloe didn't help."

"I've been thinking about that." She hesitated. "Mistress, I've found something and I think I should show someone, but not the master, not the way things are. May I show it to you? You'll know what to do about it."

"Yes, by all means, if you think I can help. Let's go into the office—we'll be private there."

We went inside, and when I offered her a mug of wine, she accepted gratefully.

"This is the first time I've sat down since we got here."

"You look tired, Selena. You've been working hard, and you've been holding everything together for the Mallius family."

"Oh, I don't mind hard work. It's the worry that wears you out. Now, tell me what you make of this." She took a folded piece of papyrus from her pouch. "I found it among Miss

Chloe's things when I was unpacking her little travelling-chest just now. Tucked in among her clothes, I don't suppose anyone was meant to see it."

It was a short note in Greek, in an elegant hand.

Lord Eurytus sends greetings to beautiful Chloe.

My dear, you must know how you have captured my heart. Ever since I saw you yesterday, I have longed for your touch, for your kiss. I shall fly to your arms this morning, my dearest. Be kind to your adoring and devoted lover when he comes to ask for your favour.

I laughed aloud. "*Merda*, Selena, now I've seen everything. Eurytus, the most important Imperial official in Britannia, writing schoolboy love letters to a child! It came this morning, presumably?"

"While I was asleep, I suppose. And I'm thinking it may explain why she wanted to leave the house."

I saw where she was driving. "She didn't want to meet him, and thought she'd take evasive action. But why didn't she come to the fort, instead of going off into the country?"

"She probably reckoned Eurytus would be at the fort himself later on."

"It may explain something else too. About Eurytus' assassination this morning…"

She recoiled in horror. "You're not suggesting Miss Chloe had any hand in that?"

"No, of course I'm not. He was found in the village, not far from Brennus' house. Quintus Antonius will know more. He had a look at the place before he went off searching for the girls. But I've been wondering, why would an important man like Eurytus be wandering about Isurium on foot, and on his own? If he was off to call on Chloe, he may have thought she'd be more likely to take notice of him if he didn't have half a cohort of bodyguards with him." I put the papyrus into my own pouch. "This is very helpful, Selena. Thank you for bringing it to me. I'll show it to Quintus as soon as he gets back."

"That's a weight off my shoulders. I'll see you again shortly then, when you come to talk to Lord Statius." She stood up, and gazed down at me for a few heart-beats. "You're looking pretty exhausted yourself, Mistress."

"I can't deny it. As you say, it's not the work that wears you out, it's the worry. I thought by now I'd be pretty sure who murdered my poor cousin. But there are still two possibilities, and I can't find any way of separating them."

"Trebonius and Nikias," Selena said.

"Exactly so."

"Well, nobody could do more than you're doing, that I'm sure of. You'll find the evil man who killed my lady and bring the Furies to punish him."

"If I don't, it won't be for want of trying." Then my brain caught up with what she'd just said. "Say that again, Selena."

My sharp tone alarmed her. "I don't mean to speak out of turn, Mistress. I just mean…"

"No, you haven't said anything wrong at all. I just…I just didn't hear you clearly. What did you say about the Furies?"

"All I said was that you'll find the evil man who killed my lady, and the Furies will punish him, like they do all murderers. Follow them and punish them for ever." She smiled sheepishly. "I suppose my lady or the master would call on them by some fancy Greek name. But the old-fashioned Roman name will do for me."

"And for me." I couldn't believe I'd missed something so obvious. Whoever tried to murder Mallius had spoken of "the wrath of the Erinyes." He had called the Furies by their Greek name. So he was either a Greek, or fluent in the Greek language.

Nikias was a Greek. Trebonius was an old-fashioned Roman, and although like all educated Romans he'd be bound to know Greek, he would never speak it from choice.

On an impulse, I got up and gave Selena a hug. She was surprised, but not displeased. "Thank you, Selena. You've just shown me how to find out for sure who killed Jovina."

"How?"

"I won't say just yet. It's a wild idea, but I need to talk to Mallius to be completely sure. I'll go and see him now."

She smiled. "There now, I said you could do it. The gods go with you."

The guard at Mallius' door recognised me, and I went straight through to see his master. As I entered the room, Mallius was pouring some wine into a beaker from a big clay flask.

"Ah, Aurelia, you've come at just the right time. I've had a present of some Falernian, I assume it's the rather good stuff they sell at the mansio. Have you tried it yet?"

"I had some the other night. You're right, it is good. And I'll take a beaker with you, if you're offering, thank you."

He poured it out for me. "I suppose you haven't brought me any news to celebrate? Nothing about Chloe yet?"

"Nothing, I'm afraid. The searchers are still not back." I took the wine and sniffed it, which is normally one of the pleasures of drinking good Falernian. "This isn't the wine from the mansio, alas. Never mind, it's welcome. Who sent it?"

"The doctor." He raised his beaker. "So I'll drink his good health…"

"Don't drink it, Marcus!" I shouted. I ran across to his table, snatched the beaker he was holding, and with my other hand grabbed the wine jug. "Don't touch a drop. It's poisoned."

"Poisoned? Are you mad?"

"No. But you are, if you drink this. It was Nikias who tried to kill you last night. It's a million gold pieces to a bowl of porridge he's trying again now."

"Nikias?" He stared at me in disbelief. "What in the gods' name makes you think that? We agreed it was Trebonius."

"You convinced yourself it was. I still had some doubt, and I've since realised that it must have been Nikias, and how I can prove it. That's what I came to tell you."

"Well, all right. You can put those things down, I'm not tempted to touch them now."

I replaced the jug and beaker on the table, but I was too tense to sit down. I began pacing the room, trying to stop myself from shaking. "You told me the words that your attacker said last night. You remembered them quite clearly, didn't you?"

He nodded. "Certainly. He said 'We both know who murdered your wife. You should have kept your eyes shut and your mouth shut. You will pay the price, and I will risk the wrath of the Erinyes.'"

"Good. Now what language was the attacker speaking?"

"What do you mean, what language?"

"It's a simple enough question," I said, speaking in Greek this time. "What exactly did he whisper to you? What were the actual words? Were they Latin or Greek? Or maybe native British, or Gaulish or Parthian…?"

"Oh, I see what you mean." He'd spoken in Greek as well. As I remembered from long ago, he was equally fluent in Greek or Latin, and switched between them without even realising he was doing it. "It's funny. Now you ask, I'm not sure. Let me think." He closed his eyes.

"Go over it in your mind," I said. "You're lying in bed. It's very dark, but you can see the silhouette of a man leaning over you, and you can feel a pain in your wrist. And then he starts to whisper…"

"Greek," he said. "It was Greek…*Greek!*" Realisation came to him in a sudden flash, as it had to me. "Of course it was. He talked about the wrath of the Erinyes. If he'd been a Latin speaker, if he'd been Trebonius, he'd have said the wrath of the Furies."

"That's what I thought." I was elated, with the excitement of a hunter who has his quarry in plain sight at last. I smiled at him. "Would you care for some wine now?"

"So Nikias killed her," he mused, still taking it in. "Gods, I never liked him, but I never dreamed he would be a murderer, especially of someone he loved."

"Jovina told me the baby was his, you know. Not Trebonius'. That's why she wouldn't let Nikias attend her as her doctor. And she also told me he was trying to persuade her to run away with him."

He put his head in his hands. "Aurelia, I've been wrong about so much. I want to be sure now." He looked up. "Are you certain all this is true?"

"I'm certain. I'll swear it if you like. The question is, what do we do now?"

"Arrest the man, of course. Confront him, see if he admits any of this. He may, once he realises we know the truth. This wine will be evidence…although it's our word against his that it's got poison in it." He looked at the flask and the two untouched beakers. "I'll tell my men to catch a mouse or a rat, there are usually plenty around the granaries. We can test the wine on one of those."

"Persuading everyone that Nikias is a murderer won't be easy. Trebonius won't want to accept he's got a killer running his hospital, and he won't want to lose a good doctor unless he's got rock-solid proof."

Mallius nodded. "But Trebonius is no fool, and he must know he's under suspicion himself. He might be glad enough to have confirmation that he's innocent."

"Perhaps. But I think we should wait till Quintus and the others come back. Quintus has clout, and once he's heard our evidence he'll insist on an arrest."

He stood up. "I have clout too, you know. I'm the deputy commander. Ajax!" he shouted, and the big bodyguard appeared at the door. "Fetch the others, all of them. We're going to the hospital."

We must have made a curious picture, the six of us, as we marched through the fort. Mallius and I led the way, and the four giant soldiers followed, one of them carrying the doctor's flask of wine. It's an indication of how busy everyone was that we didn't attract any attention at all.

We strode straight in through the main door. When we halted in the waiting area, young Onion came out, round-eyed with curiosity. He looked at all of us, decided that nobody was hurt, and asked Mallius, "Shall I fetch the doctor for you, sir?"

"We'll find him for ourselves," Mallius said. "Where is he?"

"In the store-room, sir. I'll tell him you're coming."

"No you won't, you'll stay here until we've finished talking to him. Ajax, you and the men stay here too. Don't let anyone disturb us while we talk to the doctor. And don't let him leave this building for any reason. Understand?"

Nikias was alone in the store-room, sorting some small flasks of oil. He looked up as he heard our approaching footsteps, and when he saw Mallius he dropped the flask he was holding, gave a frightened cry, and backed away. It took me a little time to realise why. He thought he was seeing Mallius' shade…he thought Mallius was dead. It was the final proof we needed.

Mallius advanced, holding up the flask of wine. Nikias retreated across the room till he stood cowering against the shelves on the farthest wall. Then he made a pathetic attempt to recover his dignity. "I'm pleased to see you, Mallius."

"I doubt it," Mallius answered in Greek. "You thought you'd killed me, didn't you? Now I've come for my revenge."

"Revenge? I don't understand." But he understood well enough.

"Yes, I've survived your attempt to poison me, and your effort to fake my suicide last night by opening my vein."

"But I assure you…" It was almost a whisper.

"Don't waste my time. I was awake enough to hear what you said to me, but it's taken me a little while to understand. You said you'd murdered my wife, and you were going to kill me because I'd seen you do it. And you boasted that you'd risk the wrath of the Erinyes. Well, let me tell you, my wrath is just as deadly, and rather more immediate."

"Oh, I know that," Nikias exclaimed, suddenly finding his courage and his voice. "Your wrath is deadly, and your poor wife suffered from it for years. I know what you put her through, and I wanted to take her away from it. I loved her so much, I could have made her happy. But she repaid me by destroying my baby. For that I killed her, killed her and threw her into the river. But you, Mallius, I thought you'd seen me. There was someone who looked like you, too near for my safety. So I had to kill you as well. You deserved it anyway, for the cruel way you treated the woman I loved."

"I didn't see you kill her," Mallius replied. "And you botched your efforts to make me look like a suicide." He held up his bandaged wrist. "You opened the wrong vein."

Nikias nodded. "I realised that this morning. A pity, really, because you don't deserve to live." He hesitated, then suddenly lunged forward and seized the flask from Mallius' hands. Before we could stop him he was drinking the wine straight from it. Some of it spilled over the front of his tunic, but most went down his throat. He stood holding the empty flask and facing us squarely, with an air of exultation, almost of triumph.

"Without Jovina, I see no point in living any more. And I don't have to face your wrath, Mallius."

He flung the empty flask in Mallius' face, and made a rush for the door. He raced along the narrow corridor and into the waiting area, but the guards there caught him easily. By the time we reached them, he was already writhing on the tiled floor, coughing and choking his life out.

I believe death came quickly, but I left before the end. I felt sickened, and desperate to be outside. Nobody stopped me, or even noticed, as I hurried away from the hospital.

But I couldn't shake off the unhappiness I was feeling. I tried to make myself concentrate on the fact that I'd fulfilled my promise and found Jovina's killer. I should have been elated, triumphant…but there was only a dull sadness. The whole tragic story of love, hate, and betrayal was such a complete, dreadful waste of emotions and lives.

Chapter XXVII

I walked blindly on through the fort, not knowing or caring where my feet took me. I found myself near the main gate, and as I headed towards it, I heard someone call my name.

I felt an enormous wave of relief engulf me as I recognised the group riding towards me: Quintus and Lucius, Titch and Gambax…and Gambax was carrying Baca in front of him on his saddle!

But Chloe wasn't with them, and neither was Vitellia.

There was a flurry of greetings, everyone talking at once except Baca. Gambax carefully helped her dismount and supported her with an arm round her waist. She was shivering, hardly able to stand, and her eyes were swollen with crying. As I went to her she said sadly, "I'm sorry, Mistress. So sorry. I couldn't stop it. I know Master Lucius must be angry with me, and Master Mallius, and I should have been able to do something…"

"Baca, you poor thing. It's all right now, you're safe." Selena took the girl in her arms. Baca let her head fall onto the older woman's shoulder and began to cry.

I looked at her closely. She appeared unharmed, but she'd obviously been badly frightened. "Don't worry, Baca. We know you did your best, and you didn't run away. We won't forget that."

"Don't cry, my dear." Selena stroked her hair softly, as if she were comforting a tiny child. "You're quite safe now, and you'll help us find the girls. But what you need first is a hot drink and something to eat." She looked enquiringly at Quintus. "Is that all right, sir? I'll bring her to you later."

"Not yet." Baca raised her head and gently disengaged herself. "I want to tell you what happened before I do anything else. There isn't much time." She wiped her eyes on her sleeve. "I'll take a drink of wine, if you're offering, but I'll sip it while I tell you."

"Good girl." Quintus smiled at her. "Come with us into our office, and tell us everything. We won't need you for long, and we can certainly find you a hot drink and some food. Gambax, you can fetch us something to eat and some warm wine, can't you? Good. Enough for all of us. Titch, get someone to see to the horses please, and then join us."

As we walked to the office, I drew Quintus to one side. "Nikias has confessed to killing Jovina and trying to kill Mallius, after we confronted him."

"Gods alive!" He ran a hand through his hair. "Was that your doing?"

"Some of it."

"Well done."

"It doesn't feel very well done. After he confessed, he took poison. He's dead."

"But Jovina is avenged, and that's what we wanted. I still say well done, Aurelia. You can brief us all when we've talked to Baca."

We sat around the table, and Quintus drew out a note-tablet from his pouch. "First I'll read the message the kidnappers left with Baca for us—for Trebonius really. It's in good Latin, an educated hand I'd say, and it's got the usual letters VVV at the end.

To Tiberius Trebonius, fort commander Isurium, from Prince Venutius of the Brigantes

We, the Brigantes of Isurium, demand that you release your hostages immediately. We are not responsible for the death of Eurytus. We have taken hostages of our own, two young girls. If you kill any Brigantian hostages, they will die.

I felt even more sick and cold than before. "Gods, I should never have come here. I should never have brought Vitellia. I should never have…"

"Enough, Relia," Lucius said, firmly but without anger. "None of us blame you for this. Don't waste time and energy blaming yourself. We've got to work together, and we've got to move quickly."

Gambax and Titch came in with food and drink. They offered some to Baca, who ate and drank eagerly, and they helped themselves, but the rest of us only picked at the food, though the wine was welcome.

"Well, now, Baca," Quintus said, "we must thank the gods that someone as sensible as you was there to try and look after the girls. Tell us what happened this morning. Why did they decide to leave the house?"

"Miss Chloe got a note from Gambax asking her to meet him by the river, where they had the party yesterday…"

"I didn't send a note," Gambax protested. "I swear I didn't!"

"I know that *now*, but this morning she thought…we all thought, it was from you. It was only short, something like 'Come and meet me by the river one last time. Your father says you are to marry Lord Statius tomorrow.'"

"That's not true either," I said. "In fact according to Selena…"

"It seemed true to Miss Chloe. It's what she's been dreading, even more since her mother died. So she was determined to go for one last meeting, and nothing Miss Vitellia or I could say would make her change her mind. So we decided we'd go with her, and at least make sure she didn't try to run away or anything silly. Then we could all go to the fort together."

"And when you got to the river there was nobody there," I said.

"Nobody we could see. We were waiting by the water quite some time. Miss Chloe was getting impatient and we were trying to persuade her we should go back to the fort. Then we heard horses, and we looked round, and three natives came down to us and grabbed us. Miss Chloe was very brave, she stood up to them and ordered them to let us go. They just laughed and said they were taking her and Miss Vitellia for a little ride in the country. They only had one spare horse, I suppose they hadn't reckoned on Miss Vitellia being there too, so they tied the two girls onto the one beast. And one man said he'd take me along on his horse, but the leader told him I'd be more use left behind with a message. So…" She stopped abruptly and drank some wine. The mug shook in her hand. "They tied me up, and the leader wrote out that message and left it with me to give you. And they rode away. That's the last I saw of them." A tear rolled down her cheek. "I was frightened after they'd gone. I thought you'd never find me."

"We'd have kept looking until we did," Quintus said. "Just as we shall keep looking for the girls until we bring them home safe."

"Were any of you hurt?" Lucius wanted to know. "Or molested at all?"

She shook her head. "The leader said the girls would be safe for today if they did what they were told, and after that…after that it would depend on what happened here."

"Did you get any idea where they were taking the girls?" Quintus asked.

"Not really. There was only one mention of it. As they were about to set off, the leader said to one of the others, 'The usual place will do nicely to hide them. How long will it take us to get there?' And the other one said, 'An hour if we use the main road most of the way, more if we avoid the road and go through the woods.'"

"'The usual place…'" Quintus repeated. "We'll have to ask around, see if it means anything to people here. It doesn't sound as if this leader was a local man, at least not from Isurium."

"I don't know. I did hear his name, though. Venutius."

She had nothing further to add, so we sent her off to her hot bath, with our heartfelt thanks and promises that we'd find the girls, come what may.

"Now," Quintus said, "the first thing I must do is go and brief the commander. I'll show him the note and see if I can talk him out of this madness. If we could get him to send out messengers announcing that the hostages won't be killed, the word would get back to Venutius, and they'd spare Vitellia and Chloe."

"They might," Lucius said grimly when Quintus had left. "On the other hand they might start asking for a ransom instead, or just decide to keep the girls anyway."

"Stop it, Lucius!" I said. "Don't even think it. We've got to stay hopeful however bad things look."

"And I'm afraid they do look bad. Trebonius has handled the situation all wrong," Lucius said. "He's completely over-reacted. I've spoken to some of the lads on patrol. The Brigantians were fairly quiet this morning. A few of them were disposed to celebrate when they heard Eurytus was dead, and there'd have been some drinking and loud talk, but the soldiers could have contained it. There are only a handful of real rebels, and most of them would rather not confront the army, whatever Prince Venutius would like them to do. But now with this threat to the hostages, they feel they've got nothing to lose and they're spoiling for a fight, any fight."

"But even Venutius won't risk an outright battle. Our boys are too well armed and trained."

"We can only hope not, and battles aren't their style anyway. You know how they operate, fighting in small bands, setting fire to anything Roman, and picking off any isolated settlers or soldiers they find."

"Have they burned Jovina's—I mean Mallius' place?" I asked.

"Probably. In the end we didn't leave anyone behind to guard it. All the servants begged to come with us to the fort; they could see which way the wind was blowing. If we'd insisted they must stay, they'd simply have run off as soon as we'd left."

The door opened and Quintus came in, stony-faced and angry. Lucius asked, "No joy?"

"No." He sighed as he sat down, and reached for a beaker of wine. "The executions start at dawn tomorrow."

We were all silent. There really was nothing to say.

"I told Trebonius how things are," Quintus went on. "I told him we'll have to go out and search tonight, and he appreciates it's urgent, but he absolutely refuses to alter his decision about the hostages. He says it'll be seen as weakness by the rebels. 'I've great faith in you and your colleagues, Antonius,' he said to me. 'You'll find those girls if anybody can.' *If* anybody can…and he won't even give us an escort. He says we can't take any men from here until his reinforcements arrive. Which may not be till this evening, or even tomorrow." He took a long drink, and put down his empty mug with a bang. "I told him we must go anyway."

Titch nodded, and Lucius said, "I agree."

I felt torn in two. Part of me wanted to argue, to tell them it was far too dangerous to set out when the Brigantians were so hostile. But they wouldn't have listened. And the other part of me knew that they were right. It was now or never. So I said, "This time I'm coming too."

Quintus and Lucius started to protest, but I ignored them. "I'll dress as a lad and carry a dagger. I can look after myself. You need to convince the rebels you're too strong a patrol to be attacked. Five is stronger than four."

"No, Aurelia, it's out of the…"

"Don't argue with me, Quintus. Or any of you. I'm coming, and that's that. Let's not waste any more time discussing it."

Titch suddenly smiled. "I remember a long time ago when you did something like this. At Oak Bridges it was. I didn't come with you, but I heard about it. You were like a tiger." He looked at Quintus. "Wasn't she? And she would be again."

Quintus smiled too. "She was. She is. I'd like her to come. But this isn't my decision. Lucius, you're the head of the Aurelius family."

"Fat lot of notice she takes of me," Lucius grumbled.

"*I'll* take notice. If you forbid Aurelia to come with us, she won't come."

"So, Relia, will you let me decide for you this time?"

"Yes, Lucius, I will. If you think my coming will endanger the rest of you, then I'll stay behind. But be honest. Do you think that?"

He sat in thought for what seemed like a long time. Then he grinned, and I saw excitement flash in his eyes. "I think you'll do more good than harm by coming, Sis. And a woman's presence might be useful, if Vitellia and Chloe have been hurt or frightened."

Quintus smiled again. "Now that we've done the really difficult task, all we have to do is plan how best to search, so we can cover as much ground as possible with just the five of us."

Gambax spoke up. "Sir, I think I know where to start searching."

"You do? Where?"

"Baca said the kidnappers talked about their 'usual place.' I've an idea where that is. And if I'm right, it's somewhere well hidden, but not too far. We could get there by tonight easily. It's an hour's ride, no more."

Quintus looked at him thoughtfully. "And how do you come to know anything about any 'usual place' used by native rebels?"

"It's a bit awkward to explain, sir. It involves another soldier. It's not my secret, but I swore I wouldn't tell. But I didn't dream they'd use the place for hostages. Anyway he's not here now, and if he were…."

"Who's not here?"

"Philippus."

"Ah. We already have some information about Philippus which we're not making public. We know he's in regular contact with the Brigantian rebels, and he may be implicated in Eurytus' death. I want your promise that you'll keep that confidential, Gambax. In other words, we share each other's secrets, but only among ourselves. Understand?"

"I promise."

"So tell us about this 'usual place'. That's an order. First of all, where is it?"

"Roughly five miles away. Four miles north up the main road, then a mile or so west through the trees. There's a small farm and a roundhouse, a couple of outbuildings, and a very large barn, much bigger than you'd expect to find on what's really only a smallholding."

"You've been there?"

"Once, with Philippus. I didn't see inside, it was closed and bolted. The peasants who owned it told me they store grain in it for paying their taxes, but they were very reticent about it, and they had a long private talk with Philippus while I stayed in the house. I'm pretty sure they use it for hiding goods they buy from him."

Quintus nodded. "Do you know what he's selling them? Presumably something illegal, otherwise why keep it a secret?"

"Yes, sir," Gambax said miserably. "Military supplies from Cataractonium, the tannery there. Tanned leather, heavy-duty stuff for body armour and shields, and some finer leatherwork for clothes and shoes. They pay good money for that, and Philippus is always broke."

"You're certain of this?" Quintus was implacable.

"Yes, sir."

"Then why haven't you reported it?"

He said nothing, simply sat there looking thoroughly ashamed of himself, as well he might. But I remembered my first night at the mansio, and I knew the answer. "It was because of Chloe, wasn't it? Philippus used to act as a go-between for the pair of you—he'd pass messages and help you arrange to meet her without her parents knowing. You didn't want to antagonise him, so you kept quiet. Is that right?"

He blushed. "I love her."

Quintus said, "You're a disgrace to your unit, Gambax. I ought to have you dismissed here and now."

"I know, sir. But that wouldn't help Chloe and Vitellia. At least let me show you where I think they are."

"All I can say is, you'd better be right about this meeting-place. If you are, and if we get the girls back safe, I'm prepared to overlook the fact that you didn't report Philippus. We can deal with him on his own later. But if we don't find them, you'll be thrown out of the army so fast your feet won't touch the ground. Is that clear?"

"Yes, sir. Thank you. I'm sorry."

"You will be, Gambax, if you lead us on a wild goose chase. Still, if you're right, it makes the task of searching very much easier." He got up and went to the window to look out at the sun, which was still quite high. "We've got probably four hours of daylight, and an hour's ride, you say…better allow two, because we'll have to go under cover for the last stage. We can't just ride up to the door. We'll leave here an hour from now. Does everyone agree?"

Everyone agreed enthusiastically. Suddenly there was an atmosphere of hope among us. We all felt that though the situation was far from good, things might have started to look up at last.

Quintus began issuing orders. "Gambax, your first job is to find clothes for Aurelia, and then get horses ready for all of us, and a small carriage for bringing the girls back. We can use it to carry a few necessary items: some supplies in case we find ourselves stuck out in the wilds all night, or in case the girls haven't had any food today. An axe…some rope…We may as well be prepared."

He nodded. "I'll pack blankets as well, and the makings of a fire."

"Fine. Anything you think we'll need. Now, what else must we do before we go? Aurelia, we need to brief you on what little we managed to discover about Eurytus' murder, and see if you've picked up anything at this end which ties in with it. But first you need to brief us." He smiled at the others round the table. "She's found Jovina's murderer, who also tried to kill Mallius."

"Who?" Lucius and Titch asked simultaneously.

"Nikias." I told them how I'd worked out Nikias' role in my cousin's life, and her death, and about Mallius' evidence. They asked a few questions, and they were impressed. That pleased me, I don't mind admitting it. When I concluded my report with Nikias' death, Lucius remarked, "Probably the best solution," and the others nodded in agreement.

"You've done good work, Aurelia," Quintus said. "Very good indeed. I only wish we had time to celebrate it properly with a good meal and a jug or two of wine."

"It's too soon to celebrate yet," I said. "Let's wait till we've found the girls and stopped the killings. Then we'll have something worth celebrating."

"You're right. So in between tracking down Nikias, did you pick up anything useful about Eurytus' death?"

"A little, yes, but I don't know how much weight to give it till I hear what you discovered in the village this morning. All I know is that he was stabbed near Brennus' house."

"His body was found not far from there, by the side of the road. But we don't think that's where he was killed, because there was no blood to speak of on the ground, and yet we could see from his wound that he must have bled heavily. I don't suppose you've had a look at his body, have you?"

"No. I will if I must, but I preferred to spend my time today with the living, not the dead."

"I can't say I blame you. The important point is, he had a serious stab wound in his neck, easily deep enough to have killed him. There were no cuts on his hands or arms, which means he didn't try to ward off his attacker. In other words he was taken completely by surprise and killed immediately."

"The oddest thing, to my mind," Titch put in, "is that he was out on his own. He always had some of his bodyguard on duty outside Brennus' house day and night, and he liked showing them off. Why weren't they with him? They're a pretty useless lot, but even they could have stopped him being ambushed and stabbed almost on his own doorstep. What was he doing out by himself?"

"I can only think of one reason why a vain man like that would venture out without his escort," Lucius said. "He was on his way to see a woman."

"You've got it, Lucius. That's something I did discover today. He was calling on Chloe. He sent her a note." I read them the note Selena had found. The freedman's ridiculous attempt at a love-letter made everyone laugh.

"Gods," Quintus said. "As a poet, he makes a very fine tax-man. 'Be kind to your adoring and devoted lover when he comes to ask for your favour.' Chloe saw this, presumably?"

"Selena found it among her things. She thinks, and so do I, that one reason Chloe left the house was to avoid having to meet him."

They were all serious again. Quintus said, "That's one puzzle solved, at least."

"What about the weapon that killed him?" I asked. "This morning you mentioned a knife with a silver handle."

"That's another puzzle," Quintus said. "The report from the soldier who found the body mentioned a knife, a small knife with a wooden handle inlaid with silver. He said he hadn't seen one exactly like it before. But by the time I got there it had gone. I suppose somebody stole it."

"Not very attractive to a thief, covered in blood," Lucius pointed out. "My guess is the murderer realised he'd left it behind and came back for it."

I opened my belt-pouch and drew out Congrio's little knife. "Was it anything like this?"

"*Merda!*" Quintus exclaimed. "That's it! No, wait, this one's new, unmarked, it's never been used in anger. But it's very like the description we got of the original murder weapon. Where did you get it?"

"Congrio gave it to me as a present."

Lucius groaned. "Oh no, don't tell me he's selling knives as well as those silly cloaks. That means everyone in the fort probably owns one."

"Quite the opposite. He hasn't sold any at all. He gave out two as presents to people he said had helped him sell the cloaks. One for me, and one for Philippus."

"Philippus," Quintus said thoughtfully. "He fits the description of 'The Greek.' And the other two people who fit best couldn't have murdered Eurytus this morning. Mallius was in hospital, attended by Nikias."

"But supposing it was Philippus," Lucius wondered, "why did he do it?"

I said, "Either as part of the plan for the Fall of Troy, which means presumably for money, or just possibly because he didn't like the way Eurytus was behaving towards Chloe."

"Or both," Quintus suggested. "Virtuous vengeance and naked greed combined?"

We got no further with this speculation, because Gambax came in. "The horses and the raeda are all ready, sir. And I've found some clothes for Mistress Aurelia. And…well, time's running on, sir."

Quintus nodded and stood up. "Yes, it is. Let's move."

"Wait now, Quintus," I said. "I must look in on Mallius before we go. Tell him the news, such as it is. He has a right to know."

"He has. And he can be a useful reserve for us here. If we don't get back tonight, it's up to him to come looking for us tomorrow, or at least get Trebonius to authorise a search."

Mallius' bodyguards went so far as to smile at me this time, and ushered me straight in to see their master. He was smiling too, and the smell of wine in the room made me fear he'd already forgotten his promise to me about not drinking too much. But he got up to greet me, steady on his feet, and his words weren't slurred when he spoke.

"Aurelia, thank you for your help today. You disappeared before the very end, but Nikias is dead, and good riddance."

"I couldn't stay to watch. You military men may be able to take that sort of thing in your stride, but not me. Of course I'm glad we've got justice for Jovina, even though I know it won't bring her back."

"No." His shoulders sagged. "And he spoke the truth about the cruel way I treated her." With an effort he sat straight and smiled. "Will you have some wine…guaranteed poison-free?"

"I can't stay, Mallius. I've come with some news of the girls, then I'm going out to help look for them."

I explained briefly, and when I mentioned the ultimatum and Trebonius' stubborn determination to continue with his reprisals, he looked stricken.

"I knew he was wrong to threaten the hostages. I *knew* it!"

"We all know it. The trouble is, he won't change his mind now. We've tried to persuade him, but he won't budge. So we've only got tonight to find the girls and get them back."

"That's hardly possible, is it?"

"Possible, though not necessarily easy. We've been given some information about a place the rebels have been using for hiding stolen goods, and we think the girls may be imprisoned there. It's not far."

"Where? Tell me."

I told him about the place Gambax had described.

He nodded. "I know where you mean, and I agree, that's a likely hiding-place."

I shot an arrow into the dark. "We've also had information that Philippus has been storing goods there…goods that he's selling to the rebels."

I expected an outburst of denial, but he merely shrugged. "I've heard the same. The stupid boy is supposed to be involved in some shady dealing. Surplus stores, that sort of thing."

"Supposed to be? You haven't tried to check whether it's true?"

"I confess I haven't. His mother asked me not to."

"Jovina knew about it?"

"Like me, she'd heard rumours. She asked me not to follow them up, she said Philo was being punished now and had promised her that he'd behave himself in future. I—well, it seemed easier to let sleeping dogs lie. No senior officer wants a scandal involving his own son."

"I can see that. But you're going to have to face it sooner rather than later. Whether we find the girls or not, we'll have to tell Trebonius why we went looking in this particular place."

"Let's cross one bridge at a time, shall we? Who's going in this search-party of yours?"

When I told him, he stood up, making a supreme effort to look energetic and fit for action. "I'll come with you. Wait, I'll get my armour and sword."

"No, Marcus, absolutely not."

"Don't argue, my mind's made up."

"But it's out of the question. Not possible."

"What, you think I'm not up to it?"

That's exactly what I thought, but I knew I'd get nowhere by saying so.

"We need you here. It's vital you stay in the fort to watch our backs. There's nobody else who can do it."

"What do you mean?"

"I think it's pretty certain we'll find the girls tonight, but we may not be able to bring them back here straight away." Or at all, the fleeting thought went through my mind, but I suppressed it. "If for any reason we don't come back to the fort tonight, it's imperative that Trebonius sends out patrols to look for us tomorrow. It's up to you to persuade him to do that."

"He's sending men out to help with your search, surely?"

"No, he insists he can't spare anyone till his reinforcements come. So there'll just be the five of us, and if we have trouble tonight, we'll need urgent help tomorrow. That's what we want you to do. Please, Marcus. It could make the difference between life and death, for us and for Chloe."

"Very well, I'll stay. And I'll make sure Trebonius wastes no time in sending out extra men to help you when the reinforcements get here."

"But even if they don't come," I persisted, "if we're not back here tonight, you must make him understand how critical the situation is, and send men out at dawn anyway."

"I will, never fear. You can rely on me. And Aurelia…"

"Yes?"

"When you find Chloe, tell her…tell her I just want her home safe. I'm not angry with her, and it doesn't matter what has been said or done in the past, we can sort things out. I just want her back safe and sound."

"So do we all. And I hope you'll be telling her that yourself by tonight."

Chapter XXVIII

It was a stupid idea, of course. I can see that now. I could see it then, if I'm honest. I expect we all could, though nobody spoke the thought out loud. We knew there was no other choice, so we tacitly agreed not to admit that we were a party of fools, letting our hearts rule our heads.

We were full of confidence when we assembled just inside the main gate. We were a slightly odd sight, all wearing hooded cloaks against the cold wind, and three out of the five were Congrio's Vulcan's Shield garments. Lucius and I were the two exceptions, he in an old army leather sagum, I in a plain sheepskin travelling cloak. The men all had swords, and I stuck a dagger through my belt, as well as carrying Congrio's little knife in my pouch.

The sentries knew where we were going and wished us good hunting. I stopped for a word with Centurion Ennius.

"You've had a long watch today, Ennius. What's the latest news from outside?"

"Everything's still under control," he said, "though I'm afraid there's been quite a lot of damage to Roman property. I wish the reinforcements would hurry up. Still, one of the patrols has just caught a couple of village youths setting fire to shops in the forum, and executed them on the spot. That should give the rest something to think about."

It was easy travelling on the main road north, though we had to go slowly because of the accompanying raeda. Gambax drove it, while Titch led his horse. Once we were clear of the village the highway was deserted except for two ox-drawn wagons and a courier, all heading south for Isurium. After four miles, Gambax halted us beside a small turning that led left into thick woods.

"From here we need to take care," he said. "This track leads to the big barn. There are twists and turns and it forks in several places, so keep close to me and stay under cover of the trees where you can. After about a mile the trees end and there's the farm, the roundhouse, a couple of small outbuildings, and the barn itself. That's bound to be guarded. So I suggest we follow this small track about half a mile, then dismount and hide the horses and raeda, and go on foot from there."

We rode slowly and dismounted where the trees were still thick enough to conceal all the transport out of sight of the track. We walked on quietly and in single file, stopping frequently to listen. The men had their swords drawn, and I kept my hand on the dagger stuck in my belt. But the woods were quiet, with just the occasional bird-call or the scuffling of a small animal darting away as we approached.

Where the trees began to thin out, Gambax signalled us to halt again. He and Titch would reconnoitre from here, and without a word they set off.

"That's far enough," a deep voice called from the shadows, and six men armed with heavy cudgels rode out of cover and surrounded us. It was as simple as that. "Keep still, all of you, and you won't get hurt."

Of course all four of our men lunged at them, but they were at too much of a disadvantage, fighting on foot against horsemen. One of the riders had his leg cut, another received a minor slash across the arm, and a third was thrown from his horse when it reared up to dodge a blade aimed at its head. But their companions wielded their big sticks expertly. Titch and Lucius had their weapons knocked from their grasp with wrist-numbing blows, and were then flung to the ground when they tried to go on fighting. Gambax was hit on the head with a force that dented his helmet and laid him out unconscious. Quintus' arm was struck hard enough to make him grunt with the pain, and stumble so that he went sprawling. I didn't attempt anything myself, because I knew I'd no chance. One of our captors pulled the dagger from my belt but didn't search my pouch, so my little knife remained unnoticed, at any rate for now.

So far the ambush had been conducted without a word after that original warning. None of us spoke, either. I looked the natives over to see if I recognised any of them, but I didn't. They were all tall and muscular, with longish hair in various shades, fair, brown, and one red-headed. They wore good leather jerkins trimmed with iron, stout hide kilts and heavy boots. Leather from Cataractonium? I wondered. Very likely.

It was easy to tell which was their leader. His jerkin was trimmed with gold, and he wore a gold-decorated dagger at his belt, as well as an elaborate torc of twisted gold at his neck. And above all he had the bearing of someone used to being obeyed. The look of a prince, perhaps? Were we going to meet Venutius at last?

Whoever he was, he didn't appear pleased by our arrival. "Someone's betrayed us," he muttered, more to himself than to his men. "Portius swore this place was safe."

Portius... Did he mean Philippus?

The red-headed man beside him nodded. "Someone's talked, Venutius. But not Portius, I'd stake my life on that. He's got too much to lose."

"And he's just lost it," the prince snapped. "By the Three Mothers, can you ever really trust a Roman?"

His men stirred uneasily and muttered together. One said, "What does it matter who talked? If one knows, they must all know."

"True enough," Venutius said. "But we can hold them all off for tonight, and we'll move tomorrow."

He looked at us the way a man inspects horses he's thinking of buying. He asked his red-haired companion, "Are any of them the commander or the deputy commander from the fort?"

"No. That one is a soldier, but nobody important." He nodded towards Gambax, who was now trying to sit up, rubbing his bruised head. "The other men are investigators from down south somewhere. The woman belongs to one of them, I think."

"I don't belong to anybody." Oh, me and my big mouth! The words were out before I could stop them, and what's more I'd spoken in British, the language they were using among themselves. How much more sensible I'd have been, I realised, to pretend I didn't understand them, then they might have let something slip.

Venutius laughed. "You do now. You all belong to us. You're hostages, and you're just what we need. Your commander is threatening to kill some of the men from Isurium he has taken hostage today. I've told him that for every one of ours he executes, we'll do the same to one of his people. But so far we only had a couple of girls…"

"The girls are here?" Lucius interrupted. "Are they alive? And unharmed?"

The prince nodded. "For now they are. They aren't much use to us dead. We've told Trebonius we'll do nothing to them until we hear that he has started his unspeakable executions, so unless he breaks his word, they'll be all right till dawn at least. Perhaps longer, if he sees sense. But there are only two of them, and Trebonius has twenty. I was anticipating having to raid some Roman farms hereabouts tonight to even up the numbers, but the gods have sent me five more. I'll be content with that for the present."

One of his men said, "If we have to execute two a day, we can start with the men here. Keep the women for a treat later."

"I've a much better idea," Venutius answered. "They can decide among themselves who's to be executed first. I'll enjoy watching how a pack of Romans choose which among them is to be sacrificed."

This was such an appalling prospect I was lost for words. But Quintus appeared unruffled. "Whoever you murder, it won't change Trebonius' mind. It'll simply make him and everyone at the fort more determined than ever. And now they all know where to find you, they're coming for you in strength. Your only hope is to release us and the girls now, so we can return them to Isurium and persuade the commander to call off the executions."

Venutius laughed again. "I don't believe you can arrange any such thing, not with that madman Trebonius in command. He wants the murderer of Eurytus in his hands before he'll release our people. But we didn't kill the man, whatever you Romans think about it. So we're not able to hand him over, and we're not prepared to suffer for something we haven't done."

"And *I* don't believe *you*," Quintus retorted. "We know you planned to kill him at midsummer. We've seen the secret message sent from Londinium, about the Fall of Troy, and Achilles and Hector. That proves it."

"It proves someone planned to kill him," Venutius was smiling like a philosopher enjoying the cut-and-thrust of an argument. "I'm not saying I'm displeased that someone has finished him off. But it wasn't my doing, or any Brigantian's. One of you Romans murdered him. Personally I hope he gets away with it, but I'll not stand by and allow any of my men to take the blame."

"A nice defence," Quintus replied, in the same casual tone. "If only it were true. But this murder was committed in the civilian village. It was done by a Brigantian, there's no doubt of it. Maybe not by you or your immediate war-band, but by someone living near the fort. We Romans can't let Eurytus' death go unavenged. So if you have any influence in the village, why don't you persuade the culprit or culprits to give themselves up to justice? If not, I can't answer for the consequences."

"Meaning what, exactly?"

"The whole fort is on battle alert. In fact the whole of this part of the province, because reinforcements are on their way from other bases, so the word has gone out. They know precisely when we set off to find the girls, and where we were bound. If we're not back at the fort by tonight, the commander will take that as a signal for open war. He'll have enough men to hunt down every last Brigantian between here and Eburacum. Is that what you want? To die yourselves, and have your women and children sold into slavery?"

I felt like cheering. Quintus was magnificent.

But the prince merely shrugged. "What's your name?"

"Quintus Antonius Delfinus. Imperial investigator."

"Well, Quintus Antonius Delfinus, I don't think you're in any position to threaten me. And we're wasting time." He nodded towards his men. "Put them with the others. Make sure they're securely tied up. Double the guard on the barn and in the woods from now on. Catching this lot might have been like picking plums off a tree, but they may try sending someone more useful."

So they marched us ignominiously away. We walked with what dignity we could. I felt frightened, not to mention humiliated and disappointed at how easily we'd been caught.

The clearing with the buildings Gambax had described was only a short distance away. We halted outside the door of the enormous wooden barn, and one of our escort stripped off our cloaks, while two more brought ropes and tied each of us up, hands behind our backs and feet loosely hobbled together so we could barely walk without falling. It was done in silence, quickly and efficiently. Then the red-haired man pulled the heavy door wide open, and we were shepherded towards it.

"Help!" a voice cried out from inside. It was Chloe's voice, shrill and scared.

"No help, my dear," Venutius said. "But we're bringing some company to make the hours pass more pleasantly."

As they pushed us into the barn I had a brief glimpse of hay piled up waist-high all along the left-hand side, an empty space to the right, and the two girls huddled together at the far end… except the far end was much nearer than it should be, the whole interior was much smaller. That back wall must be merely a partition, separating off a further section which presumably had its own entrance from outside. I could distinguish the outline of a door in the partition, but it had no handle.

"Lucius!" That was Vitellia's voice, a mixture of fear and joy. Of course, she hadn't known my brother had arrived in Isurium.

"I'm here, Kitten," Lucius answered. "It's going to be all right."

Then our captors slammed the door, and we heard two heavy bolts shoot home. We all stood still in what felt like complete darkness. But as our eyes adjusted, we realised it wasn't pitch-black, only extremely gloomy. I could make out two small windows, one on each side and very high up. They'd no glass in them, and presumably could have been closed with shutters, but you could see this hadn't been done for a very long time. They were festooned with masses of giant spider-webs, complete with giant spiders, which blocked most of the light but let in some air at least. I'm not one of those females who faints away at the sight of a spider, and I'd have been fascinated to watch them if circumstances had been different. Now they only served to remind me that I was as helpless as the flies trapped in their silken nets.

I tried to walk forward, but found it too difficult, so I sat down on the earth floor. The others were doing the same. We shuffled along on our tails till we were sitting close together, and the two girls, who were tied up as we were, worked their way from the far end to join us, so we formed a rough circle. Lucius and Vitellia sat together, talking softly. I noticed that both girls had managed to retain their cloaks, and I envied them the warmth. The barn felt cold. Our own cloaks had been flung into the barn after us, but for all the chance we had of wearing them, they might as well have been back in Isurium.

Quintus said softly, "We're glad to see you, girls. Are either of you hurt?"

Vitellia murmured, "No, just uncomfortable from being tied up all day. We've been here hours. Oh, Lucius, when I saw you there I thought you'd come to get us out of this horrid place." It sounded as if she was about to cry, but there wasn't light enough to see.

"We'll be out of here soon," my brother said. "Reinforcements are on their way."

"Chloe," Gambax said, "they haven't hurt you either, love, have they?"

"No. I'm stiff and sore, but nothing worse." Her voice was almost unrecognisable, no longer the self-confident, spoiled young lady, but a frightened child. "And I know it's all my fault. I'm sorry I've got you all into this mess. I didn't realise what would happen."

I bit back the remark I'd like to have made. Probably everyone did. There was no point in recriminations now, there'd be time enough later for telling the silly child what we thought of her. If indeed "later" had any real meaning for us…

I pulled myself together as Quintus whispered, "Listen, everyone, we must plan how to escape, but remember we're likely to be overheard if we speak in normal voices. If we want to talk among ourselves, it must be like this. But our audience will think it odd if they don't hear anything."

He went on in his normal voice, "What's done is done. Let's concentrate on the next few hours. It seems to me we're stuck here till the reinforcements come, so we may as well just make ourselves as comfortable as we can."

"Are reinforcements really coming?" Chloe asked.

"They are. There are patrols searching in the woods now. We weren't sure which of their hideouts the rebels had taken you to, so we split up into several groups to save time. We all arranged to rendezvous before nightfall. When we don't show up there, the others will know where to find us…and you. We just have to wait here and not give the natives any trouble. It's only a matter of time."

Quintus spoke firmly and confidently, and loudly enough to be overheard by whatever guards were posted outside the barn, if they were taking the trouble to listen. It was impressive, so convincing I almost found myself believing what he was saying.

In a whisper he added, *"That should reassure them that we'll be good little boys and girls, while we get ready to escape. Now here's what we're actually going to do."*

We then had one of the weirdest conversations I can ever remember. Really it was two conversations, one privately in soft whispers, the other loud and strident for the benefit of any listeners. Describing it afterwards like this, it sounds clumsy and awkward, but actually it worked surprisingly well.

Quintus began it. *"These ropes feel pretty flimsy to me, made of old hemp and quite frayed. We'll find a way to saw through them. We need something sharp within reach, so we can rub the ropes across it till the strands split apart."*

That'll take all night, I thought, but then reflected that we had all night at our disposal, so I said nothing.

"A good spiky nail sticking out of the wall, or a jagged wood-splinter," Lucius agreed. *"I didn't have time to notice if there was anything like that here. Did anyone else?"*

"There's something…" Chloe began loudly, and then remembered, and with admirable quickness changed what she was going to say. "There's something odd that I don't understand about all this." She dropped her voice to a whisper. *"By the door, Antonius. I'll show you."*

She began to inch her way towards it, and so did Quintus and Lucius. Meanwhile she continued out loud, "I got a note from you, Gambax, this morning, telling me to meet you by the river. When we got there we were ambushed. So you didn't write it, presumably?"

"No, I didn't. It was a trick to get you out of the house and stop you going to the fort. I'd never lead you into a trap, never!"

"Here we are," she blurted out as she reached the door, and added in a whisper, *"Sorry. It's here."*

"What's that, Chloe?" Quintus asked in a hearty voice.

Again the child's quick wits came to her rescue. "Here we are in the middle of nowhere. I wonder…can the gods still hear us?"

"I'm sure they can," Quintus answered.

"Then let's each say a prayer for help. I always pray to Diana the Huntress when I'm in trouble."

"Me, too," I exclaimed. "You don't have to be in a temple to call on the Immortals. Let's all pray quietly. The Roman gods are still with us, and if we ask for their help, they'll hear us, even if the Brigantian gods aren't listening."

There was a short silence. I expect everyone prayed. I know I did.

"*Good,*" Quintus was by the door now. "*Well, Chloe? What are we looking for?*"

"*There's a nail at about waist level on the left. I felt my cloak catch on it when they brought us here.*"

"*Good girl.*" He and Lucius were searching the walls, but having trouble seeing anything much in the gloom.

"*Got it,*" Lucius breathed. "*Sticks out about a finger's width, good and sharp too.*" He levered himself upright against the wall. "*I can touch it with the backs of my hands, but I can't bring the rope near enough to the nail to do any cutting. Ouch! All I'm doing is making myself bleed.*" He struggled on for a while, then stepped back and Quintus took his place, but we could all see that the pain from his injured arm made it impossible for him even to get close, and he'd then have the same problem as Lucius.

"*Let me try.*" Chloe had got herself into a standing position near the door. "*They tied us up differently, look.*" And we all realised that the two girls' hands were bound in front of them, not behind as ours were.

"*How did you manage that?*" Quintus smiled for the first time since we'd entered the barn.

"*We were cold this morning, and we asked the men to let us keep our cloaks on. So they had to tie us like this.*" She moved close to the door and held her hands out, and sure enough, she could get part of the rope onto the nail, but not the point itself. So she began sawing it across the metal, with very short thrusts back and forth.

"*Not too hard,*" Quintus warned softly. "*Slow and sure. Don't rattle the door… Well done, that's right. Let's give the audience some distraction.*" He slid down the wall to a sitting position again, and moved into the centre of the room. "I'm starving," he said heartily.

We all followed him, leaving Chloe working laboriously by the door.

Lucius joined in. "So am I. I wonder if they'll bring us any food."

"I shouldn't be feeling hungry at all," I said. "I ate far too much at the party yesterday. Did anybody try the goose with cherry sauce? It was really delicious."

We babbled on, keeping the chatter going while watching Chloe, willing her to get herself free. We must have discussed every dish on offer yesterday and were starting on the wines, and I for one was beginning to wonder if she'd ever do it. I racked my brains for another inane topic of conversation.

Then suddenly she let out a stifled gasp and stepped back from the door, waving both hands in the air. She forgot that her feet were tied and went full length on the earth floor, but she leapt up immediately and was still waving.

"Done it!" It was only a whisper, but it held a whole world of triumph.

"I think that party was one of the most brilliant I've ever seen," Quintus said aloud. We all agreed enthusiastically, trusting that our audience wouldn't realise where the real brilliance lay.

Chloe flapped her hands, flexing her fingers to loosen their stiffness. Then she sat upright, leant forward, and untied her feet. She stood up a little unsteadily, and walked across to where we all sat.

"Who first?" she mouthed. *"You, Quintus Antonius? Your bad arm must be painful."*

Quintus glanced round at us. *"I suppose nobody is carrying a knife?"*

"I am," I said. *"In my belt-pouch."*

"Excellent. Use that, Chloe."

It was, as Congrio had said, a good little knife. She had us all free in no time. The relief was enormous. We could move and walk about, and that made us feel that somehow we had a measure of control over our situation. It was hard to keep remembering not to exclaim aloud.

But our pleasure didn't last long. There was a shout somewhere outside, too distant to make out the words, then came hoof-beats, a single horse cantering through the trees. When the rider shouted again, nearer this time, we could all hear the one word "Venutius!"

"What's up?" Someone answered from close by the barn. "Who wants the prince? Oh, it's you, Katakos. What's all the noise for?"

The man was panting, speaking in short jerky sentences. "They've broken their word. At the fort. They've executed two already."

"What? Two of ours? You sure about that?"

"Yes, quite sure. Brennus' son is one; don't know about the other. The lads on watch in the village saw it. They sent word as we arranged. Stone dead, they are. So much for waiting until dawn!"

Someone else said, "Well, if they won't wait, we don't have to. We can take our revenge as soon as we like." Several of his comrades cheered.

Katakos said, "Pass the word to the others, will you? I must find Venutius."

"I'm here, Katakos. They've started the killings, you say?"

"Yes, Venutius. Two dead already."

"Then we must act now. Call the men here."

There was the sound of a horn blown long and loud, three blasts in all. As the echoes died away in the woods I heard Quintus mutter, "Gods, this is what we've been dreading. The start of open war."

Nobody else spoke for a while. What can you say when you've just listened to your death sentence?

Chapter XXIX

Eventually Lucius burst out, "How in the gods' name could Trebonius do this? After the message Venutius sent him, after we told him what our plans were…he knows we're out here searching. How could he?"

"It seems he doesn't care overmuch whether any of us live or die," Quintus answered bitterly.

I said, "I can see what's happened, and the gods know what we can do, but Trebonius has kept his word. I'm sure he hasn't killed any of the hostages from the village, Quintus. The natives have misunderstood something they've seen."

"How can it be a misunderstanding? Either two of the hostages are dead, or they're alive."

"But other Brigantians may have been killed in the fighting around the village. There have been patrols out all day, jumpy and angry and waiting for an excuse to spill blood. And some of them have spilt it. Didn't you here the centurion on duty when we were leaving, telling me two men had been executed in the forum for setting fire to Roman property? And it's late in the day now, so I doubt if they were the first."

Lucius swore. "Gods, that's probably it. We must tell Venutius, try to make him understand that Trebonius hasn't broken his word."

Quintus shook his head and put his finger to his lips, then whispered, *"Can't talk to him, he'll see that we're not tied up."* Aloud he declared, "No point, I'm afraid. He won't take our word for anything, will he? And even if he did, his men are angry and he probably couldn't persuade them that arsonists and looters being killed isn't a cause for war."

We were all talking loudly, but even so we could hear voices, footsteps, and hoof-beats, the unmistakable sounds of a group of men gathering together. I tried to estimate how many of them there might be, but I couldn't—a couple of dozen perhaps?

"Listen to me, men of Brigantia." Venutius' voice rang out, and they were all immediately quiet. He sounded quite close to us, an unexpected piece of luck, because it meant we could hear what he was saying. "The Roman pigs have broken their word and started to kill the hostages they took this morning. You all know what that means."

An angry roar rose up from the men, followed by a chilling chant of "Kill the Romans! Kill the Romans!" I felt sick with fear. I went to stand by Quintus and gripped his hand. I saw Lucius put an arm round Vitellia, and Gambax move to comfort Chloe. Titch, the only one without a partner here, stood straight and still with an expression that said anyone who tried to kill him would pay dearly.

"Not so fast, boys," Venutius called, and the chanting stopped. "Of course you're angry. So am I. But there's something else. You know that we picked up the girls by sending them a forged letter this morning. But now more Romans have come out from the fort, five of them, four men and a woman. One of them is a soldier, and they've headed directly here to find us. In other words, our base here is no longer secret, and no longer safe. It looks as if someone has talked."

Somebody shouted, "I never trusted Portius. He used us for his own schemes and plans, he never believed in what we're trying to do. He'll drop us when it suits him."

"Possibly, but not just yet," Venutius said. "Don't forget he hasn't been paid for this last load from Cataractonium, and he's still desperate for money. And we've used him too, remember. All that good Roman leather he's sent us… Settling his debts was a small price to pay for it, not to mention the information he passed on. No, he's too smart to mess on his own doorstep."

"Who's Portius?" Gambax whispered.

"Code name. Tell you later," Quintus breathed.

"Well, whoever's talked, we've got to move, Venutius," a voice called.

"Yes, we'll go tonight. Take as much as we can with us, especially the good stuff, the war gear, boots, all that. The fancy soft leather you got to impress your women may have to stay behind. We can store it all at Katakos' place for now. That's never been involved with the stuff from the tannery, so it'll be safe. All right, Katakos?"

"Fine by me."

"Then let's get to it. You all know your jobs. Guards, back in position, there may be other patrols coming our way. Wagon and mule drivers, get the animals and vehicles ready. The rest of you start gathering the leather into manageable bundles and loading it."

"What's happening about the hostages?" Katakos asked. "Do I get to store them, too? Or can I just have the women and someone else can take the men?"

"Leave them to me," Venutius said. "They won't be going anywhere. The less you all know about it, the better. Accidents will happen, won't they?"

I didn't like the way he said that, nor the wave of laughter it brought from the men. An accident…involving us?

As everyone began to move noisily about their business, it was surprisingly easy to form a mental picture of what was happening outside. Some of the footsteps moved away, while others made for the far end of our barn. We heard bolts being shot back, followed by the creak of a heavy door opening, and then curses and grunts as men began to shift the leather that must be stacked up just beyond the partition wall.

What I couldn't picture was what would happen next. Venutius meant to kill us, that was obvious, but how? From what he'd said, he wouldn't simply send half-a-dozen warriors into the barn to cut our throats. "Leave them to me…They won't be going anywhere…Accidents will happen." I was paralysed with fear, unable to move a muscle, yet my mind raced like a bolting horse.

Quintus, still holding my hand, beckoned everyone into a close circle, and there was a small comfort in feeling the others so near. Whatever we were about to face, we'd be together, we could support each other. However death came to us, we could meet it with, at least, Roman dignity and courage.

"We've not much time." Quintus spoke quietly, but there was no need to whisper now. The noises coming from beyond the partition covered his voice. "We've one important advantage, the element of surprise. We can fight our way out when they come to get us. It's the last thing they'll be expecting. We've a few weapons. Aurelia, your knife. May I use it please?"

"Of course." I handed it to him.

"And we've all got cloaks." He glanced towards where ours had been thrown into a jumbled heap near the door. Titch went to fetch them, and started handing them round to us.

"Look, we've nearly all got those Vulcan's Shield ones from Congrio," Vitellia said. "I hope he's right about them bringing us luck."

"But a cloak isn't a weapon," Chloe objected.

"It can be," Lucius said. "You can throw it over the enemy's head to blind him. Or sweep it along near the ground to trip him up." He advanced on Chloe, flailing his cloak almost on the floor and catching her ankles. She tried to move out of the way and stumbled.

"These can be good too." Titch took off his leather belt and whirled it around his head. "Catch a man in the face with the buckle, he'll know about it."

This is desperation indeed, I thought. How can we face armed barbarian warriors with nothing but one small knife and the clothes on our backs? But of course I took off my belt and whipped it experimentally through the air. The other girls did the same.

"My mama told me," Vitellia said unexpectedly, "that if I ever needed to defend myself against a man, I could knee him in the balls."

Lucius' shocked expression at the notion of his beloved doing any such thing was almost comic. "Now don't you worry your head, Kitten…"

"Oh I'm not exactly worried," she answered gravely." The trouble is, I'd have to get very close to him to do that, wouldn't I?"

She hadn't meant to be funny, but it came out like dialogue in a comedy, and everyone laughed. The atmosphere, which had been taut as a catapult-spring, relaxed to a wary alertness. I suddenly felt a rush of excitement, almost exultation. I've known it before when I've been facing danger. It's a kind of battle fever, and real soldiers must experience it often; otherwise no man would ever go into battle twice.

I looked at Quintus and Lucius, whose moods I always know so well. They were feeling the same, I was certain of it. Perhaps after all we might take the Brigantians unawares. It was our only hope, but it was at least a hope.

"Get into position," Quintus said. "Men standing against the wall there so we'll be next to the door when it opens. Girls sitting in the middle of the floor, not too close together. With luck they'll come straight in and head for you, not realising that we can outflank them. Sit quietly when they come, then jump at them once they're clear of the door, and we'll attack them from behind."

We did as he ordered. I sat between Chloe and Vitellia, who were both looking pale and frightened. I tried to think of something we could talk about that would keep our minds from brooding on the impending fight.

Chloe provided the obvious topic. "What's been happening in Isurium while we've been stuck here? Did Selena and Statius and all our servants move into the fort?"

I recounted some of that day's happenings. Most important, I was able to reassure Chloe that Mallius hadn't killed her mother.

"I suppose that's something," she said, with an attempt at casualness which didn't come off. I could tell she was relieved.

"He said to tell you to forget about the past. All he wants is for you to come back to him safe and sound."

She ignored the message and asked, "Have you found out who did kill her?"

"Yes, we have. It was Nikias."

"Nikias?" Vitellia exclaimed. "That nice Greek doctor?"

"Not so nice," Chloe said. "A slimy little man, I always thought. What's going to happen to him?"

"He's dead. It's a long story, I'll tell you about it when we're safely away from here. But I swore I'd avenge Jovina, and I have."

"Good." There was a pause, and the sounds from outside came through to us, loud and menacing.

Vitellia asked, "Is Baca all right? They left her behind. I was so afraid for her. But you must have found her, or you wouldn't be here."

"She's safe, though she's had a bad fright. It was brave of her to go with you. What in the gods' name did you think you were doing, running away like that when you knew you were meant to be moving to the fort?"

Chloe hung her head. "A letter came from Gambax, suggesting I should meet him by the river. I thought, I'll go there for just a short time before I go to the fort."

"But I never wrote any letter," Gambax objected.

"I know you didn't, love. I ought to have realised it wasn't from you, but I was desperate to get out of the house anyway. I'd had a note from Eurytus saying he was coming to call on me, and I was frightened what would happen. If Mama had been there she'd have sent him packing, but there was nobody else I could trust to stand up to him. We couldn't find Philo—he'd left the fort—and Statius is too old. When the note came apparently from Gambax, it was like a gift from the gods."

"And I couldn't let her go out alone," Vitellia put in. "The servants were all busy getting ready to move to the fort, except Baca, and she insisted on coming with us. Thank the gods she did."

There was another pause, and we all became aware that the noises from outside the barn were growing fainter. There was no more activity from behind our partition wall, and the footsteps and hoof-beats were receding. Then Venutius' voice rose above the mixture of sounds. "I'll finish off here and follow you."

"This is it," Quintus hissed.

But nothing happened, except that the other noises died out to silence, leaving only the whisper of wind, and occasionally bird-calls from the trees round the clearing.

"They've gone," Chloe whispered. "Gone and left us here."

"I doubt that," Quintus said. "Not all of them, anyway. Venutius is preparing some kind of nasty surprise, I'll bet you anything you like. So be ready, everyone. We're about to find out the worst."

Still nothing happened. We remained on the alert. I remember clutching my cloak in one hand and my belt in the other so hard that my fingers began to stiffen. Still there wasn't a sound from outside.

After what seemed like half an hour but probably wasn't, Lucius said, "You'd have lost your bet, Quintus. They *have* gone. Even Venutius. They're going to leave us here, as they think, tied up and unable to move."

"They'll come back later to fetch us, I'm sure," Quintus said. "Having got their hands on seven hostages, it doesn't make sense for them to abandon us for good."

"But we won't be waiting when they come," Titch muttered. "All we have to do is get ourselves out of here." He glanced up at the windows. "Yon windows are the best way, for anyone who's on the small side, and not afraid of spiders." He grinned. "How about it, girls? Either of you care to get through there, if we can lift you up to it? Then you can run round to the door and unfasten the bolts."

"Ugh! No, I couldn't possibly!" both girls exclaimed together, and everyone else laughed.

"I'll go," I said. "That is, if I can squeeze through either of them. They're not very large, are they?"

"I'll give it a try first," Titch said. "I'll need to climb on someone's shoulders, mind. Gambax, you're the tallest."

He was, but not by much, and the men started discussing how best to raise Titch—or even me—up high enough to get through the opening.

Suddenly Chloe screamed. "Smoke! I can smell smoke. It's coming from the other side of the wooden wall."

We ran to the back of the barn and stood by the partition, sniffing the air like hunting-dogs after a boar. At first I could only catch the smells of timber, hay, and sweat. But then I smelt the unmistakable tang of burning hay, and something else I couldn't identify…but it was smoke all right. I could see thin wisps of it seeping through some of the wider cracks in the partition wall. And was it my imagination?…no, it wasn't. There was a very faint reddish glow visible through one or two chinks, whereas before there had been darkness.

We all stood as if rooted to the ground, taking in the appalling situation. We were imprisoned in one half of a barn, while the other half was on fire. If we couldn't escape immediately, we'd be going up in smoke too.

It was Quintus who roused himself first.

"So that's what Venutius meant by 'accidents will happen.' The cold-blooded bastard means us to die here, tied up and defenceless, in what will appear to be an accidental barn fire. Only this one is no accident…and we're not tied up."

"And maybe not defenceless either," I said. "We've got several of these fancy cloaks that Congrio says will protect against fire."

"You surely don't believe in that sort of rubbish?" Lucius asked.

"We saw him try to burn one up in Eburacum, and it didn't catch alight," Vitellia said.

"Unless that was a trick of some sort," I answered.

"Well, then," Titch said, "this is our ideal chance to try them out."

Lucius laughed scornfully. "Well, I don't suppose they'll do any harm. I'm hoping we shan't have to find out whether they do any actual good."

"Everyone over by that window, please," Quintus said. "Gambax, get ready to take Titch's weight. Lucius, help me lift him onto Gambax's shoulders…"

"Wait now, Quintus." Lucius picked up the sheepskin cloak I'd been wearing. "Gambax, put this on. You'll be cut to ribbons otherwise, Titch's boots have hobnails in them."

Titch put on his Vulcan's Shield cloaks. "I tell you something, if that Congrio was lying and I get roasted, I swear I'll come out of the Underworld and haunt him until I get me money back."

"We'd all better wear cloaks," Quintus said. The girls put theirs on, and Lucius picked up his old sagum. Quintus and I took the remaining Vulcan's Shield cloaks.

Gambax stood braced against the wall below one of the windows, and Quintus and Lucius hoisted Titch easily up onto his broad shoulders. But we could all see straight away that Titch wasn't going to get through the opening.

"Me shoulders are too tight a squeeze," he called down. "I think mebbe I could force meself through with a push from you fellers below, but I'd go flying out head first, and it's too long a drop for that really. Still, I'll give it a try if it's the only way."

"Good for you, Titch," Quintus said, "but let's think a bit first. There's nothing to be gained by you breaking your neck in the fall. Before you come down, can you clear those spiders out of the way? We'll have better light, and we might be able to persuade one of the girls to try. They're lighter and thinner than you."

"The smoke's getting thicker," Lucius said softly. "I can smell hay burning, and…what's that other foul stink mixed with it?"

"I've smelt it once, on a battlefield." Titch jumped down, brushing spider-webs from his arms and hands. "It's burning leather. They've left some leather stored in there, but it doesn't burn easy. It needs the fire to be hot."

"Very comforting, Titch," I said. "Right, you've cleared the window of spiders. Help me up, I'm sure I can get through there."

"No." Chloe stepped up to stand beside Gambax. "I'm the smallest, and I got us all into this fix. I'll go."

"No, love, you mustn't think of it," Gambax protested. "Nor you, Mistress Aurelia. This isn't woman's work."

"Then what do you suggest, Gambax?" Chloe snapped. "That we all stay shut in here till the fire breaks through and we're roasted alive? Do stop arguing, there isn't time. Somebody give me a hand up here, please."

"Quintus Antonius," Gambax pleaded, "don't let her do this."

"I think she's making a very sensible suggestion," Quintus answered. "And a very brave one, too. Are you ready, Chloe?"

"I'm ready."

"Then I'll help you up."

She hardly needed his help, she leapt up so lightly that she almost seemed to fly. And we all saw that she could easily slide her slim body through. She leaned her head and shoulders out, then withdrew into the barn.

"Titch is right, I need to drop feet first. I can turn round, I think…help me, Gambax, will you?" He did as she asked, and everyone else shouted encouragement.

But by now we were only half-watching her. Most of our attention was concentrated on the partition wall, which was making loud cracking sounds. The small wooden door in the centre which linked the two halves of the barn was the weak point. Smoke was literally pouring round its edges, and it was becoming harder to breathe the air. How long before the planks of the door caught alight and collapsed?

"I've done it!" called Chloe. She sat in the window-opening facing outwards, her legs dangling over its edge. "Wish me good fortune, everyone. Here I go!"

She let out an exultant yell, and disappeared.

We held our breaths. We heard a crash, a cry, and a couple of ripe curses that shocked Gambax. Finally came a shout that was a mixture of triumph and despair. "I'm down but I've twisted my ankle. It's all right, I'll get to the door. I'll be as quick as I can."

We ran to the door, hardly able to see our way through the stifling smoke. I glanced back and saw that the light showing round the edges of the door in the partition had changed from red to orange-yellow, and that it wasn't a steady glow now, but a stream of sparks pouring through. Even as I watched a couple of the sparks flew out into the room and landed on a pile of hay. It began to smoulder.

I ran to it and I flung my cloak over the wisp of smoke that was curling upwards. When I lifted it again, the smoke was gone, and Vulcan's Shield was undamaged…but more sparks were coming in. I saw two more patches of hay begin to smoke, and then one spark landed on me.

Lucius ran up. "Give me your cloak, Sis, and get back. Leave it to us."

For once I didn't argue. I watched from a safe distance as he and Titch used two Vulcan's Shields to put out more potential fires in the hay. This didn't look like a situation that could last long. I wished Chloe would hurry.

"I'm here," she yelled from outside the door. "I'm doing the bolts. Get ready." We heard her shoot a big bolt back. Then there was a pause. "Gods, this second one's stuck. I can't move it."

"Yes, you can," Quintus shouted. "You've done brilliantly so far, now finish the job. It's getting too hot for comfort in here, so for the gods' sake put some muscle into it."

"I *am*, but it's almost too high to reach, and…"

"Listen, Chloe, you can do it," Gambax shouted. "I know you can. Haven't I always said you're strong for a girl? Now show me. Just one quick hard pull, that's all it needs. A barbarian pushed that bolt in. Are you saying you're feebler than a barbarian? Now I'm going to count to three. One…two…*three!*"

There was a grating sound and a triumphant yell, and the second bolt shot back.

"Well done!" Quintus shouted. "Get clear of the building, Chloe. When we push the door open, the fire will spread through to this side for sure. So run for your lives. Come over here, Lucius and Titch. Ready? I'm opening NOW!"

He pushed hard and the door flew wide open, so fast he almost overbalanced. I stopped him falling, and we rushed out into the wonderful fresh air. The others were ahead of us, but they slowed down to turn and look back.

"Run, you fools. Run!" Quintus yelled. Gambax snatched Chloe up into his arms, and we all pelted across the clearing as if the Parthian cavalry were after us.

From the barn came a crash and a loud roar. We'd been only just in time. None of us dared stop to look till we were in the shelter of the trees. When we turned, we saw the entire building blazing like a pyre, with long flames blowing out from it on a rising wind, and sparks flying everywhere. The trees near it in the clearing would be on fire soon. The whole wood might burn.

"By the gods, that was too close for my liking," Quintus said. "Is everyone all right? Chloe, how's your ankle?"

"I've sprained it, but nothing's broken. I'm sorry I was so slow."

"You were magnificent, Chloe. You were all quite magnificent! I wish I were a general—then I could hand out battle honours to everyone."

"I don't like the way that fire's burning," I said. "It'll catch the trees any time now. We need to move out of here. Do you suppose our horses are still where we left them?"

"And the *raeda*," Gambax said. "We'll need a carriage. Chloe can't walk, let alone ride."

Quintus nodded. "Gambax and Titch, could you go and fetch it please, and bring all our horses here. On the double. We must get back to the fort as soon as we can. I want to be inside those walls before nightfall."

"Listen!" Titch exclaimed. "I heard a bugle. In the trees, I'm sure I did."

We strained our ears but could hear nothing, which was hardly surprising amid the roaring and crackling noises coming from the fire. Even as we watched, the roof of the barn fell in with a rumble like thunder, and flames leaped up into the sky and across into the trees nearby.

"There it is again," Titch shouted excitedly, "a cavalry bugle, sounding the charge. I used to be a bugler—I'd recognise it anywhere. Can't you hear it?"

"I can," Gambax called. "It must be a patrol from Isurium, come to find us!"

"Take cover!" Quintus shouted. "We'll see who they are before we show ourselves."

But before we were properly hidden among the scattered trees, there was a third strident bugle-call, and out into the clearing burst a dozen soldiers, cantering along with drawn swords. And the man leading them was Philippus.

"It's all right, everyone," he called out. "You're safe now."

Chloe cheered wildly and rushed out of the trees as fast as her injured ankle would allow. "Philo! Oh, Philo, thank the gods!"

Chapter XXX

The rest of us emerged more cautiously, but we soon shared Chloe's joy. This truly was a rescue party, a contingent of men from the fort. I recognised some of them, and they were all grinning broadly. What Philippus was doing leading them, I couldn't guess, but for now I was happy that they were here and we were safe.

Philippus embraced Chloe and Vitellia, and Gambax slapped him on the back. Of course none of them knew of his double identity, and we four realised this wasn't the time or place to reveal it.

Having basked in their gratitude and congratulations, he came to the rest of us, shaking our hands and asking whether we were all right. We assured him we were and thanked him for coming to find us. If our responses were a little reserved, he didn't seem to notice. He probably wasn't aware either how cautious we were being in answering his various questions. It was like walking on egg-shells, blending truths, half-truths and lies as we talked with a man who combined the roles of rescuer and murderer.

"We're certainly glad to see you," Quintus said. "We need to hurry back to the fort before it gets dark. Our horses are hidden in the woods near here."

He nodded. "We heard them. The smell of smoke was upsetting them, but they haven't bolted yet. Some of my men are bringing them, then we can be off."

"How did you find us?" Lucius asked. "The Brigantians seemed to think this place was a secret."

"We've been aware of occasional native activity here," he answered smoothly. "Storing stolen property, even some illegal iron-working. We were supposed to be looking into it properly, but of course with all this Eurytus business…Anyhow, when I got back to the fort this evening and heard the girls were being held hostage, I thought of this barn at once. I persuaded the commander to let me have some men, and we came as fast as we could. I must thank you for saving them from the fire. You took a considerable risk, bringing such a small force here."

"We had no choice," Quintus answered. "The ultimatum from Venutius said the girls would be executed at dawn if Trebonius killed any of the Brigantian hostages."

Philippus asked a little too casually, "I'm impressed you knew about this place, though. How did you find out?"

"Just a lucky tip-off." Quintus replied lightly, "which meant we made our way here quite quickly. But there weren't enough of us to get the girls away on our own. Trebonius absolutely refused to let us have any of his men until reinforcements arrived."

Philippus nodded. "They've come at last, thank the gods. Ten cavalry from Eburacum, and a century of infantry promised for tomorrow. Lucky for all of us. Trebonius can be as stubborn as a mule. Believe me, I know." He grinned. "Mind you, so can…" he broke off and gave a loud and unconvincing cough. "*Merda,* this smoke's appalling." He coughed again, and added lamely, "Sorry. Let's get out of here before we all end up with sore throats."

Quintus laughed. "From what we heard of Venutius, I'd say he could match Trebonius in stubbornness, and toughness too."

"Was Venutius here in person?"

"Yes, though of course we didn't get much chance of a chat. But we could overhear him well enough, talking to his men. You should have heard what he threatened to do to the man he thinks betrayed his base here to us. Someone called Portius. I shouldn't like to be in his sandals if Venutius catches him."

Philippus turned away hastily and began shouting orders to his men. Quintus and I exchanged a smile.

We were soon on our way home. It was slow going through the woods. I remember Philippus suggested that those of us on horseback could ride ahead with a small escort, if we wanted to reach the fort more quickly, while the carriage would trundle slowly back at its own speed with the rest of his troop. We refused the offer, saying that after all we'd been through we preferred to stay together. Perhaps we were being over-suspicious…but I shared Quintus' views about that.

"As you like, of course," Philippus said. "Anyone would think you don't trust me to keep them safe!" He laughed, but it rang hollow. "I'll send a couple of men ahead of us, at least, to tell my father and the commander and everyone that we're coming."

When we reached the main road we increased our pace a little and trotted along while the escort spread out around us. Philippus stayed at the rear, chatting to the girls in the raeda, playing the part of the brave hero risking his life to save his sister. We were content to let him take the glory…for now.

The road was empty and peaceful, and as Quintus and I rode along side by side it felt almost as if we were taking a pleasant evening ride to watch the moon and stars come out. Almost, but not entirely.

Quintus edged his horse close to mine and said softly, "From what we overheard tonight, we've enough evidence for an arrest now. I'll see Trebonius as soon as we get back. Our friend at the rear must realise we know something, but he can't be aware exactly how much."

"At least he came to save his sister," I murmured. "Whatever else he's done…"

"…I know, but he's a murderer and an enemy of Rome. Don't let your heart rule your head." He turned in his saddle as a horseman rode up alongside us, but it was only one of the escort, who were taking it in turns to trot up and down along our line of march.

"Nearly there, sir," the soldier said cheerfully. "You'll be glad to get back, I bet."

"You're not joking," Quintus called. "A hot bath and several beakers of hot wine, that's what I'm looking forward to."

The man rode on, and Quintus moved even closer in. "When we get there, we must make sure our friend doesn't have a chance to leave again. We'll tell the guards to close the gates, say we think someone is following us…anything to make sure he doesn't escape."

"Make sure who doesn't escape?" Philippus had ridden up alongside us on the cleared strip of earth next to the road, so we hadn't heard his horse approaching. He was watching us curiously. "Are you about to arrest someone, Quintus Antonius? Have you discovered who killed my mother?"

"I was talking about the man who tried to kill your father in the hospital," Quintus improvised. "You've heard about that, presumably?"

He nodded. "A nasty business. But at least I'm relieved my father didn't really kill Mother." He paused, and he wasn't play-acting now. He looked so utterly miserable that I felt sorry for him. Whoever and whatever he was, Jovina's death was a tragedy for him.

Then he straightened in his saddle and said briskly, "I haven't been into the village today yet. Do you know if our house is still standing?"

"It was this morning," Quintus answered, "but now, I couldn't say, I'm afraid. The rebels burnt quite a lot of Roman property this afternoon. Tell me, where did you get to today? We looked for you, we could have done with your help. But nobody knew where you'd gone."

"I was looking for my sister, of course. Scouting around trying to find traces of which way she'd gone. She spent part of last night threatening to run away, you know, and I thought she might try to leave home for good."

"Where did you look?"

"The party field first, but there was no sign there."

Oh really? And I'm the Queen of Brigantia. If he'd been to the party field, he'd surely have seen either Venutius' men waiting in ambush, or their capture of the girls…or if he went later, he'd have found Baca.

Quintus asked, "Did you go anywhere near Brennus' house?"

"No." His voice was sharp. "Why?"

"It's where Eurytus' body was found, I wondered if you'd seen it. Or even Eurytus himself, before he was murdered. Or, of course, you could have caught a glimpse of whoever killed him."

"No."

"That's a pity. Someone must have seen the man who played Achilles to Eurytus' Hector."

Philippus gave a little start of surprise, but he covered it well with another hollow cough. "*Merda,* that smoke's really got into my chest," he growled. I felt myself go tense. That growl sounded almost like Portius, or a lion in a nightmare…

Quintus went on unhurriedly. "So where else did you check? The main road, I suppose, if you thought the girls might be leaving the area?"

"Exactly so. I went some distance towards Eburacum, then doubled back and headed a mile or two towards Cataractonium, but no joy there either. I didn't get back to the fort till quite late, after you'd gone. I went to see Father, and he told me about the ultimatum from Venutius and everything. And when I heard what they planned to do to Chloe…as you said before, there was no choice."

He turned his horse and rode back to the carriage. I whispered to Quintus, "Did you ever hear such a parcel of lies?"

"He must take us for fools," Quintus whispered. Aloud he said, "Look, here's the fort at last."

We received a welcome that wouldn't have disgraced a victorious general. It was almost dark when we arrived at the main gate, but the whole area just inside it was ablaze with torches, mostly in the hands of a crowd of people waiting to greet us. They cheered as we rode through, and milled round us, asking questions and making jokes and enfolding us in an atmosphere of warmth and congratulations. I turned to look for the gate centurion and was relieved to see his men were already shutting the big main gate behind us. I saw Quintus pause for a brief word with him and heard him say, "The commander will confirm it."

Mallius hurried forward and lifted Chloe bodily out of the *raeda*, and she clung to him and wept on his shoulder. Philippus went to greet his father, and Selena bustled up, crying and laughing at once. Lucius took Vitellia in his arms, and I saw tears there too. I'll confess I felt my own eyes prickling, as the tension relaxed and I allowed myself to realise our ordeal was over. But I'd too much to do to waste time crying now. There'd be time enough for emotion later.

I looked round to see who else was there: Statius, but he was keeping in the background, and Congrio, and Ennius, and several other officers I recognized from the party. Then the tall figure of Trebonius made his way towards us and people drew back to let him pass. Quintus and I, Lucius and Titch, Gambax and the girls and Philippus, all gathered round him.

"I'm so pleased you're home safe and sound," he said. "I'm sure you know how worried we've all been about you. Well done, Antonius, and all of you. And Philippus too, you've done a grand job tonight."

Philippus saluted. "Thank you, sir. I'll make my formal report later, shall I?"

"Yes, do that. Meanwhile, are any of you hurt?"

"I've got a sprained ankle," Chloe answered, smiling now. "I had to jump out of a window, and unbolt a door so we could all escape, and…"

"Gods alive, child, whatever next!" Trebonius smiled down at her. "And the rest of you…nobody injured?"

"A few cuts and bruises, nothing more," Quintus said. "Commander, I've got an urgent report to make about today's events. We know who killed Eurytus. May we go to your office straight away? I'd like Aurelia to come with me."

Selena spoke up. "If you'll pardon me, sir, the quicker I can get these two girls washed and fed and into their beds, the better it'll be for them. They've had a very trying day, sir, I'm sure you'll understand."

"Of course." Trebonius seemed to see the two girls properly for the first time, and take in their dishevelled clothes and dirty faces. "Off you go. You're quartered with Mallius, aren't you?"

"That's right," Mallius said. "Selena will take good care of both of them. You're welcome to stay with me too, Aurelia, if you like. There's plenty of room."

"Thank you, Marcus, I will."

The girls climbed back into the carriage, and I saw Lucius lean down and give Vitellia a kiss. "I'll come with you," he said, "and see you settled in."

"So will I," Philippus offered. They both followed on foot as the *raeda* rolled away.

"May I ask one more thing, Commander?" Quintus said. "It's imperative nobody leaves the fort until you've heard what we have to tell you. Nobody at all. Could you give the order to your guards?"

"All right, if you think it's so important." He beckoned the centurion in charge at the gate, and repeated the order to him. "Alert the lookouts on the ramparts," he added. "If anyone tries to leave here tonight, arrest him."

He led Quintus and me into his office and didn't waste time on preliminaries. "The messengers who got in ahead of you told me what a narrow escape you had. You reached those two girls just in time. I'd like the details later, of course, but for now, let's hear who killed Eurytus. The gods know I don't want to have to start executing hostages, but I can't go back on my word, especially after tonight. So if you can name the assassin, nobody will be more pleased than I."

"You may not be so pleased when you hear his name," Quintus said. "It wasn't a Brigantian. It was one of your own men."

"Go on."

"It's Philippus."

"Jupiter's balls, it can't be. You have proof?"

"We have. And I'm afraid this murder is only one of his crimes. We can also show that he was implicated in kidnapping the girls today, that he murdered Terentius at Oak Bridges, and that he's been selling army stores to the Brigantians."

He sighed. "The secret trading I've suspected for a while now. I think we all knew Philippus was up to a few tricks…but I kept putting off dealing with him. I couldn't afford to lose a very competent fighting man for just a bit of juvenile mischief."

"This isn't juvenile mischief. Kidnapping, and two murders, one of a soldier and one of an Imperial freedman…"

"Yes, yes, I know. I'll need evidence, of course, good hard evidence."

"We have it."

He got up and went to the door. "Send me a secretary," he ordered an aide in the outer office. "I want all this recorded."

An elderly grey-haired man came in with note-tablets and stylus. He sat down at a small table in the corner.

"Write this all down," Trebonius instructed. "Don't leave anything out unless I tell you."

Slowly and carefully Quintus and I told him everything we knew about Philippus. The murder of Terentius…the intercepted message to the rebels, which Philippus had managed to pass on by word of mouth…his disguise as Portius, both at Oak Bridges and when dealing with Venutius…the evidence of the knife that killed Eurytus…and finally our conclusion about how Philippus had helped kidnap the girls. Trebonius listened carefully and the secretary wrote fast.

"Much of that makes sense," the commander said slowly. "Until we come to what you're accusing him of today, which in my view are the most serious crimes: the killing of Eurytus and the kidnapping. Your only evidence is hearsay, surely. You had a report about a knife being used, but it disappeared. Another report about a forged letter, but you don't know it was Philippus who forged it. Admittedly he went off without leave, but it isn't the first time he's done that. I'm not sure why you don't believe he was searching for his sister and Vitellia all day today, as he said. After all he did eventually find them."

"Because he left here early this morning," I answered. "*Before* he could have learned that the girls were missing. I know that for certain. One of the servants looking after them discovered they'd gone, after we'd arrived here ourselves. She told me later she sent urgently to the fort asking Philippus to go and help, but he'd left. She was told he'd gone out, leaving a message that you'd sent him to Cataractonium."

Trebonius nodded. "Of course. You told me that this morning, Aurelia. You thought I'd sent him on some errand, but I hadn't. I was too busy to do anything about it…gods, why didn't I pay more attention?"

A thunderous hammering on his door interrupted him, and Titch burst in, shouting, "Commander! Can you come quick, sir, it's very urgent. Please, sir, as quick as you can…"

"How dare you come charging in here?" Trebonius began.

Quintus stopped him. "This is my assistant. What's happened?"

"Philippus is dead. He tried to escape, attacked a sentry on the rampart, and there was a fight. He fell over the wall and it killed him."

Chapter XXXI

But he wasn't dead. Not quite.

Pythis was bending over the still form when we arrived below the wall. Several soldiers stood around holding torches, and by their light the young doctor felt him over carefully, held a mirror to his mouth, and then straightened up. "He's alive, just barely. I think his back is broken, but there's breath there, and a pulse in his neck." He turned to the soldiers. "Can two of you lads bring a stretcher. We may be able to save him."

"And somebody fetch his father, please," Quintus said.

They carried him carefully into the hospital and took him to the little room where Mallius had lain only this morning. The two bearers were slow and gentle, but the jolting of the stretcher must have been agonising for a man with a broken back, and as they settled him on the bed, he groaned and opened his eyes. "Father?"

"I'm here, Philo." Mallius moved closer so his son could see him. "Keep still now. You'll be all right."

"Everything hurts, and I can't move my legs or my arms," Philippus muttered. "My back's broken. Isn't it, Pythis?"

"I'm not sure yet. Just lie still and rest for now."

"Don't worry, I'm not going anywhere." He smiled, but it looked more like a snarl. "I'm finished. And I'd rather die tonight, here, than be executed for killing a rat like Eurytus."

Mallius was shocked. He hadn't heard our report to Trebonius. "If that's what they're saying, Philippus, I'm sure they're wrong. You had nothing to do with that."

"I did. I stabbed him this morning."

"Oh, gods," Mallius moaned. "Why, Philo?"

"For money, of course. It was all arranged with Venutius. The Fall of Troy…should have been Terentius playing Achilles. But I managed to take the part over instead." He laughed, but it turned into a groan. "Can't you give me something to stop the pain? Where's Niki? He'll know what I need."

"He's not here just now. You'll be better if you rest…"

Philippus swore. "I can rest in the Underworld. Get me a drink, if you can't spare any medicine."

Onion had come in carrying a flask of wine. Pythis poured some into a mug, and between them they raised Philippus' head far enough to let him drink it.

"That's better." He caught sight of me. "It's all your fault really. I knew you were a nosey little cow, I tried to stop you coming to Isurium. But I had to get the message through to Venutius. Terentius' servant…he knew the message, but not what it meant." He coughed and spat out blood, and accepted another long drink. "I delivered it, but I didn't have the half-coin to identify myself. So they never paid the money. Cheating bastards. And I should have had more when I'd played the part of Achilles. A really big payment, they promised me. I could have given up trading. Or maybe not. I quite enjoyed it."

"Enjoyed betraying the Empire?" Trebonius said.

"You old fool, you don't see it, do you? I'm no traitor, but I'm poor, and I needed money, and that was an easy way. I knew the Empire would never fall just because of what I did. We can always beat the barbarians if we have to." He surveyed us all as we clustered round his bed, and suddenly tears came into his eyes. "Tell Chloe and Vitellia I'm sorry. I forged that note to get Chloe down by the river. Venutius told me she'd be ransomed for money. And then I found he'd lied to me. He wanted hostages."

"You did the honourable thing in the end," Mallius said. "You rescued them."

"No choice." His voice slurred, and he closed his eyes for a few heartbeats, then opened them and looked directly at Mallius.

"It's over now, and I'm tired. Too tired to fight any more. Give me another drink, boy, for the gods' sake."

But before Pythis could get the beaker to his lips, he groaned and made a choking sound. His eyes were still open, but the life had gone out of them, and we didn't need to be told it was the end.

Chapter XXXII

Tomorrow, the first day of September, is Lucius' and my birthday, and we'll be celebrating it together here at the Oak Tree. I haven't wanted to go to any sort of celebration since my trip to see Jovina. I've been busy through the summer, and I needed to let the passing days put some distance between me and the terrible events at Isurium. Now at last I feel like a party.

My brother has come up from Londinium and brought his darling Vitellia with him. They still make sheep's eyes at one another. But I don't mind, because Quintus is here, too, so I can't feel jealous of anyone else's happiness.

Albia and Candidus are staying for a few days, with the twins. When I see the chaos those two cause at nearly five years old, I shudder to think what they'll be like by the time they're grown, and I realise again how much I like being an aunt and how much I'd hate to be a mother. But we all adore them, and no Aurelius family gathering would feel right without them.

We invited Mallius and Chloe to come and stay, but they've only just got settled in Londinium, so they reluctantly refused. Mallius has a new posting there on the governor's staff, which gives them both the chance of a new start, far away from memories of Jovina and Philippus. According to Vitellia, who spends a large part of her time writing and receiving letters, Chloe swears she'll wait for her soldier-boy for ever and a day, or until her father gives consent for them to marry, which may amount to the same thing. Gambax, presumably, swears the same.

Good luck to them, if they are really destined for one another. And whatever happens, at least Chloe won't be spending her life with Statius. Vitellia has started to introduce Chloe to her own wide circle of young friends. As our grandmother used to say, there's plenty of fish in the sea and it costs nothing to sail out and look them over. It's if you do more than look that the trouble can begin. So we'll wait and see.

One marriage that will definitely happen is my brother's. He and Vitellia are more in love than ever. He still spoils her, and she still lets him. But she's grown up a lot this summer and acquired a measure of independence. She's still sweet-natured and of course stunningly beautiful, but no longer the biddable little girl he brought to Oak Bridges in June. He knows it and seems content, and so am I, because now she's much more the sort of wife I'd hoped he would choose.

They've set their wedding date for April next year. We're all invited to stay at her father's villa. Albia and I are already thinking about what to wear.

About the History

The opening of this story, where Aurelia receives an invitation to a birthday party, is rooted in fact. The Romans did invite each other to their birthday celebrations, and there's a charming example of such an invitation among the documents found at Vindolanda on Britannia's northern frontier. What's more the handwriting experts say the invitation (from Claudia Severa to Sulpicia Lepidina) was written by more than one person, the main part by a secretary and the closing words by Severa herself. There's nothing sinister about this letter, but of course it set me thinking; a note written in more than one hand could have an altogether more disturbing cause.

Most of the places mentioned in the book are factual, except for the village of Oak Bridges and the Oak Tree mansio itself. The mansio's location is at the bottom of a real hill with a steep road up to the Yorkshire Wolds—a road which still carries traffic today from York to the coast. York in Aurelia's day was known as Eburacum; the more familiar Eboracum came later.

The remains of Isurium, such as they are, lie around and beneath the village of Aldborough, but the remnants on show now are of a later and more impressive town than the village Aurelia would have known. The Romans built and rebuilt their towns, and the original fort and village of Isurium would probably have been built mainly of wood. But they have left very few traces behind, because they were in due course overlaid by a larger town built mainly of stone, with a regular grid of streets and a forum in the centre. Isurium did become a tribal administrative centre for the Brigantes, and by the 300s AD was known as Isurium Brigantum. When it achieved this important status isn't clear, but it must have been later than 100 AD, when the Romans still regarded pacifying the northern part of their province as a work in progress. So I've allowed myself to speculate about Isurium's early history, and to picture it as small and usually quiet, with occasional native unrest. One day archaeologists may prove me wrong, or even right.

If you thought that the Vulcan's Shield articles sold by Congrio were remarkably like asbestos, you're right: that's what they were. The Romans knew about asbestos and its fire-resistant properties. They called it *amiantus*, and Pliny the Elder, in his encyclopaedic work *Natural History*, mentions it more than once. He thought the fibres came from plants grown in the deserts of India. Table mats and napkins were woven from asbestos and were treated as novelty items because their owners could clean them by simply throwing them into a fire, where dirt would burn away, leaving the cloth unharmed and clean. When I learned, by pure chance, about *amiantus*, I was so intrigued that I was determined to include it in one of Aurelia's mysteries. I wonder, did anybody actually think of making clothing from its fibres? Who knows? But they could have done.

It's hard to imagine nowadays how enormous was the control of the Roman *paterfamilias* over the rest of his family. In theory he even had the power of life and death, though by Aurelia's time this was only in theory. But Lucius could certainly have forbidden Aurelia to travel to Jovina's party, ordering the mansio's staff not to give her any help, and fully expected that everyone would obey him. Aurelia's recklessness, or shall we call it courage, in disobeying him over something so important as a journey away from home would have shocked most of her contemporaries. It even worried Quintus, but not for long.

As with Aurelia's earlier mysteries, I've done a great deal of research on the history. It's no hardship; I love doing it, and I feel it's important to get the historical facts right as far as I can. Where the history isn't known or is uncertain, I've taken the author's privilege of using educated guesswork plus imagination.

I'll end with a list of some of the books I've found useful. I wish there was space for all of them.

Roman Authors

Tacitus. *Agricola.* Tacitus' account of a general and governor who spent much of his career in Britannia, and of Britannia itself and its people.

Suetonius. *The Twelve Caesars.* A wonderfully gossipy account of Roman court and political life. Most of it was far removed from Aurelia's provincial existence, but it makes fascinating reading.

Pliny the Younger. *Letters of the Younger Pliny.* Not about Britannia, but very much about the Roman mindset, and the life and opinions of an educated and likeable aristocrat.

Modern Authors

Guy de la Bedoyere. *Roman Britain, A New History.*

Peter Salway. *A History of Roman Britain.*

Alan K. Bowman. *Life and Letters on the Roman Frontier (Vindolanda and Its People).*

Lindsay Allason-Jones. *Women in Roman Britain.*

Barry Cunliffe. *Iron Age Britain.*

Andrew Dalby and Sally Grainger. *The Classical Cookbook.*

Philip Wilkinson. *What the Romans Did for Us.*

To receive a free catalog of Poisoned Pen Press titles, please contact us in one of the following ways:

Phone: 1-800-421-3976
Facsimile: 1-480-949-1707
Email: info@poisonedpenpress.com
Website: www.poisonedpenpress.com

Poisoned Pen Press
6962 E. First Ave. Ste 103
Scottsdale, AZ 85251